In Day of War, *Cliff Graham issues a call to battle. Based on the life of King David and his mighty men, this isn't just a story about swords and shields. It's about real men who struggle with more than the enemy soldier before them. You will enjoy this book on many levels. I strongly recommend it.*

—Robert Whitlow, bestselling author of
The List and *The Trial*

*If you've never read the Bible or studied Judaic history, this is a fast-paced means of exploring that time period. If you've read the tales of David and his Mighty Men, then you are in for a treat. Graham fleshes out these stories, turning them into pulse-pounding battle scenes and excursions through ancient Israel.... *Day of War *leaves us wanting more stories about these engaging characters. The Bible comes alive through these pages, while never sugarcoating violence or the struggle of the male gender.*

—Eric Wilson, *New York Times* bestselling author of
Fireproof, Haunt of Jackals, and *Valley of Bones*

An enthralling and captivating story that captured me from start to finish. Extremely well written. Brutal and honest, thrilling and powerful.

—Grant Curtis, producer of
the *Spiderman* movie franchise

This book about Benaiah, an ancient warrior who ranks as one of Israel's great unsung heroes, is both captivating and inspiring. Cliff Graham does more than write words—he paints pictures. He does more than tell a story—he invites readers into one of the most amazing stories in Scripture.

—Mark Batterson, author of
In a Pit with a Lion on a Snowy Day

Finally! A gritty, intense, and real portrayal of one of the most dynamic biblical characters of all time. The images sear into your brain like you're watching an IMAX movie. Day of War *grabbed me by the throat and would not release its grip until the last page. You don't read* Day of War, *you consume it.*

—David L. Cunningham, filmmaker
and director of *To End All Wars* and *The Path to 9/11*

They call it a war of biblical proportions for a reason! Cliff Graham brings history, faith, and fighting to life, all at the same time!

—Lt. Col. (ret) James Jay Carafano, Ph.D., director of
the Douglas and Sarah Allison Center for Foreign
Policy Studies, The Heritage Foundation

DAY OF WAR

LION OF WAR SERIES

BOOK 1

CLIFF GRAHAM

ZONDERVAN®

ZONDERVAN.com/
AUTHORTRACKER
follow your favorite authors

ZONDERVAN

Day of War
Copyright © 2011 by Cliff Graham

This title is also available as a Zondervan ebook. Visit www.zondervan.com/ebooks.

This title is also available in a Zondervan audio edition. Visit www.zondervan.fm.

Requests for information should be addressed to:
Zondervan, *Grand Rapids, Michigan 49530*

Library of Congress Cataloging-in-Publication Data

Graham, Cliff.
    Day of war / Cliff Graham.
        p.   cm. — Lion of war ; bk. 1)
        ISBN 0-310-33183-8 (pbk.)
        1. David, King of Israel — Fiction.   2. Bible. O.T — History of Biblical events — Fiction.   I.
Title.
PS3607.R337D39   2011
813'.6 — dc22   2011005889

Published in association with the literary agency of Alive Communications, Inc.,
7680 Goddard Street, Suite 200, Colorado Springs, CO 80920.
www.alivecommunications.com

Cover design: GiantKiller Pictures
Cover photography: Joel Grimes
Author Photo: Alden Dobbins
Map illustration: Ruth Pettis
Interior design: Katherine Lloyd, The DESK

Printed in the United States of America

11 12 13 14 15 16 /DCI/ 24 23 22 21 20 19 18 17 16 15 14 13 12 11 10 9 8 7 6 5 4 3 2 1

For Cassandra, L.M.H.B.
For my sons, that you may know the war paths.
And for my dad, the one who first showed them to me.

ACKNOWLEDGMENTS

Most new novelists seem to thank everyone they have ever met. I wanted to avoid that temptation. But this particular project is vast and varied, and I need a couple of pages to give credit to those who are making it happen:

Bryan Yost, design partner and friend, who leapt out with me in faith. Todd Hillard, ace writer, true friend, and mentor who has proven invaluable to this endeavor time and again. Nic Ewing, Mike Altstiel, and Jesse Ewing, for helping me shape the concept. The rest of the team at Men of War, including Lee Rempel, Jeremy Banik, Adam Haggerty, and Jerry Smith, who have all contributed more than they know. Col. (ret.) James O'Neal and the other warriors I interviewed, for giving such poignant insight into the mind of the combat soldier during the hell of battle. Julie Mecca, for seeing something in this story at its earliest stage and patiently giving advice. Jim Miller, who believed in it, worked tirelessly on its behalf, and will always be a part of it.

The Army chaplains who have given me invaluable instruction about the spiritual and psychological effects of battle on both warriors and their loved ones, and who demonstrate loving care of the souls of warriors on a daily basis: Gordon Groseclose, Mike Dugal,

Bob Hart, David Bowlus, Rabbi Henry Soussan, Leon Kircher, and Eddie Barnett.

My agent, Joel Kneedler, who took on this highly unorthodox project at the right time, guided it skillfully, and proved himself to be the missing link in the chain. The rest of the team at Alive Communications, including Donna Lewis, Sarah Ring, Lee Hough, and Rick Christian.

David L. Cunningham, Grant Curtis, John Fusco, Nicole Nietz, Jeremy Wheeler, and the rest of the highly talented folks at Giant-Killer Pictures and Global Virtual Studio who are bringing David and his Mighty Men to the big screen, for your tremendous efforts and personal enthusiasm for the project. Also to Alden Dobbins for being willing to sweat in the Negev Desert in August while figuring out ways to make me interesting on camera.

The team at Zondervan: Cindy Lambert for breaking land-speed records in acquiring it; Dave Lambert for omitting needless words in the manuscript; Alicia Mey, Don Gates, and Jessica Secord for promoting it. Especially to Bob Hudson for his careful editorial eye and enthusiasm for the material.

Michael Hedrick, for letting us spend time with you and your team in the Holy Land. For anyone looking to take a tour of Israel and the places where David and his men bled and sweated, please consider CJF Ministries.

A few people who don't know me but had a tremendous hand in shaping this book regardless, including Matt Chandler, Ravi Zacharias, and Charles Swindoll. Also to Michael Shaara, Stephen Pressfield, and Bernard Cornwell, authors of the golden standards in combat novels and the inspiration for my own efforts.

My family, including my parents, grandmothers, in-laws, and sister, for being supportive fans regardless of what I actually wrote.

Most of all my wife, Cassandra, for stubborn faith and naive optimism, which always kept me going during the trying hours.

NOTE TO THE READER

The story of David has been rehashed many times, but nothing of this length and scope has been done on his warriors, the original "Dirty Dozen" of the Scriptures. That may be because so little is known of them. They barely register in Scripture. There are two chapters (2 Samuel 23 and 1 Chronicles 11) devoted to their heroic feats. Hence this tale.

Some may take issue with my portrayal of these men. I don't claim to have completely accurate insight. But I do believe that this portrayal is, at the very least, consistent with Scripture. The Mighty Men were certainly heroic, but they were merely men—disgruntled outcasts emerging from an era in Hebrew history where the worship of Yahweh was almost nonexistent.

This novel is based on careful research and analysis of known facts about the time, but there are so many gaps in the record about timelines and other military and cultural details that I occasionally resorted to my own creative guesses. For this, I beg the forgiveness of the discerning reader. I have used modern terms for some people groups and places in order to avoid confusion. I have written the story in dialog designed less to be true to the voices of the time than to be easily understood by modern ears. I have also shortened or omitted some cultural descriptions, not out of disrespect, but to keep the story taut. Any errors or inconsistencies are my fault alone.

I have taken some liberties with the descriptions of supernatural activity. One would search the Scripture in vain for a few of the specific examples of human/angelic interaction depicted here, but although those may be extrabiblical, they are generally consistent with other recorded events in the Bible.

This is fiction. Please read it as such.

A final note: This book is extremely violent. However, it's no more violent than Scripture itself—just more violent than many previous novels based on Scripture. It also contains mature themes of sexual temptation and lust that demand that readers be mature enough to understand them. Please exercise caution and discretion when passing this book on to more sensitive readers.

David's war years were both the best and worst of his life. The Lion of War Series, by painting a picture of David and his men at that time, is an attempt to help us understand these men in their proper context as products of a barbaric and troubled era. In what ways, for instance, might the trauma of those war years have contributed to the destructive decisions David made later in life? In modern times, we label the problems warriors face after battle Post Traumatic Stress Disorder. Regardless of the name, it is clear that warriors are affected for the rest of their lives by the hellish nature of battlefields. David was no exception.

And yet he was called "the man after God's heart." In the Bible, between the episodes of vicious battle, we see glimpses of poignant and profound worship. It is a comfort to know that, regardless of our mistakes, the God who loved, forgave, and empowered David does the same for us.

Units of Measurement

reed	9 feet
cubit	18 inches
span	9 inches
handbreadth	3 inches
fingerbreadth	1 inch
talent	90 pounds
shekel	a coin, weighed about 1/3 to 1/2 ounce

Oh LORD, *my Lord, the strength of my salvation,*
  you have covered my head in the day of battle.
PSALM 140:7, ESV

I have bestowed strength on a warrior;
  I have raised up a young man from among the people.
I have found David my servant;
  with my sacred oil I have anointed him.
PSALM 89:19 – 20, NIV

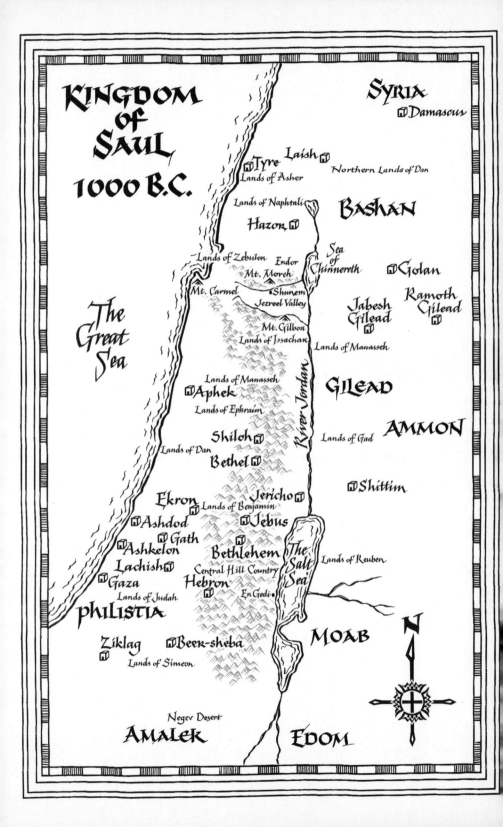

DAY OF WAR

PROLOGUE

The young man studied the bed of the creek through the sunlit ripples. It was cold water, carried from the snowmelt further to the north, cleansing the valley of winter—and shallow enough that he could see the gentle nudge of the stream against the stones.

He pulled one of the stones out of the bed and rubbed it dry with the edge of his tunic. It was perfectly round, just the right size, and smooth, free of divots and blemishes. Perfect, as though it had been created simply to be there waiting for him.

He chose five of them.

He stood in the cold water, so soothing to his feet after walking the entire day. His back was stiff from the pack he carried, and the chafing of his sandals on his ankles was worse than normal after such a journey. He let his feet soak in the icy stream and closed his eyes, listening.

The rugged gulley cut by the stream was deep enough to shield him from the many eyes that watched for him, from behind and from the front. They would be waiting, and his time was short.

He opened his eyes and looked at the crest of the bank on the other side of the brook. It would begin soon.

The mud of the riverbed covered his feet as he stepped through it. On the other side, he stood at the foot of the bank of sand and gravel. A few steps and he would crest it, coming into full view once again of the gathered masses of men on the rolling hills lining the valley. He felt their enormous presence, felt the lust for death permeating their ranks.

His breathing was shallow as he counted out his timing once more. Swing, measure, swing, measure again. Three times, then release.

He had seen five of them. The one in the field below, four more behind him in the ranks. They might be brothers. All were as massive as the one now shouting in the field.

The young man blinked. None of his own brothers had come down with him. They had responsibilities, were valuable to their father. They had not cared enough about his fate to stand with him.

And they had never known the covering.

Today he would show it to them.

Holding his staff over his shoulder, he began to climb up the sandy bank from the creek. The sun was directly overhead and his shadow was small. He spoke quietly as he climbed, praying as though someone climbing next to him needed to hear it. He spoke aloud to himself often in times of peril and all throughout the days of peace.

He reached the top of the bank and the field came once more into view. Glittering ranks of men, wearing armor and bearing standards, lined the top of the valley around him, thousands upon thousands, and the sound of their shouting and taunting now reached him in full volume, no longer muffled by the sandbank.

He had enjoyed the quiet while it lasted, but now it was time. He let the noise of the men he despised wash over him, focusing his growing anger. He clenched and unclenched his fists.

A short distance away on a small outcropping of stones, highlighted against the barren slope leading up to the pagan army, the massive warrior stood with his weapon raised.

It was the largest figure any of them had ever seen, larger than two normal men. He carried a spear that looked as big as a tree. A curved scimitar, several times heavier than a normal sword, was strapped across the back of his heavy armor. He wore greaves to cover his shins, a plated armor breastplate, and a thick bronze helmet with a crest of horsehair billowing out of the top. Chain mail resembling fish scales covered his torso and glinted in the midday sunlight, shining so brightly that the young man glanced away for a moment.

The giant's thick curses to the Hebrew god rung across the hazy field as the afternoon heat's distortion gave him the appearance of an evil spirit. His armor bearer nearby looked like an infant next to the huge warrior.

Surely this was not a human, the young man thought. It had to be a monster. A monster from Sheol unleashed as punishment to the young man's people for forsaking their God. He breathed slowly to push away the fear as it surfaced. He whispered in prayer once more.

The giant continued to taunt him, so the young man taunted him back. The giant was smiling broadly, his black beard spilling out of the opening in his helmet. He repeated his dark curses louder, raising his spear even higher to keep his army cheering.

Now, slowly, the younger man felt his fear seeping away as the covering came. He smiled at the champion, who still did not realize what he was facing.

They would all see soon enough.

He tossed his staff to the ground and pulled taut the sling made of two ropes of goat hair attached to a leather pouch. He reached into the small hide bag at his waist as the war drums of the army across the valley pounded out the summons to watch the contest.

Both kings wanted their men ready if the other side's fighter lost in order to exploit the advantage. Neither side trusted the other's promise to depart if their champion lost.

The young man pulled out one of the stones from the creek bed and notched it into the leather strap at the base of the sling. His forefinger was calloused from drilling with the weapon. It had never failed him. It would not fail him now.

The drums increased in their frenzy. The enemy soldiers were screaming behind their iron weapons and expertly forged armor, clearly the superior force in strength and equipment to the poorly outfitted Hebrews cowering on the hillside behind him. Like a pack of hyenas, the enemy could smell the coming slaughter. The young man glared at them as they cursed his God. Rage rose in his heart.

And then he felt the fire.

It swelled in his chest first. Then it rushed in a torrent into his arms. His fingers twitched with crackling energy, and he felt as though his muscles would leap out of his flesh if they were not given release. His eyes clamped shut. Listening to the war drums pounding, he let the fire course through his skin and thought that he would burst with the rush of heat filling his body.

Soon the sound of the fire roaring in his ears blotted out the rest of his senses, and he felt nothing but the heat consuming him with greater intensity than he had ever known. His sling shook in his hands. The war drums hammered, the soldiers beat their swords against their shields in time with the drums, and he heard the mass of voices shouting at him.

He opened his eyes. The monster had charged past his armor bearer and was running toward him in leaping strides, covering ten cubits with each bound, his armor bearer struggling to keep up.

The young man shouted to relieve the tension, but it only made the fire in his body burn hotter. He found himself running as well and pulling the sling tight. The stone settled into the groove in the leather and he whirled it once through the air.

Swing.

He slowed it.

Measure.

He kept running and whirled it again, even though it was difficult to sling accurately while running. He wasn't able to fight the fire.

Swing.

He sped it up.

Measure.

The giant was bearing down on him. There was no more time.

Swing ... faster ... aim!

He cried out, certain the fire would destroy him, but instead it drove him forward through the rocks. Dust flew. With a final burst, he released one of the ropes, sending the stone whistling though the air, and as it flew toward the black form of the warrior, the young man whispered in his spirit: *Cover me in the day of war.*

A powerful race known as the Philistines, or "Sea People," dominate the lands along the coast of the Great Sea. They are superior technologically and militarily in every way to the scattered tribes of Israelites who inhabit the mountains inland, primarily due to their mastery of the forging of iron, something of which the Israelites have little knowledge.

Saul, the first king of a united Israelite nation, and a tormented and troubled man, has nevertheless managed to keep the Philistines at bay for forty years. His brave son, Jonathan, is the crown prince. The two of them are encamped in the Jezreel Valley in the northern part of the kingdom, where the Philistine kings have united in an invasion attempt. It is the largest force yet assembled against the Israelites, and they have little hope that their army will prevail.

One of Saul's former commanders — David, a close friend of Jonathan's — has gathered and trained a personal army of outcasts and mercenaries after losing his position in the Israelite army, despite being the nation's greatest champion, for crimes he didn't commit. Rumors have spread throughout the kingdom for years that David was chosen as a boy by Samuel the prophet to be king after Saul one day. Fearing that the rumors are true, Saul has hunted him relentlessly for years, consumed with jealousy at David's unique abilities (which some say are bestowed by Israel's God, Yahweh) and with hatred for imagined treason. In desperation, David offered his services to Achish, the king of the Philistine capital of Gath. His most loyal warriors came with him, led by a mysterious group of fighters known as the Three.

News of David's apparent defection has divided the Israelite population. Those of the tribe of Judah, Israel's largest tribe, believe he is secretly fighting on their behalf, while those in the northern tribes view him as a traitor, regardless of how Saul has mistreated him.

But David has not been fighting for the Philistines. Rather, he has been raiding the towns and settlements of the Amalekites in an attempt to secure the southern borders. He has been sending plunder to Achish to make it appear that David has turned on his people, but secretly he has also been sending it as tribute to the Israelite tribal elders. Through

David's efforts, the Amalekites, among the oldest and most vicious enemies of the Israelites, have been subdued.

Now David marches north with his band of warriors alongside the Philistines. Many of his own men argue among themselves about marching against their kinsmen on behalf of their enemy. They wonder what will happen if David actually has to face Saul on the field of battle.

To foster goodwill among his people while continuing his deception of the Philistines, David dispatches a warrior, Benaiah, to a small town high in the southern mountains that has been ravaged by wild predators. David orders Benaiah to meet up with the army in the north when his task is finished.

It is the spring month of Aviv, the first of the campaign season. The weather has been unusually cold for that time of year.

Part
One

ONE

Benaiah the son of Jehoiada had never seen a snowstorm, and now he wished it had remained that way.

It never snowed in the south, Benaiah's home. He had only heard legends of the freezing rain as a boy. Travelers from the east would speak of it when they stopped at his village to water their camels and replenish stores for the crossing to Egypt. They told of a powerful blanket of white that fell over the land and killed plants and livestock. At the time, he had yearned for it with a boy's enthusiasm for the unknown. But, as with many of life's youthful mysteries, it quickly lost appeal once he was in the thick of it.

Cold wind whipped across his face. Benaiah held his hands over his eyes, waiting for it to pass before continuing his climb. Snow covered the mountain trail and he was forced to pick his way among the ice-covered rocks.

In the south, the month of Aviv brought the land into full bloom under abundant sunshine. The barley would be ripening on the plains, signaling the approach of Passover and its reliably pleasant weather. But the tall mountain ridges of this northern country were crested with white, and the dreary gray sky promised more of it.

Crouching next to a large boulder, he adjusted his grip on the spear shaft and listened. The wind stirred up enough noise to prevent him from hearing around the bend ahead. He knew the creature could be hiding among the many boulders and clefts along the slope. He studied each one carefully for a flash of gold fur.

Frowning, he moved up the path again. They had said it was large. Three times the size of a man, maybe ten or eleven cubits—absurd, since no creature could be ten cubits. The village elders said the beast came late at night. Perhaps they were so afraid of it that every shadow in the torchlight became part of the lion.

Benaiah had hunted lions all of his life. He knew that it took only one kill for them to realize that man was easy prey. It was better to hunt them in groups, and since the other warriors in Benaiah's band were marching north at the moment, he'd had to recruit two men from the village to come along. They were stout enough, and accustomed to harsh living on the frontier, but one of them was elderly and the other was very young.

Most of the men in the land who were of fighting ability and age were preparing for war in the north, gathering equipment and training ahead of a rumored Philistine invasion. The king had summoned them all, farmer and herder alike, leaving a shortage of men in the villages capable of defending their homes or engaging in heavy labor. Philistines tended to cause trouble in the days leading up to Passover because they knew that some of the Hebrews still observed it. Saul, the king of the Israelites, had been using Passover as the reason to build his army, claiming that their holy lands were being overrun by pagans during their holiest month. Although Saul's true devotion to Passover was, at best, questionable, Benaiah thought as he crept his way up the path.

He had almost missed the village when he'd arrived that morning out of the forest. It was small and well away from the major trading routes, but the people took pride in their buildings. Family homes were surrounded by stone walls and built with sturdy mud brick roofs similar to the modern construction in the cities on the plains. There were buildings where farmers brought their supplies to work the reaping floor. Wheat would be harvested in another month or two, depending on the weather and the amount of runoff water that gathered in the valleys, and he saw reapers sharpening their flint blades for when the time came to trim the tops of the bundles.

Even though the olive harvest would not occur until much later in the season, men were already working on the village olive press. More than likely, it was the only one in the region and would see heavy use when the time came. A man was testing the beam press by filling baskets with rocks to simulate ripe olives. The beam extended over a notched stone that sat above a collection basin. The counterweights hanging from the lever would create enough pressure on the olives that an ample amount of oil would squeeze into the pan underneath.

Benaiah could tell that the small community was primarily a herding one. Since the time of shearing was just beginning, there were hundreds of sheep from the region being prepared. First, they were corralled into a series of pools where the shepherds would scrub them clean and then let them scamper out, bleating wildly, to dry out in the sun. The wool would be cleaned again after it was shorn and then stretched out in the sun to dry while it was raked. But that morning there was no sunshine, only the cold dreariness of early spring in this country, and the frustration of the shepherds had been evident as Benaiah passed them.

He paused to watch one shepherd struggling to hold down a thrashing, bleating sheep. The man struck it on the snout, but that had no effect. He struck it harder, and the sheep finally calmed down. With strength gained from years of chasing the stubborn and foolish creatures through the highlands, the shepherd pinned the sheep between his knees, tucked his robe back into his belt, and dunked the animal underwater. When it popped up again, he combed his fingers through the matted wool to clean it of mud, excrement, and dead insects.

When he was done, the man released the sheep. It charged through the water to find the herd, agitated but clean. The shepherd wiped his brow, noticed Benaiah watching him, and nodded warily. Benaiah returned the nod and continued walking.

Some of the workers he passed had paused from chiseling stones or preparing the harvest blades and were eating *leben*, the goat's-milk dish curdled into porridge. Tough loaves of bread were dipped in vinegar and passed from man to man. A few threw handfuls of parched grain into their mouths to chew on while they worked.

Despite their labor and willingness to stay busy, fear was apparent everywhere he looked. Mothers shouted at children for going near the edge of town. Farmers and herders, nearly all of them past the age at which men ceased such work, had streamed past him, almost hiding behind their mules. Oxen, possibly sensing the presence of the terrible predators lurking nearby, refused to depart the village with their carts to return through the forest to the trade roads. Their owners beat them with reed sticks, but they would not be budged.

Benaiah was wearing a dark traveling cloak, and he imagined that he must have looked like a phantom emerging from the mist to the children watching from the rooftops. His bulky, muscled frame made his cloak billow out even more, an effect he intended. He swept his eyes back and forth while he walked, always searching his surroundings for threats. His black hair and beard had been trimmed short because it was the start of the campaign season, the time when kings could finally lead their armies to the field after being in garrison all winter while the soldiers tended their herds and took care of other home matters.

Benaiah had expected warmer weather, but at the last moment he had grabbed the heavier cloak, since it provided more comfort while he slept on the ground. Now, climbing through the snow, he was grateful for it. Under the cloak he wore a short battle tunic that came only halfway down his thighs and was laced, out of tradition, with a pattern of blue string on the fringe. When fighting, the short tunic was much preferable to the cloak. Too much loose material was a liability.

He carried a spear, a bow with arrows, a sword, and in his belt a dagger, all forged from iron, which had drawn no shortage of stares from the people in the village. Iron was rare, especially in weapons. Straps from the shield on his back hung over his shoulders.

Benaiah had approached the town's common area near the well and knelt before the group of elders deep in discussion under an overhang nearby. He briefly told them who had sent him. When they asked why no more had come along, he informed them that his own army was marching north with the other soldiers in the land and he was all that could be spared.

The elders insisted that he take more men with him in search of the lion, but Benaiah resisted, insisting that too many would make noise and alert the creature. One of the elders, Jairas, wanted to come, and Benaiah consented, believing it would be good for the morale of the town to see one of their own come along. A young man named Haratha, one of the few physically strong men left in the village, demonstrated that he could sling proficiently, and Benaiah allowed him to come as well.

Benaiah handed Jairas his sickle sword. The man's momentary puzzlement showed that this was a different design from the swords Jairas had seen before, with a longer tip and less curvature—and it was iron. Several of the veterans among the elders wanted to question Benaiah about it, but he just shook his head. They had no time.

Benaiah kept the spear and bow and fastened his shield to his back. He gave Haratha a pouch of heavy copper pellets and told him to sling them at the animal's head to distract it after Benaiah shot the first arrow, giving Benaiah time to release another. Once the creature was wounded, it would likely charge, and Benaiah told them that he would take the charge with his spear while Haratha got a safe distance away and Jairas stabbed the sword into the hide between the ribs.

The animal had already killed several people, including a small boy who had wandered off by himself into the forest to find consolation when his siblings tormented him. The grief-stricken family had been standing nearby when Benaiah and the elders were talking, their clothes torn in mourning, their faces downcast. The body had not been found and likely would not. There would be no burial ceremony. No closure. Benaiah had tried to ignore the sinking feeling in his chest, the black memories in his mind.

Several hours had passed now since the three of them had climbed out of town on a game trail, following the faint spoor. Somewhere lower on the rocky slopes, they had crossed the snow line. What was simply a cold rain in the lower valleys was falling as snow on the high ridges, accumulating on the ground and making the spoor difficult to follow and progress on the hunt slow.

The sun peeked through the gray sky occasionally, only to be quickly shrouded again in the blanket of snow clouds. Benaiah kept the men moving, fearing they would lose their courage if too much rest was given. Even though they kept to a moderate pace, sweat was dampening their clothing anyway, bringing with it the danger of freezing to death. The icy terrain was hardest on Jairas, who struggled to keep up.

The lion was following the trail cut through the pass by the people in the village to reach the higher grazing grounds. Benaiah assumed that, with the late spring snowstorms, the animal had descended to search for food in the valleys.

Benaiah studied the spoor, glanced up and down the valley, and nodded to himself. The lion must have followed the scent of the sheep, encountered the first victim in the forest, and killed him out of fright. Then, because it had been an easy kill and the flesh was sweet and tender, the lion had decided to stay near the village and take more people, most recently the boy from the night before.

The approach Benaiah was taking was the worst possible way to hunt the deadliest animal alive. He had hunted them since childhood—but on organized hunts, with many skilled men working together. Were it not for his hurry to finish this mission and get back to his men currently marching north, he would have taken a day or two to prepare. But the chief had made it clear: get there, kill the lion, establish our goodwill, and get back fast.

They stopped to rest at the top of a steep climb in the trail. To their left was the dense forest of the upper mountain, growing darker in the gray late afternoon. On their right, the slope fell sharply before leveling out just before the forest near the village far below on the valley floor. Somewhere in the distance he heard water running and guessed there was a stream flowing under the blanket of snow.

"Lions are territorial and don't stray far from their hunting grounds," Benaiah whispered to the other two.

"I assume we are the bait," said Jairas quietly.

Benaiah nodded. They resumed their climb.

Most of the afternoon slipped away. The higher they climbed, the colder the air turned. Jairas and Haratha were huffing for breath, and Benaiah began to wonder how much longer they could hold out, especially considering what awaited them among the rocks of the mountains.

The trail led toward more snow-covered rocky outcroppings. The day would be ending soon. Benaiah debated with himself: Abandon the pursuit? Return tomorrow? He strained to hear any birds or hyraxes squealing a warning. He kicked the path every few steps and checked the swirl of powdery light snow to confirm the wind direction.

Just then, around the curve of the path ahead, he heard the sound of dogs bellowing. He had seen dogs in the company of several merchants he had passed on the road to town. The dogs must have scented the lion and chased it themselves.

Senses fully alert, the group trotted carefully forward. As they rounded an outcropping of stone, the saddle between the hills came into view. Across a small cleft in the hillside, crouched against a rock in front of the yowling dogs, was the cornered lion.

Its hide was a dusty yellow and matted with gore from a recent kill. Black tufts of hair formed its mane, dotting the area around its head and shoulders. Its muscles coiled and snapped with fearsome power. The roar was now constant, and so loud that it seemed as though the mountainside shook with each echo. The elder had been right about its size—it was the largest lion Benaiah had ever seen.

One of the dogs noticed them and turned. The lion snarled and swung a paw, knocking it senseless. The other dogs howled and nipped at its hindquarters. Though heavily outmatched, they were bravely staying with it.

Benaiah yanked an arrow from the quiver. They closed to within fifty cubits of the lion, watching it strike another dog with its paw, killing it instantly. Steam rushed from its mouth as it roared again.

Benaiah saw Haratha halt in terror.

"Keep moving! We have to get closer!" Benaiah called.

Haratha bobbled his sling, dropping the copper pellet. He glanced up at the lion, his eyes wide with fright.

The lion lowered its head and flattened its ears, signaling a charge. It roared again.

Within arrow range now, Benaiah lifted his bow up and pulled the notched end of the arrow to his mouth. The motion was so familiar that he had the lion within his sights instantly.

The lion struck the last of the dogs down, then sprang from its crouch toward the terrified Haratha. Benaiah's foot slipped on the snow and he lost his target. He yelled again for Haratha to release while he struggled to stand again.

Before the creature reached him, Haratha managed to launch a copper pellet that miraculously hit the charging animal in the head. A spurt of red mist erupted from the lion's face. It snarled and paused briefly to paw at its head where the pellet had struck it in or near the eye. By that time Benaiah had regained his balance and sent an arrow into its hide.

The lion winced at the arrow but leaped again, struck Haratha, and tumbled with him across the slope. The lion slashed and snarled, but abandoned Haratha and sprang up the slope toward Benaiah.

Benaiah felt his muscles tense. The animal moved faster than he'd thought it could on the snow, but he was ready. The arrow he sent would have caught the creature in the throat if it hadn't slipped on an icy rock and stumbled.

That was all he had time to do before, with a flash of golden fur and the hot stench of rotting flesh from the animal's jaws, he felt the animal's crushing weight and infinite strength, and then he was rolling, smashed against the frozen ground, his face grinding against the icy pebbles as the monster roared in his ear.

Benaiah managed to stop by shoving his hand into a snow bank and digging his fingers all the way to the ground. He winced, waiting for the next strike, but the lion had turned away from him, lowering its head and flattening its ears. Then it charged back toward Haratha—but Jairas had stepped between them, sword in hand.

Benaiah regained his footing and rushed forward, searching for his fallen spear in the snow since another shot with an arrow would risk hitting one of the others. Benaiah shouted for Jairas to stab instead of swing, but in his panic to save Haratha, Jairas could not hear him and hacked away harmlessly at the animal's neck. The lion ignored his blows, attacking instead the one who'd ruined its eye.

Haratha screamed, the lion roared, and just as Benaiah reached the spear, the lion's claws sank into Haratha's thighs and it threw itself on top of him. Benaiah snatched the spear out of the snow and lunged toward the fight.

The lion had stretched its jaws wide enough that it looked as if it was about to swallow Haratha's head. A hard bite with those fangs would burst through the boy's skull, killing him instantly.

Benaiah shifted his grip and aimed the spear thrust at the lion's head instead of its flank. The spearhead impaled the muscles on the lion's jaws as it bit Haratha. The fangs slashed into Haratha's scalp, spraying a wave of blood onto the snow, but the bite from its wounded jaw lacked enough force to penetrate.

Snarling and shrieking, the lion twisted away and released the boy. Benaiah snatched Haratha by the collar and jerked him backward, away from the lion.

Roaring, the animal pawed at the shaft of the spear lodged firmly in its jaw. Benaiah shrugged the shield straps off his back in order to move better and dove for the spear handle, landing on top of it, ripping it back out of the lion's face.

Jairas appeared again, still trying to hack at the animal's hide. This time his aim went true, and he slid the tip of the sword into the lion's flank. Benaiah hauled the spear up and shoved it into the bloody fur. It stopped against bone. He pulled it back and shoved it again, this time finding the soft underbelly in front of the rear leg.

The lion spun in a circle, knocking Jairas over and pulling Benaiah back to the ground. Benaiah clung to the shaft as the lion tried to run away. The spearhead was now lodged in the rib cage—a killing blow, if Benaiah could hold on long enough.

The lion turned and lashed out with its paw once more. Benaiah dodged it, yelling curses and pushing the spear as hard as he could. Every muscle in his arms burned with exhaustion.

The animal snarled and slipped onto its side. It tried to stand again but couldn't. A leg kicked several times as a spurt of dark blood erupted from the spear wound in its flank. It lashed at them again, weaker. It coughed blood from its lungs, along with the coppery smell of rotting flesh and blood. With a final swipe of its paw, it bit at the rocks and the earth before lying still.

Benaiah let his face fall into the snow and released the spear shaft. The ice felt good against his eyelids. His face started to go numb against the snow, and he wished he could make that numbness permeate the rest of his body.

He took several deep breaths, then stood and walked to the lion's head. He prodded the remaining eye with his foot to ensure that it was dead. No response. Benaiah had once walked away from a kill only to be attacked from behind. He believed that these creatures were capable of hate. Satisfied that this one was dead, he looked around for his companions.

Jairas was fumbling with a water pouch next to the still form of Haratha, trying to work the frantic energy out of his hands. Benaiah knelt next to them and put his finger on the boy's neck. Haratha's eyes blinked open when Benaiah touched him.

Haratha's scalp was ripped into divots from the fangs, and blood poured from the tears in his thigh. His chest was sliced into ribbons of skin, exposing the bones of the rib cage. The dull, white gleam of his exposed skull was slowly becoming soaked with blood. Haratha clenched his jaw stoically.

"You come from hard Judah stock," Benaiah encouraged him.

Haratha smiled weakly.

"I will carry him," Benaiah said to Jairas, pulling out strips of cloth to bind the wound. "You carry my weapons. We only have an hour or so before he bleeds out."

Benaiah pulled a vial of olive oil from his pouch and poured it into Haratha's cuts while the icy wind bit at them. He emptied salt into the cuts as well, causing Haratha to swoon from pain and shock. Benaiah slapped his face.

Jairas held Haratha down while Benaiah wrapped the largest wounds with bandage cloth. He tightened a knot with a stick to cease the flow of blood, which was spurting gently onto the snow and forming a scarlet pool. Finally Benaiah sat back, exhausted, and watched Haratha's blood fill the snow. He felt the cold numbing his mind and slowing his thoughts.

"You have wounds as well," Jairas said.

Benaiah examined his arm, then felt his shoulders. "Not deep. I will wash them out. But not now. The boy will die if we don't hurry."

"Your bow and arrows?" Jairas said, nodding to a spot nearby. The bow's string had snapped when the lion pounced, along with the shafts of all of the arrows in the quiver.

Benaiah cursed. The bow was among the prizes of his weaponry, brilliantly made from something called bamboo wood by a master craftsman from lands far to the east. It had cost him a tremendous amount of gold and considerable haggling with the wily merchant. His fellow warriors, especially the archers, could barely disguise their envy. He was relieved that the bow itself had not broken, but it would take him awhile to string it properly again, and he certainly did not want to do it in cold weather.

Benaiah raked his fingers through his beard, then pulled the collar of his tunic away from his neck, a nervous habit he had picked up and could not shake. After a count, he hoisted the boy onto his shoulders.

"We are only an hour's walk above the village if we cut straight down from here," Jairas said. "It would be rougher going but a much shorter journey."

Benaiah nodded.

Snow was falling steadily now, filling the barren spaces on the ground that the previous storm had missed. After a few moments of stumbling, they started to make good progress. Benaiah became hopeful that they would make it down from the pass before the storm settled in and made travel impossible.

He had just begun to relax his breathing and find a rhythm in his steps when another lion attacked.

The animal had been lying in wait in a small thicket on the slope. The hot roar blew across Benaiah's face as the paws, with immense force, struck his head. He dropped Haratha and threw his arms in front of the lion's jaws, his throat scratching out a cry and his legs giving way. The power was overwhelming. He could see nothing but golden fur, feel nothing but the lion's crushing strength.

Like the other lion, this one wrapped him up with its paws and was trying to bite his neck. Heat and steam from the lion's breath covered him. The lion's screams made him dizzy as he fought — although all he could do was roll his body to the side, away from Haratha. Benaiah felt like vomiting as the rancid breath closed around his face.

They rolled several times down the mountainside, one of Benaiah's arms pinned to his side by the lion's weight and strength. Benaiah wrenched away from the jaws as they snapped for his neck. A fang caught his scalp and he felt hot, blinding pain.

The ground gave way on one side, and he sensed that they were struggling on the edge of a drop-off of some kind, either a cliff or a pit. Something erupted in his strength, his right arm slipped out of the lion's grip, and he shoved the creature as hard as he could while stabbing its eye with his thumb. It released its grip, slipped on the loose, icy rocks, and tumbled backward into a pit. The animal landed with a thump on the bottom.

Benaiah wiped blood from his forehead where the claws had gashed him and staggered back up the slope. He had to find a weapon quickly. The lion might leap out of the pit at any moment and resume the attack. The wounds in his skin burned like coals; he was losing a lot of blood.

The commotion had revived Haratha, who was now sitting up and insisting to Jairas that he could walk. The older man argued that the boy would further damage his body if he did not remain still.

"No, take advantage of his strength," Benaiah said to Jairas. "Let him walk with you back down the mountain. You need to get him back quickly, and it will take too long if you drag him. I will climb into the pit and get the lion."

"Don't be a fool. It will tear you apart."

Benaiah ignored him and knelt by Haratha.

"Let me stay with you," said Haratha. He still looked dazed, the loss of blood turning his skin as pale as the snow around them. Benaiah had seen these erratic bursts of energy from wounded men before. He would become delirious soon.

"Who is your father?" Benaiah asked.

"Eleb."

"Haratha son of Eleb, you fought well today. You will return to your woman if you can manage to stay awake."

"I ... have no woman. I am trying, though."

They all laughed and Benaiah clapped him on his good shoulder. He helped Haratha to his feet and the young man leaned against Jairas for support.

Roars erupted from the pit behind them. They could hear thudding and crashing as smaller rocks cascaded. Benaiah considered going back down to the village with Jairas and Haratha. Losing a man to the jaws of a lion was the last thing David's little army needed right now; every one of them would make a difference in the coming days.

But the faces of the dead boy's parents in the village appeared in Benaiah's mind. The familiar pit in his gut gnawed at him, and he knew he had to make sure this lion would die. If it escaped, it would surely return to terrorize the village. They were relentless when they had developed a taste for man.

He swore under his breath.

"Get moving. I'll catch up," Benaiah said, sliding the back straps of his shield off.

"You are certain?"

"You need to get him back. His family will need him."

"Perhaps it will die down there. It has not come out. It might be trapped."

"It might escape, and it will not relent if it does. Just get him back to the village."

Jairas looked at him a moment longer, then nodded.

Benaiah watched them disappear down the slope into the forest. He felt the sudden urge to say something else. He shouted toward them as the wind picked up.

"I have a woman. Tell her ..." But they kept walking without turning. He assumed they could not hear him over the noise of the storm. He let it go.

The clouds swirled and increased, grappling along the ridges above and tossing more and more snow onto the slopes. The weather in this high country was unnerving. And it was getting colder. He had heard of men dying from the sleep brought by cold weather.

Relief, he thought. The best way to go. Slip softly into Sheol, the faces gone at last, the pain dulled by the cold darkness.

More roars came from the pit, more pebbles scraped loose. He expected to see the black-maned monster tear out of the hole and race toward him. He clenched his teeth.

His death would not come from sleep.

Benaiah picked up his spear and walked to where an old tree was lying on its side, roots hardened by age jutting into the air. Finding a good root with a sharp end and a twist in the center to grip, Benaiah pulled down with all of his weight and broke it away from the tree. In the old days, roots such as this one were among the only weapons his people could muster. It would work well against the creature.

Benaiah checked the dagger on his belt, then discovered with dismay that his water pouch had been torn apart by the lion's claws. It had protected the flesh on his side, but now he was left with nothing to drink. He scooped up a handful of snow and tried to quench his thirst with it.

He reached the edge of the pit and peered down. It was a hunting pit, clearly dug many years before, probably by ancient hunters who had enlarged a natural cave in the hillside. Eight or nine cubits across, about the same depth. Normally hunting pits would be covered with brushwood and approaches dug so that a group of hunters could drive the lion toward a narrow cleft where the pit's covering would give way, trapping the animal. The hunters would then rain arrows on it until the animal died.

But Benaiah had none of those luxuries.

He could see the lion pacing in the corner, occasionally crossing a patch of snow that had drifted in. It huffed air in great plumes of breath, roaring and gasping in the low-pitched rumble that could be heard for an entire day's walk away. Especially at night, he remembered, when the still desert breeze brought the sound through the Nile reeds.

Benaiah tossed the root into the pit below. The lion snarled and drew back into the darkness, waiting for him. He would leap from the edge, land with the spear raised, and pin the lion as fast as possible. Once the spearhead was buried to the heart, he would grab the root and stab its neck. Then the people in the village would never perish in its jaws again.

Benaiah himself might be the lion's last kill.

He closed his eyes, pushing the thought from his mind, feeling the prickle of snow on his face. His hands clenched and unclenched. The last of the gray twilight faded. The beast roared, and Benaiah felt it watching him, waiting for him, amber eyes boring into him and craving the taste of his flesh.

This had to be done.

He nodded.

He would be free. She would be free of him.

Benaiah shook his head, trying to focus on the lion and how he would kill it, on what type of maneuver might, against all odds, keep him alive, but the black depths of the pit reminded him of a room he'd known, of the day of sorrow. That day came back to him—the day all was lost.

There was darkness, endless darkness, and screaming, and the smell of blood. Blood covering the doorway, blood in the room, bits of hair across the stone floor. He heard the sound of families throughout the town wailing and moaning in grief, the smell of smoke drifting, cries to Yahweh. A raid. How could he have allowed this?

Benaiah looked for Sherizah, called for her. There she was, his wife, in the corner, her hands over her eyes, her cries filled with anguish. He shook her. What happened? *What happened?* She shook uncontrollably. Blood was everywhere, the room cold and dark.

Where are they? Where are they? he'd yelled at her.

Gone. Killed. They are gone . . .

And he was away. He was away . . .

Benaiah blinked.

He was above the pit, in the snow, with the lion.

The wet on the edge of his eyes stung in the cold. He wiped

them quickly. The black pit gaped in front of him. He felt its darkness in his bones. He squeezed his fists and felt his hands shaking again. He pulled absently at his collar with his thumb.

There was something the chief always said.

Cover me in the day of war.

He shook his head.

Benaiah breathed a few more times, enjoying the snow and the rage of the storm gripping the pass above him.

Then he leaped over the side.

TWO

As soon as Benaiah hit the ground, the lion leaped from the shadows. The creature's hot, rancid breath, like that of the first lion, had the stench of decay. Before Benaiah could fully raise his spear, he saw a flash of bloody fur in the dusk and the lion was on him, swatting his spear aside.

They rolled over together. The spear out of reach, Benaiah pulled his dagger and plunged it into the beast's flank. The blade skipped off a rib. The jaws snapped at Benaiah's head again and again. He forced his fist into the open jaws and shoved his arm down the throat, trying to prevent the fangs from piercing his skull. The lion tried to roar again, its voice now muffled by the arm down its throat, and raked its claws painfully against Benaiah's side, crushing him beneath its weight. The paws pinned his dagger hand against his body.

Benaiah searched frantically for the spear nearby, needing it if he was to have any chance. One of his shoulders was buried in the lion's throat, the other pinned to his side. The fangs buried in his shoulder hurt so badly that Benaiah fought to remain conscious.

Something caught his sight in the snow.

The root, only a handbreadth out of reach.

The paw pinning down Benaiah's weapon arm released for just a moment, and he used it to stab his dagger into the side of the lion's face. It roared, sending specks of saliva into his eyes and ears.

Benaiah pulled free and scampered backward until he reached the wall of the pit, gasping for breath, his arm bloody and burning. The lion was pawing at the dagger sticking out of the side of its face. Its jaw hung limp. When the animal roared and snarled, it sounded almost sloppy. The blade must have severed some of the muscles in its jaw.

Despite the searing pain of the claw wounds, Benaiah leaped forward, knowing the animal would outlast him if he did not mortally wound it fast. He snatched up the root, shouted, and rammed it into the lion just behind the shoulder, near its heart.

The root pierced the rough hide and entered the soft interior flesh. The lion convulsed and shrieked with fury, twisting away and jerking the shaft from Benaiah's grip, flinging blood into Benaiah's eyes from the wound.

He staggered backward and wiped his brow. When he could see again, he noticed the lion in the corner of the pit. The root thumped back and forth as the lion darted around trying to dislodge it. Benaiah looked for the spear but could not find it in the swirl of dirt, snow, and blood.

He rushed toward the lion again, grabbing the root and hanging onto it to prevent it from snapping as the lion thrashed around. The gouts of blood pumping out of the wound told Benaiah that he had struck near the heart, but not near enough. The animal was not dying. If anything, its roaring and thrashing increased.

The shaft of the root, slick with blood, slid through Benaiah's hands. He tried to grip it harder. A rotten stench rushed across his nostrils. The root had penetrated the bowels of the animal.

The lion curled into a ball and then rolled violently sideways, catching Benaiah off guard and knocking him over. He lost his grip on the root; his head thudded against the rocks. He saw a bright shock of light. Fighting past the throbbing in his head, he reached out into the snow for something to fight back with. Why wasn't it dying? Claws, pain, burning. Where was the spear?

There was a huge roar, and the lion pinned him again. He gagged at the rotten breath. He arched his back in panic—and felt something beneath him.

The spear.

Screaming with his last burst of panic-stricken energy, he lurched to the side and shoved the lion away from him. His arm came free enough to reach the spear and swing it around, hoping to drive its head into the lion's throat.

Too late he realized that he had shoved the wrong end forward, and the dull end cap of the spear thudded harmlessly against the golden hide. Before he could turn it and try again, claws raked the side of his head, pounding him so hard that he almost blacked out. He felt numb, as though the cuts from the claws were so brutal that they had bypassed all pain.

A short flap of skin from his torn scalp now hung over his left eye. He pushed it out of the way, but it kept falling back, blocking his view. As the lion reared for another strike, Benaiah rolled out of its path and stumbled toward the wall of the pit.

With his clear eye, he saw a branch sticking out from the wall of the pit overhead. He jumped for it. He missed it on the first try and fell to his knees. The lion roared. He could hear it crawling toward him. Its wounds were finally taking a toll, or it would have leaped.

Benaiah jumped again and managed to wedge his hand between the branch and the frozen mud of the pit wall. Just as the lion's paw swiped at his leg, he pulled himself up out of reach. The beast snarled at him but was apparently too wounded to leap.

Benaiah panted. His breath curled out in icy tendrils against the darkness of the pit. The rumbling growl of the lion came from below him, and even though he was only a few cubits above the monster, he could barely make it out in the dark, with only the large puffs of frozen breath drifting upward as it roared indicating its location. Benaiah's arm shook from the strain of holding him in place on the branch.

He had to deal with the skin hanging over his eye, which was swelling so quickly that soon he would be unable to see out of it. The lion might be in its death throes, but it would live long enough to kill him if he didn't kill it first. A thought occurred to him: simply hang onto the branch until the lion bled out. But the growling below him continued. How was this possible? The spear must have ripped the lion's insides to pieces. The resiliency of predators amazed him—and how they defied the call of death to exact revenge on their hunter.

Benaiah was suddenly very cold. The snowflakes stung his open wounds.

He saw his wife's face in the darkness. She was holding out a pouch of water to him, and he reached for it ... for her.

He shook his head; he was going delirious with pain.

Benaiah fished in his belt for his second flint dagger, a smaller one that he only used for skinning game.

It was still there.

Pulling the blade out with his damaged arm while he held on to the root with the good one, he dug the point into the skin above his eye and sliced a small part of the flap away from his scalp. His head was still numb from the paw strike and he barely felt it, but the fresh wash of blood pouring down his face was a nuisance.

The lion roared again, but this time, he thought with soaring hope, it sounded weaker. He had to move now and finish it before he became too weak.

Benaiah let go of the root and collapsed onto the snow. The lion charged. Benaiah snatched up the spear with the correct side forward this time, and as the beast opened its jaws wide to bite, Benaiah aimed the spearhead into the black opening and held on for his life.

The spear slid down the lion's throat and penetrated deep into its bowels, all the way up to Benaiah's fist. His arm entered the throat again, but the jaws no longer snapped. He heard a dull rumble from deep inside the creature's throat. The bloody shaft started to slide in his hand. He tried to keep his hand clenched but his strength was running out. The paws swatted at him, but with little force. The animal was finally dying.

Slowly, when it seemed like the entire pit would fill with blood, the roars became weaker and the thrashing softened. The lion struggled a bit longer and then coughed out a pink mist and lay still.

Benaiah let his head fall onto the patch of ice next to the lion. He listened to the cold wind whistling across the mouth of the pit. He wondered vaguely how much blood he had lost. He packed lumps of snow into the wounds on his head and arm to stop the bleeding. He shivered. The great body of the lion was still steaming, so he leaned against it for warmth.

The cold weather, exhaustion from the struggle, loss of blood, and heat from the carcass made sleep nearly irresistible. He slapped his face to wake himself up. He had to keep moving so that he wouldn't fall asleep and freeze to death.

Benaiah sat up and tried to focus on the icy ground around him. It was almost completely dark now; only moments of light remained. The lion was still leaking blood onto the snow. Benaiah's spear was buried in the carcass and the dagger protruded from its mouth.

When enough strength had returned that he knew he could climb, Benaiah crawled toward the dead lion and knelt on its head while he tugged at his weapons. The dagger came out easily, but the spear needed several hard pulls before it finally came loose. He left the root buried in the carcass.

Benaiah tossed the weapons out of the pit onto the hillside above and studied his predicament. Snow still drifted in twenty cubits above. He searched up and down the wall for a route to scale on the ice and loose rock. The hunters who had dug the ancient trap had done their work well; he could not easily spot a way out. Small drifts of snow were accumulating on every surface of the wall, and it was getting colder.

He spat blood to clear the coppery taste from his mouth. He stepped up to the wall and began to climb, one carefully chosen handhold or foothold at a time, slipping backward every time he gained traction. Progress was slow, but eventually he pulled himself over the lip of the pit and lay on his side.

It was now dark. The moon occasionally peeked between the storm clouds. The snow had stopped falling but the wind was picking up, pushing another storm up through the valley and causing bits of ice to sting his exposed flesh. His mind was in a fog. His sweaty tunic clung to his back, causing him to shiver. He needed to get out of the mountains fast.

Still, he took the time first to bind his open wounds. He pulled strips of linen from his pouch and wrapped them tight. Then he wrapped his cloak back around his shoulders, wincing, strapped the shield onto his back, and picked up his weapons. He knotted together the two ends of the broken string on his bow and slung the weapon over his shoulder.

He worked his way to the route that would take him straight down the slope. He ran his finger along the jagged edge of the cuts on his head and arm, wearily grateful that he had not been eviscerated by the claws.

Around him the landscape had become a sea of white powder

and black ice-covered rock. His fingers were numb. He slipped and fell every few steps, yelling in agony as hidden branches and jagged rocks disguised in the snow stabbed him.

Benaiah came across the tracks in the snow where Jairas and Haratha had left the main path. He could make out a forest far below where he remembered seeing the creek that led back to the village. He hoped he would run into the other two before long, so that he would not have to navigate unfamiliar terrain in his weakened condition. He focused on one step at a time, trying to keep his mind as clear as possible through the cold and the pain, sensing that the storm was getting worse.

THREE

Benaiah picked his way down the pass and into the forest he had seen from above. Several times the game trail he was following split apart, and he would debate with himself which direction to take—until a brief lull in the snowfall would allow him to see which route would lead him back to the stream.

The weather changed abruptly as he stepped out of the forest into a clearing. Behind him, the boughs of the trees were heavy laden with snow, and yet where he stood everything was slick with rain. Confused, he stopped for a moment. It was beautiful—the lightning and thunder of a spring rainstorm in front and the white-out of the snowstorm further up the mountain. Rain pelted his face. He let the cold water wash through the cuts on his head, enjoying the tingling pain and letting it revive him.

He suddenly felt very weary. Before he knew it he was sitting on a rock to rest. Thunder rumbled up the valley. He vowed to rest only for a short while to let his blood-drained body recover. He rested his face in his hands, shivering in the cold.

Lightning flashed, and he looked up again. It was easy to be lulled by the thunder. Storm clouds and snow clouds mingled overhead, illuminated by the lightning. Benaiah looked over his shoulder in the direction he had just come.

He felt his neck prickle.

He had seen something in the lightning flash. Another lion? He strained his eyes, but no object materialized.

In his exhausted state he almost ignored it and kept walking, but discipline reminded him to never doubt the fear instinct, which warned of danger long before the mind. He stared at the woods and waited for the next lightning flash.

A man was standing in the path.

Benaiah could not make out the man's face. He saw what looked like a cloak similar to his own draped around the man's shoulders, but the rest of him was obscured by the snow still falling in the forest.

At first Benaiah thought it might be Jairas. But where was Haratha? Had Jairas left him behind? Benaiah waited for the next flash and gestured for the man to come, but he did not move.

Benaiah gripped his spear and slowly reached for the hilt of his sword—before remembering he had given it to Jairas.

A sickening feeling crept over him. He felt the pain in his wounds pulsing. The man was still far up the trail, but now Benaiah thought he could hear a quiet voice close by, as though someone was standing only an arm's length away. He strained his ears to understand, but the storm and wind were too loud, the voice too soft.

Lightning flared again. The figure was moving toward him.

Alarmed now, Benaiah ignored the swelling stiffness of his arm and held a spear at the ready. The wet darkness was becoming oppressive. He stared hard at the spot where he'd last seen the figure, waiting for another lightning strike. None came.

He shook his head and wiped his eyes, unable to see anything in the blackness. He kept the spear shaft tight in his grip. Somewhere down the valley the thunder was rumbling.

Suddenly the moon erupted from behind a cloud and the area was bathed in silver light. Benaiah's heart jumped. The man was directly in front of him, as tall as a tree. Fear wrapped around his throat and Benaiah found it impossible to breathe.

The figure held a shadowy sword, glowing with some unknown pale, cold light, sideways as though preparing to swing it at Benaiah's head. All was happening too fast. Benaiah tried to push his spear forward into the warrior's midsection, but his blood felt like it had frozen. Moonlight glinted off the man's armor. The figure was immense and powerful, taller than any man Benaiah had ever seen, cubits taller than himself.

But worse than the man's size and the menacing weapon he carried, Benaiah was suddenly overcome with the greatest feeling of despair of his life. Every terrible thought and sorrow he had ever felt came back. His eyes clamped shut in fright.

He tried to move but only gagged, angry at his helplessness and fear in front of this demon from Sheol.

Then he was overcome with flashes of memories: of blood on stones, of a woman, his wife, screaming and shaking, of a sun-washed seacoast far to the south, and Pharaoh's entourage gathered on the hillside watching him battle, watching him lose ground in the hot sand, growing weaker, giving way before a great mountain of a man who swung a spear so viciously.

His mind was overrun with dark images. Fear shook him, leaving him unable to strike or defend or move in any way.

The sword that stretched from the arm of the warrior slashed forward, and all Benaiah could do was watch.

A clang as the sword struck. Benaiah cringed, expecting to be dead.

Another sword, glowing hot with tongues of fire, was a hand-breadth from his face. Through the rain, he could see that it had blocked the sword of the dark figure.

Benaiah watched, terrified and still unable to move.

The flaming sword slashed fast and high, and then Benaiah saw that it was wielded by another warrior who had just arrived. The new man's armor glinted, but it was the flaming sword that Benaiah could not stop staring at. It moved faster than he thought a man could move it, cutting and striking, pushing the dark figure back to the snow line.

The two fighters contended with each other across the wet landscape, the flaming sword driving with endless power and speed until finally Benaiah lost sight of them in the mist covering the snowy tree line.

Benaiah let his breath escape. His arms shook, and the spear clattered to the ground. His eyes could not leave the tree line.

Then the moon disappeared again, the rain increased, and cold mist drew up around him. His wounds burned, rousing him from his stupor. His combat instincts kicked in. Summoning his strength, Benaiah picked up the spear and trotted down the path, unable to stop himself from looking frantically over his shoulder every few moments. The damp cold was getting to him. His muscles quivered uncontrollably. He was now so wet that conserving energy to avoid sweating was pointless, and more importantly, if he did not keep his blood pumping he would freeze. He found himself running. The path twisted down the mountainside, barely discernible in the dark.

What he had just witnessed must have been his mind tricking him. Had to be the wounds, he thought. Maybe the infection from the claws was setting in already, making him mad.

His own steady footfalls lulled him, and before long he realized that it had stopped raining. He paused briefly to look behind him up the pass. He could still see the storm in the high country. Lightning flickered in the clouds and thunder rolled gently. There was no sign of the two warriors.

Benaiah resumed his trot. Exhaustion crept into his limbs. His knees buckled each time he hopped down from a rock in the trail. A swirling, numb feeling seeped through his head, and he could feel his pulse slow.

He slipped on a wet log and pitched forward, too weak now to even hold his hand up to stop his fall. Just before he struck the ground, a hand caught his arm.

"Sit and rest."

Benaiah was too weary to argue. He knelt on the nearest patch of grass and slumped to his side. Whoever the man talking to him was, it was not an enemy or he would already be dead.

Benaiah panted a moment with his eyes closed. When he opened them after regaining his breath, a man with a trimmed beard and cuts on his forehead stared back at him. Benaiah recognized the armor: it was his savior from the battle above.

A spear and shield were strapped to the man's back. The flaming sword glowed quietly at his side, resembling a bed of coals in a campfire instead of the tongue of flame he had seen earlier.

The warrior cupped Benaiah's face between his hands and spoke something like an oath. It was in a tongue Benaiah was not familiar with, and he was familiar with many tongues.

Benaiah felt burning pain in his head for a moment. His muscles twitched with new power and energy. The weariness that had overcome him slipped away. He still saw the claw wounds on his arm, but they didn't seem to affect him; they ached just enough to remind him that they were there. His heart beat stronger. He took a deep breath of moist air and held it a moment.

The warrior released Benaiah's head and stood up.

"It will be enough for your task, in Yahweh's great mercy. Get up."

Benaiah had recovered enough to be once more confused as to what was happening. He let the man pull him to his feet and tried to study his face as he adjusted his equipment. Dark hair, dark eyes, short beard trimmed like other warriors. But he was *immense*, with massive arms and a cloak that looked as heavy as a talent of gold. He had deep lines on his face, gutted and gnarled from years of combat. His stare was fierce. Benaiah had rarely met a man whose gaze he could not hold.

Benaiah became frustrated with himself. Why was he not asking who the man was, and how he had appeared so suddenly, and who had been the other warrior back up the hill? But either the cold or his own fear was holding his tongue.

The wind started up again, whipping drizzle into a swirling pattern that made both men lower their eyes into their cloaks. Benaiah dreaded having to cover his damaged arm with the thick wool, since the wound was still open and raw, but he felt the man's gaze spurring him on. Holding his breath, he wrapped it up once more, winced, then gripped the shaft of his spear. It still hurt, but he sensed that his strength would last the night. The man's touch had affected him greatly. Somehow.

The warrior gestured toward the village. They set off, moving at a slow trot on the wet ground. The air was still bitterly cold and breathing was hard. Benaiah evaluated his condition and considered whether the shortness in his breathing was caused by the cold or by a broken rib. Likely a rib, he decided, because he could not inhale all the way without it stabbing him.

They followed the creek through the forest as it twisted in and out of wet undergrowth. Moonlight was patchy at best, but the warrior didn't seem to need it to find his way. Benaiah watched the shadows around him as much as he watched his footing, wondering whether the dark figure would reappear. Not even able to raise a blade, he thought with disgust. The battle with the lion had drained him, but that was no excuse for his helplessness.

"He has been my adversary since the dawn of all things. We will see him again," the man whispered, just loud enough to be heard over their footsteps.

Benaiah was about to ask how the man had heard his thoughts when the warrior caught his arm in a sudden movement. They crouched together and took cover behind a boulder.

They listened quietly for a moment. The rain had become a light drizzle, sprinkling on their armor and weapons. Through the trees Benaiah could make out campfires from the village; they were close enough that, were it not so late, he could have heard the noise of families cooking and talking. Then he saw what the stranger had spotted.

Lining the edge of the clearing where the town was built, silhouetted against the fires, were soldiers. Benaiah could see their heavy armor. He guessed they must be raiders who had snuck into the valley looking for supplies. But raiders from where?

The stranger pulled Benaiah's head closer and whispered, "They are Amalekites, the enemies of Yahweh's people, and you will kill them."

Benaiah's arms tensed as he held his weapons. Amalekites. The hated nomads from the south who had plagued his people for generations—the people who had destroyed his life. Anger surfaced, overpowering the pain and the weariness. He did not fight it and began to think of the pleasure of slaughtering them.

"Look at your feet."

Benaiah peered at the dark forest floor. He saw a log nearby, along with some brush and a few rocks.

"Look closer."

Benaiah leaned down, straining his eyes at the log. He saw a small foot with a sandal on one end. He winced.

The body of the boy killed by the lion.

He was grateful that it was too dark to make out many details, but it looked as though the body was mostly intact. The lion had killed him, then left him behind without eating him. As if it had killed him for no purpose, not even for food, but only to bring death and sorrow in troubled times.

The sight of the small corpse, his memory of the grief on the faces of the parents, blood on the stones of his own home, a burial he had missed, they all came to him and made him shake. He felt it coming again, the urge to vomit, to hate, to scream in agony, and run, and kill, and rush into the forest.

The hand squeezed his shoulder again, the stranger pulling him close. His embrace was firm, brotherly, and Benaiah's heart swelled with sorrow.

"I . . . ," Benaiah heard himself whisper.

The warrior hugged him tighter. His voice was soft, compassionate. "I know what you suffer. It was planned before your birth."

Benaiah recoiled. He fought to keep his voice quiet. "*Planned? By who? You were there?*"

"I have stood in the presence of Yahweh, who knows and moves all things. I have protected you all of your life."

"Who was supposed to protect my family?"

"They are in his embrace."

"What about *my* embrace? Who are you?"

The warrior ignored him and unwrapped part of his bulky clothing and handed the bundle to Benaiah, who reached out with trembling hands and took it. It was a burial shroud, embroidered with a pattern of such exquisite detail that Benaiah momentarily forgot his agony and was astounded by it even in the blackness.

The warrior pointed at the boy. "Return him to his father for burial once you have defeated your enemies." The stranger looked directly at Benaiah, his eyes fierce. "Power will come to you now to help you accomplish this task. But your heart is twisted with vengeance and hate, and the power will leave you. One will escape. "

"I won't let one escape."

"It has been decided already. The power will leave you."

"The power?"

"You have heard it called by another name."

Benaiah searched the man's eyes, but there was nothing to be revealed there. The power? He thought quickly. "The covering."

The man nodded. "Do not flee the covering, Benaiah. It is there for you always."

"Who are you? Please—tell me."

The warrior grinned slightly. "Darkness grows over the land of Yahweh. We have many battles left to fight before the end of your life. You will see me again."

Benaiah was more than a little confused. He had heard plenty about the covering from David and the Three, and at any other time he would have wanted to question the stranger further, but now he was becoming too angry to ask questions. He was already making his plans to assault the Amalekites. The desire to kill the men down the hill overwhelmed him. He would attack and maneuver fast. Take advantage of surprise and the terrain. He turned to ask the warrior how he wanted to assault, but there was no one beside him.

Benaiah looked around him, searching the forest with his eyes, but saw nothing. The man was gone, leaving his spear propped next to Benaiah. The night felt a little colder, and Benaiah's head throbbed again unexpectedly.

Benaiah tried to form a plan of attack despite the ache from his wounds. The stranger's touch earlier had not removed all of the painful stiffness, but he felt as though his limbs could move effectively.

As a boy growing up in the home of a priest, he had been taught to read and write the Law, not how to survive the bloodbaths of combat. His father had even made him copy his own scroll of the Law, something he dutifully did every week.

Since becoming a man, though, he had neglected the Law and preferred the intriguing works on warfare brought by the merchants to Kabzeel. His home had not been far from the trade routes, and he was able to sit in the tents of the merchant caravans, listening to them read tales of battle dictated by great generals to their personal scribes in foreign lands. There were scrolls on strategy and leadership, some from Egypt, some from the lands of the old Hittite empire in the north, or, on one occasion, the mysterious and savage lands east of the Jordan.

All of them, without exception, said never to attack when outnumbered, especially alone. He'd seen the sense in that—until he met the Three. The Three of David, mighty in battle and feared to the point of myth. The Three who had taken him in and trained him and shown him their fighting ways—the study of predators and control of movement, the study of power and speed. His power of death grew, power to pour vengeance on his enemy's heads.

He watched the helmets of the Amalekites, likely stolen from Philistines because Amalekites never wore armor. They were looking back and forth at one another, doubtless discussing the best approach to deal with the few remaining men in the town. He loathed the Amalekites and their barbarian ways. Their cowardly warlords loved to kill children and rape women. They had been his people's enemies from the days of the exodus from Egypt. They had become his own enemies more recently.

Benaiah touched the boy's body and felt the weight of loss all over again, the pain that never seemed to leave him and tore at him in the darkness.

He made sure the dagger was in his belt and clutched his spear. It was never his favorite weapon. He wished he had brought his club, but he had left it back with the army. No good on a lion hunt, it would have served its brutal purpose well here. He laid his bow against the tree with the intent to retrieve it later.

Just before he rose, Benaiah put down his own spear and took up the spear left by the warrior. The balance was perfect. The wooden handle had been polished smooth by unknown ages of the warrior's grip. The head, cut from a metal he had not seen before, was honed to a sharp point.

He felt something—*warmth*—permeating the weapon. The drizzle was cold and his body was shivering uncontrollably under his soaking clothes, but the shaft of the spear was as hot as a baking stone. Heat snaked through his fingertips and into his arms, and Benaiah felt it surging through his body. His muscles cramped, released. The force of it overwhelmed him.

Benaiah allowed the strength to flow into him. He no longer felt the pain from his wounds. When he shut his eyes tight, he saw images of fire—fire that came not from the spear but from the sky above, then underneath, then everywhere at once, with the spear becoming ever hotter.

The wind through the canopy of trees above blocked the faint sound of his movement as he stood and began to stalk toward the Amalekites' right flank. Benaiah still had no plan. He only knew he needed to hurry; the violent force of the heat from the spear pushed him forward. And deep beneath that fire, the familiar demand roared in his heart for the blood of these enemies.

The closer he got to the Amalekites' flank, the more the pain from the claw marks dimmed, and the more his muscles tightened with new strength. The spear burned. The shield was off his back now and fitted onto his left forearm.

He knelt ten paces or so away from the closest man. He could now see their faces illuminated by the distant flicker of the village's campfires. Arrogance spilled from them.

Crouched, body tense for battle, he looked down the slope. He saw many people moving around one of the homes—perhaps the one where they had taken the boy Haratha.

It was not good that all of the village's men were concentrated in one place. It gave the Amalekites an easy target. They would not have to worry about hidden reinforcements surprising them; they could circle the buildings and smoke the villagers out or force them into the open. Since all of the most able fighting men were gone, as the Amalekites' scouts would have reported, they would only be facing the few craftsmen, farmers, and shepherds Benaiah had seen earlier.

When the village's men were dead, the Amalekites would sweep through the town and take all that they pleased, raping the women and slaughtering several children as a warning. Others would be taken to be sold into slavery. Many lives were about to be destroyed.

There would be dead children. Bloody, brutalized women. Screams. Benaiah closed his eyes, tried to fight the memory . . .

. . . a dark doorway, screams from all around him. *Men of Amalek did this, men of Amalek did this,* she told him, over and over. *Men of Amalek did this . . .*

The burning threatened to overwhelm him. He embraced it. He studied the helmets in front of him as the spear raged in his grip.

Ten soldiers.

Ten who would enter the black depths of Sheol this night.

FOUR

In the house, Jairas looked away from the water and blood as it dripped down the side of the workbench on which Haratha lay. The boy's shouts pierced the room. Jairas reinserted the leather strap into his mouth.

The physician was probing Haratha's wounds with a bronze pick in an ineffectual attempt to remove particles of fur and dirt buried deep in his flesh. Water was doused across the wound again, but blood kept filling up the gash and obscuring the physician's work. The boy yelled and broke into tears—the first time Jairas had seen him do so.

He motioned for one of the others to take his place so that he could wash his brow, since blood and sweat were beginning to obscure his own sight. Walking to a basin in the dark corner of the common room, he picked up a ladle and poured water over his face. Its coolness prickled his hot skin. He shuddered. The grime from the day's exertions was covering his body and would take considerable scrubbing to remove.

Although carrying Haratha back down had been exhausting, the man Benaiah certainly had had the worst of it—leading them up into the pass, hunting lions, and then attacking one in the pit.

It was after dark when, carrying the youth over his shoulders, he had stumbled down the main road and called out for aid. The women and the few remaining men who had not been conscripted came running, and they laid the boy out on a workbench in the physician's home. The physician—whose occupation some of the followers of the Law frowned upon, believing that it showed a lack of faith in Yahweh—was a skilled man who had served in King Saul's army before being dismissed for stealing. He stubbornly defended his innocence of those charges at every opportunity. Most of the village people cared little about the things of Yahweh and were desperate enough for physical care that they did not mind the physician's origins or his attitude.

Jairas dipped the ladle into the water and poured it over his eyes again, then wiped them with a cloth.

Haratha's screams began to subside. Either the loss of blood or the weakness brought by fear was calming him, and he panted slightly, whimpering with delirium.

"I can do nothing further with this, so I will dress the wound and wait," said the physician.

Haratha's father, standing next to his son's head, nodded his gratitude toward the physician. He stroked his son's hair while his wife wept softly. The man's left leg was missing from the knee down, an old wound from the early days of Saul's wars with the Philistines. Jairas motioned for the rest of the crowded room to leave, then followed them outside into the night air.

The moon broke free of another cloud and hung suspended for a moment, illuminating the village and the mountains surrounding it. Jairas looked back up the mountain and thought of the warrior and the lion. Now that Haratha was back safely, Jairas wanted to form a search party as soon as it was daylight. The brave man deserved that, at least.

The other villagers were wandering down the street back to their homes. Jairas looked on while the watchman tended the flames of one of the lookout fires.

Jairas had lost a friend in the attacks of the past weeks, a good man with good children. His wife would need a husband again soon, to provide for and take care of her. The dead man had no brothers for her to be married to, and as a village elder Jairas was responsible to find her a new husband. He stared into the fire and thanked Yahweh, as all men did, that he had not been made a woman. Theirs was a hard life. He turned back toward the house to check on Haratha one final time before turning in for the night.

Noise burst from the tree line at the edge of the village. Clanking, crashing, and screaming echoed in the cold night, carried by the wind. Jairas was so startled that he caught the front of his sandal hard on a stone and fell. He leaped back up and looked in the direction of the clamor.

Village men ran up to him. "What is it?" shouted one of them.

"I don't know—but grab your weapons!" Jairas sprinted past the watchman's fire to his own dwelling, where he grabbed the sickle sword Benaiah had given to him on the lion hunt.

His wife was shocked awake in their bed. "What? What's happening?"

He never stopped moving. "Problems at the edge of town. Stay inside and barricade this door."

Jairas ran back into the night, hearing his wife calling after him but ignoring her. Joining with the other men on the road outside, they all ran toward the sound of battle.

How many were there? Who was fighting?

Sense finally clicked in his mind, and he halted the group of village men. There were ten of them.

"We should not charge them wildly. Form a wedge."

"A what?" asked one of them, a tanner.

"A wedge! Did you not serve in Saul's army? A point of three men, with the fourth behind so that the rear is covered."

He pushed them into formation, making two teams of four. They carried rusted bronze hoes and spears that were nothing more than sharpened sticks—pathetic weapons, but all they were allowed to have by the Philistines.

"You two." He pointed at the two old men not in a team. "Follow us and pull out any wounded. Can you do that?"

They nodded.

"Hurry!"

He led the first team at a steady trot toward the sound of the fight. His band of old men and farmers would not last long against trained warriors, but he would be a dog of a man if he did not try to protect his home.

The sounds were becoming spaced out. One side had inflicted losses on the other, and now they were probably growing tired, he thought. It had been many years since Jairas had heard the sound of combat, but a man never forgot it. He was terrified.

The moon, which had been hiding behind a cloud bank, was revealed once more. The sight before them stopped the group in midstride.

Several bodies lay in a trail from the woods leading into the village clearing. Fights always moved downhill, Jairas remembered, the slope carrying the momentum of men in struggle. As his eyes followed the sound of battle, he recognized the animal skins and mix of captured armor the Amalekites wore. But they were trying to encircle only one man, who was moving with great speed among them.

The man swung his spear in an arc at the level of his enemy's heads. He ducked under a swipe from a man behind him, tucked the spear under his arm, thrust it backward, and buried it in the torso of the attacker. Before the Amalekite had even fallen to the ground, the warrior slid the shield down from his upper arm and hit another in the face with it. The man staggered back from the blow, and the warrior lowered his shoulder and drove it into his midsection.

Screams resonated as the lone figure darted immediately to the next man, driving his spear so quickly that Jairas scarcely saw it. The warrior was moving impossibly fast.

The moon hid again, burying the fight in darkness, but Jairas could still make out the forms in combat. He did not know who the warrior was, but he was killing Amalekites, and for that reason the villagers needed to join him.

"Come on, left side, left side!"

Jairas sprinted forward, motioning the men in his wedge to stay tight and cover his sides. There was an Amalekite soldier in his path, facing the skirmish with the unknown warrior and paying no attention to anything behind him.

Jairas's sword thrust clinked off the Amalekite's armor. The surprised man turned, but before he could react, Jairas punched him in the mouth, hurting his hand but gaining enough time for his men to run the man through. Jairas started forward again and motioned for them to follow, but after a few steps he realized that they were not.

"Come! He needs our help!"

The group was looking past him.

"No, my friend. He does not," a older shepherd said.

Jairas turned back to the fight. He finally realized who the warrior was.

Fire burned in his muscles as Benaiah dove to the rocky ground to avoid a spear and rolled, not thinking, simply moving. His enemy's sword thrust just missed his waist. He leaped up and sprinted away from the group to draw them after him, hoping one might slip and fall, providing him another opening. He had to find the sixth man.

Reaching the tree line, he banked sharply to the left and leaped over an Amalekite warrior, then sprinted toward the village, where he could turn and face them again, this time with their forms illuminated in the glow from the fires, providing him better targets.

Benaiah saw a band of men fifty paces away. He recognized Jairas clutching the sickle sword. On the ground next to him was the sixth Amalekite soldier.

Jairas shouted something, and his men stepped forward holding their weapons out. The Amalekite attackers saw them and skidded to a halt.

Benaiah slowed. "Hit them now!" he cried.

Jairas's men, protecting their homes and families, bayed war cries like a pack of wolves and ran toward the five remaining Amalekites. Benaiah shouted for them to stay in their wedge.

After only two or three clashes of wood and metal, the Amalekite leader in the middle of the group waved his sword and shouted an order in their language. He and his men immediately spun and fled toward the safety of the forest.

"Chase them! Don't let them reach the trees!" shouted Benaiah.

Battle rage flooded him, and he cried out, the flames hot and lashing at his muscles. He bent and grabbed a discarded lance from the ground without breaking his stride and threw it in one motion. It whistled through the air and buried itself between the shoulders of the Amalekite leader.

The fire was consuming him now, making his legs shake with power as he ran, and he grabbed the impaled shaft sticking out of the still-standing man and shoved it forward through the Amalekite as hard as he could. The lance head lurched through the man's rib cage and burst out the other side. As the man fell forward, Benaiah seized the lance head and pulled it as he passed, sliding it entirely through the Amalekite's body and out the other side.

Benaiah threw the lance again and struck another man. He repeated the motion, driving the weapon into his enemy's body and pulling it all the way through the dying man as he passed. He did it again with a third.

As he ran past the place where he had planted his spear earlier, he snatched it up, holding it in his right hand and his shield in his left. Still running and very close to the edge of the clearing, he closed on the remaining two men. Their heavy armor slowed them, and he laughed at their stupidity for wearing it on a raid.

The first man looked back at him, terrified, and begged for mercy. Benaiah clipped the back of the man's leg with the spearhead, causing him to pitch forward onto the rocky ground. He leaped over the man's body and closed on the last Amalekite.

Just as the man reached the trees, Benaiah felt the fiery power suddenly leave. Weariness overcame him, the grip in the spear handle went cold, and the wounds on his head and shoulder raged with pain once more.

He threw the spear in a final effort to stop the Amalekite. It arced through the air and landed in the dirt—a mistimed throw. His enemy cursed him over his shoulder as he disappeared into the forest.

Benaiah shouted in frustration and slowed to a stop. Sweat dripped from his face, the heat from his body giving off steam in the frigid air. After catching his breath, he turned and walked to where the wounded Amalekite with the crippled leg thrashed in agony. The man cursed him in the tongue of his people.

Benaiah could speak the Amalekite tongue, having spent time among them. "Answer my questions," he said. He put his sandal on the Amalekite's throat. "Where did you come from and how many are at your camp?"

The Amalekite glared at him. "How did you get those weapons?" he asked. "Your people have no smiths or—"

Benaiah pressed hard on the man's throat. "Where did you come from?"

The man gagged. Benaiah looked at the man's injured leg. The hamstring had been cut. Crippled for life, at least, but it didn't matter—Benaiah had no intention of letting him live.

"If you tell me where your encampment is then I will show you mercy." He eased the pressure on the man's throat so he could speak.

The man reached back and felt his leg, fingering the smooth edge of flesh where Benaiah's spear had cut him.

"Tell me where your army is and what you are doing far away from Amalekite lands."

The man clutched his leg, wincing in pain. Blood covered his hand and formed a small pool near the wound.

Benaiah pressed harder on his throat. "If you tell me, I will show you mercy. This is the last time I ask."

The Amalekite spat out something inaudible. Benaiah released some of the pressure.

"There's a larger raiding army moving up from the desert through the plains," the Amalekite choked out. "We were ordered to break off and steal food from any villages in the mountains we came across. We didn't think it was defended. All the Israelite fighting men were supposed to be with Saul, fighting against the Philistines."

"Where are your spies? Who are they?"

"I don't know such things. I obey my masters."

Benaiah cursed, knowing the man was right. A regular foot soldier would not know who was feeding the chieftains information.

Benaiah thought of the city of Ziklag, where the families of most of David's men lived. An army of Amalekites raiding the south? Even after what David's men had done to them this year?

"How do I know you're not lying? It is common among your kind."

The Amalekite's replies were becoming weaker. "All of us mustered after those raids by the Lion of Judah. I knew many that he killed."

"How many of you are there?"

"I don't know. Many."

It could be true. Most commanders of large raiding parties kept them divided up to prevent total defeat if things went badly. It was easier to move a group of twenty men than it was a thousand. So the total number of fighters might be unknown to those lower on the chain of command.

Benaiah lifted his foot off the man's throat. This was troubling news. With the Philistines on campaign against Saul, and with David joining them, there was no one to watch the southern border for raids. The incursions by David's army had been so successful that entire Amalekite clans had been wiped out. No one had thought they would be able to muster an army after such devastation.

And what the man said about David's raids was true. All the women and children had been put to the sword in those villages. Their intention had been to leave no one alive to tell the truth — that it was David and his soldiers wiping them out, and not the Sea People, as they called the Philistines.

But this man referred to the Lion of Judah, Benaiah thought. They have finally figured out it was us.

"Get me help ... you promised me," the man rasped.

Benaiah looked back down at him. He positioned the tip of the spear on the edge of his eye socket.

"Don't! I will be your slave!"

Benaiah rammed the spear through the man's skull. The Amalekite convulsed violently.

Benaiah turned and walked toward the forest, ignoring the people gathering behind him, calling out. He picked his way back into the trees. When he reached the dead boy, he wrapped him tightly in the burial cloth and hoisted him over his shoulder.

Weariness overtook him. The battle rage that had kept him going all day was dissipating. Emerging from the woods. he made eye contact with Jairas, standing in the gathering. "I need water," Benaiah said.

Jairas nodded at one of the men, who broke into a run toward the well at the edge of town, where more people gathered, awestruck.

Women began to chant songs of praise for him who had killed lions and destroyed Amalekites. As more of them arrived they sang louder, their voices piercing the cold night air and encouraging the others to join in.

Benaiah saw who he was looking for in the crowd. He carried the bundle to the father and mother. When they realized what he was carrying, the woman shrieked and the father wept openly, hugging the boy between himself and Benaiah.

Benaiah released the boy to the father, who shouted praises of gratitude to Yahweh that he had his son back. He carried him into the crowd, his wife next to him, both of them clutching the body of their son and weeping.

The man sent to fetch water arrived and handed over the pouch. Benaiah poured the water into his mouth so quickly that most of it ended up on his soiled tunic. His hands, shaking harshly, were weakening, and he missed his mouth with the last of the water. He felt light-headed and knelt down on the soil, his ears ringing so much that he had to cover them with his hands.

Soon the entire village and all of those who had come for the shearing season, over a hundred people, had joined in the chanting, clicking their tongues and throwing dust into the air. The watch fires had been stoked, and the flames leaped high and bright.

In that light, images came to Benaiah: the amber eyes of the lion, a child's foot, the blood on his doorstep, the rage he poured out on his enemies.

With a final gasp, he disappeared into darkness.

FIVE

Benaiah found himself walking through sunlit corridors splashed with brilliant, colorful artwork, enjoying the scent of the Nile delta flush with spring flooding. His feet were clean. They were always clean. There was always a basin nearby to wash them in or a brush to dust them with. The Egyptians were cleaner than his people, always bathing and rubbing on perfumes at the end of every day. The great river ambled in front of every home and provided water to all who longed for it in abundance.

He entered the pool at the base of the alabaster steps. Goldfish touched the surface of the water around his feet. He watched them swirl around lazily before letting the linen garment fall from his waist. He stretched his tired muscles, first in his legs and then in his arms, taking a moment to admire how taut they had become from the desert fighting.

He was making a great deal of money in these lands. More than enough to gather holdings in the prime country near the coast. Perhaps he would become a merchant one day. But there would be no sons to pass the business along to, not unless Sherizah provided them. Two daughters, that was all.

He lowered himself into the water ... and then he was in the desert at the edge of the sea, the high peaks of savage lands standing like imposing sentinels along the shore. Not a blade of grass or growth of any kind, only the scorpions and the vipers. What did they eat? Where was life?

Before him stood a crowd that had come to watch. And they had brought their champion, a great giant, his eyes darker than night, his gaze indifferent, as though Benaiah was only another fly to swat. The daughter of Pharaoh was there, seated on a golden throne carried by Nubian slaves, and they were all watching him, this barbarian Hebrew from the north who was to battle their champion in the sand at the edge of the emerald water.

Benaiah shifted his weight, and the champion attacked suddenly, so enormous, as immense as the giants in Gath, his spear like an oak tree. They fought across the sand, into the ocean, the salt spray burning his lips and eyes, terrible harsh sunlight on every rock face. The giant was overwhelming him, and Benaiah sensed a great void behind, drawing him in, pulling him into darkness ...

There was a dim glow through his eyelids. Pain hit him suddenly, causing him to cough and clench his eyes in startled awareness. He blinked them open and waited for the light to adjust in his sight.

He was in a small room with a rough-hewn table in one corner. He was lying on some sort of mat on the floor. He was not in Egypt. He was in a small village high in the mountains, and he had been nearly killed by a lion.

Groggy and feeling like he had drunk too much wine, he tried to gather his wits by surveying the room. He guessed this to be the main room of the house, eleven or twelve cubits wide, with thick walls of stone and rubble cemented with mud. Robes and belts hung from hooks protruding from the walls, and there was a single window high on one of them with reed lattice covering it.

The light streaming against Benaiah's face was coming from the window, but the smell of food, which he was immediately intrigued by, was coming from the entrance, a large wooden door with a bolt. The door was slightly ajar, allowing the breeze to swirl across the first level of the home, covered in dust and pebbles tracked in by sandals. Benaiah was lying on the second level, two steps above the entrance.

The roof was carefully constructed of sycamore beams covered with brushwood bound together with mud. It was slightly green—moss from the continuous drip of spring rains. Seed sprouts from the mud were also blooming, contributing to the look of a forest floor above him.

Benaiah's thoughts wandered to his father's home in Kabzeel when he was a boy, fighting with his brothers about who could stay inside and scrub the ceiling and who had to work the plow. Their father wanted them to do more than sit and read, so he made sure that Benaiah and his brothers grew to manhood with calloused hands.

Benaiah felt close to his father, a man who seemed to have no vices and loved his family dearly. It was a legacy and a name to carry with honor. Benaiah simply did not want to become a priest himself. But at home, they'd studied the Law, spoken of politics, and worked their lands. He'd learned of the guilt offering *assam* and the sin offering *hattah*, made when a person upset Yahweh or deeply offended someone else. His father had taught him how someone could become ceremonially defiled and unclean, and how to be cleansed of such guilt.

So I am without excuse, he thought as he studied the ceiling.

A woman walked in carrying a ceramic pot. Seeing Benaiah awake, she startled, almost dropping it. She bowed her head curtly and continued to the rug spread out on the floor near him. Putting the pot down, she averted her eyes and hurried out the door. Wisps of steam rose from the pot.

The smell of the meat made his belly ache for food. There was a dull throb on his head and arm, but when he sat up too quickly, it flared up and he felt like he had thrown himself into the cooking fire.

"Careful, my friend, you aren't well yet."

Benaiah turned to see who was speaking. Jairas stooped over him, a smile showing through his thick black beard. A gray robe and girdle hung loosely from him, and a square of thin wool was wrapped around his head with several cords. He wiped his brow with a wet rag.

"You have been asleep for two days. Disease nearly killed you."

Benaiah thought about this a moment, then became frustrated that his mind seemed to be working slow. Everything was a haze—his thoughts, his memories, the sights in the dwelling around him.

"Two days?"

"Yes, two days. My wife and I have been up with you. So have our children."

Benaiah rubbed his slashed arm.

"You did not have to ..."

Jairas made a dismissive gesture and dipped the rag in water.

"After what you did? We should be giving you the whole village and all of our daughters as a war prize."

Benaiah looked at the other people who were suddenly in the room sitting on the floor next to him. Two girls and a boy, along with a woman he assumed was their mother, the one who had brought in the pot of food.

"You have a knack for living, my friend. First we lost you to the lion in the pit, then I thought the infection would take you. Yet here you are." He touched a sensitive part of the scalp wound and Benaiah winced.

"I confess I believed the lion had you. But our physician is quite skilled. Irritating man, though, always whining. You must tell us about the lion when you can, or my son will drive you to the point of madness with his questions."

Benaiah glanced at the boy sitting next to the bed, staring wide-eyed at him.

"The entire town knows about your fight with the Amalekites. They wish to show you their gratitude," Jairas continued.

"What about the boy? Does he live?"

"Haratha lives. The physician, as I said, is very skilled."

Then Benaiah remembered all of it. The storm, the lion, the warriors in the forest with blazing weapons ... the man who had escaped, and the prisoner who had told him about the raiding party.

He grabbed hold of Jairas's wrist. "I need to leave. I need to warn my men."

Jairas looked puzzled. "Warn them of what? All but one of the Amalekites was killed."

"Not them, the larger raiding force in the lowlands. The wounded man told me."

"You would trust the word of an Amalekite?"

"Amalekites live in small settlements scattered across the desert. They seldom join together, and they certainly wouldn't send one group of ten men alone into our territory. They must have been part of a larger force moving into Philistia."

"But you only just awoke! Those wounds are far from healed. Too much movement and they'll reopen. You'll bleed out on the trail."

"They will hold long enough for me to get back to my men." Benaiah pushed himself upright, ignoring the burning on his head and shoulder. The wounds were painful but not threatening. He should be able to function now.

"At least stay for the afternoon meal."

Benaiah looked at the eager faces of Jairas's children and nodded. He rocked himself forward and slowly stood. The creaking in his stiff joints led him to stretch his arms over his head and move his fingers. He had on a fresh tunic, apparently donated by Jairas. In one corner of the room, his spear, his sword, and his tunic were hanging from wall pegs. His dagger was propped against his shield near a doorway that probably led to a bedroom. The blades were clean and gleaming. The men must have rubbed them with olive oil and wiped them with coarse wool for him.

Benaiah thanked Jairas once more, who waved it off and maintained that there was more he wished he could do. Benaiah had heard nothing from Jairas's wife, busy preparing the meal. That did not surprise him. Women spoke only when they were directly addressed. But he was grateful for her care.

The three children stared openly at him, and he winked. The two girls giggled and the boy tried to suppress a smile. Their dark eyes were friendly and innocent. He glanced away. When they all finally gathered at the ceramic food pot in the middle of the dinner rug, Jairas spoke a blessing over the food and the man who had come to them. The meal, lentils and roasted goat, was a rare feast. Steaming loaves of bread were torn apart and used for dipping oil and scooping up the mix.

There was cinnamon-spiced water, cakes of fig and raisin, and most surprising of all, a small vat of honey to dip them in. He knew a simple family would never have been able to afford such a meal, so it must have been donated by the village at the request of the elders, as hospitality required.

Still, Benaiah could not help feeling guilty a much-needed goat had been slaughtered on his account. That did not stop him from ravenously eating his first true meal in days.

Throughout the meal, the children chattered excitedly back and forth about the killing of the lion, and Benaiah was forced to clarify.

No, there had not been forty lions. No, the Amalekites had not had an army of witches he'd been forced to fight off.

When his belly was full, Benaiah gathered his equipment regretfully. Jairas's wife was given permission to speak and gave him her own thanks, again avoiding his eyes as much as possible. He tousled the head of the boy, asked permission to kiss the girls on the head, then walked into the late afternoon sun with Jairas behind him.

A crowd had been standing near the entrance of the house throughout the meal. Now they shouted to the others on the street. Leather tanners and potters left their shops, carpenters put down their bow drills and mallets. Metalworkers told their apprentices that they could run outside, briefly, to see the great hero off. He nodded to the people and forced a smile.

The elders spoke a blessing over him. When it was finished, the crowd began to trudge back to their work, resigned to the start of another day.

"Are you sure you cannot wait?" Jairas said as he and Benaiah were left alone again. "Sabbath begins this evening. It will take several days to reach your friends anyway."

Benaiah finished tying his shield to his back and adjusted the pouch full of cakes and nuts that had been given him for the journey.

"I've lost enough time." And the Sabbath does not matter to me anymore, he thought.

The livestock in the residential stables were lowing, protesting the fact that their owners had forgotten to feed them in order to be around the fighter.

Jairas cleared his throat. "What is he like? Your leader. The Lion, as the children call him."

Benaiah paused. "He sings a lot. He is also the most terrifying man on a battlefield I have ever seen."

"What about his politics? I heard he was chosen to become king one day, that he was raising an army in the desert to overthrow

Saul. We know he is a man of Judah, which is good, but we hear that he employs foreigners and even Philistines. That he actually *serves* the Philistine kings! He also puts heavy levies on the people who work his lands in the south."

"That last is true. But he divides up the bounty from them and sends it to the tribes."

Jairas raised an eyebrow. "We have never seen any of his help here."

"I assume that nice new olive press was paid for by a donation, correct?"

Jairas nodded.

"And if I remember correctly, your lions are dead now," Benaiah said. He exhaled heavily. With his wounds he was having a hard time leaning over to tie his sandal straps. "He knows the people are wary of him. That is why he sends us out to help them."

Benaiah could sense the older man gazing at him as he worked. The outlaws were already legendary, as was their leader. David was famous everywhere men gathered because of his exploits in the king's army.

After a while, Jairas sighed and sat down next to him. He rubbed his forehead, every bit the tired, aging man he looked. "I was still in Saul's forces when he killed the champion of Gath called Goliath," he said. "I was summoned with all of the other men to the Elah Valley. I will never forget what I saw that day. Only Yahweh gives men such ability. I want to know if he is still the same man. If he is, then we are with him. You can tell him that."

Benaiah nodded. "He is that man."

That this village supported David was good news. Benaiah and the rest of David's forces had been spending a great deal of time trying to quietly convince the people that, despite how things looked, David was not a traitor serving the Philistines, that everything he was doing was for their ultimate good. "He sent me to help you because he loves his people," Benaiah said. "All of the tribes. We are not traitors, but people will believe what they believe."

"But it appears as though he is the vassal of Philistia. They are our blood enemy and the enemy of Yahweh. The tribes in the north will have a hard enough time accepting a man from Judah. Marching with Philistines does not help his case. What does he intend to do?"

Benaiah was in a hurry to leave but made sure to watch his tone in the presence of an elder. "He doesn't reveal all of his plans to us. But on my father's honor, and the honor of Israel, he is the best man and mightiest warrior I have seen. When we march with the Philistines, it is they who need to be careful."

Benaiah thanked Jairas once more, then turned and began to walk down the road out of town. "Tell Haratha I hope he finds a woman," he said over his shoulder.

The people called shouts of encouragement after him as he left, and he nodded to each in turn. From the edge of the forest, he waved a final time, then slipped into the trees.

The snow on the mountains above him was gone now, exposing the grass struggling to emerge with spring. The rolling terrain of the Judean high country all looked the same and made it difficult to navigate. He followed a path that was occasionally lost when the grass gave way to pebbles and dirt. Benaiah had to make careful note of the creek bed. Following the stream's route to the Great Sea would eventually bring him out of the hills and into the area around Ziklag, his current home.

She would be there now, rising with the sun and meeting with the other women at the community well. They would carry on and chat, the other women unaware of what she carried in her heart. No one knew but the two of them; there were wounds better left buried.

Benaiah pushed the thought from his mind and concentrated

on forming a plan. In his rush to get moving, he had not thought beyond leaving the village. His original instructions had been to meet the rest of the men in the Philistine capital city of Gath, where they would be passing through en route to the north. Benaiah had been delayed several days; it was possible that they had already made their way to Aphek in the north, nearly four days' journey from where he was, even if he ran almost continuously. Benaiah kicked a rock in frustration. By the time he got there, they might already be in the fight.

He searched for an alternative. The Amalekites must have already been in the land for some time if they were sending out smaller parties like the one he had met. There was a chance they were moving toward Gaza, Ashkelon, and Ashdod, all cities on the coast. Those Philistine cities were larger, much more of a prize to the barbarians from the south. David's small town of Ziklag might be ignored if a more appealing option existed.

The Amalekite chieftain must have good spies if he knew that the entire Philistine army, summoned from every city, was moving toward Aphek. The Philistines hoped that would be their last campaign against the disorganized Israelites, enabling them finally to destroy Saul and subjugate the people who had conquered Canaanite land so many years before. It was an ambitious military campaign, but like any other it had its drawbacks: it left the entire southern portion of Philistia exposed. The Philistines had to be relying on the hope that their rivals in the south would be too war-weary to invade before they could return.

That left Benaiah only one option. As much as he wanted to rush immediately to Ziklag and protect his home, he did not know for sure that was where the Amalekites were going. It was possible they would simply raid the coastal cities. Benaiah had no love for the Philistines; the more of their cities that burned to the ground the better.

Hopefully the Amalekites would see the incredible opportunity given to them by the Philistine army's foolishly mobilizing every soldier and abandoning their large cities to fate. And once Philistia had been sacked by Amalek, perhaps David could be persuaded to launch an open war with the Amalekites, something that would give Benaiah unending pleasure.

He would have to travel as fast as possible to reach the army. All he could do was warn David; the rest would be up to him. If he did not think it was necessary to speed back to Ziklag, then so be it.

Except for his injuries, Benaiah was in extraordinary physical condition. But he needed to stop for breath every hour. His head and shoulders burned as sweat seeped into the cuts. He sat when he became light-headed, annoyed at the effects of blood loss.

By the time evening fell, the stream he'd been following had merged with several other waterways from other valleys and become a river. The terrain had changed, telling him that the plains were not far. He made up his mind to be out of the hill country before dawn.

In the open fields of the coastal plain, he would be better able to take a more direct path to Aphek, bypassing the Philistine cities of Gath and Ekron where lone Israelites were harassed. David had been insistent that his men never travel alone through those cities.

Sitting around the campfires while on campaigns, David had confided in some of his select men bits of what he was planning. He had been anointed with oil as a boy, he told them, symbolizing that he was to become Yahweh's chosen king. Samuel, the old prophet who had recently died and was buried in Ramah, had chosen him when he was a boy. Samuel told David that he would rule over Israel someday, and in the years since then, Saul had hunted him in every corner of the kingdom. David was looking ahead, trying to subdue the enemies he would face as the ruling king over Israel one day, and his wars in the south were part of that plan.

Benaiah was among those who argued that David should kill Saul and be done with it. David had had many chances to do so and had refused each time, claiming that Yahweh did not want him to. Benaiah had long since lost patience with that way of thinking. He knew about Yahweh, had studied him in his youth, but after that day years ago, he wanted nothing to do with him.

All through the night, Benaiah was grateful to be alone with his thoughts as he ran, crawled, leaped, and jogged along the rocks next to the river, which he had guessed by then was the Zephathah. It was the main source of runoff in the spring season from this part of the hill country, but it was still too early in the season for the river to be at full flow. Later, when the rains hit their peak, the route that Benaiah was now taking would be impassable.

His wounds were finally loosening up and caused him less pain as he ran. He pushed himself hard, faster as the hours went by. The cool night gave him energy, and by the time the sun peeked over the mountains behind him, he had broken into the foothills known as Shephelah.

The forest was now full of sycamore trees. The early morning sparkle was reflecting in the dew. Moisture from the sea always gathered on the ground overnight in this part of the land, forcing him to pause once to wring out the water from his sandal straps. He ran past fields of sheep, the shepherds giving him a curious glance as he passed them. The open areas provided a great deal of freedom in choosing his path, and by the time the sun rose in front of him, he had left the rolling forests of Shephelah and passed into the fertile farmland of the plain of Philistia.

Benaiah had been running almost a full day. His body demanded that he stop for rest, and he eased himself slowly to the ground against a sycamore. He closed his eyes. Birds chirped. He felt something crawl across his ankle but was too tired to swat it. Being alone in the woods reminded him of the two warriors he had encountered high in the pass. Or had they been spirits? So many strange things to consider. He could scarcely wait to ask David about them.

Gradually he realized that he was looking at chariot tracks in the soft earth nearby. A Philistine road. Centuries before, when the great warlord Joshua was leading the Israelites into the land, they had been forced to withdraw from the coastal plain. The Canaanite nations who had been there before Philistia had chariots and easily defeated any attempt at subduing them. But in the hill country of Judea, the Israelites were able to win many battles, since the chariots were rendered useless. There had been an uneasy coexistence since that time, with neither army able to fully overcome the other.

Benaiah rose slowly from his comfortable nook before his muscles stiffened. He started trotting again, keeping his focus away from his wounds and on the ground in front of him. He resisted the temptation to look toward the south in the direction of Ziklag. Her dark hair would be tied up under her shawl with a leather strap, but it was so thick that she would need to tie it again throughout the day. He loved her hair, loved the way it spilled uncontrollably out of its wrappings.

He let his mind stay on her for a while, on the years of their youth when they had found solitude and happiness on the banks of the river, in better days. He watched her as she went about her day by the river, bundling branches and gathering provisions for meals. She would visit her sister, chatting endlessly about the goings-on in the city as only women do.

They were very young when they were joined. They would go on long walks—ignoring the work of the lazy afternoons of summer—and swim in the waters of the river ambling toward the Great Sea.

The sun had risen high enough to allow him to strip away the rest of his clothing except the cloth wrapped around his waist. This was a great relief, since the wool of his clothing had been fastening itself to his wounds and reopening them continuously. The bundle on his back grew heavier, and he stopped again to tie it down correctly. If the balance of the equipment on his back was off, his joints and muscles would overcompensate, leaving him in crippling pain each morning. He conceded that he would need to rest after dark; despite his urgency, it would do no one any good if he wore himself out and died before reaching Aphek.

That night he slept under a cleft of rock in a field, after searching for any better shelter. There were few other people in that part of the plain because it became exceedingly marshy during the spring season and swarmed with bugs. Only lepers wandered this land, cast out and shunned by their tribes.

The fluke spring snowstorm in the hill country had caused a major washout of the rivers and streams, forcing the shepherds and cattle herders to move their animals to drier ground. It would be slow going, picking his way through the mud, but at least he didn't have to worry about being bothered by anyone. He wasn't concerned about defeating bandits in an open fight, but he could scarcely afford another injury before reaching his men.

In the morning, Benaiah tied his equipment on properly for the day's journey and set off north, leaping from dry spot to dry spot as best he could, occasionally snagging his foot in a mud pit. Small streams of runoff crisscrossed his path, and he jumped over them frequently. He saw no one else the rest of the day, and by midafternoon, he found a path of dry ground that ran parallel to the foothills on his right side.

He ran past the Philistine city of Gath, following a path between the foothills to avoid the city where the giant Goliath had come from. He relished the irony of David wandering freely in their streets, deceiving their own king. Benaiah wondered how annoying it must be to the people to see the conqueror of their greatest champion coming and going through their gates as he pleased.

Benaiah remembered that there was some sort of pagan festival the Philistines were celebrating over the next few days. David's men had been given strict orders not to go near there. *Because of the prostitutes. Unclean.*

He spent another night near the city of Gezer. Benaiah was making good time despite his injuries and detours to avoid populated areas. One more day of traveling and he would reach Aphek, where he would demand a full meal of roasted meat. Although Benaiah had the supplies sent with him by Jairas's wife, he craved more nourishment.

The plains were getting drier the further north he traveled. He was now close enough to his own men that travel on the trade road was possible. He ran, desperation growing in his spirit as he thought about the helpless families in Ziklag.

Around noon he crossed paths with a caravan of merchants, who told him that the army had passed them, traveling north.

Benaiah was grateful to be arriving *behind* the army. David and his men marched at the rear of the Philistine ranks because many of the kings from Philistia did not trust them, believing that when they reached a narrow gorge David would order his men to turn and ambush them. It was David, after all, who had destroyed many thousands of their best soldiers when he served under Saul. King Achish was David's only ally among the Philistines, and only because he thought David was destroying towns in Judah.

Marching at the rear of the column also meant that they were forced to inhale the dust and feces left by the war horses of the regiments. It was intended to humiliate David and his men.

As the last rays of daylight fell over the Great Sea to his left, Benaiah finally reached the plains surrounding the city of Aphek. Exhausted and in pain, his wounds leaking a yellow fluid, Benaiah stumbled toward the tents and campfires of the army. He made his way carefully around the outskirts, looking for the distinctive tents that the Philistines had given the Israelites while they stayed in their camp—simple coverings, much less elaborate than the Philistine battle tents.

At the southern edge of the encampment, he found them. He stumbled toward the nearest fire in the middle of them and collapsed next to a man sitting bare chested and eating bread, who called out for help. Benaiah heard voices, commotion, and then nothing more.

Part TWO

SIX

The terrified man, muttering in fright, was escorted toward a small cluster of tents tucked deep in the forest behind the lines. When they reached the command area, the escort pulled the flap of the center tent aside and announced the man, then darted back to his post.

The questioning went on for an hour. Eventually the chieftain decided that the tent was too full, so he ordered everyone out except his senior counselor and the bedraggled figure sitting in front of him. There were complaints and grumbles, but the men slowly filed out the flap of the tent and huddled together for warmth a short distance away.

The chieftain rubbed his eyes and cracked the knuckles on his hand. "You say that he used both sword and spear, and that he gave orders in their tongue. Was there anything else about him that you noticed? Clothing, armor?"

The man replied, "No, master. He moved in the darkness, and moved too fast ... though, as I said, he had a shield, an armored one, unlike what they normally use."

The chieftain was a head taller than any of his men, with thick black markings dyed everywhere into his skin. Scars covered his face, many obscured by the black beard tied in braids. Thick arms strained against his leather armor studded with bits of copper. Gold bracelets dangled around his wrists.

He pulled the armor off and set it against a tent pole. The tent was a luxury, one that he knew had no place on this mission. But he didn't care. The troops would do all the dirty work. He had earned his keep, put in his time in the mud-soaked troops. He was the chieftain now, and he wanted to sleep in a tent; he wanted female slaves, and he wanted gold. That was why he was here. Anything that got in the way of those things annoyed him.

The chieftain looked at his deputy, who thrust his head outside the tent and called for a servant to remove the man. The lamp was down to a flicker. The chieftain ambled toward it, lost in thought, and readjusted its wick. The flame sparked anew. He turned to watch the servants hauling the lone survivor out.

"Do you believe him?" the chieftain asked his deputy.

"I don't know, master. No reason for him to lie. I have heard the Hebrews have such men."

The chieftain nodded. Regardless of what the foolish kings told the troops, the Hebrews were not cowering women. The raid had gone too easily up to this point. The gods would not let them have it without a challenge.

Other than the troubling news of this messenger, though, the chieftain and his large force of Amalekite warriors had much to be pleased with. The weather, which had been plaguing them for over a week with cold rain and high winds, had finally cleared out and left behind a brilliant night sky. Food was steady, disease had not crept among the ranks yet, and the land in front of them was full of so many women, they were told, that a man would have to tie them up just to be able to control them all.

The Amalekites were encamped for the night, spread out along a defensive front atop a ridge, each man's position oriented to cover what the others could not see. Troops were crouched behind stones and fallen trees, eyes alert to any movement in the pale light. It was rumored to be a haunted land, this Judea, and superstitions were flying among the ranks. Everyone hated the Hebrews and thought them cowards, but the Amalekites were also aware of the many tales of their god destroying his enemies.

Each unit of one hundred men, under its senior commander, was strategically placed to better ambush any approaching forces. They had left their desert clothing behind and wore stolen armor in an attempt to mimic the military success of other nations. All carried an iron weapon and had been drilling day and night with them, aided by mercenaries who sold the expertise they'd gained in foreign armies.

The Amalekites had always been a nomadic people, wandering through the deserts of Sinai and the Negev, raiding trade routes and hoarding gold. Now they looked to the north and the fertile lands of their enemies, desiring revenge for the defeats inflicted by the Hebrew king Saul.

This force had been rapidly mustered from any remaining towns not already plundered by the Lion, the Hebrew warlord who had been inflicting terrible destruction on them, given that name by the troops out of admiration of his ruthlessness. When a spy reported that the Philistines and Hebrews were marching to war, and that the Lion himself was likely with them, the Amalekite kings had put aside the arduous task of butchering each other and stealing live-stock and sent men to be united under the only chieftain remaining who had not been killed by the Lion. This advance force was to burn towns and steal, supplying them with the gold and goods they would need to organize a larger army.

The atmosphere in camp had been excited earlier in the day,

when reports were coming in about the success of raids into southern Philistia and the border of Hebrew territory. They found little resistance anywhere they went; they moved with great speed into small villages whose men were on campaign with the Hebrew king. Since the Philistines were absent from their territory as well, the entire coastal plain was open to them. With every good report, the men became more confident and gave thanks to their gods for easy victory.

Then it all changed earlier that evening.

Instead of a feast of dates and meat captured from the Hebrews, each man in the raiding army now had his weapon in his hand, tensely waiting for word from the command position at the rear of the lines about the lone soldier who had stumbled in just before dark, shaken up and unwilling to tell his story until he saw the chieftain. No, a deputy would not do, he had told the watchmen. There were demons in the hills north of them, he kept repeating, demon warriors from the land of the dead.

The watchman who had first spotted the messenger spread the news that the man appeared exhausted and disoriented, that he had been running continuously for several days, never stopping to eat or drink. There was blood on his clothing. He said that all of the men in his party had been slaughtered by a demon and would say nothing more until he saw the chieftain.

The rumors had passed up and down the line, growing to become a fantastic tale of demon armies leaping out of the ground and bearing down on them during the night. The section leaders did their best to calm the men, but even the leaders felt an extra chill in the night air.

The sorcerers had warned of this, the troops whispered to one another. There were not enough lights visible on the horizon to give them permission to invade. The gods never allowed armies to prosper if the lights of the war gods' targets in the stars were not visible. They had not even brought priests to appease the gods.

In his tent, the chieftain was pacing. "But there was only one. The Hebrews fight in teams of three or four."

The deputy placed his hand down on the table, looking at the map of the region sketched on parchment by his spies. "He may not have been sent for us. But you're right; they would not have sent one alone. Their best men are with Saul in the north."

Both men remained silent for a moment, each trying to piece it together.

"He may have been on another errand and stumbled across them," said the chieftain.

"Possible." The deputy shifted his weight and looked up hesitantly. "What if it *was* a demon?"

The chieftain shrugged. "The priests would have warned us. I am no fool; I know there are demons in those hills, but I also know not every shadow is a demon."

"The priests were against this campaign. Maybe they asked the gods to send the demon."

Someone scratched gently on the tent flap.

"What is it?" demanded the chieftain, irritated.

"Master Karak, the officers want to know what to tell the men to calm them down," came the voice of his armor bearer.

Karak looked at his deputy. "Well?"

"Tell them it was an ambush and there was only one survivor. It is the truth, and it will let them know what we are up against in these hills. Not demons, but dangerous fighters."

Karak liked it. "It will help prepare the men for what is ahead." He said to the armor bearer, "Tell the officers to tell the men that he was ambushed with his squad, there was a fight, and he alone escaped. Tell them to be ready and alert at all times."

The armor bearer left. Karak walked to a cushion in the corner of the room and gestured wearily for the deputy to join him. It had been a long day. They had been jubilant at the early successes, but both men, seasoned warriors who held no illusions of war, knew it was bound to end. This was unwelcome news.

They settled onto the cushions and lay their heads back. The wineskins abandoned earlier were replaced. The chieftain held the wineskin against his forehead, lost in thought. He closed his eyes for a moment.

"He said the unknown warrior used both sword and spear. The only Hebrews I have heard of who do so are Saul and his son. Most Hebrews learn a single weapon in their tribes like our people do. They would not have time to learn more if they are plowing for crops and fixing oxbows."

"But some elite fighters might learn them. You have learned three, master," the deputy replied.

The chieftain sat up and stared forward. "It must have been one of the men with that warlord called 'the Lion.'"

The deputy frowned. "Is he real?"

"You remember those tales about a Hebrew boy who killed one of the giants from Gath."

The deputy nodded. "David. Hebrews on the borders would try to scare our people with tales of him. Do you think he is real?"

"All of our spies say they encounter talk of him in Hebrew lands. And someone highly competent has been leading raids against us. David might be the Lion."

"He would surely be marching with Saul. A Philistine invasion of that size into the land of his people would draw him out."

Karak scowled. The stories of David made him a terrifying figure to the Amalekites. One hundred boys under the age of ten had been sacrificed a few years previously by the priests in order to beseech the gods to strike David down. The kings and tribal chiefs had tried to appease their people by claiming he was a myth spread by Hebrews.

As Karak thought about it, it began to make sense. The stories about David claimed he was leading a band of criminals and foreigners and had trained them into elite fighting units. He might have sent one of his best fighters to the village on an errand, who then encountered the raiding party and dispatched them. A group of regular soldiers properly ambushed by a highly trained warrior under the cover of darkness could be defeated. It was not unthinkable.

"Master, David's exploits really might be myth, something spread among our ranks by foreigners to deter us," the deputy said.

Karak shook his head. "No, there is too much on him. The Philistines even speak of him." He settled back into his rough lambskin cushions. "They are going to be vulnerable in the south. One man may have stopped a raid, but he won't stop an army." He paused a moment, thinking. "Bring the commanders back in. I want to move out as soon as the other advance parties return. We will hit that Philistine town the scouts reported earlier. Ziklag."

The deputy stood up and walked to the opening.

"Also send in my share of the prize today."

The deputy nodded, opened the flap, and stepped into the darkness. Karak rubbed his eyes, piecing it together. Of course, the man could have been lying. The raiders may have simply been defeated by old men with sticks. Either way, Hebrew warlord or not, the nearest army was days or weeks of travel away. If they moved fast enough, the gold and women of the southern regions of two kingdoms would be theirs to choose from.

The tent flap opened again and the group of men who had left earlier ducked inside. They were all large, with thick, dusty beards, and wore dull-colored clothing like their chieftain. His orders had been to dress in subdued garments to blend with the rocks and bushes. Behind them, panting in humiliation and terror, were three young Hebrew women captured during the day's pillaging. They wore nothing to protect them from the freezing night and tried vainly to cover themselves in front of the group of men. There were loud laughs and comments.

Karak stood up from the ground to his full height, towering over the other men and causing the women to close their eyes in fright. He grabbed them by the hair and dragged all three across the room, while the officers laughed and made animal noises. He threw them onto the pile of animal skins that made up his bed. They shrieked in pain and clung to one another.

The Egyptian watched quietly from the corner next to the other commanders.

He despised these filthy Amalekites. They paid well, but most were lazy and undisciplined compared to his old regiment. When he was in Pharaoh's armies, his warriors would have crushed them in an open war and laughed at their womanly ambush tactics.

Many important preparations for campaign were omitted in favor of needless luxuries, such as this large and cumbersome command tent. Only a fat ruler wishing to look powerful by touring the front lines would make his men carry such an unnecessary burden.

The chieftain appeared to be a skilled fighter; the Egyptian had sparred with him in workouts. But not all effective fighters made good generals. Karak seemed to be here not out of duty to his kings but rather out of a desire to grab as much plunder as he could after years of obeying the bidding of others.

The Egyptian didn't begrudge the chieftain such a motive. It was what he himself was doing, after all. There were mercenaries from many lands in this army. Most were here as spies, of course—as was the Egyptian himself. They would offer services for hire to the Amalekites, claiming they had abandoned their homelands, and then promptly return and offer information to their own kings. It was dangerous but highly profitable.

The Egyptian turned away from the scene on the animal skins and stepped out into the night. His white linen robe glowed in the moonlight. He did not care what the chieftain had ordered about subdued garments; he would not stoop to wearing barbaric clothing. The colder he became, the more linen he would drape around his shoulders. Only shepherds and other wretches wore raw animal skins as cloaks.

An Amalekite soldier walked past him, his head coming no higher than the Egyptian's elbow. The man's eyes darted toward him quickly, and he picked up his pace. The Egyptian's great size had been the subject of whispers in the ranks; his elegant grooming, the use of kohl and galena to paint his eyes, and his fine white clothing would have been openly mocked were he not the largest, most intimidating man in the raiding force. He had gleaming bronze skin, bulging oiled muscles that rippled with veins, and a clean-shaven head; there was no hair on his body of any kind.

The Egyptian had overheard the conversation about the Hebrew warrior. It reminded him of the only time he had fought a Hebrew, on the coast of the sea when he was among the pharaoh's bodyguard. There was a Hebrew mercenary in the bodyguard as well, and on a whim one day while hunting with his falcons along the coast of the sea near Aqaba, the pharaoh had ordered them to fight for his amusement.

And they had fought. Across the sand, under the sun, into the sea. The Hebrew had talent, but he was untrained and rough, wielding his weapons heavily like an infantryman instead of nimbly like a master of arms, and the Egyptian had defeated him. Disgraced, the Hebrew had departed.

The Egyptian walked back to his own small tent, enjoying how he towered over the other soldiers as he passed them. Once inside, he laid down, resting his head on the wooden pedestal that served as his pillow, and listened to the light breeze moving through the camp.

It would be an interesting report to make to Pharaoh when he returned. The god-king would want to know about Hebrew warlords and skilled fighters before any invasion commenced.

SEVEN

Far to the north, deep in the mountains of Gilboa along the southern side of the Jezreel Valley, a campfire burned. The night was bright and clear and brought an occasional chilly breeze, causing the fire to flicker lazily. A good night for a fire, the soldiers all agreed, and they had been given permission to make one, despite being on the march.

Another, smaller fire burned just inside a small stand of trees on top of the highest ridge, with the commanding view of the Jezreel and of Mount Tabor. The two men who warmed themselves by this fire were dressed in the typical clothing of a soldier in the Israelite standing army on campaign: light wool tunics cinched up for when they put on armor before battle, covered with cloaks to ward off the surprise spring chill. They each had neatly trimmed beards. One of them was of noble birth and the other was a commoner, but they were talking and laughing like old friends.

A young man named Eliam sat in the forest nearby, trying to listen to their conversation as he quietly stitched his tunic, damaged during the day's training. In his twenty-fifth year, Eliam was keenly aware that he was serving Yahweh's anointed king only through the good graces of his well-connected father. It was an opportunity purchased by a great many head of cattle and not through any merit of Eliam's. He had narrow shoulders, felt like he plodded awkwardly when he walked, and had not noticed any servant girls looking at him. In all, Eliam was unsure of his place both in the court and in society, but he had determined to make the most of any opportunity he was given.

Eliam had been in the court of King Saul since childhood. He was not a slave or typical tent servant, spending his hours in menial labor. He was, more or less, an understudy to the various soldiers coming and going from the court. Eliam's father wished him to become a great war leader, like the legendary prince Jonathan, in order to attain the highest positions of respect and influence in the kingdom.

Eliam had been privileged several times to sit under Jonathan for instruction. Tall and strong, looking every bit the great hero he was renowned to be, Jonathan taught Eliam about the foreign alliances their nation faced—the tension with the Moabites, the tribal bickering between the north and the south, the bloodthirsty Amalekite frontier, the ever-looming shadow of the Philistine colossus.

The lessons were grand and Eliam soaked them in, but they were remarkable for what they did not contain: any descriptions of the man David and the bond of brotherhood that most of the kingdom knew David and Jonathan shared. Whenever Jonathan began to describe a particular battle or encounter that Eliam knew involved David, the prince would catch himself and go silent or change the subject.

It was David who dominated all comings and goings of Saul's court, held at the tamarisk tree on a hilltop in Benjamite country, as it had been for forty years. Even though David had not set foot under the tamarisk tree in a long time, everything about him seemed to be on Saul's mind. Where was he? Who was sheltering him? How large was his army? The questions were tossed around war councils night after night. The generals, led by Jonathan and a brilliant commander named Abner, pleaded with Saul to leave David alone. There were far graver threats, they said. Philistia would eventually come at them with everything in its power, and the Israelites still had not learned how to forge iron to compete with them.

At first, Eliam was not bothered by the king's erratic behavior. He wrote it off as the stress of leadership and believed that Saul would eventually forget about David and come around. But as time passed, Eliam saw the king lash out unprovoked and ever more violently. Eliam heard things beyond simple screaming and shouting. He could swear that he'd seen strange images in the darkness of the royal house, heard voices and utterances from unknown and terrifying depths. He had sometimes seen the king stumble along the hallways, staring vacantly, talking with someone who was not there.

David was in hiding, but that didn't stop the people of the kingdom, many of them fed up with Saul's irrational behavior, from choosing sides between Saul and David. Eliam had noticed that even the ever-cheery Jonathan had become morose. The presence of his own son sent Saul into rages. Eliam would often wake up late at night and hear the sounds of the king thrashing about his palace, screaming and shouting at his heir, accusing him of aiding their enemy and denying himself his own throne. Jonathan did his best to calm him but was frequently rewarded with a hurled jar.

Now, sitting near Jonathan himself, Eliam hoped to learn more about what troubled the king. Instead, he found that he was listening to old war stories. The man with Jonathan was Gareb. He had arrived just before they set out from Saul's court, saying that he'd heard Prince Jonathan was going to battle and that he'd be a lesion on a leper if he would stay behind pushing a plow when he did.

Eliam had been watching them laugh together for hours, like brothers. He continued mending the tunic and tried not to show that he was listening.

"That was Michmash, not Jabesh-gilead," said Jonathan.

"No, it was Jabesh-gilead. I remember the fool who thought he could make the shot with the arrow at four hundred paces."

"I forgot about that. Then which one was Michmash?"

"As you killed that man with the rock and he screamed for his mother." Both men erupted in laughter once more. Eliam was wondering what was so funny about that when Jamaliel walked up. He was the chief cook and oversaw the foreign laborers in the camp.

"What are they talking about?" Jamaliel whispered.

"Battles. Michmash. What really happened there?"

"What do you mean?"

"I know we won, but I always thought Jonathan was behind the front, overseeing the equipment and cleaning up."

Jamaliel put down the bowl of stew he had been carrying and peered at the men around the campfire. "Did you hear that from the king?"

Eliam nodded. "Jonathan has never spoken of it. I know about most of his other campaigns, but that one seems to be forbidden."

Jamaliel sat down next to Eliam, rubbing his legs as if they were tired or sore. "The first time Jonathan fought was against the Ammonites in Jabesh-gilead, in the lands of Gad. He was very brave. Saul knew that he needed a standing army, so he rewarded Jonathan with the leadership of a division."

"How many men were in the army?" asked Eliam.

"About three thousand. Jonathan led a division of a thousand in a campaign against Geba and Gibeah, held by the Philistines. This didn't sit well with the Philistine rulers, so they ordered chariots and men to establish a garrison at Michmash after traveling up the Beth-horon pass."

"Why there? There's nothing out there."

"It's where our people have always mustered for battle. The Philistines knew if they could establish a stronghold there, it would demoralize our troops. It's also right near the center of the lands of Benjamin—"

"—where Saul is from," finished Eliam.

Jamaliel nodded. "It was embarrassing for Saul to have his hated enemy camped out in his homeland, openly challenging his authority. He began to lose many of his conscripts to desertion. No man wanted to die in a hopeless cause. I think he only had about six hundred men left in that force when he took his position opposite the Philistine fortress at Michmash.

"Jonathan had secured Gibea with the regulars, so that was where Saul decided to encamp. The Philistines have good spies. One of them must have reported the fighting between Saul and Samuel."

Eliam nodded. He had seen the old prophet and the king bickering many times. Samuel had even told Saul that he would lose his throne one day because he had angered Yahweh. Saul had in fact angered the Lord on many occasions, but the one most frequently mentioned was when he failed to destroy the Amalekites after being commanded to do so.

Jamaliel dropped some herbs into the bowl, then continued. "Knowing there was trouble in our leadership, the Philistines decided to press the advantage and sent several invasion forces into the land. This left Michmash with only a handful of defenders, but Saul was afraid to attack it even then. He could only move his army a little closer, to a hilltop called Migron.

"The Philistines taunted them across the ridge. Jonathan got tired of listening to it and came up with a plan. He and Gareb, the man sitting next to him over there who used to be his armor bearer, decided to sneak out of the camp to the south, alone. Neither Saul nor anyone else knew what they were doing. I suspect the Philistines noticed them but must have assumed they were just deserters from the main force, so the two of them slipped into the gorge behind the camp, forgotten. There are cliffs in that area so steep that one could assume they could not be climbed.

"They made their way to the base of the cliffs beneath the Philistine outpost, then climbed up. It must have been scary, weapons weighing them down like that. When they reached the top, they ambushed the outpost."

"Just the two of them?" Eliam asked in disbelief.

"Just the two of them. Wish I could have seen it. Worthless Philistines probably ran like women when they heard the commotion."

A voice behind them broke in. "You left out a few things, Jamaliel."

It was Jonathan, who had walked over looking for his delayed food. There was a slight grin on his face in the firelight.

"Forgive me, lord." Jamaliel hurried to finish the bowl.

Eliam concentrated on his stitching. Jonathan watched them a moment. Gareb had joined him.

"What was it I said to you before we climbed down into the canyon?"

Gareb replied, "You said, 'Perhaps Yahweh will be with us.'"

"And now all the men chant it. Did you know what I meant by it, Gareb?"

"You told me once. Yahweh does not want us to be meek in battle. Once we are certain it is his will, we attack and pray that he delivers us."

"How many of the men know that?"

"Probably only a few. Troops forget things easily. They chant it because you said it, and they love you."

Eliam kept his eyes focused on the stitching, wincing when the tip of the copper needle poked his wrist. He wiped the small trickle of blood off on his waist and noticed, after nothing more was said, that Jonathan continued watching him.

"Come join us by the fire," Jonathan said after a while.

Jamaliel and Eliam stopped what they were doing, made eye contact, and then slowly stood. Jonathan gestured toward the fire, and Gareb returned to the rock he had been seated on. The two servants followed. Jonathan took the bowl of stew from Jamaliel and returned to his own boulder.

The four men listened to the sounds of the Israelite army around them as soldiers prepared to settle for the night. Men were digging sleeping spots in the rocky forest floor, taking no particular pains to muffle the noise of their digging. Most assumed that since they would die soon anyway, it did not matter who knew where they were.

Eliam watched the fire nervously, afraid to look up at the men across from him. Out of the corner of his eye, he noticed that Jonathan had his eyes closed, as if savoring the familiar sounds. Loud, crass jokes were being shouted back and forth among the camp; fires crackled; the wind dusted the treetops overhead every so often. The night was idyllic. One would never know what waited in the valley nearby.

"This was back before anyone besides my father and I had iron weapons," Jonathan said quietly, not opening his eyes. "I decided to ask Yahweh for a sign, so I told Gareb that we should go pay a visit to the Philistines. If they shouted for us to stay where we were so they could come kill us, we would take that to mean Yahweh did not want us to fight them. But if they demanded that we come over, then it would be a sign that he wanted us to destroy them. Yahweh does not care about numbers, you know.

"When we came out of our position at the bottom of the cliffs, one of the Philistines shouted over the side, 'Look, the Hebrews are crawling out of their holes! Come on up here and we will teach you a lesson!' So that was our sign."

"I never was a good rock climber. Too stocky and well muscled," said Gareb.

Jonathan ignored the joke. "I told him to follow me up the cliffs because I knew we were going to defeat them. When we reached the top, we split up. You don't normally do that when you fight in pairs, but I wanted to destroy them.

"I killed the first man with a single thrust, then tossed his weapon to Gareb. We attacked them without mercy. There were twenty of them. All died quickly."

Eliam glanced at him. This was a different story than he had heard the king tell the historian.

"Yahweh sent an earthquake, surprising all of us, but we kept advancing because we knew it was from him. The Philistines, who were poorly led despite their strength, began to panic. Lookouts across the gorge in my father's camp saw the enemy fleeing, and we watched as our countrymen began to chase them.

"The three Philistine divisions that had been sent out from Michmash were so terrified that they began to fight among themselves. Gareb and I were separated from the rest of the army by the canyon, but we kept pursuing them.

"The battle went on for hours. The Lord was bringing a great victory. As the Philistines fell, our men took their iron weapons. At some point in the afternoon, my father gave an order that no one should eat until evening. I don't know why he—"

Jonathan abruptly stopped. Everyone waited, unwilling to prod him on. After a while, he stood and walked to the edge of the firelight, looking out over the army encampment.

"If I had known he had given that order, things might have been different between us."

Jonathan turned to look at Gareb. Eliam was stunned at the depth of anguish on his face.

"I would have stopped. I would have never eaten again, if that was what he wanted. I would have done anything for him."

"It was a foolish order. You saved the kingdom that day. Your father should have taken the crown off right then," Gareb said.

"Don't say that. He is the Lord's anointed."

"Then the Lord anointed the wrong man."

Jonathan's eyes flashed with anger. "The Lord never makes mistakes! His purposes are his own. Never say such things!"

Gareb only stared, his jaw clenched in silence.

Jonathan turned away to face the valley far below. "The Lord did not make a mistake. The right man has been anointed to rule, and nothing can be done to stop him."

Eliam did not know what that meant, but it was as though the mountains and the forests and the stones in a thousand fields had collapsed onto the shoulders of this one man. He could feel the weight of his sorrows just by standing near him.

Shouts and mocking laughter erupted in the night. A soldier was regaling his friends at a campfire nearby. No one could actually hear any of the story, but the laughter seemed to calm Jonathan, who raised his face to the sky and inhaled deeply several times.

Eliam waited desperately for him to continue, but Jonathan did not appear interested in saying any more, content to watch the darkness and campfires.

Jamaliel said, "They say David gathers men in Ziklag, lord."

Jonathan's shoulders hunched a little as he exhaled a deep breath, but he still said nothing.

Jamaliel prodded. "You were close to him, lord prince. Why do you remain here?"

Jonathan did not look back at them. "We had a tremendous victory that day. We should have butchered all of them like oxen. Phi-

would have been subjugated, the plains finally the property of Yahweh's people—it was all within our grasp." His voice dropped enough that Eliam had to strain to hear it. "Don't ever speak of David again to me."

The fire crackled loudly, diverting Eliam's attention. When he got up to stoke it, a man approached them and asked to speak with Jonathan, who listened to him and then turned to the group. He looked at Eliam.

"That garment looks good. Make sure it is stitched twice where the leather rubs it." He turned to Jamaliel. "As usual it was bitter, but it will suffice," he said, then winked. Slapping Gareb on the shoulder, he said, "The king calls a war council. I will be back in a few hours." With that he strode out of the light of the fire, followed by the messenger.

Eliam watched them disappear into the night, then added another log of cypress to the fire, staring at it while steam hissed.

"That log was too wet," Jamaliel said.

"Wet like your pants when the fighting starts, right, Jamaliel?" Gareb replied.

"I wasn't always a cook. I was a shield bearer too. "

"Right. And how did that go for you? Last I heard your master still had the arrow in his loins."

But Eliam paid little attention to the banter, the conversation with the prince still on his mind.

EIGHT

*There are flames. He is testing us, those of us who came to him in the
cave. Only the strongest can join him. The ground is on fire all around
me. He is testing us, testing us. But we can do this. Run faster now!
The log on the rope swings again, almost hits me; I need to keep moving.
Faster! he shouts, his sword cutting the ropes, sending more logs toward
us. Will this never end? Will he never let us rest? But I will not quit.
More logs swing toward us. I can do this. Keep moving, faster . . .*

*The javelin flies at me. Dive quick, roll, keep running. Too many
things, so very tired. One more hill to climb. My legs are burning, they
will not hold up. Breathe again. Wipe the dust. He is shouting at us
again, I fall, more boulders coming down the hill. I can do it, I can do
it, she needs me to do it . . .*

David's voice rings across the mountainside.

*"You will be the greatest fighting force in the world, or you will
be dead before the month is out. Either way, you will learn to move
quickly."*

How do we survive this? Have not eaten in days, I need water, I need rest. Keep carrying this rock, Benaiah, do not quit, no matter what happens, do not quit!

"Praise to our God!" David shouts.

"Arrows to our enemies!" we shout back.

Keep running. I cannot run up another hill. Sherizah, forgive me, I tried for a better life for us. But I cannot run up this hill. I fall forward; my face scrapes the dirt. That is all I have. No more. The others collapse next to me. They are finished as well. David wanted one more hill. We cannot give it. But keep moving, he said. I can keep moving. I will roll if I need to. I will not quit! Keep moving! Crawling over the stones and the heat, I am so thirsty, I need water. Rolling now. Blackness, cannot see anymore, need water, I cannot do it, but I do it anyway, I keep moving.

I feel a hand on my back. "Well done, man from the south," says the voice of David. "You have a home among us, if you wish." He is smiling at me. So are his men. We can join them. A new life for us. A new start ...

"Well, it looks like Benaiah, son of the priest, valiant man from Kabzeel, has once again fallen prey to his weaknesses. Probably has some excuse like his back gave out. Your father was a tough man. What happened with you?"

"No, it'll be better than that. His eye hurts. Or maybe the child he was fighting stuck him in the leg, and he needs it to be kissed."

Benaiah felt his head clearing in the cool evening air. Had he passed out? He became aware of dirt on his face. No, it wasn't dirt; it was sand. No, dirt. Then the pain closed in with pressure behind his eyes, and he felt queasy.

"Don't worry, we're going to get the physician for you. He'll be here in a minute. Don't know if he'll kiss it, though. You need me to kiss it and make it better? Bet I kiss better than your woman does."

"That cut on his arm needs a better kiss than you can provide."

"Bring your woman over here and I'll show you."

The voices sounded familiar. His eyes were not working yet; was it because of the blood loss? He rubbed them with the arm that still worked. The other one wasn't doing anything he wanted it to. And why weren't his eyes working? There was laughter. Yes, he knew those voices. They were standing next to his head, and a few of them had their hands on his back.

Finally his eyes opened, and he saw a large, husky face staring at him. Next to that face were others. The Three.

"Well, they're open now, so I guess that rules out the bad eye. Any other excuses, Benaiah?"

He saw the curl in Josheb's mouth as he said it. Always joking. Benaiah coughed out the dirt in the back of his throat and narrowed his eyelids. "Lions will do that to a man."

"Lions, is it? And when did the bear attack?" This was Eleazar, running his fingers through his beard.

"No, the bears went down first. Twenty of them. Followed by twelve prides of lions. I let them have at one of my arms so it would be more of a challenge."

"Just one arm? Thought you were more man than that. My infant daughter would have given up at least a leg," said Eleazar.

"Well, that will spare her from being chosen for marriage. At least there will be a reason other than her face," Benaiah replied. Everyone laughed loudly.

Josheb prodded Benaiah's forehead, making him wince. "You never had a beautiful face to begin with, but you look awful now. Like you slept on a pile of arrowheads."

Benaiah forced himself to sit up. The men cleared away from him to give him room. There were a lot of them around. Josheb shouted for the group to return to their meal since there was nothing more to see. Benaiah felt relieved that he would not have to tell his story to a crowd. They meant well, but he was tired. And in pain.

He pressed his arm with his hand, hoping to relieve the pressure from the wound, which was surely infected by then. There was a physician on the way. He hoped it wasn't a Philistine. Then he remembered that David had brought a physician along with them, another man who had deserted Saul's army. He was a battlefield physician, accustomed to cuts and heavy bleeding. That was good. There would be a lot of that soon.

Josheb finished shoving men out of the area and returned to kneeling down beside Benaiah. He was an averaged-sized man, smaller than Benaiah, and it would be hard for anyone to pick him out of a crowd of soldiers. Nothing about his physical appearance, including the constant twinkle in his eyes as he prepared his next round of teasing and joking, would convince anyone that he was probably the most lethal warrior in the kingdom. His body was not large, but it was hard, and he could move it quickly. Josheb was wearing a dark war tunic with elaborate stitching, which, to his lasting ridicule by the men, his wife asked him to promise to wear.

"We were a little worried about you. Thought you would catch up to us in Gath. By the time we reached Ekron, we figured you were hurt, but after all, we couldn't abandon our Philistine sisters — sorry, *brothers*."

Benaiah took the water offered to him and poured it over his face. The cold splash felt like new life. "As long as you didn't weep for me."

"So it was a lion after all? I am glad Yahweh spared you, my friend," Shammah said as he leaned against a small tree. Shammah was the dourest of the group. His inability to make a humorous remark frequently left him out of conversations. Benaiah was a kindred spirit, but even he realized that a man rarely enjoyed life in an army if he could not come up with the occasional witty comment. Where Josheb was physically unimpressive, Shammah was immense, even larger than Benaiah. He walked awkwardly, and his social interactions were even more so. He muttered to himself when he was alone, saying he was praying. He would have easily been mistaken for a large, bumbling oaf were he not able to fight ten men at once with such control that he would scarcely be panting when all lay dead around him.

"Two of them," Benaiah said. "Had some help from the village. A brave man named Jairas; a kid was with him. The boy girded his loins, though. He took a charge and was wounded pretty badly."

"Did he make it?" asked Shammah.

Benaiah nodded and took another drink of the water. "He did. He was pretty sad that he didn't have a woman to look after him, though. He told us so. Said he was trying. Made me think of Shammah."

Josheb laughed. "That definitely puts him in the same camp as Shammah. How long have you been trying, Shammah?"

Shammah scowled. He fidgeted with a stick on the ground. "A long time. It fails to be funny." There was more laughter. "No, I said it fails to be funny."

"Why wasn't the last one acceptable? I heard she came from good stock. Her father had more than enough for the bride price. She even had good, wide hips for childbirth."

Eleazar, the third man in the group and usually the one who held his tongue until it was most appropriately used, had hung out ripe bait and everyone knew it. They all waited to see who would bite.

Josheb could not help himself. "Width was the *least* of her worries."

Shammah punched him. It was a stiff blow, but Josheb was laughing so hard that he did not even mind the blood on his lip.

"I told you, I will marry when it comes time. The Law forbids a man to marry unless he can stay a year with the woman."

"May the Lord spare me from such a fate," said Josheb. "A year with a woman. I would rather wash Philistine feet. My wife kicked me out after one day. David has *two* of them. Perhaps he needs our prayers."

"It isn't all that bad. Some are worth it," replied Eleazar.

"That's because yours is good and submissive. What do you do if they behave like unruly mules? I'd never want to face my own wife in a fight."

"Saul must have conscripted even more of the men because there were hardly any left in that town." Benaiah had a way of interrupting the fun, much like Shammah, and he knew it, but his mind had begun to wander again. The other three looked at him expectantly for a moment, then realized he was not being humorous. They all stared back into the fire.

"They say he is already in the valley. Has camps stationed near the Gilboa range," said Josheb.

"Makes sense. We always fortified the valley before campaigns," answered Eleazar.

Josheb frowned. "But David was always the one holding the pass. No one got through the Jezreel if he was there. He was the only one capable of it. Who do they have who can do that now? Abner? He doesn't have enough men."

"Jonathan," Benaiah said.

"But he won't leave the king."

"They might all be there. Even Saul."

Eleazar bit into a raisin cake that was apparently so hard that he shouted and spat.

Josheb threw a rock at him. "Here, eat that. Better than my wife's cooking."

A man walked up to them carrying a satchel, and Benaiah held up his arm. The physician unwrapped the cloth from around the wounds, saw the oozing pus, and sat back on his heels.

"How long ago did this happen? And what did it?" he asked.

All of the men pretended to ignore him. Physicians were never popular in the army, or in the rest of the tribes for that matter, since many saw it as a lack of faith in Yahweh to have their illnesses tended. Fighting men just saw it as weakness.

"Six days and a foul beast. Sounds a lot like Shammah's week with a woman." Josheb ducked the blow this time.

Benaiah winced as the physician began to massage the wounds with a pasty ointment. It burned. A few moments passed with the physician probing the wounds and testing his reflexes.

"Did a physician treat it before?" he asked. Benaiah nodded, embarrassed to admit it. Josheb smirked at him.

"Good," the physician said. "There is infection, but if you lie still for a day or so, you should be ready. It will hurt, though. Hurt so badly you will want to die. Fool thing to do, chasing beasts."

"Your speeches would inspire armies to victory," Eleazar said to the man.

A new voice cut in. "At least we would not have to listen to the endless whining of all of you." A new form had arrived next to the fire; a man with a loosely wrapped gray cloak. He took a seat next to Benaiah and gave him a glance.

"Word has it you attacked several lions by yourself. Did you even think about the rest of us? We need men right now." The man turned his eyes to the fire again. Benaiah felt something in his chest flip. *Steady it. Not now.*

"I thought the children of priests were smart," the man said, the hint of a smile on his lips.

"Usually they are, but with our friend Benaiah, something went wrong somewhere," said Josheb, quick to speak before Benaiah could.

The physician wrapped the wounds on Benaiah's arms and head. It really did hurt. He could not let these men see it, though.

The man continued. "David has been called to the tent of King Achish. We should hear something soon. Keep yourselves ready for my orders."

He waited for a response, then rose and departed into the evening toward another campfire nearby.

"He's a brave fighter on his own. Doesn't need to prove anything. No one thinks less of him just because he is David's nephew," Benaiah said as he watched him leave.

"Joab hates losing control. He didn't like that David sent you instead of him. Thought he should have been the one," Shammah said, gnawing on a chunk of roasted goat dipped into a pouch full of olive oil—made for him, as Josheb had loudly and mockingly pointed out earlier, by his mother.

"If he had, he would be half digested in that lion's belly right now. Can't say I would miss him," said Josheb.

Benaiah let it go. He would be annoyed with Joab later; he was too tired now. It was evening still, so he must not have been out for long. The camp was beside the trade route known as the Way of the Sea, near the base of a mountain range crowned by towering Mount Carmel on the far northern edge of Philistine lands. It was a day's walk around the base of the mountain into the wide mouth of the Jezreel Valley. The other route into the Jezreel, and the one he suspected they would take, was through the pass by Megiddo to Shunem, only a few hours on the march. However the Philistine army chose to close in, it would be a dangerous breach into Israelite country. Benaiah heard a stream nearby. He could see the flicker of torches and watchtower fires of the town of Aphek in the distance.

Something nagged at Benaiah, something hidden in the back of his mind. Something that he should have been telling the Three. What was it? He felt like his mind was full of mud, his thoughts sluggish and inconsistent. The fever made him sweat. He remembered the lion, and the village with the shepherd and the dirty sheep. Other strange images surfaced: darkness and fire, and figures roaming the deep woods. None of it made sense to his exhausted mind, but it felt urgent.

"How has it been here with the Philistines?" he asked, trying to find something to focus on.

"Lovely," said Josheb. "We get to walk behind them on the roads and inhale the dung from their pack donkeys and chariot horses. We get to camp along the bottom end of the stream so that all of their filth and waste floats past us, ruining our water. They even go out of their way to urinate in the water next to us while we're filling up skins. Great bonding and camaraderie taking place."

"Makes you wonder why we're marching with them," Eleazar said.

"David has a plan. He always does," Shammah said.

"He needs to tell us that plan, then. It's unfortunate enough to lose men from the northern tribes, but I'm not going to spear a fellow man of Judah," said Josheb.

"Yahweh's army has men from all of the tribes. Yahweh loves all of his people the same. They don't deserve slaughter at the hands of uncircumcised Philistine sea-filth," said Shammah.

"The Philistines can have the northern tribes," replied Eleazar. He was the smallest of all of them, but the quickest on his feet, and his skill with small weapons was unequaled. He was a restless man, always wanting to move and take action, intolerant of the long hours of mindless speech-making that characterized war councils. Josheb joked that if David ordered Eleazar to attack Gath alone with a rock, he would do it just to avoid sitting still in a war council.

Benaiah sighed. Politics got them nowhere. If it had not been solved in centuries, they were not going to solve it tonight.

Josheb, always the peacemaker, changed the subject. "Speaking of the tribes, you arrived at an interesting time, my friend. We have more men coming from all over the land. Many have bows and slings, good scrapping fighters. There are even Benjamites."

Benaiah actually turned his head toward Eleazar in surprise. "Saul's tribe? They left him?"

"Yes. Good men, too. Said they were tired of how they were being treated, heard a man could make a lot of money out here with us."

"Don't forget the Gadites," Eleazar said. "We gave them shields and spears when they requested them, and they know what they are doing. They even crossed the Jordan. Two weeks ago."

"Impossible," said Benaiah. "The Jordan is over its banks now."

"You haven't met these men yet. You'll believe it about them. They look like the lions you just got done fighting."

"What about the men from Manasseh who left Saul?" Benaiah asked.

"Philistines wouldn't let them come," said Josheb. "Thought they would have a change of heart and betray them in the fight because it's close to their own land. David sent them back to wait for us outside of Gath. It's a wonder we're even here. I have no idea how David does it. He kills their best fighter and slaughters them by the thousand as a youth, and yet one of their kings trusts him enough to lead us to war with them. I wouldn't trust us if I was a Philistine. There are a lot of suspicious characters in this camp. Shammah most of all."

"The point is," Eleazar said to Benaiah, "there are a lot more men here than before. Even some foreigners. You speak some of their languages, so I think David has his eye on you as their commander."

Benaiah nodded. He was fading. His head swam with confusion and pain, but he tried to hide it. "I figured that would find me one day. Seems a little odd, though, that David trusts foreigners so much." Even to himself, Benaiah's voice sounded increasingly weak. "I thought the whole purpose of this was to get rid of them."

"Only in our land," Josheb said. "Beyond our borders he wants to make alliances. At least, alliances with those not named 'Amalekite' or 'Moabite.'"

"Yahweh wanted Israel to purge the land of pagans. But Saul never did it. David will. David reads the Law," said Shammah through another mouthful of roasted goat. Shammah ate all day and read the Law all night. Benaiah wondered when he would pull out one of his beloved raisin cakes, also made by his mother. Likely not until Josheb was gone.

"As long as that purging includes acquiring gold, then I'm happy," said Josheb.

Benaiah felt himself being lulled by the conversation around him. Jokes, serious talk, then jokes again. Then there was silence, each man left to his own brooding.

The breeze felt good on his head. The bandages were wrapped tightly, but the physician had left enough gaps to let the dry air in. Night had come quietly while they'd spoken. The sky looked clearer than ever tonight, with not even wisps of cloud to ruin the display.

It was their way of handling the pressure, the laughter. Josheb knew it. That was why he was the one they admired most. He was the funniest man in the army. He was also the deadliest. His spear had brought death to many desert bandits.

Although his thoughts were vague and foggy, Benaiah knew that, for all the Israelites in David's band, the pressure they were feeling came from the same thing: they were marching with heathen Philistines against Israel, Yahweh's chosen people. Something about it was so inherently wrong that surely Yahweh would send lightning to split open the earth to swallow them.

It was getting cold again. The fire crackled, and Eleazar stoked it. Benaiah loved the campfires at night on campaign. He loved the jokes. Loved the way a man could forget things and rest. The way he could bury heartache in the ash and coals.

His eyes drifted away from the flames, and he stared at the smoke rising to the stars, so bright tonight. He thought that perhaps the rain and snow had finally left for the season. It had surely surprised the armies. Kings went to war when they thought the bad weather had passed.

Sounds of men laughing were everywhere across the camp. A man at a fire behind them was telling another lewd story, to applause and laughter every few moments. Laughter could be counted on. No matter how many men may have died that day, there would always be laughter. Josheb would always find it for them.

A voice broke through the darkness at the edge of the firelight.

"He wants a meeting with us in the morning. Pack your things tonight. We will be leaving." It was Joab.

"Leaving? Where?" asked Josheb.

"Our alliance is over. He will explain it more tomorrow. Tell your men that we move before daybreak."

The young man disappeared again with a flippant wave of his hand. Benaiah despised his arrogance.

Then, suddenly, it all crashed back into his memory. The lion, the pit, the warriors battling one another in the snow ... and the *Amalekites*. How had he forgotten? His face flushed with blood and shame at his delay. Had the lion's claws raked his mind out?

"Amalekites are raiding in the hill country!" he all but shouted. "I killed nine of them, but one got away. There is a larger force somewhere." The heads of the Three snapped toward him.

"Amalekites? How? They couldn't possibly be ready for a campaign," Josheb said as he stood.

"Might be mercenaries. They never stopped raiding the trade routes," Benaiah replied. "They might be near Ziklag."

The group went silent. Amalekites. Their families. It sank in deeply.

"There's nothing we can do until morning." Josheb began to walk out into the darkness for his turn to inspect the night watch. "Give your report to David in the morning. And try not to let the spiders and scorpions scare you, son of Jehoiada. I won't hold you if you are afraid."

The others dispersed from the fire as well, leaving Benaiah alone. He was angry at himself and his foggy mind that had forgotten about the threat in the south. He rose and set about finding a tent of his own. Perhaps the foreigners would become his company after all. Where were they from?

Sleep first.

NINE

Karak, the Amalekite chieftain, hidden by the poor light of dusk and by the wall of the waste ditch near Ziklag, watched and counted how long it took the night-shift guard to replace the other man. They were lazy and far too slow. By the time the first figure had departed the shadow of the gate, Karak could have moved twenty men through the entrance without a word of warning. He smiled. It had happened just this way last night too. In another hour there would be another rotation, and that was when they would strike.

By a stroke of luck, the watchmen at the city gate had foolishly left the massive doors open to allow the cool breeze from the desert through. In the narrow corridor just inside the gate, there was a series of sharp-angled walls one had to pass through to actually enter the city. The most important rule in the defense of towns was to never *ever* leave the gates open at night, not for any reason. And yet here they were, blessed by Baal or whichever local god had seen fit to assure that lazy men would be guarding the gates that night, men unfit to march to the north to war.

Ziklag was perched at the top of a round hill with barren slopes. The countryside surrounding the Philistine city rolled gently away in all directions. Though they were at the edge of the great Negev Desert, the hills of cooler lands sat to the east, and the Great Sea was only a two-day walk to the west. Ziklag served as both a town and a watchtower for this part of the trade routes. The guards would be able to see an enemy threat coming from a long distance.

Karak could make out the paths the women traveled to get water from the nearby creek bed. The scout had watched them the previous day and counted how many women fetched water. If each woman hauled water for one family group—and Philistine households could be large—then the number of women reported hauling water was a good indication of how many people were inside. The scout also reported, to the delight of the chieftain, that almost no men were seen either leaving or entering the town.

He looked to his left and checked the rows of soldiers lying still in the drainage ditch hewn from the side of the hill. The city's refuse and waste water was thrown out near the gate and trickled along the very area they were waiting in. It would have been checked frequently by true soldiers—it was too obvious an ambush position—but the Philistines had sent all their best men north. Old men and worthless men guarded their cities. The old men were too tired to search the ditch; the worthless men, too lazy.

Next to him was his deputy, and next to the deputy was the Egyptian mercenary. Karak would have enjoyed the mercenary's job more than his own. Able to fight and capture plunder and never having to obey a king. He suspected the man was a spy for the ruler of Egypt, but that did not matter to Karak. For now, he was a good fighter and a terrifying presence on the field, worth the gold.

The Egyptian was the greatest fighter Karak had ever seen; no man alive could stand with him in single combat. Not even the vaunted Hebrew warriors they had heard about in the legends. He would decide the fate of nations if he rose up from the ranks and taunted his opponent. No enemy king would have a warrior capable of meeting him.

The night watchman had settled at the entrance gate and was no longer visible, sitting in the shadows. The chieftain wondered if it was an old man, sleepy from the day, unable to see past twenty paces in the darkness. He was amazed again at how fortunate they were that all of the fighting men in the land were in the north.

His troops would move quickly. There were two hundred of them, with the rest of his army waiting in the hills above. They would be difficult to control. None of them had ever been formally trained in the movements of armies, preferring instead to attack small outposts from the backs of camels, swinging their blades across the throats of women and farmers. But they had been attentive to their training for this mission. The promise of gold and women made for good fighters, and the Philistines had both.

He had not wasted manpower and time raiding many Hebrew settlements. They were poor and not worth the effort. But the kings of Amalek wanted vengeance for Hebrew raids along the borderlands. There was said to be a significant Hebrew population living in Ziklag, and since it was the furthest outpost of the southern borderlands, Karak had decided it was worth taking. It would be the perfect way to finish their raiding. And if they were successful, they would have captured so much bounty that they would need to return to their own lands to deposit it all and sell the slaves.

The moon was extremely bright, checkering the land with black shadows from all of the objects in the desert. City walls gleamed. Karak imagined the nightly rituals going on behind the walls. Workmen were probably stoking fires to heat and forge iron, the mysterious metal that had only recently been seen in his lands. Merchants were wrapping up their goods from the day of bartering and selling, women were putting children to bed. The women. Philistine women did not resist like Hebrew women did. He thought of them and smiled.

An hour passed. The men were getting restless. A squad or two could lie still for hours and never even breathe loudly. But large groups clustered together for long periods of time began whispering and complaining. It was like moving a herd of cattle.

Karak saw movement at the gate. Another watchman changing shifts. It was almost time. They would go at the end of the new man's shift, when he was most tired and eager to get back to his warm bed. Better get them moving.

He looked at his deputy, who was lying in the ditch behind him and waiting for a command. The man nodded and moved down the line. Each commander would be given the order.

Karak looked at the Egyptian, lying next to him watching the city gates. The Egyptian looked back and nodded. The warrior only spoke a few words of their tongue, so Karak let him operate alone. If he fell, he fell. Karak wasn't going to put him in command of others.

Karak pointed at himself and made a gesture as if he were about to charge. He then pointed at the Egyptian and tried to indicate that the man should go through the gate first when they approached. Karak planned to follow him through. The mercenary nodded slowly and looked back at the city. Karak hoped the man had understood. When they breached the walls, there would be enough confusion and disorder. Faced with an abundance of helpless women and treasure, Karak had no expectation that his men would maintain discipline. But that was all right. Their greed and lust would get the job done.

The Egyptian's spear was enormous, larger than even his. Enormous like the man was enormous. He stood a full head and shoulders above the chieftain, who was larger than any other in the army. Dark muscles were tightly strung all over his body. He kept himself very clean, as if more concerned with dressing well than fighting, but he easily dispatched a dozen Amalekite warriors at a time when they sparred. His monstrous spear swung with such force that two soldiers had their lungs crushed through their armor during one contest.

The deputy had returned from alerting the officers, and now it was time to wait again. A thick bank of clouds was settled on the horizon, distantly visible as a gray wall. It had not moved much during the night, unfortunately for them, so their approach would be far too obvious in the moonlight.

Cities in this land, Karak knew, usually focused their defenses on the gates. Single combat between champions was decided in the shade of the watchtowers during sieges, and the city elders often conducted business or held court between the towers. Kings stood on them to watch for messengers returning with news of distant wars.

Inside, the market would be near the entrance, crowded into narrow streets that allowed only three men to walk abreast. The market would maintain a festive atmosphere during the day, with caravans arriving and new wares being tested, wedding festivals being celebrated, and children chasing each other through the tight alleys and back passages overflowing with broken pottery shards and around the public oven and well.

Dwellings would be further in, some crowding the narrow streets and others, those of the wealthiest classes, along the walls. The governors and rulers of the city would have their quarters near the back, furthest away from the gates and from the common people. Now the rulers would likely be gone, seeking glory in the north against the Hebrews, while their cities burned and their cattle were stolen.

The moments passed and then it was time.

Karak reached down to tighten the leather straps on his footwear. The iron-studded shield was fastened to his arm, the captured iron sword at his side. He fingered the hilt. Glancing around at the officers, he stood, spoke aloud to his gods, and began to run.

The Egyptian watched the chieftain leap over the lip of sand and followed. His spear was in his hand, he carried no shield, and he ran in long strides behind the Amalekite warrior. Behind, he heard the smattering of footsteps as scores of soldiers crawled out of their hiding places and followed their officers. They had shown poor noise discipline during the wait. The Egyptian worried that the town's defenders might have heard them, but thus far there was no sign of activity.

His great height made him stand out in the crowd of running men. Long legs carried him fast, and he forced himself to slow down and follow the chieftain. Better to let an arrow from a hidden tower guard strike Karak first. Ahead, in the black shade of the city entrance created by the moonlight, the shift change was taking place. The invaders were in the open now and could easily be spotted, which happened as soon as he thought it.

A guard had stepped from the darkness to greet his replacement, then, seeing the rushing horde, cried out a warning. The two of them scurried to shut the gate. The Egyptian ran faster, pouring all of his strength into running. Since neither of the watchmen appeared to be an archer, the Egyptian set aside any concern about being first and sprinted ahead of the Amalekite chieftain. The gate was shutting, the two men shouting and working together. No one else from the city had come yet. He ran harder.

When he was ten reeds away, he saw that he would not arrive in time and threw the great spear toward the entrance. It flew through the entrance of the gate and buried its head in the sand. The wooden doors stopped against the shaft, protruding through the opening. The watchmen shouted and pushed harder. The gates did not move. They kept pushing, unaware of what blocked them.

The Egyptian reached the doors at last and lowered his shoulder, slamming into the opening and prying it wide enough to squeeze his torso through. He let out a terrible shout, grabbing the shaft of his spear and twisting until he finally burst through to the other side. He swung his spear toward a watchman, an old man, to his left, slamming him against the wall before his partner could react. The Egyptian did not wait; he swung the spear again, smashing the side of the other Philistine's head with the iron tip.

The Amalekite chieftain and his men burst through the gate behind him, forcing the doors completely open. Karak shouted, urging the men to move faster. The Egyptian wiped his brow with the hem of his tunic and ran down a street that angled away to his left.

There were a few torches and lamps being lit in windows as he passed. A woman screamed. He stooped to grab a handful of sand to dry his palms and kept running. He wanted to reach the Hebrew quarter. He had seen it on a scout of the town, before offering his services to Amalek. He'd pretended to be a slave in order to wander the streets.

To his amazement, he had discovered that the town, though Philistine, was owned and dominated by a Hebrew warlord whose men had been raiding trade routes. There was a storehouse in their quarter that would be a great prize.

He followed the wall, hearing the sounds across the city of the Amalekites destroying everything they touched. Men on a raid were filled with lust and violence. There would be great chaos in Ziklag tonight.

———

Karak urged his men forward through the darkened streets. They were setting fire to the buildings and shops of the market and breaking into homes. He ordered the men to douse the flames; it was not time yet. He bellowed at a man who had already seized a woman and was tearing off her clothes. "Not yet! Wait until the city is in hand!"

The soldier cursed and threw her down.

He had ordered the men before they set off to capture the city first, then plunder. The chieftain knew what happened to a man when he was raiding, but they needed to keep running. It would be impossible to control eventually, so he had to control it while he could. There might be more soldiers present to defend the city further in.

The two companies of men under his immediate command split, shouting and running. He looked around for the Egyptian, did not see him, and kept running. He had tried to tell the man to secure the northern part of the city—hopefully he had understood. Karak stayed a little behind the main assault force, the better to control it. Several men ran with him, waiting for instructions. He felt his sweat stinging his eyes.

They pressed on, street after street, clubbing every man they saw. Some tried to surrender, and they struck them as well. His orders had been clear: There was to be no killing if possible, because much of the bounty would be the high prices brought in the slave markets of the south.

Children who had awakened during the commotion ran outside. His men hit them with the shafts of spears and kept running, trying to penetrate deep into the city, trying to reach the far side before sweeping back through again. As each block was taken, he left behind a group of men to guard it until they returned.

One Philistine took command of a group of others and holed up in a stone building used as a meeting hall. They blockaded the doorway from inside, then threw stones and fired arrows from the roof. But they were untrained, and their efforts were futile. The chieftain simply sent men around to scale the back of the building.

There were screams. The fighters on the roof had thrown a vat of oil over the side and lit it on fire. It burst into flames as it hit the ground. His men ducked out of the way, and remarkably, miraculously, none had been touched by the fire. He shouted orders. Men moved.

After a few moments, more heads appeared on the roof—his own men. An officer reached over the side, pounded his fist, and shouted the signal. The chieftain bellowed another order, and the men kept running. They had to move, had to move quickly, and he urged them on with shouting and threats and curses. Flames were everywhere on the buildings now, and he cursed at his men for setting more fires. He had wanted to clear the buildings of plunder before setting fire to them, but once the tide had begun, he could not stop it, only direct it. They kept rushing forward.

Men began ignoring his orders. They pulled women out of homes, screaming, tearing at their clothing, and assaulting them in the open of the street while their children howled. He raged at them to keep moving, but he needed to stay with the main assault, and so he left them behind.

The tide struck the far wall at last, near the stone houses of the city rulers and elders. There was no more resistance. After sending a squad into the city governor's home, he turned the flow of men toward the northern part of the city, where the Egyptian had presumably gone. He would search for the man along the wall, as agreed—if the mercenary had even understood what he was being told.

They kept running. He had fewer and fewer men around him as each block passed, and he was forced to post a rear guard in case a counterattack emerged from the shadows. But there were no opposing fighters, hardly any men anywhere, and those they found, they easily captured. The wave of his soldiers pressed hard down the dark streets and alleys of the Philistine city. He felt his sweat and blood racing, and despite the stress of controlling his men, he could not contain a shout of pleasure.

The Egyptian listened to the growing storm of rage in the distance; they were still a good distance away. An occasional Philistine man had emerged from a dwelling as he'd passed, but he'd raced past them. Women shrieked from windows but he ignored them. He needed to reach the Hebrew quarter.

And there it was at last, a separate area of buildings, storehouses, and tents along the northern wall of the city. He recognized the multicolored shawls and caravan covers as Hebrew, the garments and clothes required by their bizarre god who claimed to be the only one. He'd never understood such a concept: Why would a man choose to follow only one god when there were so many other areas of life where he required the gods' services?

Women looked out from the openings of their homes. It was inexplicable that no men would have been left behind to protect them, especially while they lived among enemies. As he ran past them, he heard more shrieks and screams.

When scouting the town the previous winter, the Egyptian had seen a large building along the wall. It looked like a row of shops from the front, but the size of it aroused his curiosity. He'd had to leave after only a day; even though he'd worn the garments of a slave laborer, his size always aroused suspicion. But in that time he had seen men coming and going from the building, passing a sentry in the doorway each time they entered.

The Egyptian came around a corner and saw the building ahead.

He pulled at the handle, but it was locked. He lowered his shoulder and crashed through the doorway, breaking the hinge.

He was astonished. It was an immense storeroom of gold, jewels, and precious metals. It was hard to see much in the dark, but the room was so full of treasure that its contents gleamed and sparkled in the splash of moonlight seeping through the doorway. It was everything he'd suspected it would be. Mounds of loot gathered from hundreds of caravans were heaped in every corner, as though a great king of Egypt had been buried in his throne room full of gold. There were fine cloths, woven garments, precious stones and metals, and countless other luxuries like those he had coveted in the palaces of the pharaoh.

Whoever this warlord was, he had done well for himself.

The Egyptian saw another doorway in the corner at the far end of the moonlight coming from outside. He could only make out some of the items inside: a rack of weapons, a stack of greaves, other pieces of armor. He assumed the room was full of them. He pulled a sword off the rack and tilted it so he could examine the craftsmanship.

Iron.

The Egyptian replaced the sword. He stared, thinking. Most interesting. Hebrews with iron weapons. Were they forging them or capturing and hoarding them?

He smiled, wiped his face, held his spear across his shoulders, and walked back outside. He had found the storehouse first. Claimed it. Any man who disputed this would be dealt with.

Moving it all was impossible, of course. He would carry the best of it and be content to return later when the pharaoh's armies invaded. They would sweep through Amalekite lands, capturing any treasure that had found its way into their filthy tents, and then push into Hebrew country. There would be more storehouses like this one. Pharaoh would reward him with lakhs of gold for his spying, more than could be pulled by a hundred oxen.

He stood silently and looked at the moon, large in the sky. Nearby was the sound of crying and whispers, and he nodded. They would cry louder when the barbarians arrived, as they would soon. The rape of the city had already begun. It was most inappropriate, most unbecoming a man of the River Kingdom. Cold night air basked him. He listened and waited.

TEN

In better days, before the darkness:

She holds the child and looks at me. The baby girl stirs in her arms. Another daughter? But there must be sons. Two daughters? I need sons! Her hair is tied up. I love it that way. Perspiration on her face. She smiles at me, confused.

"Are you not pleased, lord?"

"I am pleased."

Am I? Daughters bring dowry. I will need dowry if I have no sons to work the land. I will fight wars for money the rest of my life. Daughters guiding oxen? They could not lift a yoke. She is still smiling at me. Better look at her. My hand on her head. Such soft hair.

Sherizah says, "Forgive me, lord. I know we need sons."

Her eyes watch me. She is beginning to cry again. I never like it when she cries. So very tired after a long night of waiting. She cries. She pulls the bundle close. I am not upset, am I?

"It is not your fault, Sherizah."

She lets out a long breath. Looks away. Tears are staining the front of her shawl. Of course I love the girls. There will be more. Sons will come eventually.

Benaiah gazed at the inside of the tent as it shook with the morning wind. It was still dark out. Something had awakened him. Unable to get to sleep again, his wounds aching, he had lain helplessly while the nightmares found him in the dark, even awake.

Benaiah heard someone clanking cookware nearby. Time to move.

The cold air bit at his skin while he stood and pulled a winter tunic over his head. The wind picked up again and violently whipped the campaign tent. He was grateful for the tent; normally they did not have them because they weighed too much and were too cumbersome for the lightning pace of David's army. They moved in and out of a town before anyone knew what happened. Like a lightning strike. That had been Josheb's description, and Benaiah liked it.

His wounds had solidified, turning into something like slabs of limestone knitted into his scalp and arm, and they roared with such pain that he had to sit down again. After stretching his arms out again, Benaiah finished dressing and gathered his weapons next to him: spear, sword, shield, his prized bow, and a lance swiped from a Philistine rack the night before.

He held the spear shaft and felt the balance. The spear was a thrusting and swinging weapon, thrown only when it was unavoidable. The lance was the throwing weapon. He picked up the lance and held it over his shoulder as if he was about to toss it. His shoulder and arm were stiff; he would not be able to put much force into it.

There was another weapon to go into the bundle, and he relished sliding it from the satchel that covered it, running his fingers along the shaft. He had found this root growing with the rock sunken into it. No one could explain how it had happened. But it worked—a perfect war club. He held it lightly against his forehead, feeling the cold knob of rock.

He knew all of the weapons. Few men in this herding and farming culture knew weapons well; even fewer knew more than one. Benaiah knew every weapon—but this, the simplest one, was his favorite.

The others were iron, a benefit of having lived among Philistines. The men of Israel gathered at that moment with Saul in the Jezreel Valley had such weapons, stolen from captured enemies, but they did not know how to maintain them and had no instruments to sharpen them with. Some had figured how to grind the blade on stone. It was slow, and frequently chipped the edge. David's men were encouraged to keep their weapons in top condition, though it was becoming more tedious using the Philistine smiths to forge their weapons.

He straightened the weapons on the ground, then after grunting in pain a few more times, decided to go for a walk to loosen up. His wounds felt better once he was moving. Outside the flap of the tent, a cold blast of wind sucked the air out of his lungs, choking him. He hated this weather. Spring near the mountains was never one season or the other: cold one day and hot the next.

He heard Josheb shout, "Good morning, brother! Glad to see you awoke from your fainting. There is someone here you must meet."

Josheb was draped in wool blankets and beaming with his usual good cheer. Next to him stood a man with a cropped beard and fierce eyes. He looked to be in his thirtieth year—as Benaiah was—with a thin scar stretched across his forehead. He was larger than Josheb; he looked at Benaiah from the same eye level. He wore his hair long and had tied it in places, with the locks hanging off his shoulders. His ornate cloak signified that he was a man of wealth. He did not look like a Hebrew. His skin was too light. He was from the north.

"Benaiah son of Jehoiada, this is Keth of the Hittites."

The man nodded and Benaiah did the same. Hittite lands were in the north of the kingdom. In ages past they had been an enemy to the Hebrews, but some scattered tribes had begun to follow the Israelite religion. David accepted such men. Benaiah gave Josheb a questioning look.

"Keth joined us a few days ago," Josheb said. "He's a brave fighter, renowned along the northern frontier as a killer of Philistines, so we're hiding his identity in the camp. He is even learning our tongue. I told him that we would circumcise him tomorrow, and that Shammah would do the honors." Josheb laughed at his own joke. Keth seemed to miss the reference, and Benaiah smiled in spite of himself.

Then Josheb shifted somewhat, as though he were trying to keep his next sentence from being overheard. "And Hittites are good with iron, so he has made fast friends with our leader."

"I have heard about you from your fellow warriors, son of Jehoiada. It is my pleasure to meet you," said Keth, holding out his arm. Benaiah grasped it and slapped him on the shoulder, then winced when the man did the same. Keth pulled his hand back apologetically.

Josheb chuckled. "Forgive Benaiah; he was butchered by a band of savage rodents a few days ago."

"Lions. And I won."

"Winning entails receiving no wounds and hanging their tongues around your neck as a prize."

The three men walked together through the gloom, picking their way around sleeping men and those just now arising. Benaiah looked across the camp to the Philistine position and saw no one up there yet. The wind must be keeping them inside their tents, he thought, then grinned. David never let weather deter him. Everyone in David's army would be up and moving quickly, despite having, as yet, no specific orders. One can never move fast enough, David always said.

They passed men chewing on hard cakes of dried bread and, seeking a little variety in their dull wartime diets, bartering with one another to swap fruits and nuts, freshly picked and delivered to them before the strange cold snap had blown in. Several grumbled about being up so early; others complained about the cold morning. One group was tossing pebbles to see who could land one inside the nostril of a soldier who had not yet awoken.

A section leader walked by, saw the sleeping man, and kicked his jaw lightly, causing him to startle awake and swing at his imagined attacker, only to miss and career over sideways. His pebble-throwing squad mates laughed hysterically.

They came to an opening in the center of camp and stood in front of a set of three tents, held down by ropes but threatening to fly away in the wind. The tent in the middle was larger and designed for meetings. Benaiah saw a crowd of men already gathered in the entrance. He held open a flap, and they stepped inside.

In the orange glow of several torches, he saw Eleazar and Shammah standing around a circle in the dirt where a crude outline of the countryside had been sketched. Josheb bid them farewell and made his way toward the spot. The tent was crowded with leaders of companies, logistics men, and section leaders, all talking at once.

Joab, who had been speaking to Eleazar, arms crossed, shouted for everyone to quiet down. Benaiah searched but did not see David anywhere.

Joab spoke again, loud enough to be heard over the powerful

wind outside. "He will be here soon. Stay close and stop cackling like hens."

The group quieted a little but continued murmuring. Joab was tall and, Benaiah thought once again, insufferably arrogant. Always right there when David looked for a volunteer, stepping in front of others who offered. It was good for a man to be eager, but not at the expense of the efforts of everyone else.

Benaiah turned to Keth, who had been standing quietly in the corner behind him. "What brought you to us, my friend?"

Keth said, "I heard of this *apiru* named David."

Benaiah nodded. He had heard the same response from many of the six hundred or so men who had come in from different lands. "Well, we are an interesting group. Half of us are in debt over our heads. Others stole cattle. Some are mercenaries. A more worthless bunch of men you will never meet. But they fight."

Benaiah was sure that the conversations Keth had heard around campfires the night before had reminded him more of pagans than pious Hebrews. It was an odd bunch for the man who would be king of a united Israel to gather around himself.

"I noticed your men have iron weapons," Keth said. "I thought the Philistines prevented Israelites from learning the skill."

"True," replied Benaiah. "There isn't a smith allowed in our lands. We have access to smiths because we live in a Philistine city. That's why David chose Philistia to hide from Saul—he wanted to learn the craft of forging. We still haven't mastered it, so we threaten to kill a blacksmith's entire family and that persuades him to keep us armed. David welcomes men like you because his army cannot fight with bronze anymore, and we won't be able to use the Philistines forever. One day we will have to fight them. Already have, a couple of times. King Achish overlooks it. Philistines bicker among themselves just like we do."

"I know the forging process. It will be my honor to help however I am able. Although I still do not understand what his purposes are," Keth said.

Benaiah thought about it a moment. Keth might be a spy. He weighed his words carefully. "He was told by a prophet that the throne of Israel would be his one day. King Saul didn't see it that way, so men started showing up to join David while he was on the run."

"On the run?" asked Keth.

"From Saul. He has spent years running from him. Pretended to be insane so that he could hide among the Philistines. He was the greatest soldier in the king's army, but he was forced to live like a wilderness hermit. A lot of us heard about this and decided that he was our man. We could ... understand him. Criminals on the run and all. But he had done nothing wrong. Unlike everyone else here.

"Many are here because they believe Yahweh is with him. Others are here for the money. Others for women. Some want to be in positions of power when David takes the throne," he said, then looked at Joab again, who was pointing his finger at the table and arguing with Josheb.

"Yahweh is your god," Keth said.

"He is. He has many names, like El Shaddai. Some are not allowed to be spoken. I have even heard David call him ... well ... '*ab*.'"

"El Shaddai. I like that. 'Dwells among the mountains.' There were beautiful mountains in my homeland. But isn't *ab* what children call their father?"

"David says that Yahweh *is* our father."

"And you? You are a follower of Yahweh?"

Benaiah hesitated. "Hebrew men are circumcised when they are born, as a sign that we are set apart to Yahweh for his use. But not all of us follow the Law of Yahweh as closely as David does. For many of us, like me, it is simply an old custom of our people."

"Then why does David have men around him, men he trusts his life to, who do not even worship his god?"

Benaiah smiled. "That is one of many things that cannot be explained around here."

Benaiah watched Joab rudely pointing directly into Josheb's face, as though he were a stable boy to give orders to. He frowned.

Keth eyed a soldier in front of them thoughtfully. "There are rumors of a better forging process than simply hewing iron. Some races already possess better metals for their weapons."

"Perhaps that is why you were welcomed here. Have you met David yet?"

Keth nodded. "Briefly, when I first came. I heard about his fight with Goliath of Gath, even where I am from. The storytellers sing of it."

"I was not there, but I have spoken to some who were. Goliath had four brothers, did you know that?"

"I did not."

"He ran out against Goliath with just a staff and a sling. Alone. Against what he thought would be five of them. He assaulted the giant and was ready for the brothers. The brothers must have thought better of it around the time David cut off the Philistine's head and yelled his challenge to them, covered in their more powerful sibling's blood."

"How did he do it?" Keth asked.

Benaiah waited for some shouting in the tent to calm down again. He spoke hesitantly, remembering his encounter with the warrior in the woods. He also wondered again if Keth was a spy. But something urged him onward, to keep telling this man what he knew.

"He calls it 'the covering.' I think he is referring to Yahweh, or some type of power from Yahweh. He asks for it just before a battle. He told me once that he asks for it all day long, even when there is no war. He used to, anyway."

"Used to?"

"I haven't seen him do it in a while. We've been fighting continuously for almost a year, raiding up and down the frontier, and he hasn't mentioned it. He is more brutal than even he used to be. He even lies to King Achish, our little Philistine overlord. Most of us wouldn't have a problem lying to a Philistine, but normally David would have."

"You mentioned raiding. Raiding against Philistia?"

I should not be telling this man everything, Benaiah thought. But then another voice responded, *Tell him.*

Benaiah felt his neck prickle. He glanced around to see if someone had whispered in his ear. No one there.

"No. Mostly Amalekite country," he said. "Also Moab and Ammon. I ran into a band of Amalekites several days ago. I think there might be a larger force of them moving into our lands, but they're so scattered and disorganized that the more I think about it the more it is hard to believe that they could muster enough cooperation to do any real damage.

"We're fulfilling the command to destroy them that Yahweh gave Saul many years ago. But it also works out well for David—he will give his own men control of the borderlands so that they have even more reason to fight for him. They don't want their own crops burned by Amalekites."

"So your god is a god of war, then? Total destruction of your enemies?" Keth asked.

"Yahweh is not close to me. I would not know."

Keth nodded. Benaiah was grateful that he let it be.

"I have known many great war leaders. Most only want more gold and property. How is David different?" Keth asked.

"He is not a man of peace. He wants to be, but he once said that Yahweh has not willed that for him. Our lands are torn apart. Many suffer, not only from outside threats but from the constant squabbling and bickering between our own tribes. Men die over who owns a quarter of a hillside. Our people need David. He is ruthless enough to stop our enemies, and compassionate enough to judge our people fairly."

"You seem to admire him greatly."

"He always puts his men first, genuine destiny pushes him forward ..." Benaiah paused. "And he took us in when we had nowhere else to go."

The two of them watched the frantic activity of men in a foul mood and awake against their will. The tent was becoming increasingly crowded.

Then the tent immediately went quiet. Benaiah turned toward the map where the leaders were arguing and noticed another man among them.

David had entered.

The most remarkable aspect about him, after all the legends had been told, was how young he still was. Some of the men present probably had sons his age. Benaiah himself was older than David, but he felt young when David was around.

David's beard was lighter than any other man's beard in the tent, and cropped short for the campaign season, like his troops'. His auburn hair was trimmed short as well. The hair made him stand out. Every man present but David had black hair. His clothing was a simple gray cloak and battle tunic.

His arms, strengthened by years of battles fought long before most boys were old enough to swing a hammer, rippled with hard muscle. Yet he was of average height and did not immediately stand out from other men in the crowd, unlike his tall king. His face was marked by old scars, but he had striking features, much more so than any other man present. Amber-colored eyes looked across the room.

He could play the lyre. He could sing melodies so achingly beautiful that even the hardest warriors would pause and listen. His compassion to the wounded had earned him renown. He prayed loudly and passionately into the night. But there was something in his face during times of battle, such as this, that reminded Benaiah of death. Violence and death. A good face for a warlord, he thought.

The room was still in the presence of the chief. He had that effect, as most men of authority did. There was something about the confident manner with which he carried himself, and the assurance that he knew exactly what he was doing at all times. That no matter what befell them, he would find victory.

And part of it was his amber eyes. The eyes so similar to a lion's, giving him the title that all around the countryside knew him by — the Lion of Judah. It was a look of power, primal and fierce. He had a lion's face.

The outlaw commander elbowed his way to where Joab and the other leaders of his army were standing. He nodded greetings, caught Benaiah's eye, and nodded to him as well. He ran fingers through his beard a moment. They all waited as the wind pounded the tent.

"My gratitude for your perseverance, brothers. I know you have been without information for some time. King Achish has told me that we are not welcome among the other Philistine rulers."

This was greeted by cheers. David smiled in spite of himself. "As that is so, we will not go to war with them. We will return to Ziklag." Half of the tent erupted in cheers, the other was silent. Several cursed aloud. Someone shouted over the sound.

"But sir, why bring us all this way? Why won't they let us come?"

"They don't think we will be loyal. I couldn't convince them otherwise. They saw how many of us were riding out to war, and they became afraid. With good reason." He nodded at the gathered men. "I would be afraid of you as well."

The soldier was not satisfied. "Then can we do a flank march around the valley and come up on the Israelites from behind? They would be glad to see us. Saul would realize that he needs your help." This caused voices to rise up again.

Josheb said, "If we flank march against the Philistines, then we jeopardize our homes in Ziklag. Surely they will send this same army against us in the south. Saul has written the fate of his kingdom in his own blood. I like us returning home better."

Joab glared at him and then at David. "If we go now, we can strike fast. Yahweh will grant it to you."

Keth leaned in next to Benaiah. "He lets his commanders argue in front of the men?"

"David wants the men to feel like they have a part in their fate. You will notice," Benaiah nodded toward them, "clean and well-behaved hardly describes our little band. It works for now."

Keth tilted his head. "He trusts them that much?"

"Some of them he would trust with his life. Some he would spear if they looked at him wrong. He loves them all, but he is a hard man. The only one who could lead them."

Keth looked back to the front of the tent, measuring this. No sense in hiding it from him, Benaiah thought. He needed to learn their ways if he was to have a home among them.

Joab kept repeating that Yahweh would give the victory. It must have irritated David, who raised his voice in anger.

"Have you asked him, Joab? Did he visit you in your tent this morning and tell you that?"

Joab's face fell a little. "No, but surely we would win. We have never lost."

The multiple voices clamoring in the tent had gone quiet.

"I see no priestly garments on you. There is no ephod on your belt. You presume to speak for Yahweh? You speak his name aloud so lightly?"

Joab changed his approach. "But lord, if we just up and leave, what will we do when we return home? Continue raiding barbarian settlements?"

There was some murmuring, but David made no reply. It was his signal that debate could resume. Josheb was about to say something else when Benaiah, deciding the time had come, spoke up. "Lord, I returned from Judah last night. Amalekites might be moving against us."

David jerked his head up and found him. "Amalekites? How?"

"I fought a raiding party in that village you sent me to. They said they were moving into southern Judah and Philistia." Benaiah had to shout over the commotion this news caused. "Perhaps as many as a thousand. Mercenaries might be with them."

David nodded, concern darkening his face, and knelt to examine the sketch on the ground in front of him.

"Lord, that is impossible," Joab said. "Amalek has been crushed under our feet. No large army could move in such short time."

"I do not know if the larger force is real or not, but I know I fought a band of them. And as I said, they could have mercenaries with them." Benaiah glared at Joab long enough to make his point, then looked back at David. "Lord, I agree with you. We need to leave. Now. Our women and children are defenseless in Ziklag. Even if it's not a serious threat, we need to be sure."

"I agree, Benaiah. If this Amalekite army exists, then we will meet it. That is all. Get your men. Move quickly." He thumped his fist on the ground and left the way he came, the tent flap blowing wildly as he walked out into the wind. A noticeable uneasiness descended on the group with the news of Amalekites near their home. Benaiah motioned for Keth to follow him outside.

The army was ready. They walked past men sitting on their bundles of animal pelts and weapons and various other pieces of equipment, waiting for any word from the commanders. Several of the men exiting the tent began to shout the orders, and the men formed up into ranks. Benaiah led Keth to his own tent and spoke to him as he cleared it of his things. The worn-out tent belonged to the Philistines, and he would not need to pack it. David's men traveled light.

"I know that was strange for you to see," Benaiah said. "Like I said, we function differently than most armies."

Keth nodded. "I slept next to a man who was running from a bad land sale. Another was accused of killing a man over a woman. He did not deny it."

"They probably won't make good administrators in the royal palace one day, but if you want dead enemies they do just fine," Benaiah said. He wrapped the last of his things in a wool blanket, covered it with an oiled and tanned hide to prevent water from leaking in, and tied it shut with leather straps.

They stepped back out into the raging wind of the early morning.

Keth asked, "His deputy, Joab? Is he a fighter?"

"He is a fighter. He's also annoying."

They walked for a while in silence. "Amalek moves, then. It is surprising," said Keth as they walked back to the command tent.

Keth wrapped the wool cloak around his shoulders a little tighter. Benaiah decided that he liked Keth. He had a hard grip and steady eyes. And he probably was not a criminal—a relief among these men.

The two of them stopped at the command tent's entrance and waited.

"Are there no horses for David and his commanders?" Keth asked.

"No. He moves like his men. Eats after they eat. Sleeps after they sleep. The terrain in our lands makes chariots and horses worthless for war. He rides horses only when he needs to cover ground quickly. He wants the men to have 'feet of iron.'"

"He rode on a horse while marching with the Philistines to this place," Keth said.

"Maintaining appearances. He wanted the Philistines to think he will fight as they do." The wind stung his eyes, and he blinked away grit.

David walked out of the command tent, his equipment neatly packed and rolled. He watched the movements of his men with a slight scowl and did not notice Benaiah and Keth nearby. Benaiah recognized the look and decided to leave him be. Joab was nowhere to be seen, probably sent off on some errand so that David could enjoy a moment alone. Benaiah did not envy David what must be a lonely life.

It made him wonder about the odd relationship between Joab and David. Benaiah suspected that David was pressured by his tribe to tolerate him. But Joab was a fighter, he conceded. He could move men.

David noticed them and smiled warmly. He walked over and embraced Benaiah, who did his best to hide his stiff wounds.

"I missed you, brother," David said quietly. Benaiah could not hide his smile. He knew that David meant it.

Keth stood with his hands clasped behind his back politely. David turned to him. "Hittite, as I said before, we are honored you are here. Yahweh has shown us mercy by blessing us with your presence. Did you find your other countrymen?"

"I did, lord."

"Tribal men are usually mixed into the companies to avoid playing favorites on the battlefield. Most are from Judah, our largest tribe, but there are equally valiant fighters from the smaller territories. I try to remind them often that while they serve me, tribal identity does not matter. I want you to be my chief armorer and train an entire company in the craft, if you will accept the position. We will fight no more wars with bronze weapons. I am tired of blades that bend when they strike shields."

David paused a moment, distracted by the way a soldier was packing his gear. "Elon, you'll never last the day on the march if you wear it like that. Your load has no balance. If you don't fix it, I'll be forced to give your crippled carcass to the Philistines. You'll be no use to me, but you might be their best man."

Several hundred men had gathered in formation nearby. Those closest, who had heard him, laughed.

He turned back to Benaiah. "That business with the lion. I trust it ended happily for all involved."

"It did. Took a little of me with it, but I was able to sort it out. Nothing like you in the old days, though." David smiled at the reference to his shepherding years. Benaiah continued. "More important was the band of ten I found. The wounded man could have been lying about a larger force, but it didn't feel like he was. Also, Saul has conscripted most of the men. I saw only a few in that town. Mostly old or lame."

David looked at the ground and nudged a rock with his sandal. They watched while the army finished its preparations. Benaiah could see the mass of men, divided into rows of twenty and columns of fifty. They were cold, stamping their feet and jumping up and down, occasionally grumbling and complaining. Some did their best to keep the laughter going. Others stared quietly and waited for the orders to march back to their homes. The rumors had already begun to fly down the ranks that their families might be in danger.

"I want to reassign you, Benaiah."

"To a company?"

"No. You will still function mostly alone, but yes, there will be men with you. I need you to organize a personal guard for me." David continued pawing at the rock on the ground with his sandal. "I don't like it, but it is necessary for command and control. I will still lead assaults, but once they have begun, I need to see what is happening on the field. I can't command my army when I am forced to fight through the entire battle."

It was clear that David hated saying it, Benaiah noticed. It was against everything in him.

"We will still be in the middle of it. I just don't want to be making command decisions while being impaled on a lance. Our little band has grown too large."

Benaiah tried to soften the blow. "You honor me. Can I pick who will be in it?"

"Of course."

"Then I would have foreigners. No men of the tribes."

David and Keth turned toward him.

"Foreigners," David repeated. He nodded, looked out at the men, then nodded again. "Interesting. As you wish. Have them for me before we return to Ziklag. It really is good to see you again, Benaiah."

Benaiah saw weariness and stress in the amber eyes. David nodded and walked off to inspect the companies.

"Good thinking on the foreigners," Keth said.

"We have enough tribal fighting, no need to get into spitting contests about who guards the chief."

They stood in the gray morning, watching the wind swirl through the camp before pelting them with grit and dust that forced eyes to shut and bodies to shiver. The sun was finally up but hidden.

Somewhere someone gave an order, and the great mass of six hundred fighters began to converge into one snakelike stream moving forward toward the trade road.

Following the marching men, Benaiah's mind wandered. He

thought about his new responsibility. The personal guard needed to be good men as well as foreigners.

He wondered about the Hittite mercenary marching next to him. A friend? Possibly a spy. What kept telling him to trust him?

ELEVEN

Eliam, still groggy from the night's sleep, tripped over a branch as he followed Gareb and crashed to the ground. Several men laughed loudly and whistled at him. He stood and tried to look as if he had done it on purpose, then sprinted, blushing, after the man who had awakened him moments before.

"The men are lazy these days," Gareb said. He was walking in great strides across the encampment, shouting orders and finding other subordinates who needed to be briefed. The rising sun was hidden behind a dreary bank of clouds, washing the campsite in gray, milky light. The fires of the night before had smoldered into tiny wisps of smoke, and sleepy soldiers crawled out from under their wool blankets, fumbling for their equipment. Those who had been caught sleeping during the morning watch were forced to endure punishments from their section leaders. Eliam watched a man struggle to hold a rock over his head while his leader screamed at him.

Men were unwrapping the packages of food sent by relatives,

eyed enviously by those who had to beg their rations from others. Some didn't eat for days at a time. The men who received food were forced to share it with those who did not, but most saved the choice portions for themselves. The cheese was always moldy, but if it was sliced carefully, some could be spared. Cakes of hard bread usually lasted the longest.

Eliam had become accustomed to the food in the field. The king's tent fared better. He and other workers usually found enough leftover meat and fruit to eat well. The king didn't eat much anymore, and his dreary countenance had its effect on the army, which moved sluggishly every morning.

Gareb stopped walking so abruptly that Eliam nearly bumped into him. He was looking at a sword propped against a fallen tree near a fighting position on the perimeter. The soldier nearby was stretching and chatting casually with his battle partner. Gareb quietly picked the sword up, then motioned for Eliam to follow. After a few more paces, he saw another discarded sword and stole that one. Five swords later Eliam began to wonder why exactly he was removing the weapons from all of the men days before a battle.

"If these careless fools want to give back their swords to the uncircumcised Philistines, then I'll help them," Gareb said over his shoulder.

His eyes searched the camp for any other violations. Eliam studied the gray flecks in Gareb's beard. He was not an old man but acted like he was. Scars of many wars covered his body. The men shied away as Gareb approached; his temper and hawk's eye for discipline infractions were highly feared. Word must have been passed around the night before that Gareb was back in the ranks; Jamaliel had told Eliam that he was a legend.

Eliam had no idea why he had been summoned to come along on this little walk. Earlier that morning, while Eliam had been lying awake thinking about the conversation the night before, Gareb had stuck his head into the tent and told him to join him for an inspection of the camp. When Eliam asked why, he was ignored. The more time he spent around these men, the more he realized that eloquence was not part of the battle drills. Speech and instruction were thankfully short, but Eliam often found himself confused about what was going on around him. Entire conversations included only a couple of words. Some of the men seemed smart. Perhaps they simply found no use for pretty language.

He shivered under his layers of wool and wondered again why the weather was so cold. At least the rain and snow had stopped. The army was always so slow when the weather was bad. Everyone was in a foul mood; the men were slow to get moving each morning, which was probably why Gareb was personally seeing to it that Jonathan's regiment was prepared.

"The men are lazy these days," Gareb said again. "Didn't used to be that way."

Eliam was unsure whether he should respond, so he remained silent. Gareb had told him earlier in the morning that Saul's war council had gone on late. Spies had reported Philistine movements into the Jezreel Valley, now visible in the husky gray morning with a layer of mist settled in it. If they had moved faster and followed Jonathan's advice, Gareb huffed, they could have closed off the pass near Megiddo from Philistine incursion.

Now the area was swarming with the Sea People, and their camp across the valley at Shunem grew daily. If conditions were right, Eliam could see the village where the Philistines gathered. Today as he looked in that direction, all he saw was a bank of clouds.

"Spies tell us the main force isn't even here yet," Gareb said. "The king still won't act. What in a mule's hind leg he's thinking by letting them pile into the pass like that I'll never ..." Gareb bit his lip. He looked at Eliam from the edge of his eye.

Eliam had not taken offense at the remarks against his king.

Instead, he took the opportunity to ask a question. "What happened at Michmash?"

Gareb ignored him and watched the men around them continue preparing for the day. The morning meal was taking too long. He shouted a few more times and men scattered. Then he said, "You are going to take my place. Not for this war, but later. You're not ready yet, so he'll need me against the Philistines, but I want you to begin preparing. You will probably run water out to us during this coming battle, but you need to learn how to carry the armor. I'll teach you how. Of course, that assumes any of us make it out of this."

At first Eliam thought Gareb was talking to a man nearby, a soldier rolling up his blanket. He wondered why the man did not respond. Eliam looked up at Gareb, who was scanning the hillside.

"Well? Say something."

"Me?"

"No, the scorpion by your foot. He'd make a great armor bearer. Nasty jab, I would guess." Eliam looked down by his foot instinctively and immediately regretted it.

Gareb chuckled. "They raise them dumber by the year now. Where are you from?"

"The ... Hebron area. My father owns land near there."

"Judah's land?"

Eliam nodded.

"Shame. They need to be getting smarter down there. Hope you're not the usual." He rubbed his nose. "Yes, I was talking to you. He wants you trained up and ready. Don't ask me why."

"But I've never even seen a battle. Why?"

"I just said don't ask me why. I don't know. You weren't my first choice either. But that's what he wants."

"Who?" asked Eliam.

"Jonathan. I came in from plowing dirt so that he didn't get himself killed, but I'm done after this. He wants you to replace me. Only the Almighty knows why. Just stay with me—move that pile out of here!—stay with me in the fight to come so you can see what an armor bearer does. We don't just bear the armor."

Gareb didn't look at Eliam during most of the conversation and kept interrupting himself with shouted orders to others. One of the men who had lost his sword to Gareb's thievery approached them nervously and asked if they had seen his sword. Gareb made him stand nearby holding it over his head, with orders that he could lower it only when his arms fell off.

"I know your section leader, and I know he has taught you about weapon security before. You had better have this weapon with you every hour of the day. I'd better hear your woman complaining that you take it to bed with you."

Gareb spoke to Eliam again. "We have no blacksmiths, so every weapon is precious. Only strong and smart men are given the chance to carry an iron sword. This fellow isn't smart, so we'll see how strong he is." Gareb folded his arms and finally looked at the stunned Eliam standing next to him. "Like I was saying, you won't be formally trained, but you'll be fine. When I started we only had rocks and sticks, and I still managed to kill Philistines by the dozen."

Eliam stared. His father would not believe him when he heard. Armor bearer to the future king of Israel. He repeated it inside his head to make sense of it. He still had questions but wanted to make sure he did not look like an overeager fool.

Soft dawn light covered the ground around them. The noises didn't change: clinking and occasional commotion. The soldier holding the sword over his head was panting now, beads of sweat dripping down his nose. He looked at them pleadingly.

Gareb glanced at him. "Gets heavy after a while. Good way to build up the arms. Sometimes I make them hold twigs over their head. They laugh it off at first. Eight hours later they aren't laughing anymore."

He motioned for Eliam to follow, then said to the soldier being punished, "Drop your arms and I'll have you speared. Swords are precious. When your arms finally give out I want you to turn that weapon in to your commander and tell him that only men carry swords."

Gareb moved on and Eliam followed him, stepping over rocks the whole way. *They are everywhere in this country,* Eliam thought absentmindedly. *A man couldn't even lie down for a night without moving rocks out of the way. There were rocks underneath the rocks, and digging them out only produced more rocks.*

Gareb spoke in his gruff voice again. "All right, might as well start now. The rule is: never leave your master in battle. Don't run from the field. It will get bad, and then it will get worse, and you still never leave him. There will be times everyone will run but the two of you. Stay next to him. Sometimes you're going to fight the best man the enemy has, along with his armor bearer, just the four of you face-to-face. Stay next to your leader. Other times it will be you and him alone against hundreds. *Stay next to him!* Don't expect to just hop out of the way and let him do the work."

Gareb was speaking while picking up discarded weapons. Eliam had many questions but was afraid to stop him for an explanation. The cloth wrapped around his shoulders sagged, and he straightened it. He would have to build up muscle. This made no sense. Yes, he was taking lessons, and Jonathan had seemed to take a liking to him, but armor bearer? The position of honor?

"What happened on that day at Michmash between Jonathan and the king?" The question was out of Eliam before he could stop it.

Gareb glanced at him and rubbed his head, gesturing for him to sit on one of the rocks. "You're not going to quit asking, are you?"

"No, lord. I need to know. I need to know as much as possible if I am to do this."

"Don't call me lord. I'm not some prince or war chief." He sighed. "You can know, I guess. Most do already; don't know how you missed it."

Gareb breathed a moment and looked at the soldiers moving. They were fully awake now, with more purpose in their steps. Eliam watched him, wondering what was going on in his mind. Gareb seemed to hate the cold weather and became fouler every time he had to adjust his cloak.

"He woke me up before daylight. Said there were two swords in the entire army and that he had one of them. His father was not going to do anything about the Philistine army threatening us, so he told me that if we hit them hard and fast, Yahweh might bring about a great victory.

"I thought he was crazy, but told him I would be with him no matter what. We snuck out of the camp, and you know the rest. After we crossed the gorge and climbed up, he hit them so violently that I thought the war would be over before I even blocked a single attack to his flank. There never was a man who could fight like Jonathan, and on that day he didn't even have his bow. We ran hard and we killed Philistines. You never saw so many terrified sea-drinking pagans. It was just the two of us, and they ran like we were warriors sent from the presence of Yahweh himself.

"It was hot, really hot, so after the entire garrison at the outpost was dead, we decided to chase the rest of them down the ridge. He wanted to destroy them before they could form up with the rest of their army, but that battle was never in doubt. He could have wiped out their entire flank by himself, that's how stunned they were. Speed and maneuvering, son. Live it all your life."

He paused a moment to shout at the man holding the sword up, still visible in the distance across the camp, telling him that his arms had not fallen off yet and to get it back over his head. The man was crying out in agony but managed to hoist it up.

"Looking back across the canyon—you remember how we crossed the canyon and climbed up the other side—I could see the rest of the army of Israel charging down the slope. They had seen what Jonathan and I were doing, and that must have inspired them, because what was once a bunch of clucking hens immediately became a group of fighting men. That's the thing about leading men, Eliam. They're always going to follow the man who leads from the front.

"Soon afterward, the king gave an order that no one was to eat anything until the end of the day. Vowed it to Yahweh. Said that if any man stopped to eat something he would be put to death. It was a foolish thing to do, one of many—"

He cleared his throat, as if regretting it. Eliam was listening quietly but fighting impatience.

Something clattered. The man being punished had dropped his sword and then fallen over when he tried to pick it up. Gareb glanced at him and then stared at the tree line in the distance.

"Jonathan didn't hear the order not to eat, so as we came to the trees—remember it was really hot—we needed to rest. Hours had gone by. I remember swatting at a bee, then another, and then I looked down at my feet and saw a beehive in a hollowed log. Honey is hard to find, despite how it always makes it to the king's table.

"He reached in and grabbed the honey and started to eat it. I was too hot to eat, and I don't like to eat when a fight is going on. It was just honey, and who could have known about an order like that?

"The day ended, the Philistines ran, and there we all were back at the camp with the king, and all I heard him tell Jonathan was how angry he was at him for charging out without orders. Even after all that we did, driving out a Philistine garrison by ourselves. He said Yahweh was not responding to the ephod, and that someone must have sinned, and it was Jonathan's fault. I heard later that he was trying to manipulate the ephod. So he called all of the men up to see who had sinned. The lot fell to Jonathan—"

"Sinned?" asked Eliam. "How did Jonathan sin by eating honey?"

"The king had made a vow that no one would eat, had made it to Yahweh, so the sin was in breaking the vow. It would have never happened if the fool hadn't ..." Gareb remained silent for a while, as if thinking. Eliam waited.

"Saul ordered the men to execute Jonathan," Gareb continued at last. "I'd be fed to the vultures before I let that happen, and others felt the same way, so we all shouted to the king that he would have to execute all of us if he touched Jonathan. Yahweh's anointed king or not, there would be blood before such a great warrior was put to death over something like that. He relented.

"That was only the beginning. Other things have happened through the years. The son of Jesse, David, was the main reason they fought."

"Do you think David is a criminal?"

"He is a criminal. He leads a band of criminals."

Gareb stopped. Eliam shifted in his seat. He did not want to push Gareb. He was learning much.

"Jonathan is loyal to his father and will die because of it one day. Probably soon. But his heart is with David and those criminals. I see it in him. He would leave this evening and join them if his father was not the king. I don't know why." Gareb noticed Eliam's confused look. "They were relatives once. Saul gave his daughter to David as a wife after killing Goliath. I know you've heard *that* story."

Eliam nodded.

Gareb continued. "Saul wanted David dead. Thought he was a threat to his throne. Which he is. He will have it one day. Even Jonathan, the heir, said so once. Said that Yahweh had determined that David would rule Israel.

"Jonathan and David are close because they fought many battles together. You'll learn about what happens among men who fight together soon enough. No words for it. Not love. Far beyond that.

"But he doesn't talk about David anymore. Doesn't want us to mention it to him, but as I watch him, I know that his heart left his father's tent a long time ago. His heart is in the desert with those criminals." Gareb shook his head. "There was a time when I would have joined them also. But David could have returned to save our lands and never did. He ran from his responsibility. But much worse than that, he is with the Philistines now. Our scouts tell us that he was marching with them to battle against us.

"He is a brave fighter. But he is also a selfish and arrogant man who deserves nothing but the poison of an asp. Jonathan should have forgotten about him." Gareb nodded and looked back at Eliam. "That is enough for now. You still need to learn this role."

Without another word he began to walk again. Eliam leapt up and followed him, picking his way around the rocks, wondering what it all meant.

TWELVE

A dog chewed on the leg of a dead woman.

In the harsh sunlight of the field outside the city where the raiders had taken them, Sherizah watched as the dog snarled and pulled, trying to separate a piece of flesh from the leg. She watched numbly, impassively, trying not to care but still feeling revulsion. It was a Philistine woman who had died when the raid began, probably of fear since no soldier had killed her. Before the raid, she had been a foul and ill-tempered woman, frequently stirring up trouble at the well, always inciting people against the Hebrews. *She deserved it.*

Sherizah squeezed her eyes shut. She would have been appalled at such a scene at any other time, but after the previous night's terrors it was just another sight, just another horrible image that ran together with the previous one.

There was the image of her home being burned. And the sight of her friends, women she was close to, being pulled away by heathen men who said and did awful things.

The images flashed by, one and another, and there were screams, and there was no end of it, the images of last night running together with those of a time long ago, and there were her girls, lying in bloody heaps, defiled, and her hair kept slipping out of its tie, and it made her so angry so suddenly that she cursed, loudly, drawing faces toward her.

She lowered her eyes to the sand. The terrors and the death had found her once more, even in the place they had gone to escape them. The smells were everywhere, and the screams. Smoke rose over the walls of Ziklag in dark plumes. The distorted air made the sky look like a bed of coals. Their men were gone. The other wives tied up elsewhere. Nothing was left but the dog eating that poor woman's body. *She really had been a wretched woman, though.*

Sherizah shook her head and retied the hair over her neck. He always liked it that way. He was gone, though. In the north, away to war, where he always was. Out with the men, away from her and the memories she probably brought to him. She'd once heard that men used to stay with their wives a year after marrying. It was written in the Law. She'd never had the year with him. She did not even know him.

Blinking, she turned away from the dog and curled up on her side, deciding instead to watch the movements of the raiders. They did not behave like Amalekites usually did, running wild with lust and bloodthirsty violence. There were clear orders given by officers who maintained control. It was an army.

One of them, a large man with black markings covering his body, seemed to be in control. He stood nearby, watching it all. Sherizah lay in the sun, in a row of women, and watched the continuing destruction.

The Egyptian prodded a mound of gold coins and pieces of silver with his foot, then walked across the treasure room. This was more wealth than he had ever seen in one place, other than the palace that was Pharaoh's future tomb. These Hebrews had been very good at their work.

He kicked a stack of gold coins over and watched it spill among the sand on the floor. Dust rose lazily and he wiped his eyes. The gold was good, as was the silver, but those things did not interest him like the iron. He ducked under the beam and waited for his eyes to adjust to the still-dark interior.

In the daylight now streaming through the doorway he could finally see what he'd missed last night. There were piles of it — scraps of discarded weapons and shards of wheel casings from chariots. Scrap iron covered an entire room of the storehouse. Much of it was rusting and no longer useful, but clearly someone had been trying to work it. There was a table in the corner with tools the Egyptian recognized as the tools used in forging. But the room was not an iron forge. There were no signs of a blacksmith shop. It was a mystery.

The Egyptian had been well educated in his homeland and was familiar with the working of metals. He even knew how to smith his own blades if necessary. But this was very odd. The Philistines had plenty of their own blacksmiths that the Hebrews could have used. Why the secrecy? His painted eyes searched the room in the stillness for any indication of purpose.

The Hebrew men living here fought with iron weapons, that much was obvious, and it was also clear that they had them serviced by local blacksmiths in the city. A room full of old and discarded metals, blacksmithing tools without a forge, all of it hidden away. The treasures of gold and silver were in full view, so why were worthless pieces of old iron hidden? With willing and able blacksmiths only blocks away?

It bothered him. Hebrews were an odd race, so unrefined and barbaric. They didn't even use chariots. They were also one of the oldest enemies of his people and had once been slaves of the glorious Nile Kingdom. The pharaoh had not said so, but the Egyptian suspected his purpose in this country: Pharaoh wanted intelligence for an invasion to reclaim the Hebrews as slaves again.

He walked back outside. Was there some kind of sacrifice to their god in the iron? And why were there Hebrews in this city at all?

A soldier shouted, and Karak turned. Another round of captured females, this time Philistines. Karak had given his men strict orders not to harm any of them, especially the Hebrews. Hebrews were the most valuable slaves when trading because their women never lost spirit. Many foreign kings liked women in their harem with plenty of spirit.

When they made it back to Amalekite lands, the children would be sold, the women put in harems, the men sent to work in the fields, and Karak would be a wealthy man.

As he watched the huddled mass of Philistine women being lined up next to the Hebrews, he reflected on the night before. It had been an incredible, unprecedented success: No men had been lost and an entire Philistine city completely captured. All of the gold and valuables would be removed and the buildings burned. It was too perfect to be believed. And wine! Wine was rare among the Amalekites. The Philistines made marvelous wine. His army would not even be able to continue their campaign without first returning to their lands with the captured bounty.

There were enough captured wives to supply an army. The final count was two-hundred and thirty. Including the children, there were over four hundred captives. The weapons and plunder the

Egyptian had found were enough to convince Karak that the city's men were raiders, and the only explanation was that the rumors of a warlord named David were true. David must have been living among these people, as they'd suspected; he may have been the governor himself and may have marched with his men to war in the north. That explained why a Philistine city was dominated and populated by Hebrews.

On the ground next to him was a Hebrew woman hiding her eyes. He searched for what she shied away from and saw the body of the older Philistine hag who had died in the street during the raid. Except for the Philistine woman, no one had been killed, difficult as it had been to prevent it.

He had heard that the heart can stop in fear. He had never seen it himself, until then. He had often feared that it would be his fortune for the gods to let him die in such a way—no honor or glory on a battlefield, just falling to the ground and dying before his enemies like the old Philistine woman.

He looked down at the Hebrew wife. She was attractive. He had examined all of them. Karak reached down and pulled her up by the hair.

The woman gasped and closed her eyes. Karak pulled her face close to his and smelled her. He waited for her to open her eyes, but she kept them closed. Most women he captured begged and pleaded with him.

He ran his hand up her chest. Then he held her throat.

"Where are the wives of the ruler of this city?" he asked. She did not respond.

Karak ran his hand over her body again. He would enjoy her one night soon, when it was her turn. Destroying Hebrews and burning their cities and having their women. He was a happy man.

Karak threw her down and walked away, searching for the Egyptian.

THIRTEEN

She is weeping. Yahweh has allowed this. Why? I feel the sorrow, but there are no tears in my eyes. It burns, though, burns—and I feel very tired. There is no escape from this sorrow.

Sherizah stumbles blindly into my chest, I place my hands in her hair, press my face against her head. Both of them gone. Amalekites have done this.

Amalekites.

I yell then, I push her away, I find the club . . .

In the town, the first Amalekite dies loudly, screaming, his throat filling up with blood. I grab his jaw and break it, then club him again. A warrior rushes toward me, and I strike him too, feeling anger and hate and power. I fight more of them, one after another, two or more at a time. Many are dead and I have killed them, and I want to kill more of them. I see an Amalekite child, and strike him down. He would have become one of them one day, and Yahweh desires them dead—not that I kill them for that reason. Yahweh has left me; he is gone. I will kill them anyway. I will kill so many of them that the desert will fill with *black blood, and the vultures will greet me, knowing that I bring them more dead Amalekites.*

A man surrenders to me, dropping his weapon, pleading for his life. I strike his face, crushing his head. And then I move on to the next with a roar of anger, a wail of grief, and I swing my club . . .

Benaiah rested, staring at the ground. Three days into the march, and still nothing. No word, no fresh rumors of Ziklag.

And still no bodyguard. He had been drawing up plans for formations and experimenting with the old methods. Guarding a man on a battlefield was difficult enough, but when that man desired to be fighting himself, it became impossible. Benaiah had to throw out much of what was taught regarding bodyguards. Kings and nobility, under normal circumstances, rarely sweated on the front lines. While serving in Egypt, Benaiah had never seen the pharaoh so much as mount a chariot to ride to battle—the reason his sons were plotting against him. David was different.

The foreigners Benaiah had selected for the bodyguard were good fighters, but he could not shake the suspicion that they would prove untrustworthy. They might be assassins sent by rival kingdoms—or worse, sent by Saul. He had no way of knowing who was loyal.

Word flew through the ranks that an elite guard was being formed, and as had undoubtedly been the case since the dawn of warfare, men sought to compete with one another for a spot in it. Men who had been with David for a year or more had been selected first, since they had already demonstrated their loyalty in combat.

For their service, Benaiah had proposed that David's bodyguards receive a tremendous wage, more than, to Benaiah's knowledge, any mercenary had ever made. This was to drive the men to compete with each other for positions and enable them to resist the temptation of being wooed away to a higher bidder. When Benaiah had presented this plan to David, he had heartily agreed. Of all the things David held dear, Benaiah had noticed, money did not seem to be among them. And David was an exceedingly wealthy man after all the raiding—even though he had sent most of the plunder to the villages of southern Judah, there was a storehouse in Ziklag full to the ceiling with treasure.

Benaiah decided that he would worry about it no more until they reached home, only a few days of marching away. The men were anxious to *charge* toward the city as quickly as possible and told their officers so. But David wanted them to rest and eat. There might be fighting soon. This was wise, Benaiah knew, but he was running out of ways to take his mind off Sherizah.

It was the middle of the day. The sun had finally begun to feel hot as they marched, and winter clothing had been abandoned for lighter, cooler garments. Now men were stripping to their bare chests. Those not worried about their families compared muscles and argued over who was better endowed.

Benaiah, kneeling, looked up at Eleazar, studying the hills on their left. Someone shouted, and all of the men rose and prepared to move. Benaiah strapped his gear back on and waited as Eleazar did the same. The two of them looked around for someone to walk with. They led no companies or squads, so they tended to wander freely among the columns of men. They saw Keth at the front of the Hittites and made their way toward him. Josheb and Shammah appeared as well.

"Where is Joab?" asked Benaiah.

"With his brother Abishai," replied Josheb.

"Did you not hear? He finally gave up his independence and stitched himself into David's tunic," said Shammah.

The humor was so unexpected that the entire group of them halted and stared at Shammah, who looked back at them awkwardly.

Wide-eyed, Josheb said, "It cannot be. Not Shammah. "

Shammah scratched his face and looked at the ground.

Eleazar said, "That was actually funny. Tell more jokes like that and you will finally get a woman."

"You do not have a woman, Shammah? No wife or slave girl?" Keth asked.

Josheb chuckled. "Shammah has killed entire troops of men with only his hands but bumbles all over himself when a beautiful woman walks nearby. We can't even get him to talk to them. I offered him my sister just to put him out of his misery, and he still refused."

"Because your sister looks like you," said Eleazar.

"One day the right one will come. Yahweh will guide me to her," said Shammah.

"Just don't be guided to the camels; you look desperate enough to make love to them if left alone," Josheb replied.

They roared at that one, and despite his best efforts, Shammah could not disguise his own smile.

"I'm still not convinced that an Amalekite army is waiting for us, Benaiah," said Eleazar.

"I'm not either. But I fought ten, and one of them said there was. How large a force would they need? Every Philistine king marched north with that army. There won't be a man in the south to stand between them and all they want to take."

They resumed their march in thoughtful silence. They had gradually made their way to the front of the ranks, alongside David, who had been marching alone. He was the only man among them who spent most his time alone, and each of them wanted to provide him company.

David looked up from the road and smiled. "Hope you are all ready for whatever we find."

The other men nodded.

"Where is Joab?" asked Josheb.

"I sent him to the rear."

"Sir, if I may ask ...," said Keth.

David nodded.

"Could you explain your relationship with your deputy Joab? So that I am fully aware of the line of command."

"Of course. Joab, as you probably heard from the men, is my nephew and reports to me. He and Abishai, his brother, ensure that my orders to the line units are carried out. You all," David gestured to the others in the group, "will be independent from him. All of you report directly to me, as Joab does."

David adjusted his pack. Benaiah loved him for carrying his pack like the others. No special treatment.

"Keth, you will eventually command the armorers, so your role will be slightly different because I don't want the armorers engaged in battle. It defeats the whole purpose of trying to get iron workers if all of you fall on the battlefield. But if your reputation is accurate, you will inspire the Hittite men who will not be able to win glory in the field," said David.

Keth did not answer. Benaiah wondered why he did not complain, having just been told that he would have to stay in the back with the gear when the fighting started. No honor could be won while defending baggage.

"Sir, what will we do if there is trouble in Ziklag?" asked Shammah.

"We do not yet know if there is trouble. If there is, I will choose a course of action when the time comes."

FOURTEEN

Later that evening, Benaiah stopped to check his sandals for rips, trying to hold his shaking hands steady. He had been wounded by the lion's claws worse than he was admitting to the others.

The city on the horizon was partially obscured by the heads of soldiers marching in front of him. His own head and shoulders were in such pain that he had sometimes wished, with all his heart, for death to take him. He'd even considered being dragged on a litter behind a donkey but had decided not give Josheb the pleasure of that joke. The whole army would have been laughing at him by evening.

Mighty Benaiah, killer of lions, hanging off the back of an ass.

Three days had passed since leaving Achish. They'd received no word yet of what was happening between the Philistines and the Israelites, but the further south they marched, the less the men cared about that battle and the more they worried about their homes in Ziklag. They inquired at each town they passed, but no one had heard of any raids.

The troops slept in the open each night, grateful to be without the burden of pitching tents. David had ordered them to move in fast-traveling formations, and he conversed with his officers on the trail to reduce the amount of time they would need to spend in camp.

At night, they slept in fighting positions dug into the ground with piled rocks bordering them, forming a tight perimeter, two men to a position. In enemy territory, one slept and the other lay awake, but as they were now in nonhostile lands, they were permitted to have only a fourth of their number awake at any time during the night. Each man carried his own provisions, so there was no need for a rationing staff.

Usually the perimeter of the camp was the ditch dug by the warriors who, to their everlasting ridicule, had slain the fewest men in the year's fighting. In this ditch, the men relieved themselves. When a new man would join the army, the others would pretend they were being attacked and order the newcomer back to take cover in the ditch, and the hapless fellow would dig himself in and wait while sitting in excrement. Benaiah had seen foreign armies dig the ditch in the middle of the camp where it was safer, but David still followed many of the old laws about cleanliness.

No pranks were played on this trek, and the jokes snapped with less venom. Men coughed, waited, and spoke about their favorite games. The weather had remained cool and sunny. Grasslands and forests slipped along the horizon as they passed, blocking their view of the Great Sea, but they still felt its presence. Benaiah wondered, as he often did, why men sailed it and what was on the other side.

Benaiah finally recognized the upcoming town as Gath. The city of giants, of the family of Anak, capital of the hated Sea People. David had instructed them to march directly through each city, in plain sight, to cut down on rumors. They may have been dismissed from the battlefield due to the mistrust of the other Philistine kings, but Achish had staunchly defended them. David wanted to keep the alliance intact. He wanted to remain in good favor with King Achish as long as possible, while he learned the forging of iron.

That led Benaiah's thoughts to Keth, walking next to him. Keth noticed his glance. "What?"

"What are your thoughts, foreign devil?"

Keth smiled. "Women and weapons."

Benaiah nodded. That was about all of it.

Benaiah pulled at the collar of his tunic as he marched. Men walked ahead of him in monotonous motion, mesmerizing him and forcing him to look away to ward off dreariness. If it had been hot—and if much of his body had not been throbbing in pain—he might have fallen asleep walking.

At the front of the column was David, speaking with Joab. Josheb and Eleazar were with them. Shammah lagged a little behind.

"What made Saul become David's enemy?" Keth asked.

"Saul was jealous of him, even after David won incredible victories for him. The giant you heard of was only the first. He and the Three led troops of men into battle after battle against overwhelming odds and never lost."

"I am anxious to see the Three in battle. I have heard much."

"You will never forget it."

"What makes them so effective?"

"They call it the *abir*—a fighting art developed many generations ago. It is a powerful style, and I have learned much from them about it. But Shammah will tell you that it is Yahweh and his power that leads them. Josheb and Eleazar are more practical, but they agree."

"Tell me more about Saul."

"Saul has a son named Jonathan, and Jonathan and David were closer than brothers. In fact, they *were* brothers, after David married Jonathan's sister Michal. She was given to David as a prize for killing the giant, but when Saul began to hunt David, she was given to another man. It wounded him, but he doesn't speak of it. Despite all that, David stayed loyal to Saul because he was Yahweh's chosen king for the people."

And that's why it's better to let David worry about Yahweh, Benaiah thought. He bit his lip before continuing. "He ran from Saul into the desert. That was when we started showing up to help him. We spent time raiding enemies of Judah while convincing Achish that we were *destroying* Judah. Someone told Saul the same thing. The foolish man believed it."

"You speak of your king that way?"

"He's a wicked and foolish man. It's the truth, so why would I say differently?" Benaiah knew the consequences would be steep if David heard him say it, but he no longer cared. "When the people in the town of Keilah in Judah were about to have their harvest stolen by lazy Philistines, David asked Yahweh if he should save them, and when Yahweh said yes, we attacked the Philistines.

"Even after that, after saving Israel's lands from the pagans, Saul hunted David. The king threatened harm to anyone assisting David, and many turned on him then. And still David fought for them. Now, we have Philistines attacking our lands in the north and Amalekites in the south. We cannot be everywhere at once to stop it."

"I still don't understand why David has not assassinated Saul," said Keth.

"He says that it would be revenge. That his time has not yet come. It doesn't make sense to me either."

"Where do the Israelites stand on David now?"

"Divided. We are folk heroes to some, enemies to others. We alone have stood between them and destruction at the hands of their king or raids from our enemies. But there will be a new king one day. David."

Benaiah stopped, thinking he'd said enough. More than enough. But Keth waited expectantly. "What else?" the Hittite prodded.

Benaiah thought about it. "He killed a bear and a lion when he was a boy with only a shepherd staff. He has perfect skill with every weapon ever forged, more so than even the Three. He still loves his sling and fights with it occasionally. The men think he is odd, and for good reason. He speaks aloud with no one around. He raises his arms to heaven at strange times. He dances, alone, when no one is watching. He fights with the sword of the champion Goliath that he killed in his youth, and it terrifies his enemies."

"Why doesn't he carry it now?"

Benaiah grinned. "Traveling with the Philistines? No, he left it behind at Ziklag. Carrying it in front of Goliath's people wouldn't help our cause among them."

"He took it from the field that day?"

"No, from the priest of Nob. Something else you should know is that David carries terrible guilt and goes into long periods of despair. For many reasons but especially about what happened at Nob. While David was running from Saul, Doeg the Edomite, chief shepherd of Saul's flocks, spotted David in Nob and reported back to Saul, who flew into a rage and believed the priests at Nob were sheltering David. But no Israelite would obey Saul's orders to kill an entire priestly household, so Doeg, foreign filth that he was, slaughtered the village. Innocent men, women, children. David speaks of it painfully."

"I am having a hard time understanding your people," Keth said.

Benaiah nodded. "It's my blood, and it makes no more sense to me."

Benaiah had told Keth much about the Israelites on the days of march. He had described the tribal system: how Joshua had divided the land among the twelve tribes from the sons of the patriarch Jacob centuries before, how Benjamin's small tribe had befriended the powerful tribe of Judah, and how Benjamin's tribe was chosen as the royal line because it was the least likely to cause controversy.

He had told him of the people's desire for a king to unite them. He had explained the Hebrew Law and why hardly any of the people followed it anymore.

"Yahweh gave the Law to Moses after our people left Egypt, but after the warlord Joshua died, the people turned away from Yahweh. They wanted to be left alone in the land and not have to worry about clearing out the Canaanites. So, for many years, Yahweh raised up heroes to save our people from invasion. But now, after demanding a king, we are under Saul. I suppose we deserve our fate."

Benaiah had thought about telling Keth his story. He felt like he was supposed to tell him, but when he tried, it would not come out. There was pain in his chest, and his throat closed, choking him.

They slept next to one another in the perimeter holes. Keth told him about his own lands and his own people and why he wanted to serve under David. He said a voice had told him to pack his things and join David's army.

"A voice?" asked a skeptical Benaiah.

"A voice," Keth had nodded, "a clear and strong voice. While I was up in the mountains. I can't say who it came from. Perhaps your Yahweh. I have not heard from my own gods in many years. But I listened to it."

Benaiah had not attempted to make sense of it. Each man came in his own way.

FIFTEEN

The three men set out from the encampment early in the morning before the sun rose, dressed as ragged peasants, carrying nothing but a dagger apiece. The leader had ordered no food or provisions, and the two who accompanied him, accustomed to his increasingly bizarre behavior, thought little of it.

They became more concerned when they realized that he was leading them around the edge of the massive Philistine army gathered on the slopes of Mount Hermon. As the men crept through the forest, the flicker of enemy campfires speckled the treetops overhead. The Philistines were close enough that the sounds of an army rousing in the early morning could be heard. Cooking ware and weapons clanked, and commanders shouted orders. The Philistines were preparing for the first watch of the morning, when most ambushes took place.

The leader was careful to lead them far enough away from the perimeter to avoid being spotted by the sentries. He was in a hurry. Despite the proximity of their enemies, they needed to pass through this forest to reach their destination in time, and they needed the cover of darkness.

After an hour of picking their way across the rocky forest floor, guided only by the leader's confident knowledge of the area, the three slipped over the shoulder of the Hermon range and, as the rays of sunlight began to appear in the sky, found themselves facing the desolate Endor region.

The forest gave way suddenly to a barren landscape that contained nothing but gray sand and rocky hills. Caves pocked almost every hillside. The large man pushed them hard, many times having them crawl on their bellies through ravines to avoid being spotted by roving patrols. The distance they covered was not great, but the need for stealth slowed them.

Once a Philistine foot patrol nearly stumbled over them, but the dust covering them from their crawls sufficiently camouflaged the men against the hillside, and the patrol passed unaware. They picked their way across the harsh environment until just after dark, when they came to a bank of limestone cliffs running north and south.

It was cold, and as they made their way toward the cliffs looming in the moonlight, the leader—a very tall man—kept wrapping his cloak around himself tighter to ward off the air. He approached a dip in the ground and leaped across a small stream without even pausing. The other two were forced to remove their thick woolen sandals and wade across, but their leader did not delay his pace for their sake. They grunted in frustration as he nearly disappeared from sight. After retying their footwear, they sprinted to catch up.

The trail took a slight turn at the base of the cliffs, and the group followed it, shoving branches and overhanging limbs out of the way as the thicket near the base crowded around them. After a while, the branches suddenly cleared, and they found themselves at the edge of a small open meadow. The cliff walls created a semicircle in front of them. The forest they had been walking through formed a border to their left, all the way to the edge of the rock wall. The ground sloped gently to the base of the cliff, where a black cleft in the rock broke the smooth face.

"What is this place, lord?"

The leader's thoughts were interrupted, and he glanced at his companion. "It was used by the pagans many years ago, before the time of Joshua."

He stepped forward into the clearing and made his way among the rocks scattered across the ground, eventually stopping near what they now saw was a small dwelling built into the cliff face. In a small corral nearby were several cattle. Chickens clucked softly and wandered around the house.

His two companions waited in silence, nervously eyeing the surrounding forest, almost expecting a winged demon to leap out at them from one of the caves. Through the window they could see flickers of orange from a fire inside.

The man waited a moment longer, then called out, "I seek counsel."

They heard nothing for a moment, then a slow scuffling inside the house. The man pulled the wool hood over his head a little tighter as someone appeared in the doorway.

"What business is this?" It was a female voice. The two companions were expecting a bedraggled old crone, but to their surprise a young and attractive woman stood before them. Her dark hair was heavily braided, and she wore sets of copper bands around her neck and arms. She stared at them.

"I need you to bring someone back for me. Conjure him up. I will give you the name."

The woman looked at the tall man in front of her and then at the men who accompanied him. It was awhile before she responded. "You know what Saul has done with the mediums and spiritists, cutting them off from the land. Why would you ask me that? I would be killed immediately if someone found out."

"As Yahweh lives, you will not be punished," the man replied.

She watched him carefully, occasionally glancing at his companions as well. It seemed to them she took a long time, but finally seemed to come to a decision. "Come inside, then," she said. She turned and disappeared back into the house.

The tall figure looked at his companions. "I will go alone. Find food if you need it." He ducked under the beam at the entrance of the house and went inside.

They were confused for a moment, then shrugged their shoulders and enjoyed the quiet. The night was perfect and crisp. All the sounds of the woods around them were amplified against the cliff face. One of them fidgeted his foot, then spoke. "Who is she?"

"Not sure. Strange that he would come here."

"Yes. Mediums. Thought they were all gone."

"No, too popular. The people hide them. It doesn't make any sense that he came here, though, when he was the one who banned them."

"Not for us to say. We are not the king."

"I wish we were. We would have perfect happiness and peace all the time. And women. Lots of good, plump women."

"Plump?"

He nodded. "Plump."

They stamped their feet and paced. One of them squatted halfway to the ground and held his arms out in front of him.

"What are you doing?" his partner asked.

"Keeping warm. It keeps your limbs working and the blood flowing. I learned this in David's army. Try it, Jehu."

"You were in David's army? You never said that."

"No, not if I was interested in keeping my head attached to my body. He's not very popular in some circles."

"Ever speak with him?"

"Of course," said the larger one. "He always came to check on us when we were out on the perimeter. Never missed a night. Impossible discipline."

"I heard he would do that."

"What else have you heard?"

The tall man kept the hood of his cloak pulled over his head so that the woman would not recognize him. She seemed not to care, going about her preparations quietly.

He gazed at the fire pit against the wall and followed the smoke up through the hole in the ceiling. The warmth of the fire against his face made him feel old. He was hungry, and that made him feel even older. Too old even to stand up and put one more foot in front of the other. The flames seemed to speak to him, to tell him that his days of walking were soon to end. He sighed.

The woman knelt next to the fire. He wasn't sure what he expected her to do, assuming it would be some sort of heathen ritual with bones and blood, but she only held her position by the fire with her eyes closed. He waited.

The fire flickered brighter a moment; he felt the hair on his arms raise. His eyes went dry. He blinked.

"Who do you want me to bring up?"

"The prophet Samuel."

She lowered her eyes and stared at the ground, swaying and muttering. This went on a few moments. He felt himself relaxing.

The woman shrieked and dropped to hands and knees, her face turned up at him. Her eyes were black as death, black as a starless night. "You are Saul!" she screamed. "Why have you deceived me?"

He sat forward. "Do not be afraid. Just tell me what you see."

She glared at him with her black eyes, then slammed her face against the floor. She stared into the depths of the earth. Her hands scraped at the dirt, her fingernails snapping with the pressure. "I see a spirit coming up out of the ground."

She had bitten through her lip; blood leaked onto the dirt by her face.

"What does he look like?"

Her eyes went wide with terror. She looked back up at him, blood streaming down her chin and neck. "An old man with a robe."

Then she stood and wandered out of the room into the night, as if dazed.

Saul was overcome. He laid down, face to the earth. He heard something shuffle, and then a log on the fire crackled. The ground became hot under his face, and he felt someone standing over him. It was the prophet. He could feel the power of his presence.

"Why do you disturb me and bring me up?" Samuel's rich, heavy tone resounded in the room, even more pure than it had been in life.

Saul could not raise his head to look at him; he was too afraid. His own voice was weak and frail: "I am in great distress. The Philistines are coming against me, and Yahweh has turned away from me. He no longer answers, either through prophets or through dreams. I have summoned you so that you can tell me what to do, as you did in the old days."

He heard the prophet sigh. "Why do you consult me now that you are the Lord's enemy? He has done what he predicted through me. The Lord has torn the kingdom from your hand and given it to another." Samuel's voice became louder. "He has given it to David."

Saul felt tears on his cheeks. He wanted to protest, but there was no point.

Samuel continued. "Because you did not obey the Lord or carry out his judgment against the Amalekites, the Lord has done this to you today."

Into Saul's mind flashed the image of the Amalekite king, Agag, kneeling before him, at his mercy, the orders from the prophet clear: spare no one. But Saul had wanted so much—he wanted the prize, wanted the Amalekites as slaves. Surely Yahweh would understand. But all that followed had been darkness. Saul began to weep.

Samuel's voice became even louder. "The Lord has handed both you and Israel over to the Philistines. This time tomorrow, you and your sons will be with me. The army of Israel will be given to the Philistines."

There was a breeze, a footstep, and the fire flickered again. And Saul knew he was alone.

The two men outside and the woman came into the hut not long afterward. They found their king lying on his face, weeping. They lifted him up to a sitting position and tried to get him to drink while the woman set about relighting the fire.

"Yahweh has become my enemy," Saul muttered to his men.

They looked at each other, then continued steadying him. He rocked back and forth, tears trickling down his beard.

The medium had reignited her fire and now walked over to where Saul sat, still quaking, his teeth chattering. Nervous, clearly desperate for them to leave, she spoke quietly. "Your servant has obeyed you and summoned the prophet. Now honor me and eat some bread before you go."

He shook his head. "I will not eat."

"Lord, you need nourishment for our journey back. Please consider eating," one of his companions said.

Saul's entire countenance had changed. He no longer carried himself with authority; he now looked like a deserted and lonely old man. The gray in his beard had seemed to increase. "I will eat something," he conceded dejectedly. "Perhaps some bread and meat."

She set about preparing a meal while the two men helped their king to a bed in the corner. Saul collapsed onto the bed and lay still. The woman slaughtered a calf outside and began preparing a platter of meat and bread, unleavened in her haste. When the meal was ready, the men ate, helping their master with his own meal. He went through the motions and said nothing.

The hour was late. When the men had finished, they helped Saul stand and wrap himself in his traveling cloak. The food had revived him somewhat. One of Saul's companions gave the woman a shekel of silver for her trouble. They stepped with their master into the night.

The medium watched them leave the meadow and disappear into the forest, then returned inside.

The fire was roaring with the fresh wood that had been laid on it. She settled onto a stool next to the flames and stared at the fire. The events of the evening had shaken her. Before, when she'd consulted the *ob*, the spirit who consulted the dead, she had been in complete control. Her customers were always impressed.

Tonight, when the figure had appeared, it had been something outside of her power. She'd felt terror in its presence, not control. Something deep had been awakened.

Her mind wandered back to the tall king. He'd looked even more frightened than she had been when the old man suddenly appeared from the bowels of the earth. He had not told her what the prophet had said to him; perhaps it was something so awful that he could not speak it. This was something far beyond her understanding, and as she felt the shadows of the deepening night begin to creep through her window, she threw another log on the fire and began her preparations for bed.

Her sleep that night was fitful, full of images of an old man angrily emerging from the land of the dead with blazing eyes and a draped mantle.

SIXTEEN

"We will camp on the other side," David said as they approached the gates of Gath. "It would be better to go around, but we need them to see us and tell Achish that we did not defect to Saul."

Benaiah and the Three nodded, though Shammah looked concerned. "There is a festival to Ashtoreth, the Philistine goddess of fertility, being celebrated tonight," he said. "It might be dangerous for the men. It is unclean for warriors to touch women in time of war, and—"

David waved him off. The fiery evening sun hung suspended between the clouds and the earth. "We will move quickly through the city."

They entered a very different world as soon as they passed the city gates. Thousands of people thronged around them, pouring wine over them, showering them with goods and services to purchase and taste and delight in. The festival had brought many from the plains of Philistia, all coming for the carnal delights offered. Merchants tried to pull them to their tables and barter for captured treasures. David had given the men strict orders not to speak with anyone, and David walked at the front of the army, leading the columns forward through the crowd.

Music from every instrument echoed through the torch-lit streets as nightfall enclosed them at last. There were instruments that resembled the Hebrews' pipes bored out of wood and bone like a *halil*, bronze trumpets and a stringed instrument that resembled a harp, which Benaiah knew his own people called a *kinnor*. There were other instruments he did not recognize made of bone and wood that produced a sound Benaiah considered too chaotic to be actual music. The air seemed filthy and burdened with the noise, as though one could not catch a clean breath of cool air in the city.

There were statues of Dagon, the chief Philistine god, half man and half fish, leering through the shadows at those worshiping him. The stone idols were carved with such tremendous detail that Benaiah was half afraid they would awaken and chase his men through the streets, driving out those who worshiped the God who claimed to rule over the desert, the mountains, and the sea. There were statues of Ashtoreth carried everywhere, along with idols of Baalzebub. Women stripped off their clothing and clung to the idols, as though willing the statues to lie with them and conceive. There were screams of ecstasy, many people engaging in sexual acts of worship dedicated to the idols in the middle of the narrow streets, and the army had to march around them.

Benaiah shoved and elbowed his way through with Keth beside him. Prostitutes clung to his chest and begged for money. Some covered his head with their garments, but he pushed them aside and shouted to the men around him to keep the ranks tight and their satchels close. Even so, he saw the eyes of the men darting to each female body they passed. And hundreds of women swarmed them, some not even prostitutes but women of the city worshiping their gods and drunk with wine.

David let Joab take the lead in the march and walked back down the ranks, calling out to his men, clapping them on the shoulders, reminding them that they would be home soon and needed to keep marching, needed to make it to the other side of Gath. There would be enough prizes to take later; there was no time for distraction now. One soldier ducked away from the ranks and followed a prostitute, but David ran after him, yelled into his face, and pointed at the column, and the man returned to the march.

Benaiah did his best to help. There were too many. It was too dark. Music, strange music, pounded his ears. He tried to ignore it. He saw Keth, his own face tense, pushing away the flocks of women and merchants who pressed them and would not give up. A woman clung to his neck; he shoved her. Another grabbed at his waist, and he shoved her as well. He shouted orders to the commanders nearby to keep their men close.

Josheb, Shammah, and Eleazar moved among the ranks and protected the men as David was. But it was too dark, too hard to see what was happening. The men would fall. *We should have waited until morning. What was David thinking?* That cursed music kept playing, louder now, joined by more lyres, instruments of hollowed bone, and drums made out of skin. His eyes clouded, and he pushed away another prostitute. There were so many of them, dressed in red and purple. Spices and perfumes filled his senses, and he desperately tried to escape ... but Sherizah was not there, only darkness and red and purple.

Despite all this, they passed through most of Gath, through the music and colors, with David calling out to them in his loudest voice to follow him, just keep their eyes forward, and they would make it. He pleaded with them. To his surprise, Benaiah found himself believing they were going to come through this and emerge on the other side.

But then they passed a large and ornate house, with many

impossibly beautiful women beckoning from its windows. It was too much. Many of the men finally broke ranks and ran inside it, able to resist no longer. Even Keth looked longingly at the house. It was covered in cloths of purple and red, and now many of the women issued from the house's doorway, offering themselves to the outlaw army for their price.

Benaiah shook his head violently, trying to clear it. The doorway of the house was dark and opened into more darkness. Benaiah could see torches inside, casting an orange and red glow across the walls and into the street. Music and pleasant fragrances poured from it, and he slapped his own face in despair.

David shouted, but most of the men seemed to no longer hear him. Soldiers continued to break ranks and run into the house. Josheb, Eleazar, and Shammah tried to pull their troops back.

Keth, Benaiah saw, was gazing intently at the house. He was muttering something. Benaiah strained to hear it over the noise. What was he saying? Keth repeated it again and again, louder, and finally Benaiah heard it.

Just when the army seemed to be disintegrating and the officers could control it no longer, the noises and smells and clamoring music went dim, and Benaiah, startled, found himself lost in a sudden, strange haze. He did not know where it had come from, only that the glow of the torches went blurry, the music faded, and a woman was standing in the street directly in front of them.

She was beautiful, beautiful far beyond what he thought a woman could be. Her dark hair and body were wrapped in deep green linen, and her eyes were as green as the stones found deep in the mountain caves. Standing before the army, in the middle of the throng and yet somehow separated from it, she held out her hands to them.

Oddly, Benaiah felt no lust for her, no carnal desire at all—he simply yearned to follow her. He felt cooler, as if a breath of desert wind had found its way into the street and refreshed his soul. He stood still, spellbound by the mysterious woman.

The men who had not fled into the house stared at her as well. All of the noises continued, all of the revelry and worship to pagan gods went on, but it was as though it had fallen into another world, and the remnants of David's army holding fast against the scarlet and purple house were standing in an oasis of goodness, clear and cool to the mind.

The woman's hands were outstretched. She beckoned them. Benaiah stepped forward again, suddenly desperate to follow her at all costs. All of the men seemed spellbound, watching her, the lady wrapped in the brightest green, and all of them knew, instinctively, that they should follow her. This woman was different from the revelers in the street; her beauty pure, her skin delicate, her attention desired.

Follow me, and I will pour out my heart to you, and let my thoughts be made known to you.

Benaiah knew that she had not spoken aloud, but he also knew that all of the men in the narrow street, straining against the pull of the crowd, had heard the same words he had. Tears glistened below the woman's eyes of green fire. And she appeared to be staring directly at David, reaching for him, begging him to hear her.

He did. He was transfixed. But he was also glancing back at the scarlet house, still near them in the night. David looked from one to the other, grimacing. Benaiah was about to run toward him to seize his tunic and prevent him from crumbling as well.

Then David yelled his war cry and pushed them forward. Benaiah shouted as well, as did the Three, and Keth. They moved their men together, clapping them on the necks and crying out to them to follow the woman. She melted backward through the crowd. Agony filled Benaiah's heart as she moved away, but she was not leaving them, only beckoning them to follow. They would have to fight, they would have to push hard through the dark of the night, but they would follow her, and she would not leave them.

Above and beyond her, amid the hazy glow that had come over them, Benaiah saw another figure. It was a man, a warrior, judging by the great sword gripped firmly in his shadowy arm. He looked immense, but Benaiah could not tell if he was truly large or just looked that way in the darkness. The woman was trailing behind the warrior, facing Benaiah and his men, and the warrior was moving through the crowd ahead of her, clearing a route through the awful noise and heathen worship.

And David's army followed them.

It was not long before they exited the city through the gate on the far side. Cold wind struck them hard in the face, and Benaiah sucked it into his lungs. It cleared his mind like a swim in the icy waters of the spring melt. He forced his feet forward, exhausted from the long day of the march and weak from his unhealed wounds. But the cold felt so good, so much purer than the heat of the city he had just left. Other men shuddered and pulled cloaks back on to ward off the night air, but Benaiah let it cover him in its cold embrace.

Light from the moon covered the landscape all around him. He opened his eyes again to search for the woman and the warrior who led her, but they were gone.

Men began to stream back to the camp hours later, the ones who had followed the prostitutes in the city. Their commanders lashed out at them. They would be punished in the morning. Most staggered drunkenly, some tripping and falling into the waste ditch, to snickers of laughter from others.

He and Keth watched their line, unable to sleep. Each had

offered the other the chance to rest and the other had refused. Now they waited. A figure approached from the position next to them. It was David, who knelt down and placed his hands on their backs.

"Why are you both out here? Commanders and officers usually stay in the center."

"We like being among the men," Benaiah replied.

David nodded. Noises of animals and insects from the night sang among the rocks and trees near the edge of the encampment. David listened to it with them, hearing the beauty as they did. Sound carried much better in cold night air. The three men sat in silence for a long time, not one of them wanting to ruin it with further speaking. No stresses and worries and fears; just the gentle sounds of the night.

"Who do you suppose it was?" Benaiah asked softly.

David looked up and down the lines of his men several times before responding. "I suppose it was from Yahweh, though I have never seen the covering in that form." He gazed thoughtfully across the plains, toward the distant tree line. The hills to their west gave off a gentle white glow from the bright stars.

"We might have walked through during the day," Benaiah said.

"It is sin to lie with a woman during war. I was testing them." David sighed. "My arrogance nearly cost us everything. I was not listening to the covering."

A thought occurred to Benaiah. "Can you to explain the covering to Keth? I tried, but ..."

David was quiet for a bit. His hand dropped to his side, where his sling hung from his belt. He fingered it before replying.

"The day I used this against the giant, I knew clearly what to do. Their champion was blaspheming Yahweh, and Yahweh wanted it to end. That was Yahweh's victory, not mine. When he speaks to me before battle, fire comes over me. A heat and a fire that pushes me forward and that I cannot control."

David paused a moment. Laughter and taunts rolled up from the camp. "In times of battle, he sends me the war covering. But the covering also comes when I am composing songs. A soft flame touches my throat and warms my soul. I call it the counsel covering. It gives me the music of the heavens. It tells me how to act, and what decisions to make that please the Lord. I wish I could explain it better. I often long for another person to speak about it with.

"But there is more to it than that. When I am acting selfishly or out of vengeance, or I am running from him, the fire leaves me. I can still perform my duties just as any other man, but there is no fire in it. I become the same as a man who does not know the covering, and it is the loneliest feeling you can imagine. I miss that touch more than anything when it is gone. It fades away and my soul is empty without it."

Benaiah had asked the question for his own benefit as much as Keth's. He let the silence return. He did not wish to annoy David, but he had so many questions. Heat. Fire. He had felt it briefly battling the Amalekites outside of the village, when the stranger had left him the spear. Was that the covering?

Benaiah thought about the man in the forest that night. It seemed a lifetime ago. Had he been a messenger? A helper?

Benaiah shook his head. He was so very tired, unable to make sense of love and hate and covering. The faces of the girls tore out at him from the darkness. He tried to shut them out, but they were screaming.

David stood and walked away along the perimeter, continuing his inspection of each fighting position before returning to the center. Benaiah watched him go, marveling again at how he never seemed to sleep.

He lay back. The stars were out vividly. The warrior of the stars was visible now, his mighty bow drawn. Across the galaxy, the lion roared his challenge, and the warrior met it, for all time, placed there by Yahweh for men like him to see.

The foreigner beside him was still, watching the deserted grasslands around them, eyes flicking to the hills occasionally. He had spoken, near the house draped in red, the den of lust, just before the emerald woman had appeared, and Benaiah had heard him.

He had spoken a prayer: *Cover me in the day of war.*

Part Three

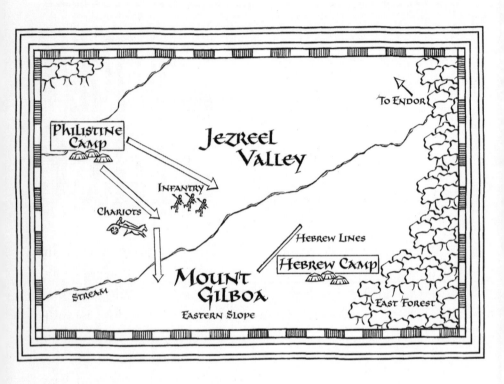

SEVENTEEN

The shield came in lower than his staff, thumping loudly as Eliam failed to avoid it. It knocked him sideways, and before he could recover, Gareb had swung at him again, and he had to duck so quickly he lost his balance. He collapsed in a cloud of dust. Humiliated, he was grateful that they were doing this outside the camp, where no one would see.

"Your reflexes are good. Too slow, but still good. You have potential."

After Gareb had completed the army's final preparations, he had informed Eliam that he needed something to distract him from the thoughts in his head, so he ordered the young man to appear in a small grove of trees outside the perimeter with nothing but a staff and a simple wooden training shield, and wearing only a loincloth.

Eliam had climbed along the ridge of the Gilboa highlands and slipped into the cool trees after the midday meal, apprehensive that he was about to become the brunt of a prank, but when he arrived, he saw Gareb sitting sullenly on a log.

They began when Gareb roused himself from his stupor and ordered Eliam to start leaping into the air, holding the shield and staff over his head. When Eliam began to sweat from the exertion, wondering what the point of it was, Gareb attacked him without warning, shoving him to the ground and giving him a hard strike with his own staff.

"Good work, now attack me," he said, and Eliam, temper rising, lashed out clumsily toward Gareb, who easily parried the thrust and tripped him up, sending the young man crashing to the ground once more.

"I am not making sport of you, if that is what you are thinking. I just want to know how skilled you are so that I don't waste time training you at a level you are beyond. Attack me again."

Eliam reigned in his emotions and tried to perform dispassionately, with measured effort. When he fell again, Gareb nodded his approval and grunted that it would be necessary to start him further along.

Eliam was not prepared for compliments—he was convinced that he was performing worse than a servant girl would have. "Sir, I thought trainers of war were angrier," he ventured to say, as they paused to drink from their water satchels and rest in the shade of the trees.

"Bad ones are. There is a time and place for striking terror into the hearts of your troops, the soldier who left his sword out yesterday being a good example, but usually you see better results when you inspire men. Beckon them beyond what they think they can do—don't just yell at them."

"Did Jonathan teach you that?" Eliam asked, a little bolder this time, believing Gareb was warming to him.

"No. David."

"You knew him? I thought you hated him."

"I told you he was Jonathan's friend, so of course I knew him. And yes, I hate him. I wish it was only Jonathan who could be credited for much of what I know about leading men, but David ..." He paused, took a drink, and wiped his brow. "David was a genius at leading men. A true genius. I have seen battle all of my life, and I have never seen anyone inspire troops on a field like he could, even when he was just your age. He was always the first to attack, the last to eat. He only slept when his men slept and only wore what they wore. He usually refuses to ride a horse even to this day. Says that since the men don't ride them, neither will he. Those who followed him loved him so much that they would have probably slit their own throats if he asked it of them. Of course, now he runs an army of mercenaries and bandits—not so easy to lead." Gareb smiled slightly. "It was probably the woman who started all of it. It always is."

"A woman? What woman?" asked Eliam.

"David was given Jonathan's sister Michal as a wife after he won the battle against Goliath in the Elah Valley. They loved each other deeply. She helped him escape when Saul tried to kill him, but then betrayed him to her father afterward. I never heard why. Who knows? Women are foolish.

"But they say he never stopped loving her, even when Saul gave her to another man as his wife. I hardly saw him after that, but he wasn't the same. Angrier, maybe. And who can blame him? Stay away from women, Eliam. Don't even think about marrying one. You'll deserve whatever you get."

Eliam wished there were unbiased accounts of David. People seemed to either hate him or love him. How Jonathan could adore him while his armor bearer hated him was hard to understand. Everyone agreed he had been the mightiest of heroes, but his intentions were so unclear now. How could he march with the Philistines against Israel?

"That's enough training for today. We will likely be slaughtered by the Philistines tomorrow, so there's no sense wearing ourselves out and making it easier for them. If you make it out, and somehow Jonathan does, you will fit him well. I meant what I said about your abilities. You have potential."

"Could you explain tactics and troop movements? They told me that I will be bearing water tomorrow, but I have no idea how to see the field," Eliam said.

Gareb rubbed his thigh as if massaging out a muscle knot. "In the old days, it was more complex. There would be more involvement from the priests, more rituals of worship for Yahweh. Sacrifices, that sort of thing. But just like in the villages, no one really follows that anymore. Who knows, maybe that's why we are having such trouble now.

"Philistia is made up of people who live on the plains near the Great Sea, along the Way of the Sea, the trade route to Egypt. Their armies are accustomed to fighting in open fields with chariots and horsemen. Do you know what infantry is?"

Eliam nodded.

"Their infantry is set up in regiments like ours," Gareb continued. "Groups of five thousand are led by a general, who delegates commanders to lead companies of two hundred. Each company contains troops of twenty to thirty warriors, with section leaders in charge of ten men each.

"The infantry is divided between heavy and light. Heavy infantry carries large armor and weapons; light infantry uses short swords and small shields. In our army, the light infantry is usually split up according to tribal specialty. Judah trains with the spear, Gad the heavy staff, Benjamin the bow, and on and on. Bows are either the first wave of an attack or cover the rear of the retreat.

"There are really only three types of battle—a raid, an ambush, and an assault. Raids and ambushes are pretty simple, but the assault is the battle in the open field, or a siege of a fortress. That's a lot trickier to understand.

"Every general on a field of assault has one objective: to get around the enemy's flank. Sometimes they try to accomplish that through a direct, frontal thrust, but usually it's a matter of maneuvering. It depends on who is commanding, but the goal is the same: penetrate the lines and capture the center. An army that is split apart can't coordinate its attacks, so the opposing army simply has to isolate the remaining troops and destroy them.

"If the battle is being fought in mountainous terrain, the advantage rests heavily on the side holding the high ground, since troops attacking uphill are easier targets and will tire quickly. On the plain, whoever is superior with chariots will almost always win. But we tend to leap through the mountains like goats instead of risking it in the open plain against chariots.

"A siege," Gareb continued, "is when you have a fortress or an outcropping of rock being held by a force. There are a few fortresses in our lands, like the Jebusite one in the mountains, but the Canaanites on the plains have most of them. Philistia builds them next to the trade routes on the coastal plains in order to charge merchants passing through heavy taxes. So if we were ever to control that land," he gestured to the valley where the Way of the Sea trade route crossed, "we would become wealthy beyond measure. That's part of the reason we're about to fight them. They want control of the trade road, we don't want them to get it.

"But enough about sieges. Tomorrow will be a field assault, and since we arrived first, we hold the high ground. If we weren't outnumbered and outmatched in every way, we might win." Gareb chuckled at his own morbid joke.

"The Philistines are masters of iron. It's a new metal that is harder than bronze and easily penetrates our armor, and that's one of the reasons they control our lands. They've dominated us since the days of Joshua. Our one chance to survive the next few days is to prevent them from using their chariots and war horses. We do that by staying on these mountains and not being baited out into the valley. The king needs to see that, though."

"You don't mention him much," Eliam said.

"Who?"

"The king."

"You already know about him, you live in his quarters."

"But I don't know what to believe about him anymore. The past few days have confused me."

Gareb, who had been discussing military tactics with great intensity, became quiet. Eliam watched him stare hard at the forest for a moment, as though trying to hear someone calling for him through the woods. His face was heavily scarred from disease and battle, giving him the appearance of an old man. The scars and damaged flesh must be from protecting his master, Eliam thought. He wondered if he himself would have the courage, when it came to it, to sacrifice his own flesh for his master, especially if his master was King Saul.

"Saul never wanted to be king," Gareb said at last. "Even hid from the people when they called him out to rule. For a while he got by on his size and his courage, which he used to have plenty of, and they say Yahweh was with him. Perhaps. I know he started out better than he's finishing, and if Yahweh was ever with him, he's not with him now. Besides, his son is a better man than Saul ever was."

"Then why does Jonathan stay with him? I know you said he is loyal, but why?"

"I suppose that is how fathers and sons are. A father can do much evil to his son, and his son still searches for his approval. One of the mysteries of men."

Eliam let his head rest against the staff and thought of his own father. He was a good man, a loving man, good to his servants and his children. They had many sheep and even cattle. He was wealthy enough to buy his son's way into the royal court, and although Eliam had not dwelt on it previously, he wondered if he would ever be accepted as a man apart from his father. It was odd indeed, how fathers and sons were. Jonathan's father had become a miserable wretch, and still Jonathan sought his approval, even to the point of certain death. Eliam wondered what he would have done in the prince's place.

Through the dense forest, he could see the plains of Esdraelon stretching below them to the far blue horizon, notched with occasional grain fields. He had heard that this was good, fertile land, abundant with life, the gateway to the northern part of the kingdom. The Philistine army was somewhere far below them at the base of the mountains, and though their numbers were great, the beauty and vastness of the mountains and the plains stretching to the distance made them seem insignificant.

Eliam did not blame the Philistines for wanting to take this paradise from them. He was young, but he shared the love all Israelite men felt for their land. Even those who did not follow Yahweh's covenant believed that this land was meant for them.

Eliam had heard the stories of his people as a boy—of the great feats of Abraham and Joshua, and how Yahweh brought them his fire if they would only love and honor him. He hated the thought of bloodshed on these emerald slopes, and he wished more men in their lands would heed the law of their fathers so that peace would come again.

"Tell me of battle," Eliam said quietly.

Gareb sighed. He let his head drop a little. "Every man wants to be there. No one wants to stay there. You'll ask yourself things. Can

I stick my blade into a man's guts and feel the blood on my arm? Will I wet myself in fright?

"I have never been in a battle I did not vomit my guts out after. My mouth gets so dry it feels like I swallowed the desert. My whole body gets tight. You can't bring yourself to drive that blade forward one more time and kill one more man. When you impale a man on a lance, he wets himself. Every time. Every man I ever stabbed wet himself, right in front of me.

"I was in battles before you were pulled off your mother's breast, and it never changes. You only think three things afterward: get the men moving, recover lost equipment, then go find a rock to vomit over. And clean off the urine from your enemies. It stinks after a while."

"Men don't follow speeches, Eliam. David gave terrific speeches, but his men followed him because they loved him. Speeches don't make you stab a man in the guts or slice through his neck while his blood sprays over you. If you ever lead troops, remember that. Be there with them. Suffer with them. Bleed with them. *Then* they will follow you."

Gareb went silent. Eliam did not prod him anymore. As they sat together, each man enjoyed the gentle, dry breeze as it glided up the slope, filtered by the scent of the forest. The bright sunlight warmed the rocks around them. Eliam wondered if he had what it took to slide a blade into a man.

The sound was imperceptible at first, neither man realizing it was beginning until its steadiness made them vaguely aware that it was not a natural noise. Eliam held his breath and strained his ears against the wind passing through leaves. It was a thumping sound, like the distant striking of a drum. A few moments passed, and Eliam became convinced it was, in fact, a drum.

He looked at Gareb, whose eyes were closed, and Eliam was

about to check to see if he was sleeping when the man suddenly sat forward, finally hearing it. He stared at the dark forest below them, then leaped to his feet.

"They are attacking."

EIGHTEEN

As he watched them come, Jonathan deduced what must have happened.

The remainder of the Philistine army had crossed the pass near Megiddo the day after leaving Aphek and set up camp near the small town of Shunem. The men had engorged themselves on whatever was found there, livestock or women, while their commanders plotted the assault. While the bulk of the force had remained in sight, that night a regiment had snuck across the valley and waited at the base of the northern slope of Mount Gilboa. It was this regiment that was attacking first.

Jonathan could see the bulk of the Philistine army only now making its way across the plains to provide the second wave of the attack. They looked like a wave of hot metal from the horizon all the way across the plain and around the base of Gilboa. Jonathan watched it, feeling its presence, feeling the awesome power and majesty of such a force, and closed his eyes, wondering if Gareb knew they were coming.

He turned and looked at his men. They were frantically preparing weapons, those who had them, while archers were testing the bow lines and foot soldiers were tying fresh leather straps around the grips of spears and swords. They were stretched in a line along the middle of the mountain, their backs to a deep forest bordering the barren slope they were stationed on. They had the high ground and would be able to hold it for a while. If the Philistines overcame their lines, they could fall back over the ridge and disappear into the forest.

Good men, all of them, Jonathan thought. They did what they were ordered. Those who remained, anyway. Others had left, and he guessed they were probably with David by now.

He shook his head, then walked down the row of his men, letting them see him, letting them feel his presence; they would draw strength and courage from it. The tide of metal in the valley grew, but he felt calm.

Jonathan moved along the line to the north, toward the dark forest, noting that the sun was quickly approaching the last part of its journey. It was remarkable how fast the Philistines had broken camp and assembled their attack march. The advance regiment was already on the Gilboa slopes, the rest only a few hours behind.

They must be confident, and why would they not be? He looked across the waves of so many men. He would have been just as confident.

It was different now. Before, when he knew he was protected by the covering, numbers had not mattered. They had not mattered when he climbed the cliffs at Michmash, and they had not mattered in the years since then, when Israel walked with a proud swagger in the confidence of Yahweh's blessing.

But they mattered now. Deep in his soul, they mattered, and he did not want them to. He walked to the forest, trying to ignore them.

On the farthest edge of his line, he saw a young man, a boy, he realized, with no beard on his face. He was hastily fashioning the tip of a root into a point with a skinning knife.

"Find something metal."

The boy blushed and looked down. Jonathan clapped him on the back and continued walking. He'd come to the end of his line of men now, and he glanced back. There were a paltry few hundred of them. He sighed as he thought about how many hardened Philistine soldiers awaited them below, then turned back and moved into the tree line.

It was immediately cooler, and he shivered. The undergrowth was thick, forcing him to leap over shrubs and tangled branches to get further in. After fighting through it a moment longer he reached a clearing, full of boulders, and sat down on one, still in the shade.

It was very calm. He listened to birds over his head and felt the chill of shadows across his neck and body. There were several pebbles in his sandals, and he took them off, emptied them, then let his feet air out for a while. It was wonderfully quiet. Few sounds of the army made it through the wall of trees. He would not have even known a battle loomed. Jonathan liked the quiet.

David was probably going back to his fortress at Ziklag. Spies had not seen him with the Philistine army in days. *He must have been ordered away, but why? Why would they send him off? To attack our rear? Surely he would not do it. Not his own people.* Jonathan left that thought buried.

It had been years since they'd fought side by side. They had not spoken in a long time, nor had any other contact. He nodded. It was better that way. David might have gone to the other side, and if he had, Jonathan would not have blamed him. Not after the way he had been treated.

Birds chirped wildly over his head in the canopy somewhere.

He leaned back, found a tree trunk, and gratefully rested against it, enjoying its strength.

And then he felt the drums. They pounded through the forest, animal skins being struck with clubs. The war drums of the Philistines. The battle would begin within the hour. He had to get back. No time for rest.

Roots for spears.

But the dark calm of the forest held Jonathan, and he gave in to it. His eyes remained closed, and he thought of wooden spears and running and sparring and laughter. There was always laughter in the camp when David was there. There was no laughter now. It was all out in the desert with David and Josheb and the others. Along with the pleasant camaraderie around the campfires. That had departed as well.

The incessant pounding of the drums had lulled him. He sat up and blinked, then shook his head to wake up. He desperately wanted to sleep, but not now. Sleep would come soon. The memories came as they always did before battle ...

... lying around a campfire. David is there. It is a brilliant night of wondrous stars, deep and black and cold. I take the pieces of the lamb and set them down. David looks at me, confused, and I dip my hand into the warm depths of the animal and pull out flesh and blood and press it against his face. Then I take his wrist and clench it, feeling the hot blood stream through our fingers. From this day on, my brother, I will fight your enemies as if they are my own. A covenant of blood between us, to pass down through our sons and their sons ...

But the days grow darker. David becomes too vicious, too coarse, too many women, too many vices. Yahweh, protect him from himself. He is your anointed. He does not know the depths of your covering yet. Be patient with him, God of my people, be patient with him. He will seek you ...

The years pass and we must part. My soul has been cleaved. It is a clear night in the desert. Perhaps he will be able to make it to Samuel, who can help him. He will not tell me where he goes, because he knows I would help him, knows I would follow him. I would follow him anywhere. He looks at me; he knows how this hurts. But this is as it should be. We have no more wars together. Go, brother. Yahweh will be between us forever, in your line and in my line. Remember our covenant. Spare my children when you reign one day. He is weeping; he is still so young, and there is great anguish in his chest. He runs. My heart has left me, my brother ...

Jonathan felt the burning in his own chest, strong now. He could stifle it in front of the men, but not in the quiet of the forest with the sound of the war drums. There were no tears at first, just a gasping for air at the pain of loss and sorrow and at the memories.

He gagged on his own coughs as if about to wretch. But there was nothing in his stomach; he had not eaten in a day because he had given all of his food to his men. He waited until the heaving in his gut calmed.

It would not be hard. Just run, right now. No Philistines, no roots for spears, just run and go. Join him. Restore the land. He desperately wanted to go. He could make it in a few days. He would disguise himself, go into Ziklag, and find David's men. He would tell them he was a criminal looking for help. When David came out, they would embrace, and all would be right.

They would plan the rescue of the kingdom together. They would drive out the uncircumcised pagans together, capture Philistine cities and raid the Amalekite barbarians, and crush the enemies of Yahweh. They would establish peace in the land.

The tribes would unify immediately if they knew the two of them were waging war on their behalf. Judah and Benjamin, together at last. Philistia would become a vassal in a fortnight. And there would be laughter again. He would get to sit around the campfire like the old army days and listen to Josheb's jokes as he teased Shammah. Eleazar would pace, and David would sing one of his new songs on the lyre when all went quiet for the night, and they would be able to feel Yahweh's very presence among them because of it.

Then he sighed. He would not leave his father, could not leave his brothers. His troops. It was his destiny to be here, with these men.

When Jonathan reached the edge of the forest, there was the boy with the root spear at the end of the flank, packing his stores and hiding them under rocks as the men were trained to do so that the enemy could not steal them. A section leader was giving orders, and the men were listening. The boy was terrified but trying to disguise it. He clutched the handmade spear to his chest.

Jonathan knelt, feeling the coolness stinging his sweat. He needed to listen to Yahweh. Yahweh had spoken to him before and might do it again. Perhaps he would be with them. It was only Gareb and I against many, he thought, and he was there then.

Jonathan prayed, eyes locked on the line of men, on the boy with the root trying to look brave to the older warriors. Jonathan had not felt Yahweh's covering in a long time. It had been many months since that warmth and strength were there. He had allowed himself to slip into the gloom of his father.

Just as he and David used to ask for it together, he asked for it now, when his heart was empty.

Gareb had heard nothing from Jonathan.

Watching from the farthest western flank of the Hebrew lines, he cursed and spat. The command area was empty, and the king was nowhere to be found. Most of the top generals were actually *hiding* themselves behind their men. Only Abner, the senior general of the army, seemed anxious to begin the fight. Gareb watched the valley fill with more Philistine foot soldiers.

Saul's army was full of hardened veterans who had engaged many times, up close and where it mattered, but their ranks were thin, even more so now than several days before when he had walked the encampment with the servant Eliam. Many had deserted, going back to their farms and herds while they still could.

He glanced at the water rack. Eliam was staring wide-eyed at the mass of armed and trained soldiers gathering below them. Future armor bearer to Jonathan. He laughed at the thought. Well, it would not be necessary anyway. They would all be dead by evening, loyal to the last. The disloyal ones had fled and would live, and the loyal ones would die this day. Wonderful.

Deciding to make himself useful, he started counting battle standards. The Philistines were arrogant and proud and clearly informed any opposing army exactly how many of them there were. Each group of marching soldiers in the valley was divided into companies, with each standard suspended over the head of the commander.

He lost track after five thousand men. Their own pitiful force would be outnumbered ten to one. Never had it been a problem before, but here they were, out in the open, about to fight using the very form of warfare that had led to their destruction in ages past. No conferring with the priests, no briefings from commanders. It was unlike Jonathan to leave the men stranded and without knowledge of their strategy.

There were a few bright spots. The Philistines had taken the bait and were attacking uphill. The arrogance of their generals would not let them bypass the Israelite army and fight defensively. Of course, a massive assault to the front like this one would probably end in Philistine victory as well, Gareb thought. Either way, the nation would change after today if they lost. No more united tribal loyalty. No more monarchy. Even if he escaped, Saul would be able to rally few supporters.

Finally, after hours of movements and pounding war drums, the vast array of Philistine companies and regiments ceased their movements, resembling a monstrous serpent lining the valley back toward Shunem. He could not see any of their giants or champions, which meant that they did not intend to leave this contest up to the gods. That had gone badly for them the last time. He chuckled. It would be nice to have David with them today.

The chariot companies sat in the rear. What for? To chase them in the valley if they fled that direction?

There was brief shouting down the lines, and Saul emerged from behind a group of men. Much taller than anyone else, he easily stood out against the rocky slopes. Even now some of the men still believed in him. Men of the tribe of Benjamin, most likely.

Gareb watched Saul make his great strides to the front of the line and then turn toward the troops. He waited. This was the point where the king gave speeches to rally them, but Gareb did not hear any words. The king only stood silently, back turned to the enemy, his armor bearer next to him.

Gareb looked back at the Philistine lines, about a hundred reeds away, and saw archers making their way forward. They shouted and waved their standards, taunting the Israelites. He could hear them all the way up the side of the mountain. The sound easily carried across the boulders and rocks. The Israelites answered.

The sun glinted on the shields and swords of the Philistines. Gareb laughed. Swords. How nice it would have been to have more of them.

The Philistine archers would follow the first line of assault, waiting until they were close enough to use the foot soldiers as cover and volley arrows into the Hebrew ranks. It would be devastating. There would be enormous casualties immediately. The Philistine arrows were heavy and iron tipped, and his men were protected only by thin shields and leather armor, with bits of copper stitched into the vests.

While the archers reloaded their bows, fresh Philistine troops would push forward in a surge behind the first ranks. They would repeat that cycle every half hour, supported by constant barrages by the Philistine archers, until the Israelites were destroyed. There would be heads and weapons captured as war prizes. The throne of Israel would be without an heir. David would lead his rebel army on raids and continue to get rich, and the people would suffer as they always had in these lands.

Gareb had supported David once. He'd thought what Saul had done to him was awful, but that was years in the past. Now, he could not understand why the man would abandon his brothers to slaughter at the hands of pagan Philistines. He knew Jonathan wanted to join David—he could tell when they spoke—but he didn't understand it. Jonathan was more a man than David could hope to be: loyal, true, and faithful to his fellow Israelites until the end. Which is today, Gareb thought. Faithful and loyal and dead.

Saul continued facing his army silently, then turned around, raised his arms, and shouted something. A challenge. He wanted the Philistines to come. He was provoking them.

Water bag in hand, Eliam watched Saul yell at the Philistines. He rehearsed in his head everything he was supposed to do: Run the water to the lines when men retreated for rest, pull out bodies as they fell so that no one tripped, and plug the hole in the lines if one opened nearby. And watch what the armor bearers did. Every major leader had an armor bearer who would be supporting them. But surely that was madness. How would he possibly see them in the fray?

There were more Philistines than he could count, against just a handful of Israelites. Eliam watched the Israelite soldiers mutter and joke and laugh nervously. Strange, how they did that right before battle.

Eliam clutched the water skin in his shaking hands. He was cold. The sun was out, but he was cold. Everything Gareb had said was coming true.

Then came a massive yell, and the echo of it rolled among the rocks, sounding as though it was everywhere at once. The Philistines were yelling, advancing now at a run. But it had happened so quickly! That was it? No other buildup? He had expected a long, drawn-out series of taunts and silences, but now there was yelling and the first ranks of Israelites were rushing downhill to meet their enemy. They moved in close formation, with shoulders touching. Then they met the first ranks of the Philistines and began to strike low.

It all seemed slow and unreal. Numb, Eliam watched helplessly as the men struggled and pressed, then started moving so slowly that Eliam half thought they would eventually sit down and take naps together. From where he was sitting, it looked as if there was nothing happening at all, just men swinging shiny objects and scuffling as if playing together.

A shout. Someone pointed at him, and he stood and ran forward, seeing the first ranks of Israelites falling back for rest. He reached a man, and immediately the noise of battle finally hit him. Screams and shouting and cries for help, clanging of swords and axes on shields and flesh.

The soldier took the water pouch from him, his face covered in thin bright blood, his breathing raspy. He drank, then threw the skin back. Eliam picked it up and ran back to the supply tent to refill it.

He struggled for balance among the rocks as he sprinted, expecting to feel an arrow bury itself between his shoulders at any moment. He reached the tent doubled over, panting, exhausted from the uphill sprint. Eliam wiped his face, heard the screams, wiped his face again, and snatched another skin. He made eye contact with the boy refilling the water skins from larger containers they had filled from the spring below.

Back down the slope, he saw the fight spreading along the side of the mountain. But where were the archers? No arrows had flown.

Eliam climbed to the top of a boulder in several quick steps. Finally able to see over the heads of the Israelites, he saw that only part of the Philistine army was pressing up the hill. They had still not sent the full force. Even the archers were still down the slope. He leapt from the boulder and ran downhill, filled now with dismay. The men were fighting hard, holding their lines, but there were not enough of them.

The sun relentlessly drained him of energy. He ran better in the evenings and in the cool of a forest, not in the brightness of the sun.

Another man shouted over the noise, close by, and Eliam ran to him, water splashing over his chest and sand spraying his face. The soldier took it, thanked him, poured the water over his head, took a long drink, and handed it back to him. The battle moved even slower now. The men were getting tired along the front ranks, and the replacements were slow to move forward. The Philistines would be putting fresh troops in at any moment.

Eliam turned and ran back up the slope.

———

Jonathan looked back toward the forest and shook his head violently. Put the thought away. Never again.

He ran from the tree line and into the open field, ashamed of his hesitation. The battle had begun, and he was angry at himself for hiding in the trees. With leaping strides he reached his equipment, checking as he ran the progress of the Philistine push. His father was in command, a short way behind the lines, but Jonathan's regiment was moving sluggishly and chaotically.

He picked up his sword and shield. No armor this day—he needed to move quickly, to finish well. He snatched up his bow and quiver and ran down the mountainside to his lines.

The men were disorganized and tired but holding. They were good men, and he would not abandon them again. Forget the desert.

Jonathan stopped himself by planting his foot against a boulder and pulled an arrow out of the quiver, fixing it in place and releasing in a single motion. The shaft spun through the dusty battle lines and hit a Philistine officer so hard that the breaking of the man's ribs could be heard across the field. He fell sideways, his face wide-eyed with shock, unable to shout or breathe from the impact.

Another arrow, another officer crashed to the earth, and Jonathan screamed with anger as he fixed a final arrow and drew the bow back as far as his strength would allow. Across the haze of the slope he saw several rows of officers wearing fish-scale armor. They were pointing at him and ordering their men to advance, assuming they were too far out of his range to be endangered.

Jonathan held the string next to his cheek, feeling the wispy sinews on his lips, and aimed the tip two cubits over the head of the closest man. He watched the dust to gauge the wind direction and moved the tip slightly to his left. Two cubits high, two cubits left.

The officer he aimed for was clearly the one in charge of that side of the front, driving his men forward and almost penetrating the

Hebrew lines. Next to him was an armor bearer. Jonathan's elbow ached from the strain, but he held his breath once more to steady it. He thought of the old saying David's warriors used.

Praise to our God, and arrows to our enemies.

The tip whistled away suddenly, disappearing in the immense dust cloud obscuring the battlefield. Jonathan could not follow its path, but as he began to run again, he saw the officer's head jerk to the side. As he pulled out his sword and ran in the direction of his own lines, a gap formed in the center of the Philistine rank.

The arrow had sliced through the neck of the first officer, almost severing his head, and embedded itself in the throat of the shield bearer.

Philistine discipline broke for the moment, and the troops pulled back from the assault, terrified by the warrior who had struck down two of the mightiest fighters on the field from such a distance.

Jonathan reached his own men and elbowed his way forward, shouting encouragement and trying to reach the front. Some who saw him cried out in relief and gave the regiment's war cry. Jonathan forced his way through the ranks past his men and came out directly in front of a Philistine's shield.

He raised his own shield and struck hard, shattering the man's teeth and knocking him backward into his troops. He slashed downward with the sword and killed him, then leaped away from a blow by another.

He darted straight ahead, across the short gap between the two armies, and past and through the surprised ranks of Philistines, until he was directly behind their first line. It was so bold a move that the Israelite soldiers believed him slain and began to wail, until at last he emerged between the helmets of their enemies, alone and moving fast.

The enemy soldiers still faced toward the Israelites, unaware of the break in their ranks. Jonathan was free to dart behind them, severing tendons that crippled their legs forever. He moved so swiftly that none of the Philistines even noticed him, and many fell, clutching their useless legs. He ran hard, ignoring the sweat in his eyes, and swept his blade again and again.

As he ran, on his left up the slope was the first rank of Philistines he was attacking, and on his right down the slope was the second wave making its way up the mountain. Philistines in the second wave pointed at him and shouted, but he ignored them, yelling and cutting. An arrow flew past his head and buried itself in the back of the Philistine soldier next to him, then another arrow did the same. The archers were firing at him foolishly as he ran among their own men.

Jonathan's heart was pounding blood through his veins so hard that he thought it would erupt from his chest. He sliced, bringing down many men without them even being aware of him. A sound penetrated his concentration: the Israelites cheering him. He looked back. The entire left flank of the Philistine assault had been beaten back. Keep moving, don't stop, need to move, he ordered himself.

The next wave of assault came, but he was still behind the first rank of Philistines, and the commanders of the Philistine archer regiment had ceased their men from firing. Holding his bloody sword over his head and waving his shield, muscles burning, Jonathan bellowed a war cry to his men, who returned it. They fought harder.

He turned slightly to the right, down the hill, and before the startled Philistines could react, he burst through the second wave of them, another one-man attack right into the mouth of the monster, calling aloud, calling for the covering, shouting and swinging his sword at any exposed flesh that came in front of him.

He reached the last of the second wave and shoved through it, feeling a sudden burn as a blade cut across his side. It wasn't deep, so he ignored it and turned back uphill, toward the forest, and staying behind the second rank of men, starting to run and cut once more. Men fell screaming, and he screamed also.

His blade moved and flashed. Philistines dropped. Their archers, waiting for their chance, were nevertheless held back by their officers, probably because they saw how thin the ranks of the Israelites were—too thin for archers to be effective.

Jonathan ran, swung his sword, and stumbled over rocks. His arm ached, but he willed it up again. The fire was coming. He felt it increasing and burning and raging into his body.

The archers began firing arrows at him again, and he held up his shield, hearing the clanking and pounding against it from the iron tips, and feeling the sweat blur his vision. Keep moving, keep moving, keep moving.

He drove his sword into the neck of a terrified archer and felt the wash of blood as it sprayed him. It felt warm and good, as it had in the old days. He laughed deliriously. Before he realized it, he had reached the flank of the Philistine line.

One last man, another archer, stood at the end of the line. Jonathan feinted as the Philistine stabbed wildly with the staff of his bow. Then the Philistine turned and tried to flee, but Jonathan ran up behind him, thrust his sword through the man's back, and forced it upward. The tip exited the man's throat. The Philistine seized violently, shaking and coughing blood.

Jonathan let the man slide off his blade and drop. Battle rage had taken over. He charged up and over rocks to his men, who faced him, shouting.

The Philistines had ceased their assault for the moment, regrouping after the surprise attack from the rear. Commanders, afraid to lose even more troops to the Hebrew demon warrior, pulled their ranks back and reformed skirmish lines. There was shouting, but for now it was calm on this side of the field.

He threw the sword to the ground and fell forward, collapsing onto his shield, too tired to look up, letting his face fall into the dirt. Around him were the cheers and shouts and the war cry of his regiment—his men, the regiment he had trained and led and fought with, called out to him. But he lay still, listening to his breath, letting himself heal.

Gareb had seen Jonathan rush out of the forest, press through the line, and crash directly through the ranks of the Philistines. It was an attack worthy of a madman, and now he shouted alongside the other men in jubilation. There was a man, he thought, and he charged forward. There would be no one left among them at the end of this day to write the song about it, and none of their own people would remember, but it did not matter.

It would be remembered by the Philistines.

Eliam struggled to pick up the water again, unable to believe that he could make another trip back up the mountain. Blisters and raw skin covered his hands, and his toes were bloody from striking against rocks. He had no idea how long it had been since the battle started, but he was surprised to see the sun a good distance lower in the sky. It was confusing—how could it have gotten so much lower?

He cursed the pain in his foot from the arrow that had struck him during his last climb up the mountain for water. He'd managed to break off the shaft, but the head was still buried deep between the bones of his foot.

And then he was angry—angry that the stupid arrow had managed to fly perfectly toward his foot. It could not have been aimed at his foot, only fired randomly through the air by some lazy Philistine archer, and it had been a perfect shot. Of all the ways to be wounded, he thought, furiously biting down on the broken shaft he had put between his teeth to control the pain.

He stumbled and fell, dropping the water skin, then watched in horror as the precious liquid disappeared into the sand. He cursed and beat the ground with his fists, then bit down harder on the wooden shaft. He reached down in another effort to loosen the buried arrowhead, but if anything he only pushed it further in. The point had exited through the bottom of his foot, and he could feel it stuck into the sole of his sandal. There was screaming and shouting all around him. He was closer to the lines than he'd thought.

Eliam rolled over in the sand and let the sweat drip off the bridge of his nose. He hated the screaming of dying men. His foot burned terribly. Men scuffled and fought very close to him. Smoke? Was something burning? He was afraid to look up, but finally did. He saw no fire. *But something is burning because I can smell it.*

Suddenly he wanted to run, straight away from this mountainside. He wanted to disappear into the forest and never feel another arrowhead sink into his foot again.

He sat up. There was the forest, nearby. All he had to do was run. He could reach the spring, he could—

There were louder shouts. He turned to the right and saw the Israelite line, blurry in the dust, pushing the Philistines back down the slope with the force of higher ground. Eliam coughed and blinked. The Israelites were pushing them back? They were advancing! Not possible.

The Philistines were pulling back to regroup, and the Israelite troops yelled and thumped their shields with their weapons. For the first time in many days, they sounded ... exhilarated. He could sense it in their faces and in their cries. He searched the field desperately to see what was causing it.

It was Jonathan, staggering back up the hill from behind the Philistine lines, dozens of enemy dead behind him.

NINETEEN

David's troops saw smoke on the horizon when they were still half a day away.

Some claimed it was a fire in the grasslands, started by herdsmen trying to clear bad ground or a carelessly tended campfire. But Benaiah knew exactly what it was, and through a fog of descending darkness in his mind he sprinted ahead.

This was just how he had come upon it before. He had approached from the Way of the Sea, weary but eager to see his neglected children and wife, and the smoke had appeared, and he had run, found the people crying, screaming, fires burning, and smoke filling doorways. He had burst through his door, and there in the corner was Sherizah, shaking, blood on the stones of his entryway, no daughters.

And now Benaiah found himself staggering through the burned and broken gates of another city, and he found himself again shouting for Sherizah, calling for her as he stumbled down the alleys and corridors that led to his home. Every building had been burned.

There were no people anywhere, all were gone except for the corpses of a few Philistine men, older ones who'd been allowed to stay behind. The flames had died, but smoke poured from every opening and smoldering ash heap.

The door of Benaiah's burned but still-standing home stood open as he ran up. He looked for the blood on the stones and realized that he had vomited all over his tunic. He threw aside his weapons, screamed for her, picking his way through his home, kicking away charred logs. Sherizah was not there.

He fell back through the doorway and lay in the dirt and ash of the street, gasping for breath. Around him, sounding muffled, were the sounds of the army searching the destroyed city of Ziklag for their loved ones. He heard no happy reunions, no shouts of joy. Only the hollow yells of men in despair.

Benaiah shouted to Yahweh then. He screamed curses and blasphemy and every angry thing he could think of. Twice this had come. Twice Yahweh had abandoned them.

He let his head roll, weak, feeling the wounds from the lion's claws inflame with new agony, as if his body had been waiting for his worst moment to remind him he had been cut to pieces.

Out of the corner of his eye he saw his sword glint. He stood up and snatched it. He walked to the doorway, propped the hilt of the sword between the entry stones, and prepared to fall on the tip.

He felt the sword tip prick his chest as he leaned against it. His weight was not yet on it. Just a little harder, just a little further, and it would end. He would descend into Sheol with the others he had slain, the others who had been slain, to where his wife and children were. And even if it was nothing but darkness, at least he would have them to hold, and promise never to leave them again.

Benaiah leaned against the sword. Sweat fell from his brow and splashed on the blade.

It was as if something was holding him back.

He threw himself harder against the blade. The tip pierced his flesh, but not more than a fingerbreadth.

Something *was* holding him back. A hand. Benaiah looked .behind him.

It was Keth.

"Do not do that yet, my friend. Come with me."

TWENTY

Jonathan's ears rang. He didn't have the strength even to lift his face from the dirt at first, but as the ringing he heard resolved into laughter and shouting, he willed himself out of the haze and lifted his head up.

There were his men, all of them, formed into rows across the mountainside, looking away from where he lay near the edge of the forest. A man was clapping his back, and he looked up. Gareb.

His old armor bearer said, "That was foolish! The most foolish thing I have ever seen, sir. Look at the mess you got us into. The Philistines are reforming their ranks, making them stronger, and they're going to come with more precision this time."

Jonathan looked down the hill and saw that Gareb's words were true. Leaders of companies and squads were replenishing their ranks with fresh reinforcements and new weapons. What Jonathan had done was indeed foolish beyond compare, for the leader of an army. The commander is never supposed to leave the place where he can best control his troops. Flying through the enemy lines like a hero only caused massed confusion. They would pay for his stupidity and probably lose the flank.

He sat up and began to tighten his leather. He needed to reassume control and enforce order. There would be no fresh reinforcements to fill their own lines.

Gareb, still watching him, said in a lower voice so that no one else would hear him, "It *was* foolish, sir. Violated every law of command and training—and it was exactly what we needed."

Jonathan looked up at his friend and saw him smiling. The shouts of the men all around him kept repeating the regimental war cry: "Perhaps Yahweh will be with us! Perhaps Yahweh will be with us!"

Perhaps Yahweh *would* be with them. *As long as we are with Yahweh.*

He looked at his men. They were *warriors*. They were here, sticks and all. They had not deserted. And he would not desert them.

He got to his feet and raised his sword, and the cries grew even louder. There was fire there now. He had lit it. They may not win the day, but at least there was fire.

Perhaps Yahweh will be with us.

Jonathan, arms still raised, pushed once more through the ranks of Israelites and began to walk the length of the front. He was exposing himself to archery fire, but he did not care. The Philistines had pulled back everywhere, reforming all of their ranks, not only the ones decimated by his charge, so the entire line of Israel's army was free of battle for the moment.

The men shouted, affirming him, and he began to run down the ranks, slapping their faces and pounding them on their chests. The war cry never let up, and while the Philistines reformed their ranks, Jonathan reached the end of his line and shouted to the men under his brother Abinadab's command. Abinadab and his soldiers waved and cheered him on as well, so he kept running, harder, shouting until he was nearly hoarse. The men returned his shouts, and the sound was more beautiful than anything he had ever imagined. In the midst of blood and death, he saw beauty in their ugly faces.

He leaped over fallen warriors and slipped on bloody rocks, but he kept running because they loved it. He laughed and ran until he reached the ranks of his brother Malchi-shua, who also rallied his men to shouting.

Then Jonathan turned and moved back to the center of the mountainside at the front of the entire Israelite army and turned toward the Philistines, holding out his spear. He knew there were good fighters down the slope, but not like his own. He loved these men and felt the burning of tears in his eyes.

The Philistines raised their own weapons and yelled, waiting like leashed animals to be released by their commanding officers. Jonathan spat toward them in hot anger. He turned and looked back over his army.

And then he saw his father.

The tall form of Saul was brooding on a rock far behind the lines. He was alone, watching his army. As the men shouted and gave their regimental war cries and pleaded for another chance to fight, Jonathan watched his father.

The twisting in his gut returned, and he looked away, trying all over again to forget the desert.

The men were rallying, and Eliam dared to hope that they might make it out of this after all.

He trudged back up the mountain toward the water tent. The arrow in his foot seared him with every step, but he kept moving. If those men could rally, so could he. But he was very tired, and the foot hurt terribly, and after a few steps, he had to kneel.

The sun was now approaching the edge of the Gilboa range behind them; it would soon go down. The sky was becoming more amber as the day wore on. Eliam watched it, listening as the void behind him filled with men's screams.

His head felt light. The wound in his foot bit at him fiercely. He realized that blood loss was finally taking its toll. His foot didn't look as if it was bleeding excessively, but looking back along the path he'd just followed, he saw a steady red drip within each footprint. It was an hour or so since he'd been wounded. Plenty of time to lose enough blood to pass out.

After what felt like an entire generation had passed, he reached the water tent and called out, but no one was there. Up the hill, far away, a boy was running. Coward, Eliam thought. He dipped the skin into the water and began the return toward the lines, hands stinging and raw.

The battle was beginning again. The Philistine ranks were now moving in a blunt formation. Eliam crawled up on the rock he had climbed earlier to get a better view.

The enemy soldiers now moved in many columns, one after the other, advancing toward the center of the Israelite lines. Heavy infantry with pikes and shields led the way, followed by lighter infantrymen with smaller swords, followed at last by the archers. There were no chariots or cavalrymen to be seen.

The formation continued to grow in mass until it was beyond counting, and the left and right flanks of the Philistine army seemed to disappear in the failing light. Behind the massed assault, shaped like an enormous spearhead, the thousands of reserve troops were forming another sweeping line. He couldn't understand what they were doing, but knew that the Israelites' situation had become more urgent. Israel's officers began sending messengers and aides to different portions of the lines.

He saw Jonathan dart back through the Israelite lines, shouting orders. The men at the far ends of the Israelite ranks didn't imme-diately react to the new Philistine movements. Word took awhile to reach the flank ends, especially when no one was watching the signal garments or listening to the ram's horn call. It was only when the first of the Philistines reached the front ranks of Israel that the men on the sides moved into position. The Israelite commanders maintained a line of soldiers on the left and the right, but they hur-ried their secondary ranks toward the center of the line, behind the point targeted by the Philistine blunt strike.

Eliam tried to gather it in, but so many things were happening at once that he was unable to comprehend any of it. Then the dust and screaming rose in clouds once more. The attack had begun again. He could see nothing more.

With his head swimming from blood loss, he half fell off the rock and made his way back to the battle.

The battle had started to shift in intensity after Jonathan's surprise attack. Gareb watched their men surging forward into the Philistine ranks, darting effectively behind the small boulders and ditches on the hillside, a type of fighting they were accustomed to and good at. The lowland-dwelling Philistines, on the other hand, were unable to gain solid footing on the steep mountainside.

Then he saw the Philistine chariots, out on the plains, suddenly burst into movement. Dust clouds rose as the horses pulled their riders swiftly east, converging on a wide opening on the eastern slopes of the mountains.

Gareb could only stare hopelessly as their chances at victory began to flicker out.

———

Jonathan saw that all was lost. One moment there had been jubilant war cries and hope, and now there was nothing but the inevitability of catastrophic defeat.

The fighting had spread out across Gilboa all the way to the eastern slopes, where the ground was more level and broad. Jonathan and the other commanders had not realized that the Philistines had simply been drawing them to where the Philistines' chariots could finally be used in the attack.

There would be no getting out of this today. Yahweh had willed it.

His eyes sought out Gareb, still carrying instructions to their flanks. Gareb caught Jonathan's eye and read his intent. They looked at each other silently for a moment while shouts and clanging swarmed the air around them.

"Gareb," he shouted, "I must do this!"

Gareb did not reply, only looked back at the Philistine chariots charging up the mountain on their left. He started walking toward Jonathan.

Jonathan shouted again. "I need to hit their flank and delay them! If our army goes down, escape and find David!"

"David? I will die before that!"

"Honor my orders!"

Gareb kept staring. Jonathan felt the anger ebb as he looked at his old friend. The two men had drawn closer together as they talked, and now Jonathan lowered his voice. "Only he can save the nation from this, and he will need your help. Yahweh is with him. Do it for me."

Gareb looked as though he had been speared. Jonathan nodded once and then turned and ran, unable to look back at his friend. Both men knew what was coming now.

Jonathan sprinted toward the far left flank. The crash of metal told him that the tip of the Philistine formation had struck Israel once more.

He shouted encouragement to the men and urged them forward. When he reached the far side of the mountain field, he stopped a squad moving in from the flank and asked them where his brother Abinadab was. A young man pointed up the slope, and Jonathan spotted his brother, directing the reforming of the Israelite lines. Jonathan ran to him and tugged his arm. "Come with me."

Abinadab nodded, told his armor bearer to direct the fight in Abinadab's absence, and followed Jonathan as he flew along the rocky slope across the rear of the Israelite lines. As they ran, Jonathan to the left, the Philistine chariots were almost all the way up the slope and ready to crush their flank.

He collided with a boy stumbling down the slope, and both of them crashed to the ground. It was Eliam. "Are you all right?" Jonathan asked.

Eliam nodded, eyes blurry and unfocused.

Jonathan saw the blood on his foot. "Get to a physician immediately."

Eliam looked back at him, confused, and then Jonathan remembered that there were no more physicians. They had left for David's army.

Jonathan pulled the boy to his feet and gripped Eliam's arm. "Be strong." He held Eliam's arm a moment longer, then motioned for Abinadab to follow.

Malchi-shua, their other brother, was below them, trying to reform the thinning ranks of the center. He saw them and sprinted up to them.

Jonathan knelt with both men, all of them panting and sweating, each far beyond the limits of his body. Jonathan picked out a group of small stones from the ground and laid them out in the formation of the battlefield.

"I will be in front," he said, pointing to the stones, "and we will rush down the left flank, in full view of the men. Make sure they see you. When we hit the Philistine side, we will try to isolate their archers and infantry from the chariots."

Abinadab and Malchi-shua looked at the rocks and said nothing.

Jonathan was irritated. "Well? Do you understand?"

"You have done this sort of thing before, brother. We have not," said Abinadab. He had the height of their father, and Malchi-shua had the face. As boys, they had teased Jonathan because he more resembled their mother, and they claimed that he was sired by another. Happier days, long gone now.

Jonathan saw the defeat in their faces and let his shoulder sag a bit. The line was still holding beneath them and the reinforcements from the flanks were converging successfully to the center, but it was only a matter of time until the chariots overwhelmed them and broke through their line, and when that happened, it would all be over soon.

"We will not live through the day, you both know that. Neither will our father. Yahweh has ordained it. But many of our men will. And our men must fight again one day. We must show them what courage is."

His voice wavered, and his brothers looked away. They had never seen him so emotional. He wiped his face and blinked, then shook his head to regain his focus. Though the sun was now hidden behind the hills, there was sweat pouring from his face, burning the corners of his eyes.

Malchi-shua, who had been looking furtively down the mountain at the battle, said, "I am not leaving our father's side. Yahweh be with you both, but I cannot join you."

Jonathan nodded. He had forgotten about his father in the past hour. How was that possible? Was their father of so little value in the battle? Jonathan had not seen him since that brief glimpse earlier, and he had no guess as to where he might be now. If Jonathan was to die, then let him die before he saw his father again.

Malchi-shua gripped his hand, did the same with Abinadab, and then ran toward the fray. Jonathan was overcome with sorrow at the last glimpse of his brother, then pushed it away again. He looked at Abinadab. "Are you with me?"

"Until the end."

He meant it. There was no scorn or resentment. Neither Malchi-shua nor Abinadab had been close to their older brother through the years, resentful that Jonathan always seemed foremost in the people's minds. But here there was none of that. Here they were two brothers who loved each other, regretting how petty their past arguments had been. Jonathan let the moment linger longer than he should have.

Then he rose with Abinadab after him. After adjusting his grip on his sword and asking if Abinadab had a worthy enough blade himself, he ran down the mountainside yet again that day.

Gareb thrust his sword forward, pulled it back, then thrust it again into the first face he saw emerge through the opening in the line. Someone screamed next to him, a lance in his belly, and Gareb jerked away from his own target and caught the falling soldier. Dust and sand flew around him.

He lowered his head and backed away from the ranks, pulling the wounded man behind him—less out of concern for the man than making sure no one tripped over his body. When he was far enough away, he dropped the legs and rushed back to the center. The wounded man cried out for help behind him, but Gareb ignored him. Mercy would come soon enough.

Gareb shouted to the men around him to close ranks, and they obeyed, but the surge of relentless power kept pushing them backward up the mountain, rendering useless every advantage they had in terrain and defensive maneuvering through sheer force and number. Soon they were pushed back over the fallen man, and, screaming, he was trampled to death. The line would burst at any moment. The sound of the chariots thundering up the mountain was getting louder and closer.

A few things went right. The Israelites had been able to reach a small boulder field near the crest of the Gilboa summit, and the chariots were forced to swing farther to the east, delaying the onslaught, since the horses had to pull the rigs up steeper ground.

The ground was so rocky that the Philistines were unable to penetrate the ranks fully, being forced to scramble and climb over boulders, which were savagely defended by Hebrew fighting teams. Whenever an opening would appear, Gareb would plug it, but he knew that eventually they would be overrun. The Hebrew archers were firing into the Philistine column, but the pagans wore so much armor, it was having little effect. Eventually the archers turned and ran, and no amount of yelling stopped them.

Gareb kept the men moving and fighting, shouting at them and kicking them when they needed it. When one unit was exhausted, he replaced them with another. Still the Philistines came, and he hated them. Even though his arm felt as though it might fall off, he put the full weight of that hate into each strike.

Unsteady on his feet, Eliam tried to grasp what had just happened with Jonathan. He watched the Israelite prince run from him and felt inspired to move again. He would get water down to the line or die doing it. The loss of blood left him strangely brave and free of fear. His mind did not process things quickly anymore, only pain and sounds. Sounds hit him again and again: clanks, crashes, screams, gurgling as blood erupted through the throats of dying men. He found himself at the line once more, near the fiercest fighting as all the ranks tried to hold back the penetration of the Philistine bludgeon formation.

It finally occurred to him what the Philistines were doing. By concentrating all their forces in one spot, they would break the line and then split, each side of the wave enveloping the remaining Israelite soldiers. The Philistine chariots would prevent any retreats.

Eliam fretted and worried over it through foggy thoughts, then gave up and decided that whatever else happened, he would bring the water.

A soldier bumped into him, knocking the water from his hands, spilling it out in the sand. It seeped into the ground and disappeared as Eliam watched in horror. Something about the empty water skin, the sound of death nearby, pain in his foot, and now Eliam was frozen.

Eliam could see and hear nothing but the flash of bodies moving and hoarse shouting. Now everything was happening so much slower, even slower than before. How odd that battles seemed to slow down so much right when they were about to be decided. He thought vaguely that there was enough time to escape.

Fear—awful, consuming fear—crept into his heart. With every lance thrust into bowels, every sword cut across a neck, courage fled from him. Eliam suddenly did not want to feel the pain. He was horrified of death. Sheol awaited him if he died, and he did not know what it would be like.

He started to reason with himself. There was no point in dying this day. There was no chance for any of them anyway. If he escaped, he might be able to come back later. Jonathan might survive, and he would need an armor bearer.

But not one who abandoned his brothers on the field. Not one who escaped.

He tried to shake off the thought but couldn't keep his eyes from the hills to the north. If he left now, there would be time. The line would hold awhile longer, and no one would notice his leaving. His foot would need tending, but he would undoubtedly pass through some village.

He felt the sudden coolness of the evening on his face. His eyes stung, and he wiped them, cursing his sweat and the dirt. And then he wanted to run, so quickly and so far away that it surprised him how selfish he was. He wanted nothing more than to turn and leave that field of despair and death and flee to the woods and deserts.

He looked up the slope, past the abandoned water holding spot, to the very top of the mountain. The forest bordered the field on all sides the entire way to the peak of jagged rocks far above. He could make it to the shelter of the forest if he went now, then he would get to a village for help.

Weak, desperate, slow of thought, Eliam reasoned and prodded until at last he gathered a plan of action. He would leave. Others were leaving; surely it would not be cowardly. The pain was too much now, and he did not want to die. The cause was lost.

The decision was made, and having made it, he was too tired and weak to reconsider. Eliam simply could not bear the thought of a blade piercing his gut. Gareb had said that many men die because they choked on their own bloody vomit. The vultures would eat them and peck out their eyes. The Philistines would cut off heads and arms, then parade them around the streets of their cities as sacrifices to their heathen gods. Perhaps Eliam himself, a member of the royal court, would have his body torn to pieces while still alive.

He looked at the battle one more time—the lines of brave men, still holding together, driving their weapons forward with weariness and heart. They deserved songs and honors and praises. He felt a throbbing in his head.

He deserved none of that. He could not disguise from himself his cowardice. How he had wanted to be brave. He would leave them on this field of honor. He would not disgrace them with his presence. He hated himself. His father would be angry. No, not angry. Only sad.

Eliam took a bandage strip from his waist pouch and tied a new knot on the arrow wound in his foot. It would be enough to show that he'd been here. He would tell the people of the brave warriors who died in this place, how he had been charged with carrying the message of defeat.

In a fog, Eliam staggered toward the distant trees. He shouted at himself to turn around and die like a man. He cursed his foot. He was thirsty.

He gave a last glance to the lines where the brave men were and then walked into the forest, sobbing.

Jonathan felt it once more. It had not been there in so long, but it was there now, as the suddenly cool evening breeze revived him while he and his brother leapt from rock to rock back down the mountain. The great army winding up the valley below them was biding its time, knowing it could not fail. The chariots lurked.

Jonathan had not felt the surge in his breath and quickening of his heart in so long that he almost did not recognize it at first. But it was there, and it spoke to him and pushed him forward to his death.

The covering had returned.

The men saw Jonathan and Abinadab running along the edge of the Israelite lines and began to shout. Their voices were weaker than before; after the afternoon's slaughter, fewer remained. But they sensed his heart and fire. His body protested, but he kept it moving because he needed it one last time.

The Philistine archers were ready for them. They had learned a lesson earlier, and this time Jonathan was in the open where they could fire freely. They did. He saw the swarm of arrows rise up from the metallic snake of the enemy forces and descend on them. It would be over soon.

But as the arrows landed, nothing happened. He felt no piercing of his flesh, no thrust of force knocking him back. Not a single arrow had struck them; they only clanged harmlessly against the rocks. He raised his eyes and screamed to the sky, feeling the covering in his blood and courage in his step. Shouts and war cries reverberated everywhere from his men up the slope, and he drank them in like cool water, letting them fuel him as he descended with his brother on the black masses of soldiers.

He hit them at full charge, an attack so brazen that the Philistines shirked away. A few men tried to swing a blade at them but were quickly cut down. The two brothers kept close and penetrated deep into the lines of the enemy, neatly separating the archers from the main force for the second time that day.

Jonathan tore at them with his sword. The power was coming, ever more, wrapping him in its terrible strength, and many Philistines fell before they knew they had been hit. The enemy was so intent on what was in front of them that they were not expecting an attack by two men on their flank twice in the same battle.

Jonathan and Abinadab breached the far side of the line. The archers had backed away from the fight and regrouped while the infantry pressed on ahead unaware. Jonathan's men saw him again and the yelling continued louder. He laughed with battle rage and looked for his brother—then saw the body lying on the ground behind him.

He turned away and kept running. Abinadab gone. Soon he would be gone himself.

Jonathan felt his terror return. His attack slowed. Many Philistines lay dead in front of him. Suddenly, oddly, he regretted their deaths. It was a strange thought, and he pushed it away. The smells of blood and metal hung in his nostrils. He charged again.

This time they were ready and formed a line on their flanks to receive him. He stumbled toward it, picked up a spear, and threw it into the ranks. It struck a shield and fell harmlessly to the ground. He raised his own shield to dodge the lances that flew toward him in response. Then a group of men broke away from the Philistine ranks and charged him. The shouting from the Hebrew lines died. No doubt they thought this was the end. And no doubt they were right.

He found strength and swung the blade. As each man came, he dodged just enough, ducked enough, and avoided each blow while delivering his own. He was weaker now, but he aimed well and men fell. The fire of Yahweh poured through him in a final rush. There was a line of men directly in front, and he crushed them, picking up a broken shield and flinging it at an officer's head, then driving the end of a lance through the eye socket of another in one motion.

Philistines died all around him, terrified of him but sent forward with the threats of their commanders.

Jonathan was not on the slopes of Mount Gilboa but out in the valleys with David, living in the days of fire, the old times, feeling the warmth of springtime and hearing the songs of his friend as they plotted campaigns and admired women in the villages. He saw his father in the old days as he destroyed the enemies of Yahweh, back when he was worthy of the crown, and the good times when David came and went from the royal court with tales of his exploits.

Jonathan no longer felt the impact when his sword struck. A dull throb had entered his head, blocking the noise of the clanging metals and the smell of dead flesh and smoke. He killed them, these brave men who had families, but he struck them down regardless. David was there smiling with him, and they gazed at the fire and talked of Yahweh and things too deep for words.

There was a shout and a grunt, and he felt the shaft of a lance enter from behind and exit his belly.

All fight left him, and he fell to his knees. The Philistine who had impaled him gave another shout. He heard, dimly, the line of Philistines cheering his demise. He tried to move his arms, feeling the need to kill the man who'd killed him, but they would not move. All strength was gone.

Jonathan's face struck a rock as he fell, and it put him in a mist, sounds no longer cohesive and his body suddenly numb. He tried to resist, tried to yell, but it came out as a mumble.

The Philistine pulled and wrenched the lance from his body, and Jonathan felt no pain, only the dull sensation of the shaft tearing loose. The soldier ran back to his place in the lines. There was no more shouting from either side then, only the grim silence of men trying to kill one another. Jonathan listened to it, the mosaic of noises that told him the battle was almost over and there would finally be rest.

He was so very tired. No pain, just exhaustion. He was relieved that the lance had ended this war for him, for he would not have stopped. But now there would be rest. There would be warmth and fires and laughter again. His blood was filling the earth around him. He did not care. He only wanted rest.

Yahweh had been there at the end. Jonathan had felt him in his spirit and let him move the blades. The covering had given him one final charge for the men to see, for his father to see. He chuckled, blood filling his throat.

His father would not have watched. His father had never been proud of him.

But perhaps his father *had* seen. Perhaps he *had* been proud.

Perhaps there had been a moment when his father watched him run courageously through the ranks, trusting only in the urge of the covering in his spirit that had so often come upon him, and was proud of him. Jonathan's father no longer understood that urge. He did once. Not anymore.

The sounds were gone at last, and Jonathan was thankful. He was weary of the sound of war. He had known it all his life. He wanted rest now. Perhaps his father had seen him.

Perhaps Yahweh will be with us.

TWENTY-ONE

In his daydream, David was climbing, but he had paused to peer up and around a tangle of wet brush that clung to the edge of the rocky face. The sun and the smell of salt; he could see far to the distant peaks of Moab, and he was calm for a moment. Calm because the place was perfect and beautiful, as though Yahweh had dipped a mighty finger into the nearby sea and shaken it clear of the death salt before touching this wadi, its bright water erupting out of the stark side of the mountain. He tried not to think of Michal and her touch, her skin, her soft body that he had taken so much delight in, before she was torn from him.

He touched his cheek to the moss, letting the cold stream cleanse his head as he clung to the brush. Then, in an instant, he remembered where he was and what was happening, and panic gripped him. He froze, listening. The sound of water, birds, hyraxes squealing nearby.

And he heard voices, violent and full of anger, coming closer, and he scrambled up the rocks beneath the waterfall as fast as he could scrape his fingers into the moss.

They were coming.

They were coming! *He was coming!*

David slipped on the moss and was twisting as he struck the pool at the base of the falls ...

And now he was in the cave, and men were there, his men, telling him to strike, telling him in desperate whispers that could not be heard over the roaring water to kill this man who hunted them. David *wanted* to kill him now and end it once and forever, to capture the crown and hunt for leopards with Jonathan again, just the two of them, building fortresses on the trade roads and building Israelite ports on the Great Sea, driving the Philistines from their own harbors, and all he had to do was kill this man in the cave only cubits away.

And how he wanted to. But then the dream shifted, and he saw the giant in the hot sun wearing the shining armor, and the flames roared through David's muscles, burning away his fear with the heat of the fiery desert sun ...

Grip the stones tight. No other movement behind me. No other men coming. So I will do it alone.

Cover me, Yahweh, in the day of war. I am alone.

The monster is coming! No time. These stones will do. Hurry. Fit the stone.

I feel you; give me the power now. He is so large. There is the shield bearer, not a small man either, he will move quickly to protect the flank.

If it is your will, Father, put the fear away.

He is coming ...

If it is your will, Yahweh, that I am hunted all of my life, so be it, just cover me in the day of war ...

David roused himself. He realized he was clenching his knees tightly to his chest, alone in the corner of the burned-out room. A pale band of sunlight streamed through the window of his bed chamber and left a golden strip directly beneath the pane. He watched the small swirls of dust dancing in the light. Some particles disappeared, then moved back into view, carried by an unseen current.

There was noise outside the walls. Arguments. The men were not screaming anymore, though. They had been demanding that his head be cut off.

He closed his eyes and tried to listen. Nothing yet. Sometimes he heard it alone, sometimes he needed the ephod, but he nearly always felt it.

The men were demanding him. But he could not face them unless he heard the message. It would not work anymore to simply kill troublemakers; from now on, they would need to be convinced. They would need to be led.

David searched himself for any remaining darkness he had not confessed that would prevent the covering from coming. There could not be vengeance or sin in his heart or Yahweh would not speak.

Their families were alive. He believed it. There were no Hebrew bodies, except that of the old woman whose heart must have stopped beating. Slavery must have been the goal of the Amalekites. His wives, Abigail and Ahinoam, had been taken. Abigail was his favorite, and he wanted her back. She looked much like Michal had once looked. Young, lush, beautiful, but wiser.

Vengeance began to heat him, and he resisted it, knowing that it would block the covering and the word from Yahweh.

David knew he had been avoiding the covering for too long. It was too easy to propel himself forward in his own power. He had been successful for so long, had never lost a battle, but despite that he felt like he was running from Yahweh. That he had been too harsh, that too much blood had been spilled.

He wiped sweat from his forehead and released his legs. It always felt good to stretch them, as it always felt good to be alone.

He had been alone a great deal back in the days tending sheep. He had been alone in the deep woods of the hill country—no brothers, no chattering people coming in and out of his father's home. The trees and the rocks and the mountains were part of him.

He hadn't minded tending the sheep. They were a pleasant audience as he tried out his songs. David smiled. Their response was somewhat lacking, but they were supportive.

In the woods, alone with the sheep, he had always heard the covering. There had never been doubt. He had heard it in the bleating of a newborn lamb, heard it in the terrible lightning storms, heard it in the roar of the lion before it struck.

Yahweh was in all of it; and away from his brothers and politics and armies and work, in the quiet wilderness places, David always heard him. How he longed for it again, those years of training, before he became the leader of outcasts and reprobates, before kings wanted his death for no reason. Better days.

The shepherd's staff he had carried as a boy was across his lap, reminding him of the day of his anointing. The old prophet had been firm but reluctant, wary of another mistake. David had been very young then—although he had felt older than he was. More had happened in his short life than many men ever saw.

Samuel's anointing oil had been fragrant, thick with olive scent, and the prophet had let it flow over David's eyes and along the side of his mouth. The prophet's hands had touched his face, and his thumbs covered his eyes as he kissed his head. He had prayed aloud in the ancient tongue of their people. The oil soothed David, and he let it stream down his chest and soak his garments. The eyes of the prophet were piercing, making David feel uneasy.

A sudden, inexplicable burning tore at David's face, forcing him to fall backward. Fire was everywhere, consuming the air around him with impossible heat. It snaked into his chest, and he felt as though it would erupt out of his lungs. David yelled in pain, and then realized that it was not pain but something else. The burning poured out of his ears. He opened his eyes, although the oil stung them, and saw the prophet, one moment facing him and the next lying on his face wailing aloud.

His brothers and his father were watching him, bewildered, and he could not understand why they did not run from the flames engulfing the room, but he had no energy to speak. He let himself lie with his face buried in the dirt, reaching for anything to hold on to.

The images of fire, so real, flowed through his mind and chest. Etched in flame against the darkness of his mind's eye, he saw the Lion. It roared at him, and in the quiet of the room he fell through its open mouth, helpless to resist ... and then he was in the woods once again ...

There is a monster, a black mass moving toward my sheep, and I am running. I have only my sling. The stone is ready. I am terrified—terrified that I cannot get there soon enough. My yell chokes in my throat. I throw the stone, a hit! The monster rolls to its side. There! A branch on the ground, grab it! Leap onto its back. It struggles and tries to toss me, but I reach around its hideous neck and pull the piece of wood hard against the flesh. The bear swipes and claws, and I keep pulling as hard as I can. The fire pours into my chest, and I scream with it. The fire comes and comes and comes, and I shout more. The bear struggles for breath ... I hold ...

The lion comes at me. The sheep are behind me, and it leaps. I miss with the stone and feel the stench of its breath right before it collides with me. It crushes me; I cannot hold it off any longer. Find the weapon! Hurry! There it is! Fire races into my lungs and through my eyes, and I seize the golden hide and throw it away from me. It rolls. I am upon it. I strike it with my fist, and the creature shrieks away from me. I catch it and squeeze the throat, claws and roars covering me, and I pull as hard as I can. No, the fire pulls through me. I have his neck in my hands, Yahweh cover me. I hear and feel a snap. The beast goes limp ...

Fire again. Through my arms it rages this time. The stone flies and strikes the giant. He grabs at his face, blood everywhere down the front of his armor. Need to hurry, need to run, I reach him and kick his knees. He falls to the ground, screaming, cursing. His sword. I grab the hilt from the scabbard. Fire in me, your fire Yahweh, let me slay this man who would curse you; let me show these people what happens when you are profaned. The armor bearer moves to flank, aware of the blow, and he is running from me as he should, for I will slay him and all his brothers. Fire burning through my heart and out my arms. His sword lies at his side. I seize it, so very heavy, swing with the fire, and it severs his neck, bright red blood spraying my face, warm and good. The armor bearer is gone. I grab the hair, hold up his head, and feel the blood drenching me, drenching me like the oil, and it feels good. But then the fire leaves, flickers away from the depths of my soul, and escapes my mouth. I am standing with the head, with the sword, with the shouts of the armies behind me. They are running. We will slaughter them; we will kill so many of them that no man of Philistia will ever be bred again. Behind me comes the army ... free men ... send the fire again ...

There was a gentle scratching at the doorway, startling him. His eyes were blurry at first, and he blinked to clear them.

"Come in."

A man wearing elaborate garments came in. Abiathar, the priest who traveled with the army, who had loyally followed David everywhere he had fled, bowed his head. The two had been together a long time, and their affection was warm and genuine. Abiathar was one of the few men David could completely trust, and he was grateful for his companionship now.

"How are you?" David asked.

Abiathar hesitated. "The men are distraught. You will not live this day unless you have answers."

"That is why I have you."

"The ephod?"

"Yes, I need the Urim and Thummim," David said.

The priest nodded. His beard spilled over the front of a multi-colored breastplate embroidered with elaborate threadwork. Jewels and gold were spaced apart in the cloth. The breastplate hung over his shoulder by two straps, fastened to a girdle with golden rings, giving the exact appearance of a gilded suit of armor.

Below the breastplate was an ornately woven pouch that hung directly over the priest's loins. Gold rings attached it to the belt around his waist. Blue, purple, and scarlet threads of fine linen were woven with precious stones, ending with a dark opening facing upward toward his chest. There were two jewels on the straps, inscribed with the names of the twelve tribes.

David held his breath a moment and looked away from the brilliant craftsmanship of the priestly garment. It was never easy for him to do this. His fists were clenched. He looked at the priest and nodded his head slightly. The two men knelt and held their arms out while facing each other. David closed his eyes and let the silence of the room cover him. The priest held still as well.

David searched his heart for any remaining hate or vengeance, anything that would prevent Yahweh from speaking to him. He repented of it once more in his spirit and listened to the quiet murmur of the insects in the window.

Tentatively, David spoke. "Should I chase them? Will I catch them?"

There was more silence. The priest moved. David opened his eyes and saw the man's hand go into the pouch. Only one stone would be in his hand when it came out. Would it be the black one? The white one? Everything depended on it.

Abiathar shuffled the contents, then came out with a black stone. Urim.

Yes.

David held himself as still and as reverently as possible. Yahweh was speaking, and he did not want to anger him. He wanted to know details, but he was afraid to ask. He meditated on the meaning of it. With his eyes closed, he prayed silently that Yahweh would reveal something else to him.

Then, in his spirit: *Go after them. You will recover everything that was taken from you.*

Many times in his life David had wondered when it was really Yahweh speaking. There was no question now.

"Thank you, great Father. Your name is above all others," he said aloud. The cloud in his mind dissipated immediately. He had heard. No more sulking and waiting.

David stood, as did Abiathar, who smiled at him. "Follow Yahweh, my future king, and we will follow you."

When the priest had left, David walked to a corner of his room and saw the men in the streets below gathered with their weapons, waiting for him. They had been ready to butcher him earlier in the day and might still be. His own men. It was the blackest day of his life. His wives were missing, his town destroyed, and his own war brothers were plotting against him. He had told them he would ask Yahweh about their situation, and when his words were reinforced by the threats of his most loyal troops, they had conceded. But now it was time to face them again.

He felt older than he was. So long ago were the days of tending sheep. The men acted like sheep sometimes, and leading them was not so different, but he was coming to realize how much he had been behaving like a foolish sheep himself.

He picked up the enormous iron sword captured that day in the Elah Valley, the one he had used to behead the vanquished giant. It too would have been taken, if the raiding Amalekites had found the secret compartment in his bedchamber.

There was no practical purpose for this sword: too large to maneuver for quick blows between the ranks and too heavy to use in open combat. Without the covering, he would not be able to use it.

But David did not rely on practical purpose.

Joab grabbed the man by his vest.

"Say it again and you will die. My vow."

The foreigner glared at him but said nothing further. The rest of the group was crowded around the entrance to David's home. The Three, along with Benaiah, Joab, and Keth, stood shoulder to shoulder at the entrance. Stone walls twelve cubits high were wrapped around the dwelling, but the gate was missing. David had entered soon after they arrived at the ruined city and had not been seen since. The men were plotting to kill him out of grief, and the only thing that had spared him was their fear of his Three.

It had been hours since their arrival at Ziklag, to find their worst fears confirmed. All order and discipline was lost when they reached the city, each man wandering off to his home to suffer alone. The men had wept and shouted, tearing at their clothing in grief.

Many yelled about David's alliance with the pagan, uncircumcised King Achish. Others, usually loyal, had fastened on this accusation and spread it throughout the ranks.

Benaiah was surprised that he was not angry with David himself.

He felt too numb to be angry; besides, he knew it was not David's fault. It was his own. He'd had many chances to be there for them. He never was.

A man shouted that David had better come out soon or he would be stoned.

"Stone him, and I will send your head back to your father with my condolences," Josheb answered calmly. Even though his own wife was missing, Josheb was keeping his usual casual demeanor.

There were fifty men demanding to go after David. It was stunning that so many would turn on their leader so quickly, especially after all they had been through. To Benaiah, the worst of it was that the men of the tribes had been the first to threaten him. The foreigners were more loyal than his fellow Israelites.

A few of them charged toward the burnt doorway. Those still loyal to David pulled their weapons and prepared to make their stand, but just then an enormous sword crashed into the cedar beams in the doorway. It struck with such force that the men running stopped on their heels. The shouting died. Heads turned toward the doorway of the house.

There was David, holding two spears, aiming one of them at the mass of men and holding the other over his shoulder.

David propped one spear against the gate and pulled the great sword out of the cedar beam. The men had gone quiet. He walked in front of them, eyes blazing, terrifying, and the fighters backed away.

"Do you know what this is? Anyone. Tell me." He held up the sword by the blade.

"It is the sword of the Philistine giant you killed," said Joab, loud enough that the men would know he was pointing it out for their benefit. David walked down the line of men, showing each of them the sword. Most had never seen it, some only from a distance. No one had ever known where it came from. Benaiah felt the tension begin to ebb.

"Many of you are not from the lands of our tribes. I understand that. You have served well and been rewarded well. You have nothing to complain about. You came of your own accord, and I have always dealt with you fairly.

"Was it a mistake to go with King Achish? Perhaps. It very well may be that I have sinned against Yahweh, and this is his punishment to me. You are free to go if this is unacceptable to you."

Soldiers were gathering quickly now in front of David's house. Word had passed through the streets that David had emerged, so the Judeans and other men of the tribes began to circle behind the group, unbeknownst to the foreigners. Benaiah watched his leader anxiously, desperate for the word given to him about their loved ones.

David kept pacing, eyes never leaving the faces of his men. He held the sword in front, and he made everyone look at it as he passed. When he reached the end, he sheathed it behind his back. The sun emerged from behind a cloud and warmth flooded the area once more.

"I am not here only to raid like barbarians. You should know that by now. I want to help our people escape their oppression. Those of you from distant lands are not aware of our history, so I will tell you. If anyone speaks before I am finished, I will kill you myself and mount your head.

"Our people, the twelve tribes of Jacob, lived among the Egyptians for many years. Times were good. There was food, wealth, and our people grew to a great multitude. It looked as though we would stay there along the banks of the Nile.

"But a king emerged in Egypt who feared what our people would do if they revolted, so he enslaved them. They labored and toiled under the whip for generations. They worked for other men. They served other men. They brought about the dreams of *other men*! In their minds was the lie that they were only worth slavery.

"Our God, Yahweh, the one you hear me sing to, the one who is the only God, heard their cries. He called a man named Moses forward. He told Moses to go back to the people and tell them that it was time to reclaim the promise he had made to their ancestor Abraham, the promise that they would inhabit the lands we are in now. He performed many signs and wonders and crushed the Egyptians with his outstretched hand.

"Moses led our people out of bondage in Egypt and delivered them into the wilderness and the desert. No longer were they slaves, although they still lived like it. A new way of life came to them, a wilderness existence of wandering, so that Yahweh could discipline them and show them that he wanted them to rely only upon him. He so desperately desired to be among them that he even had a tabernacle built so that he could inhabit their camp. It was a hard existence. Forty years they wandered, learning about Yahweh, and yet Yahweh provided for them.

"Many in that generation were wicked, so Yahweh did not allow them to enter the land promised to them. Moses, like all men, did not follow Yahweh without fault. He made a terrible mistake and doubted Yahweh, so Yahweh told him that he would not enter the land either.

"But a new leader had come, the man who had been a faithful servant to Moses. His name was Joshua, and he was a mighty warrior, a valiant man who had crept into the land of the enemy many years before and told the people of the wonders that awaited them if they served Yahweh.

"Joshua led the people. He formed them all into an army. They crossed the Jordan, brothers, at full season when the water was highest, on dry land! You men of Gad know how hard that is. Try to move an entire nation more numerous than the sand across that river!

"They attacked Jericho, assaulted Ai, and for years they waged war on these hills and in these forests. A new existence had come. A conquest existence!"

Benaiah looked at the faces of the men. They were attentive. Many had never heard these things.

David's voice was rising, blood rushing to his head and turning him flush. Even Joab had turned away from watching the warriors and was listening.

"Conquest! They were to take the blessing Yahweh had promised them! Would it come easy? No! Would they appreciate it if there was no hardship?

"Now our land is being torn apart. If we do not act, we will lose the promise. Foreigners, you can come and go as you please, but we would be honored if you stayed with us. You have a home with your families in my court. Brothers, I have consulted Yahweh, God of our fathers, and he has promised me that if we pursue the Amalekites, he will deliver them into our hands.

"As I live. As long as my line lives. As long as there is blood in the veins of an Israelite man, we will never be subjected again! You will never live as slaves again, serving other people's dreams. We have been in the wilderness, brothers, and now it is time to conquer!

"So here's your choice. You can follow me, and we will destroy the Amalekites and take back what they stole from us. Or you can crawl out of here on your bellies like snakes and disappear back to where you came from, and you will have never seized the promise Yahweh has for us."

He stared at them hard. No man spoke.

TWENTY-TWO

Eliam felt a buzzing, as though millions of insects were crawling through his ears and out of his eyes. He realized that it was dark and sluggishly tried to sit up. The swimming in his head continued. Cool night air circulated around his face and revived him a bit, so he managed to clear enough fog away in his mind to recover his bearings.

He cried out as his foot burst with pain, rudely reminding him of the wound. The iron arrowhead had taken a bit of leather from the sandal strap into his flesh with it, and it had already started to fester. Yellow pus leaked around the jagged edges of the wound. It smelled foul.

It took him awhile to remember what he was doing and where he was. There had been a battle, and running, and water. It came together slowly. He remembered making it to the forest and climbing over the pass, but beyond that he could remember nothing else. He had obviously passed out between two boulders but did not know where exactly he was. Crickets and other night insects chirped all around him. A bug crawled out of his hair and down the back of his neck, and he smacked his hand on it sloppily. Then he remembered escaping.

Shame washed over him. He had run away from the field when they needed him the most. Like a baby. Eliam groaned aloud, causing the crickets around him to cease, leaving him alone in the depressing silence. He could not even think of what his father would say.

It had been going so well. He had faced the enemy, done his duty, hauled the water, and never stopped, even when the arrow hit him. Then he had run away without reason. Men were dying bravely, and he was running up the mountain away from them. There was no excuse. He had run like a coward because he was a coward.

He desperately wanted to know what had happened in the fight. Had anyone survived? He gathered his strength and forced himself to his feet.

No water.

He had forgotten water. He had run from the field and not even bothered to steal water. So he was cowardly *and* stupid.

Any day, his father would hear from someone that his son was a coward, and he would spend the rest of his life ashamed of his own son, a coward who wasn't even smart enough to steal water as he fled like a woman.

Eliam considered killing himself. He would end it right then and die, alone and cowardly. He felt the arrow tip in his foot. Proof of what should have been his bravery, a proud wound to show his grandchildren one day. What happened? Where had his courage gone? He didn't even have the courage to kill himself. Then came tears and sobs, and he let himself weep for several moments while he massaged the wounded foot.

After a while the crickets started chirping again. Despite the parching in his throat for water, he managed to start walking. There would be a village if he headed south. He would ask for a physician, and he would drink water, and he would hope that Yahweh would kill him as soon as possible.

Picking his way through the woods, Eliam looked for someone or something to blame for his cowardice. His father had been a brave man. So had his brothers. What had gone wrong with him?

He thought of Jonathan, charging so bravely and futilely into the Philistine ranks, desperate to show his soldiers one last display of courage before he died. Eliam was angry now. Angry at what? Who?

David.

He stopped walking.

David was responsible for this. He was the one who'd brought so much suffering into the land. David was responsible for Jonathan's death.

Eliam cursed. And then he knew what he would do.

The stars were brilliant that night—the most beautiful night in a long time. Despite the horrors of the day, a day of many sorrows that would haunt his thoughts as long as he lived, the night was a wondrous sight.

Gareb crouched on a boulder and watched the fires of the Philistine army in the valley below. He was perched high on one of the peaks of the Gilboa mountains, so high that the wind was constant even when it was calm elsewhere. He loved the high ground and had gone to it in his despair.

Even from high above, Gareb could hear the sounds of revelry and celebration from the Philistine camp. Their awful music wailed incessantly. He heard laughter and shouts and screaming women— women they must have captured before and brought along for the victory celebration. *Which is well earned. We did not have a chance.*

Throbbing pain from the slashes on his back made him wince.

Philistine blades had reached him. He cursed himself. Never expose the back. There was no excuse, not even losing sight of Jonathan. Not even watching him fall.

He pulled his spear up from the ground and stared at the shaft, trying to make out the lettering in the vivid starlight: twenty. The number of men they had killed on that day so many years before at Michmash.

He watched the stars move over the valley of the Philistines, wondering how Yahweh could allow such depravity and idolatry in their land and yet still give them such a beautiful night. The wind carried with it the scent of cedar and terebinth. Many of the Israelite women had put sprigs of saffron in the men's garments before they left to war, to inspire them and remind them of home. Lot of good it did them. Made their bodies smell good over the next few days while the Philistines let their flesh rot in the hot sun. Saffron and rotting flesh. What a smell that would be.

Gareb looked down the pass at the field of battle. He was too far to see the bodies in the darkness, but the patch of grass near the edge of the forest was plainly visible. He had watched the last of it take place in that patch of grass: Saul cornered by the archers, his armor bearer with him. It looked from a distance as if the king had impaled himself at the end. No glory to the enemy. Finally did something noble. Or perhaps he was too cowardly to take the blade while facing his enemy.

The Philistines would cut off Saul's head and display it, along with those of his sons. Jonathan's head would be a fine prize.

The thought disgusted him so much that he retched down the front of his clothing, the bile in his gut rising too fast to be stopped. He choked on it, smelled the sour scent of vomit and blood, and watched it stain dark against the wool. When his gut stopped heaving, he spat out the taste.

He did not look at the other side of the field, just behind where the Israelite lines had broken at last. The hope of Israel had died in that spot. Gareb had seen Jonathan fall, and he wanted never to see the spot again. Yahweh had willed it, and that was that. It had taken an entire company to bring the warrior down. They wouldn't have been able to do it if I had been with him, he thought. He cursed the prince for ordering him away from his side, cursed his rotting flesh to Sheol and so be it. Above all, he cursed Jonathan's foolishness for remaining loyal to his father when he could have seized the throne and restored order.

Gareb had followed Jonathan's final orders; he had run from the field when the final line of Hebrew warriors broke, exactly as he'd been told to, and now he would live with that decision until Yahweh chose to kill him. He wanted that to happen before he had to drag himself into the camp of that cowardly man living among the Philistines. Perhaps he was cursed.

Never leave your master in the day of war. It was the armor bearer's first rule, and he had broken it. Although Jonathan himself had ordered him away, Gareb's heart was heavy with guilt. Many men had with honor died on the field. He should have been one of them, and now Yahweh was punishing him by making him go to David with all the other failures of Israel.

He threw down the spear and watched it clatter across the rocks. The army, what remained of it, would be leaderless. Philistia would subjugate the northern tribes, and eventually the southern tribes would fall in line. Most of the royal line was now dead. The only men worthy of inheriting the throne lay slaughtered in the fields below him. Unified Israel had lasted for the lifetime of only one king. It was an embarrassment to the world. The Egyptians, the Philistines, the Assyrians—all of them would mock and scorn the pitiful band of tribesmen who had briefly tasted freedom after years of chaos.

Only he can stop this ... Yahweh is with him.

Gareb shook his head to forget Jonathan's words and drank in the windy night around him, enjoying the brilliance of the stars over his head for a while longer. He would grieve for the men tomorrow. There was no time for it now. He had to go find the man who brought this upon them all, and he would do it for Jonathan. He would hate it, but he would do it.

He crawled off the boulder and headed south.

Abner, Saul's general, sat on the same ridge.

He fingered a deep cut on the side of his leg, felt the warm blood as it seeped through the wool bandage he had tied around it. The pain had stopped earlier, but the bleeding would not let up. Until it did, he was forced to sit against the tree and wait. He was good at waiting.

When the Philistine archers and charioteers from the valley had found the gentle, unguarded slope that allowed them to attack Israel's army from behind, ending the battle, Abner had slipped away in the confusion. By the time he'd reached the hilltop the battle was over. His army was gone.

His relative Saul was no more. He would need to see to organizing the remnant of the army. When all the generals but himself were dead, he had left the field, as was customary, since it would be up to him to restore order. There were undoubtedly only a few hundred fighters left, but whatever was out there would gather, and he would find them.

Ish-bosheth, the remaining son of Saul, was weak and easily swayed. Abner knew he would need to stiffen him up for the throne. Philistia may have won the day, but the kingdom of Israel would remain as long as Abner had something to do with it.

Abner checked his bleeding again, and thought about David.

He had been there the day the young man killed the giant, had been present in the war councils during reports of his victories. He even respected him. He knew David would come for the throne at any time. That was why he had been serving the Philistines. He would be their vassal. Abner nodded. If he took the throne, David would make a worthy king. But the tribe of Saul, Abner's own tribe of Benjamites, needed to retain the throne. As the smallest tribe, they had the best chance of unifying the people. David was a man of Judah, and Judah was too large and powerful. The northern tribes would never submit to David without another long and bloody civil war.

Abner was getting older. Intrigue and political maneuvering seemed inconsequential to him now. But he would do this final service. He would reorganize the army and retreat with it into the hill country, and once they were strong again, he would hit the invaders harder.

If the usurper from Judah interfered, he would hit him as well.

Part Four

TWENTY-THREE

Benaiah watched the dust rising in front of him, disturbed by the feet of hundreds of men. There was no talking, no noise except the pounding of sandals on the ground. Not the usual laughter. Officers did not even shout orders. David had ordered silence and speed.

Benaiah was at the front of a column formation three men wide. There were twenty soldiers in the bodyguard, assembled in haste and told that they were to follow the chief wherever he went. Benaiah had had no time to organize them yet. Officers had recommended these men based on their service so far, but he would need to conduct a better investigation of each man when they were finished. A foreign king would pay handsomely for an assassination attempt from the inner circle.

David trotted next to him, eyes focused on the road ahead, the great sword strapped to his back. Benaiah watched it rise and fall with his stride, and the effect was calming. It distracted him from thinking about his wife's hair, and how it was probably slipping out from under her shawl in the way he loved. And then the image distorted into smoke and darkness and terror, and rough men were grabbing her, tearing at her. He saw himself leaning against the blade, trying to kill himself. He would have done it, if not for Keth.

When David had spoken to them outside the house, the men had responded. Benaiah had never seen David so determined, and his determination had made the men eager to give chase. A few still whispered threats under their breath, so the Three were tasked with keeping an eye on them.

Outside the city, they had passed through a corridor of valleys that led to the south. There were occasional forests and hills, and they used these to screen their movement from spies. It was land they knew well, having passed through it many times en route to raids. The sun was directly overhead—noonday. There was more than enough light for an assault if they caught up with the Amalekites soon.

He flexed his arms to keep the blood steady. They traveled light, only a ration of water and a bag of food apiece. They would eat what they captured when they captured it.

Benaiah stepped closer to David. "Did those tracks farther back look fresh to you?"

David nodded without looking at him. "They did. They are lazy and sluggish, and they think all of us are still in the north. They have no reason to hurry. They might only be hours ahead."

Benaiah glanced back over his bodyguard and was satisfied that no one had heard him. Too much information given too soon only spread rumors among the troops.

Their marching pace had gradually quickened over the day. His joints and muscles were still tired and painful from the ordeal of the week. His wounds from the lion's claws ached, as if to remind him that they were still there, though it felt like three generations of his family had passed since his fight with the lion in the pit. The Amalekite raiding party he'd destroyed, the days of hard march, the destruction of his home—it was taking its toll, but he pushed it away. None of it mattered. There would be enough there when he needed it, just as there always was.

On his back Benaiah carried his rations and the spear from the strange warrior in the woods. He also carried his war club, the root of solid oak with an embedded stone in the top. It did not kill cleanly. He had chosen it for that reason.

The road followed a winding path through the lowland hills and eventually reached a gorge. Along the creek in the gorge, David ordered the men to fill their water bags and dip their heads. Benaiah sank his own face into the icy water, grateful for the shock, then shook his hair, slinging water over the men nearby. A few muttered at him. He saw that his men had broken into two squads, one staying with David as he paced among the soldiers, the other taking their water break. They would rotate positions. Good men. He had not even told them to do that. He nodded.

As the men lined the banks of the creek to drink, Benaiah heard the voice of a foreigner rise above the noise of the company.

"Is he insane?" the man grumbled. "We've been marching like this all day with no rest. Water or no water, I'm not going any further." The rest of the man's squad seconded him. Within moments, the growing chorus of discontent had spread along the creek bed next to the squad, until the entire company was complaining loudly that they could not go on.

At first, Benaiah could not comprehend how men whose families had been taken as slaves could say something like that. Then he realized that many of those complaining did not have families, and others had only recently joined their army. They were not in prime fighting condition; their feet had not yet developed the calloused soles that could tread upon rocks for weeks. They were the hired blades, and they cared only about loot.

Benaiah whistled for the leader of the bodyguard following

David. The man came back, tunic dirty and scuffed from the days of marching, and nodded his head in respect.

"Tell the leaders that we have trouble," Benaiah said quietly. The man nodded again, with a quick look at the complaining men around them, and walked toward the far side of the clearing at a measured pace to avoid raising suspicion. He pulled David and Josheb aside to give them the message.

Benaiah sighed and turned to the men along the stream near him. "Anyone who does not want to continue, raise his hand," he said in a loud voice.

Dozens of arms rose. Benaiah was stunned at the number. Almost two hundred, easily.

"Why did you come in the first place, then?"

A soldier said, "We're too tired, and the march from Aphek has ruined our feet." He held up a foot, and Benaiah saw that it had indeed become a bloody stump of flesh pocked with blisters and splinters of wood and thorn. He softened a bit. A foot soldier without the use of his feet was worthless. The men without families would not feel compelled to suffer like this.

David walked up beside Benaiah. "What is it?"

"Our pace has been too fast for the new troops. Their feet are ruined. No condition to fight. Look at them."

David perused the ranks. Some of them stared at him carefully, wary of seeing the sword unsheathed against them once more. Many eyes refused to meet his. He inspected them for a moment, then nodded. "All who wish may stay here. You are no use to me in the fight—you would probably only get more men killed. We will bring the families back." There were sighs of relief from the ranks.

Joab stepped up, shock plain on his face. "Sir! You cannot let them—"

David raised a hand. "Contradict me again when I am giving orders, nephew, and you will pray for death. That is my vow."

Joab was taken aback by the rebuke and did not respond. David's face was murderous. Even Benaiah was startled.

Louder, to the group, David said, "Men with useless feet are equally useless in battle, brothers. Do not hold it against them, because your feet might suffer a similar fate before this march is over. It is Yahweh who will give us a victory today, so the size of our force will not matter. Does anyone know the story of Gideon the Judge?" Nods scattered across the group. "He winnowed out his force until there were only a few, and Yahweh crushed the Midianites before them like a man crushes a scorpion."

David called for those who were continuing to reform their ranks. Daylight was limited, and they would need to reach the Amalekite encampment early to plan an assault. Refreshed by the water, men sprang up. Some even called out to their wounded fellows that all would be well.

Benaiah had to smile. Despite their near mutiny back in Ziklag and everything else that made them society's reprobates, most were good troops.

They gathered and moved out, leaving a few officers behind to keep order until they returned. Four hundred of them crawled out of the ravine and kept pace with the jog David set at the front, following a trail of slightly trampled grass and dirt. Benaiah guessed that this path would eventually take them to the trade routes into the south and the lands of Egypt.

Besor Brook, the water flowing beside them in the ravine, would eventually cross the trade routes to the south as well. Whoever led the Amalekites was taking no precautions to cover his trail, apparently assuming no one would follow them. That lack of care led David to allow his men to run in the open, with the scouts ahead and in the forest keeping an eye out for enemy stragglers.

Someone shouted from a field to their left. Two men, road scouts who had been sent ahead to spy the route, were carrying between them a young boy, bedraggled, his head hanging and unmoving. His hair was trimmed short, and he wore only a wrapped cloth around his waist. David motioned them over.

"Sir, this boy was lying in a field along the road ahead. He is alive."

They let him down next to the road and splashed water over his face. It revived him a bit, and he blinked a few times trying to focus on them. Benaiah recognized that he was an Egyptian.

They brought the boy some cakes of figs and clusters of raisins, and he ate them sloppily. David must have recognized his race as well because he began to question him in that language. "Whom do you belong to, and where did you come from?"

The boy, obviously scared, said nothing at first. When David knelt down next to him and repeated the question a little softer, he stared around the group and replied, and Benaiah translated.

"I am Egyptian. An Amalekite slave. I got sick, and my master left me behind three days ago. He was raiding the Kerethites in Judah's lands. And we were in Caleb's lands too, and we burned the Ziklag fortress of the Philistines." When he said the last, some of the men who had been crowding around began to shout angrily, threatening to spear him.

David raised his arm to calm them. "Will you give me details about them?"

Even though the boy hadn't understood the threats, he seemed to sense that he was in danger. "If you swear by your god that no one will hurt me. And do not give me back to my master."

David nodded. "By Yahweh, God of Israel, no harm will come to you."

TWENTY-FOUR

Sherizah watched the debauchery in front of her without emotion. Men paraded around without clothes, pulling at the women among the captives. Men passed around wine, danced heathen dances around campfires, and played on their instruments songs that seemed to Sherizah to have no order or structure.

Benaiah was north, far away. She was the captive of the barbaric man in the tent now. And that hard man had been watching her. She knew that her time with him was coming. She was too weary and frightened to care. She thought about making a run for it, hoping to be brought down with a sword stroke. She might even welcome death.

Benaiah had grown cold to her. His words had been soft once, gentle, soothing her with love. Those words were gone now, as he was always gone. He'd wanted sons, and she had not been able to give them to him. She had given him daughters, but now their faces were lost to her, buried in a part of her mind that she no longer looked into. Their lives had been short, and she hoped that perhaps they had gone to Yahweh. She had long since understood that Benaiah found better company among the men than with her. Grief would be difficult for a man to understand.

She pushed the hair from her forehead. There was nothing to tie it back with, so it flew freely across her face in the slight breeze. There was noise in the tent, and a man emerged, pulling a woman out of the entrance. The woman clawed at the soldier pulling her by the hair and screamed. Dezir, the wife of one of David's men.

Had she been violated? It did not look that way—yet. That had been the strange and nagging thought that followed her all the way from Ziklag. Not one person had been hurt among the Hebrews. No woman had yet been violated, no child harmed, no animals slaughtered. It was impossible to know the raiders' intent.

A guard approached her, and Sherizah saw that it was her time. Before the guard could lay rough hands on her, she stood and walked inside.

The Amalekite chieftain was stuffing roasted pig and bread into his mouth. Next to him was the large man who had first been seen at the city. He was different than the rough Amalekites: his skin was bronze like a burnished shield and gleamed with oil. He wore paint on his eyes and face, and he was almost elegant-looking in his fine linen garments. Were it not for his tremendous size, the largest man she had ever seen, she would have thought him to be a musician or entertainer. He regarded her, as did the chieftain.

"You have a husband?" asked the chieftain. She was startled that the chieftain could speak her language and nodded a response.

"He is a warrior? David's man?"

She nodded.

"They are in the north?"

She repeated her nod but did not look at them. Benaiah had told her long ago that if she was ever captured, to simply obey everything they asked her to do. Just stay alive, he had told her. But for what? To live for what? He was gone anyway.

Another Amalekite walked in and tilted his head in respect to the chieftain. The two men chatted in the Amalekite tongue a moment, and she allowed herself a glance at the furnishings of the tent. It was sparse, except for a pile of cushions stolen from some Philistine city; she recognized the craftsmanship. A torch flickered in a bracket on the center post. Maps were scattered on a short table, and the two men were reclining on the floor against the brightly colored cushions. The chieftain reached up and tore at the meat every so often.

Pigs. Unclean animals.

Sherizah stood, arms crossed at the wrists in front of her, waiting for them to question her again. Her eyes flickered to the giant, then away when she saw that he was watching her. She had sensed him watching her since she entered the tent. He made her uneasy. She seemed to him someone who was to be feared more than any of the others.

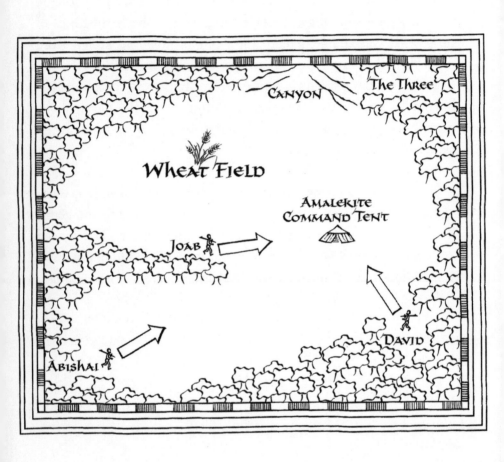

TWENTY-FIVE

There is blood on my face. I wipe it. I see Joab by the burning roof, hold-
ing something in his hand. A head. He smiles.

War, son of Jehoiada, he says. Love it. Drink it deeply.

I nod. Should be harder, killing. Especially women, children. Sher-
izah always asks me if I regret the bloodshed. Yes, Sherizah. No,
Sherizah.

There is David. He speaks to Josheb, Shammah, Eleazar. His mighty
Three. Does he not trust me? Why am I not held in the same regard?
Salty, coppery taste. My blood or enemy blood? Does not matter. Warm
and bitter.

Next to Joab is Abishai; an Amalekite man is kneeling before them.
He is begging for mercy. None would be given. It never is. David is
silent as the sword plunges into the man's neck. Joab spits, pulls the
blade out. Abishai stares at his brother's blade. I hear screams behind
me. Children are watching. I curse their fathers, because I will spend
the rest of my days bringing death to Amalekites. I will make them run

in terror from me, and go to the grave with my sword in their chest, and they will regret the day they took my daughters from me.

Make it quick, Benaiah, says David. Do not drag this out. Club them first, don't let them feel it.

I nod. But I will make them feel it. I will never relent until every one of them is dead.

My beautiful girls gone forever ...

David touched Benaiah on the arm and pointed toward an olive grove at the far right side of the field. "I sent the Three to block their retreat at the mouth of that canyon. They can hide, then step out and defend that narrow gap. We need to let the Amalekites think they can escape that way."

Benaiah nodded. Funneling so many of the Amalekites straight at such a small force would be certain death for lesser men. But that was why they were the Three.

Benaiah and David sat on the edge of a small rise overlooking an enormous wheat field. A grove of trees jutted into the field to their left in the shape of a lance, and from there Joab would lead the attack. The wheat had been trampled and destroyed by the raiding army without regard for martial discipline. The Amalekite camp sprawled across a vast area, all the way to a distant ridge scored by canyons.

Music, played by drunk musicians, wailed without any semblance of order or rhythm. Men laughed and kept the noise coming as if making it louder would solve the problem.

The scouts, men of the tribe of Issachar highly skilled at spying, had given a thorough report. The Amalekite commander had allowed his men to scatter and break ranks for the celebration, and David intended to make him pay for that mistake. Men roved about drunkenly. The sentries posted were staring back toward the fires, envious of their comrades, unwittingly ruining their night vision.

Benaiah scanned the camp for the rest of the captives. There was a tent pitched hastily in the center, and a line of women sat outside. He could not tell if they were the Ziklag captives or others stolen earlier. Children were playing in the dirt nearby, oblivious to the pressing danger. Twilight was coming, and the soldiers in the camp were drinking even more freely, a good thing.

When David and his men had first discovered the camp, they'd all been elated that the captives were still alive. Now they were focused and ready.

Benaiah looked at his fading shadow stretching across the rocks in front of him. The insects had begun to emerge for the night. Not much light left for the slaughter. David whispered something to Joab on his left, who grunted and crawled away with Abishai behind him.

All was now ready. The Three were undoubtedly already sliding forward on their bellies through the trees to their right, outside the view of the sentries, who were not watching anyway. They would wait for Joab while he moved one hundred men through the trees to the left. Abishai would split off with his hundred-man company and post between David and Joab. The two generals would begin their assault into the field of the Amalekite camp, killing everything that moved except the captives and livestock.

When they'd successfully crushed the raiders' left flank and made it to the middle of the wheat field, they would form a perimeter around the surviving captives, and David would lead an assault from the center to meet them. When the Amalekites retreated— running blindly in terror, most likely—David's men would try to funnel them toward the entrance of the canyon, where the Three would be present to block them. They would all spend the rest of the night sweeping the surrounding forest for stragglers.

As they waited for the troops to get into position, David and Benaiah watched the tent around which the women sat despondently. Guards were choosing women to go into the tent so the commander could choose among them. No doubt the rest of the men would split up those remaining among themselves. Benaiah strained his eyes against the distance to see Sherizah, but the women were letting their heads sag in defeat, and he could not spot his wife.

Then he did, at the front of the line near the entrance of the tent.

He seized David's arm, and David patted his hand, as if he'd noticed her already. David was probably searching for his own wives.

Sherizah was barely visible between the celebrating soldiers. Benaiah fought the urge to rush forward as he stared at her, feeling something wrench in his spirit. He felt the weight of all the years he'd neglected her. The times he had abandoned her for the company of his men, the times he had left her alone for months after the births of the girls. *Do not think of that now. Kill Amalekites first.*

Joab crawled forward on his chest, feeling the scratching undergrowth across his face. His men were disciplined and followed him without complaint through the roughest terrain he could have chosen. Their sentries weren't even watching, but Joab led his men with caution anyway.

Joab finally stopped, and Abishai, crawling behind him, halted as well. The older brother pointed to his right, toward the field of the encampment and a hedge of thick brush. Using hand gestures, he indicated that Abishai should line up his men in that hedge. Abishai nodded and gave the signal for "I understand." He then repeated the orders back to Joab, who dismissed him with a pat on the shoulder when he'd finished. Abishai turned to his adjutant and relayed the commands, repeating the process.

When both of them had turned to go, Joab continued leading his men along the dry creek bottom he had found on his scout. It disguised their movements perfectly. Bramble undergrowth and thorns snagged his tunic. Rocks scraped his bare legs, but he did not notice, his mind intent on preparation for the first assault. Sweat dripped down the side of his face and stained the collar of his tunic. He wiped it from his face, smudging the dirt into his eyes. Sounds poured through the woods, awful wailings of strange instruments. Joab ignored it and focused on the movement of his men.

One hundred men. A full company. They needed to hurry to the grove of trees David pointed out earlier, sticking out into the field like a peninsula. They needed to attack before light was fully gone. Once the ambush had been ignited, darkness would be their ally, but maneuvering was critical in the opening moments, and for that, all David's troops would have to be able to see.

From those trees, Joab would launch his men forward in a lightning strike, cutting the camp in half and preventing them from regrouping. He would be at the command tent before the Amalekites even knew what was happening. Joab thought of his iron blade gliding through the rib cage of the barbarian leader, and the pleasure of it made him pull himself even harder through the undergrowth.

David would be impressed with that. Joab would become commander of the army that would set David on the throne. If David let him, Joab would control Judah with ease and then set out to subjugate the northern tribes. Benjamite men upset with Saul would join them. They would need Benjamin's skill with bows and slings.

There were good soldiers in those parts. Joab had fought with them. They could be ruthlessly effective if properly led. He would unite them under David eventually, but first he would teach them a lesson. Saul had made many friends early in his reign, and many would remain loyal. Abner, Saul's general, would need to be won over. He would make a dangerous enemy if not.

Jonathan frightened Joab. Of all the problems that might stand between Joab and his ambitions, Saul's son was chief among them. David would want to give him mercy because they were old friends, and David would appoint Jonathan commander of the army. Joab was sure of it.

Jonathan will need to be dealt with, Joab thought as he crawled forward. An accident could be arranged, perhaps a hunting or a training accident. Asahel, Joab's younger brother, was eager to prove himself. Joab would put him in charge of coming up with a plan. Female assassin? They used them in Egypt.

Joab wiped sweat from his brow. *No, Jonathan is not susceptible to women like David is.* In fact, Jonathan had no vices that Joab was aware of. Loyalty? He was blindly loyal. That could be used. Joab let it go, deciding he needed more time to think about it. The battle came first.

He reached the edge of the grove. The deepening dusk had covered their approach. No one among the Amalekites looked even remotely alert. From this point, he could at last see the entire field. They were spread out to the right of the forest peninsula, in the direction of David and across the center of the field where the command tent was. Now he saw that the Amalekite camp extended to the left farther than they originally guessed.

The anxious eyes of his men watched him. Many had families in that camp. The light was almost gone. Amalekite sentries nearby guzzled wine from skins, arguing over female prisoners, playing the peculiar game with sticks and rolled hide he had seen them play before in their towns. They were woefully unprepared. No defensive strike teams, no preparation of any kind.

He mentally walked himself one more time through the plan. Archers would fire first. A ram's horn would blow, signaling the charge, and they would sprint into the camp, heavy weapons in the front ranks, closely followed by light infantry who would kill any enemies who had survived the charge. Then they would form a perimeter around the tent, shielding the women and children from the battle, so that David's company could fight with more abandon. Wait for David. Then flank outward and clean up.

He made each of his officers repeat the plan in a whisper since it was getting too dark to see hand signals. Satisfied that they had it, he let them relay it down the line.

Moments passed. Noises and music continued.

Blood was about to be spilled. Blood for Judah. For a new Israel. Blood for his beloved land.

Benaiah hated the waiting before a fight, that intolerable time after the orders had been given and all they could do was sit until all of the pieces of the attack were ready. It left him alone with his thoughts. Something he did not want.

He tried to think through the plan again to distract himself and kill time. Touch nothing unclean. Take no plunder—yet. Don't stop moving, at any time or for any reason, no matter who dies and no matter what you hear. Cut off heads when possible; Amalekites are terrified of going into the afterlife headless. Word needs to reach their homeland that an attack on David and his God is certain violent death, carrying on into eternity.

Benaiah was confident that each man knew his duty. The Gadites were particularly enthusiastic about the urge to remove heads. Benaiah liked them, truly hard men who had crossed the Jordan in full flood.

Don't think of Sherizah. Focus.

The teams were in place. They were well trained and motivated, driven far beyond what they had ever experienced, since it was their loved ones in the valley below. David's orders had been clear: finish the battle before finding your wives. Any man caught lingering with his family while the fight was going would be speared.

Would she still want him? After all?

He shook his head. *Focus on something else.*

The Hittite regiment was kneeling in a line to his right. They had the inglorious but necessary job of weapon resupply, and Keth had them ready. They would run weapons to the front as needed, replacing those that would dull or break from cracks and defects. This was a new, untested tactic of David's invention, and this would be the first chance to deploy it, to determine if it would be used in the future.

The Hittites were an unexpected provision in the race to master ironworks. Bronze was out for good; no more bronze spearheads bending against shields. They needed iron. Now they had hope that the rumors of a new method of forging were true and that they would be able to eventually battle Philistines with iron of their own rather than beg them for it.

David was sitting still as stone next to him. The waiting never seemed to bother him.

A strange man, Benaiah thought as he studied David in the growing darkness. Even now he was humming. Probably another song of praise.

"Does Yahweh ... forgive a man if he fails?" Benaiah had asked it aloud without thinking. Thankfully, he saw that none of the other men had heard him because they were too busy preparing themselves, closing their eyes against all distractions and emotions that would dull their weapon strikes.

David did not avert his gaze from the impending battlefield but nodded. "He does. None more so than myself."

It was an odd and unexpected response. Benaiah waited.

"Many black things hide in my own heart, brother," David said. "Perhaps that is why I am so grateful for his mercy."

Benaiah watched the lines of Amalekite troops pitching tents for the night, those who were already drunk with wine, unaware of the death about to befall them. Sherizah had disappeared into the command tent not long after his glimpse of her—at least he believed it was Sherizah, but he could have been wrong.

The slope was open ground and flat; they would be charging onto the flats, leaving behind the high ground against a numerically superior force. Not a good battle plan.

Perhaps that is why I am so grateful for his mercy.

"How do you know when he is speaking to you?" Benaiah asked.

David searched the grove for Joab's men before responding. "Sometimes he tells me my path as clearly as I am talking to you now. Other times, I have to decide the best course of action and then pray for him to stop me if it is not of him. I learned that from Jonathan. Consider it carefully, pray for mercy, attack violently."

Benaiah raised the subject no one ever wanted to with David. "Do you miss him?"

"I do." David answered quickly, as though it had slipped out before he could filter and measure it.

"And Michal?"

"And Michal."

"When did you first know the covering?"

At first he thought David had simply chosen to ignore the question, since several moments went by before the chief even acknowledged him again. David seemed to have forgotten their conversation and was staring intently at Joab and Abishai's position, as if he did not trust them to follow his orders.

"When I was a shepherd," David said at last, "in my youth, I saw my brothers dealing with problem sheep. I thought it was harsh, what they did, but later I saw why it was necessary.

"The ones that are particularly rebellious need special attention. If the sheep wanders away or walks toward a cliff, the shepherd normally strikes it on the nose gently with his staff and warns it not to continue. This works for many of them.

"Other sheep need to be punished more strictly. Some need to be whipped. I used to take a branch of sycamore and strip it bare, then whip the legs of the sheep until it stopped running. Most of the time that worked.

"Every few years, though, a sheep would need more drastic punishment. During the year I left my father's house to join Saul's army, one in particular would not stop going into the forest. I would strike it, hold it, never let it out of my sight, but it kept fleeing to the darkest part of the woods.

"It wandered out into a storm one night. I was huddled over my fire in the cave, stranded when the wadi overflowed, blocking the path home. I pulled all of the sheep into the cave with me to wait it out. That sheep was not among them, of course.

"So I went after it. Left the others in the cave and stumbled through the lightning and the heavy rain. I finally saw it huddled under a tree. Any predator could have killed it. I picked it up and sang to it to calm it down as I walked back to the cave.

"When I arrived, the first thing I did was snap its leg over a rock. The sheep was bleating and terrified, but I just let it flounder for a moment.

"When I was sure the leg was truly broken, I sang to it again. A silly little song I had composed for them one night after a bear attack in order to calm them. And as I sang, I wrapped the leg tightly with a cloth.

"That sheep couldn't walk for days. I had to carry it. But I carried that sheep until the leg healed, and for the rest of that sheep's life, it never left my side. It went where I went and did what I did. It grew quite old and produced a large amount of wool for us.

"That night was the first time I understood the covering. The covering is the fire. It is the strength, courage, and power Yahweh equips us with. It girds a man's loins when he needs it and lets a man know that Yahweh forgives him when he fails. It snaps our legs when we need it. It speaks Yahweh's wise counsel, like the woman in Gath that we saw that night. It comes only from Yahweh, who alone is the shepherd that we need."

Benaiah shifted his weight against the rock and shivered at the unexpected chill. He wondered at how strange the weather had been recently, wondered what the story of the sheep had meant.

"Something happened several days ago before I returned to the ranks," Benaiah said. "When I fought the lion in that village. There was a figure, a huge man, black as night, and I was frightened by him.

"But then another warrior came, and the dark figure left. The warrior spoke to me and encouraged me, gave me orders to rescue that village, then disappeared. Do you know who they might have been?"

David replied, "I have seen dark figures as well. And I have seen men who helped me. I do not know who they are, but I know that they come from someplace outside of us, from the presence of Yahweh himself. There are good and bad among them, and I have been helped by some, as you have described. We will see them again.

"I think that the warriors who have aided me are sent to us much like the covering is. Yahweh determines what we need and sends it in the day of war, sometimes even without our asking, though I have found that asking is what he wants from us."

Benaiah was confused by the answer. "But why the day of war? Why do we only ask for it then? Why not when a man is in his field plowing? Why not when he is with his family, or when he has left them and wants them to be safe and protected? Why not every day?"

"Every day *is* the day of war."

Benaiah lowered his face into his hands. The wasted years of his life crept over him in the quiet darkness of the trees and the ridge. His neglected wife. His children. The arms of his mistress. War. Death. Vengeance. *They* had been his mistress, and their embrace had been warm.

He was glad that the wetness around his eyes was hidden from view. Joab would be attacking at any time, and he needed to prepare.

David checked the line of men behind them and counted them once more, eyes searching for any of the stragglers as if, Benaiah noticed, he was looking for one of his sheep.

TWENTY-SIX

Josheb strained to hear over the noise of the camp. It had sounded like a ram's horn, but he wasn't sure. He looked at his two companions and gave a slight shrug. If it was the shofar, then—*there it was.*

A volley of stones and arrows poured out of the woods, piercing and pummeling the surprised Amalekites. Darkness was close, and the smoke from the celebration fires obscured his vision, but Josheb could see the far side of the encampment just well enough to sense the confusion and panic. The attack had come as a complete surprise to the Amalekites. Joab's men were pouring arrows into the camp, and the men close to the trees were dying noisily.

Josheb saw the soldiers nearest to them look up from their fires, as if they heard something across the camp but were unsure if it was just a rowdier celebration by their comrades. Those who had been drinking stared dumbly at each other, but the sober ones were instantly alert.

There were shouts; men began pointing. A few of them finally started looking for their weapons. But all evening they had been dropping them in irresponsible places, and the drunken soldiers would never find their weapons now that darkness had fallen.

Josheb relished it. This was the least-prepared army they had yet faced. Surely Yahweh was going before them into battle, and it would be a slaughter. He closed his eyes, listened to his spirit, told himself not to be overconfident, but to focus. Focus on the speed. *Speed is everything.* His arms and legs were ready from the fiery proving ground of David's army. They would not fail him if his mind was right. Eleazar was on his left, Shammah was on his right, Shammah praying aloud. *Wait for it.*

Eleazar said something. Josheb did not hear it. "What?"

"When they reach the tent?"

"Yes. Or if they start retreating this way."

The spear was steady enough in his hand, and it felt good to him. The spear had a point on both ends. Better for sticking and removing quickly. Better for engaging multiple enemies. *That is what we do: we engage multiple enemies and show the men that Yahweh is in the battle and that numbers do not matter.* Drive the spike through the armor. Hit, withdraw, check the man, engage again, move faster next time.

When it began for the three of them, it would be about instinct and speed. His conditioning would hold all night if necessary; many hours of training runs up the mountains with the two beside him had assured that. The arrows abruptly stopped, and then came the cry of a hundred angry warriors charging out of the woods and smashing against the left flank of the perimeter. *Don't move yet, just listen. It will come.*

Joab was attacking.

Joab flung his shield forward and struck the first man's skull. As the man fell, Joab planted his foot on his chest and swung the sword across the man's throat. He kept moving. "Stay in the line! Stay in your line!"

The men were already through the perimeter, but darkness was making it difficult to stay in a line as they charged. They couldn't see obstacles until they were on top of them, and some of the men tripped over discarded satchels and weapons.

Another man appeared. Joab stabbed at him quickly but missed, and he was forced to duck the return swipe. There was a shout, and the man swung again, but Joab was ready. He dove to his left side and crouched. The fighter was skilled. A lance flashed by out of the blackness, glancing across Joab's hip.

Joab clutched the wound, forced to retreat momentarily from the fight. There were screams and sounds of men dying everywhere around him. Smoke blew across from a campfire, clouding his vision. There was the Amalekite—charging him through the night again. Joab parried and brought his small shield up to the man's face, but his opponent saw it coming. With a grunt, he dove low himself and plunged the tip of a sword into Joab's thigh.

The Hebrew yelled in frustration at his inability to kill the man. His fighters were pressing hard toward the command tent, encountering little resistance—but lacking leadership from Joab, they were beginning to slow down. Joab tried to shout commands to them but was forced to stagger backward from the Amalekite's attacks.

Rage flooded his mind. He threw his shield forward in a feint and aimed low with the sword—but missed. The small man moved impossibly fast and never let Joab slip a cut through. *Feint, catch the blade with the shield, retreat a step.*

Joab too was fast but found himself feeling strangely weaker. Only a few moments into the battle, he was tiring. It made him furious. The man was too quick and too skilled. Joab spun to his right and ran toward a small tent, hoping to get a barrier between them.

Joab's troops called for him, and he could see their confusion through the flaming light of the camp. They were losing the advantage of surprise! They had to keep moving! He reached the small tent, searched for the relentless soldier, and spotted him appearing out of the darkness. Joab had a good angle this time, but again the man disappeared. Joab shouted and spun, searching for him.

Behind him! The lance struck Joab's side, an indirect hit, just a cut in the flesh, but he felt warm blood erupt through his war tunic. He finally landed a blow with his own blade against the man's face. It was with the blunt side, not lethal, but enough to buy him a moment to regroup as the man clutched his shattered nose.

The Amalekites wore heavy armor, stolen; that should have given the Hebrews a speed advantage, but Joab couldn't get his body to respond as quickly as he needed. This warrior was halting the entire flank charge almost by himself, and Joab felt angry and embarrassed.

He checked his wounds while the man spluttered. Surface only, nothing serious, but the blood was dripping down his thighs. His wounds burned, and he was annoyed at the unexpected pain. Thick dirt kicked up from the fighting caked around his wounds.

The Amalekite warrior had recovered from the hit and was now glaring at him from twenty paces away. Despite the blood from his broken nose, the man did not look tired or concerned in any way. And the more Joab looked at him, the less he looked like an Amalekite.

David pointed toward the left flank, where Joab was attacking. Benaiah saw them crush through the perimeter almost without slowing, but then Joab's men stopped. The surprise had been complete—why had they stopped? *Press it, Joab, now!*

It was too dark to see individual warriors; he could not make out Joab from that distance. The enemy was still so bewildered by the surprise assault that, despite the slowed attack, some stood looking at one another, mounting no defense. A few carried on laughing and eating, some were so drunk they kept pulling at the female captives, unaware they were under attack. Only a few began to search for weapons and shout warnings.

The assault led by Abishai was still pressing hard. Benaiah and David searched hard for Joab through the smoke and darkness, seeing only glimpses of men's faces as they ran by a campfire.

David leapt up and shouted over the noise to Benaiah as he ran, "Wait until you see them reach the tent, then attack!"

Benaiah jumped up as well, wincing at his legs' stiffness from the cold night of waiting. "Sir, we are your guard; we need to come with you!" he shouted back.

"Later, not now! Meet me in the center!"

Benaiah saw him disappear into the hedge of shrubs down the hill toward Joab's position.

Sherizah had been in the tent for hours.

Other women had been brought in, groped, inspected, and removed, but she was kept inside the whole time. She kept her face toward the ground as they continued to question her, stealing occasional glances from the corner of her eye. No, she had not seen them forging iron. No, she did not know when they would return. No, she did not know if they were planning more raids.

The giant never spoke. The Amalekite chief was letting a deputy question her, because he was getting drunk and was no longer very interested in what she said. He grabbed a fresh wineskin, looking increasingly groggy after filling his belly with the offensive meat. She held her left hand tightly with her right, as she always did when she was nervous. The Egyptian stared at her body the entire time she stood in front of them; she could feel his eyes on her, and she gripped her hand tighter.

She had finally guessed him to be Egyptian. Egyptians frequently traveled the trade routes near Ziklag, and she had seen their caravans come through many times with exotic spices and colored linens. They were an elegant race in speech and dress. This man was no different, but his tremendous size seemed very odd to her. Such a large man, carrying weapons twice as big as normal, looked strange wearing delicate garments.

The shouting outside the tent grew louder, and then a man burst through the tent flap. He blurted out a sentence, and the reclining men immediately sat up, then leaped to their feet, the chief slower because of the wine. They charged past her and through the flap. After pausing a moment, she followed them outside.

The Amalekite army ran around scattered, drunk, wailing noisily, swinging at phantoms. To her right, she heard the unmistakable sound of metal clashing. An attack? The Egyptian darted past her toward a tent a short distance away. Sherizah was too shocked to move and could only listen to the growing fray at the edge of the camp, growing louder. The sound of men dying and screaming in death was everywhere. Bodies scuffled through the dust and the night, the dust glowing eerie orange as it reflected the fires.

The women from Ziklag, several hundred of them, were lying on the ground next to her. David's wives, Abigail and Ahinoam, sat holding their knees to their chests, faces anxious.

There was a horrible crashing sound nearby. A soldier had tripped over a log, knocking over a rack of spears and shields. Chaos and confusion everywhere. Who was attacking them? She finally spoke loudly to Abigail. "Who are they?"

"I do not know. Keep your head down, Sherizah!" She spoke with authority, and Sherizah obeyed. She knew that even David listened to her when she spoke, and David was a hard man.

Sherizah fell to her knees and crawled next to them. Abigail rallied the captive women and children toward herself. She shouted for everyone to lie still and not flee, to avoid being hit by arrows and blades.

The Egyptian appeared with a bundle tied to his back and in his hand a spear that looked as if it weighed more than she did. His enormous palm closed painfully on her arm, and she screamed as he pulled her up as effortlessly as if she was a doll. He dragged her stumbling behind him, and the other women screamed her name.

They wove through the tents and campfires. Sherizah tripped, biting her tongue and tasting the coppery blood taste. His grip was painful.

Sober Amalekites, charging toward the commotion, stopped when they saw them. The Egyptian bellowed. "You are finished here—but if you come with me you will live!"

Several of the men turned without pausing and ran beside them through the camp. Sherizah tripped every few steps over a spear shaft or passed-out soldier, but the giant kept holding her up, seemingly without effort. He steered the group away from the battle toward escape. She heard a scream and turned.

Two of the Amalekite soldiers following the Egyptian had grabbed Deborah and Rizpah, the wives of Josheb and Eleazar, for themselves. Deborah screamed again and stuck her finger in her captor's eye. The man cursed and threw her down. He slapped her hard across the head, then pulled her by the hair and dragged her after the group.

Sherizah felt like she was running through a mud bog. Her limbs and thoughts were moving too slowly. Everything around her was too slow and yet so very fast at the same time, and she could not force herself out of the bog to think clearly.

They leapt and ran, the women crying and the soldiers cursing, between tents, around passed-out soldiers, past the noise of battle and toward the black edge of the encampment.

Shammah's eyes were still closed. Eleazar paced behind them. Josheb was standing and staring at the camp. Joab's men had not yet reached the command tent; too much time had gone by, and now surprise had been lost. "We need to hit them. Now," Eleazar said as he walked back and forth.

Shammah opened his eyes. Arrows filled the quiver on his back, and a blade was tucked in his belt. He had been concentrating on the weapons and how to move them efficiently. Not slow, not fast—efficient.

All of them had trimmed their beards that afternoon while they waited for nightfall, and Shammah, regretting it now because he believed Yahweh blessed a man with a full beard, combed at the remaining hair on his face. "No, the tent must fall first. Do not be overeager."

Eleazar swore. "I always hated ambushes."

Earlier, Josheb had pointed out a group of figures slipping out of the camp and disappearing into a wadi some distance away. They had decided to let them go. It was only a handful. If they moved from their position too soon, the Amalekites might be able to escape into the canyon behind them.

Shammah closed his eyes again, concentrating on keeping his

breath steady. It was always this way, he thought. Even the hardest man needed a few moments before the fight.

You train my arms for war, you train my arms for war.

David pulled the second sword off of his back and prayed louder as he ran, feeling the fire beginning to come over him. *Yes, Yahweh, bring it to me now on this day.* His sandals were steady on the rocks. Black everywhere. He could see the flames through the trees and ignored the slapping branches. Both swords were in his hands and ready as he ran.

Bursting into the clearing, he saw a warrior facing away from him, toward the command tent. He was not watching his position, and David made him pay for it with his life. The blade flashed, and the Amalekite flew backward.

He took careful aim at the next man and drove the Philistine sword between his ribs. He spun with both blades and dropped two more as they tried to defend the camp.

He saw the line of Abishai's men to his right and decided he would scold them later for missing the four soldiers he had just killed when they swept through the area. Sloppy soldiering he could not tolerate.

You train my arms for war. By you I can run upon a troop. By you I can pass through the valley of the shadow.

Joab's line was ahead to the left, still fighting their way forward but far too slowly. The command tent should have been taken already, but David could not see what was stopping them, and he could not find Joab.

Then he spotted him. Joab was circling an Amalekite warrior, and even though he could not see him clearly, David felt a tug of apprehension in his spirit. The fire raged in his heart. Danger? Warning?

He slowed to a trot to make sense of it. The fire roared so heavily that he was forced to stop. His ears rang, and his skin crawled with restrained power waiting to be loosed.

He felt his body pulled between two forces that wanted to burn him or push him forward. There was no pain, only the sensation of desperate struggle within him as he watched the Amalekite fighter circling with Joab. Then the heat spoke to him as it always did, and he closed his eyes and felt it, and knew what to do.

He gathered himself, afraid but ready. *You promised victory, now let me claim it, God of my fathers, and do not let the adversary prevail.*

Joab, clearly distraught now, tripped over a bundle of pelts hidden in the dark and thudded to the ground. David hurled the smaller sword through the night toward the enemy warrior, who saw it coming and blocked it with a shield.

David leaped over Joab, dodged the warrior's first attack, and swung the sword of the Philistine giant toward the man's side. The fighter saw it just in time to roll away, and the great sword struck the dirt. David yanked it back and took several quick steps away from the fighter.

The man was illuminated clearly now. This was no Amalekite soldier he was battling. He had seen these figures before.

Joab had regained his feet and charged into battle alongside him, but David held up his hand and shouted, "Go to your men. You will die if you remain here!"

Joab started to protest, but David turned on him, anger flashing, "Get back to your men!"

Joab left.

The fighter charged, and David dodged low and away. He stuck his leg out, missed the trip, then had to pull it back as the other man swung down a weapon with straps that he had pulled from out of nowhere. It kicked up dust as it missed and struck the ground. David saw metal shards attached to the leather straps, and the thought of them ripping his flesh open made him blanch.

The fighter began to set his feet for another strike, but David leapt toward him, caught him off balance, and the two of them fell together. David hit him on the mouth with the hilt of his sword, then pulled the leather weapon out of the warrior's grip. He pushed himself off the man and rolled. David tossed the leather straps into the darkness.

But then the warrior was on him, attacking relentlessly, too fast to be controlled. David felt sudden desperation. The man moved too fast, was not tiring, and David felt the heaviness of Goliath's sword suddenly return—it felt like it weighed as much as a yoke. His wrists burned.

The warrior slowed the assault for a moment, and David caught the man's leg and tripped him, then spun away to get some distance.

"Adversary," David said, "Yahweh has declared this day as holy for victory. In his name, be gone!"

The fighter crawled back to his feet and stood silently for a moment, watching David, blood smearing his face, which showed no expression. David held Goliath's sword at eye level, strength returning and warming his wrists. He stared hard at the man's eyes. The warrior rubbed his hand across his beard and wiped the blood off on his armor.

David shook his head quickly to fling the sweat from his brow. His eyes were blurry from the wind swirling from the escarpment above. "Adversary, in the name of Yahweh and by his great power, be gone!" David's free hand fell to his waist and he pulled out the sling. He held the cords between his fingers and let the pouch drop next to his knees. David saw his enemy's eyes glance at the sling. David had not intended to use his old shepherd's weapon this night. It was too dark and the combat was too close. But it had the desired effect. *So that none will ever forget that the battle is the Lord's.*

The fighter tipped his head slightly, as if acknowledging him, then walked away into the darkness.

David lowered his sword and took several deep breaths to steady his nerves. *You train my arms for war, you train my arms for war, bless you for your covering. Thank you for testing me. Forgive me for leaving your council fires.*

He prayed quickly and with urgency. Whatever came into his head, he gave thanks for. He stood a moment to breathe, then sprinted forward, tucking the sling back into his waist and keeping out the blade of the giant he had slain in his youth.

Benaiah watched the dimly lit blanket of the Amalekite command tent begin to waver. Joab's men had begun to slash at the ropes holding it up. The firelight was failing, since the fires were no longer being stoked, and it was difficult to see, but Benaiah could tell that Joab's men had surged forward again, so whatever David had done had worked. The two companies on the flank were annihilating the drunken raiders. Any who tried to surrender were butchered.

The clanging and clamoring increased. There were shouts, and then the dark shadow of the command tent collapsed in a terrific burst of dust and fragments of animal hide. Joab's men had finally formed a line.

He bellowed aloud and jumped to his feet. The men echoed him, and surrounded by the sound of battle, they charged down the hill. Benaiah choked away the fear and ignored Sheol, because his turn had come and the men would be counting on him. There was nothing left to do this night but kill Amalekites.

It was the only thing he did well.

TWENTY-SEVEN

Joab cut the final length of rope holding the tent up and darted out of the way as it collapsed in a great, heaving pile of animal hide. The smoke increased as the fires caught hold of the material. There were more shouts, and the sound of men coughing while dying, but the only ones dying were Amalekites. He had not lost a man yet, a development so shocking that he had yelled at the officer who reported it to him. But a check of the squads revealed that it was true. To have lost not a single man? Was Yahweh present after all?

Abishai rushed up. "Where have you been? What took so long?"

"Never mind. Keep the perimeter formed and wait for the second strike."

He ignored Abishai's confused look and stepped over the tent ropes toward the circle of captive women and children. In the firelight, he recognized Abigail sitting at the front of the group.

Relief washed across her face when she saw him. "Joab! Where is my lord David?"

"He attacks behind us. Is everyone here?"

"No," she replied, looking around. "Deborah, Rizpah, and Sherizah were taken when the assault began. By a huge man, not an Amalekite."

Joab swore. He walked past her and grabbed another soldier eyeing the group, probably searching for his own family. "Hold this line. Go nowhere until the orders come."

The man nodded absently, eyes still searching the huddled women. Joab kept walking, then began to trot, anxious. When he reached the other side of the group, he had a clear view beyond the smoldering ruins of the tent.

The line formed by his and Abishai's men was tight, and despite his delay earlier, things had gone exactly according to plan. Both companies were wound in a circle. Each man had ignored the urge to wade through the crowd of captives to find his own; instead, they readied themselves by facing the battle.

Joab looked toward the shadowy hills and forest from which they'd come. He heard the commotion of Benaiah's flank attack but still could not see it. The Amalekite soldiers had abandoned all discipline and were actually running away. He smiled.

Out of the darkness behind him walked David, Goliath's broadsword drawn. Joab watched him stride past the group of women and nod at his wives Abigail and Ahinoam.

Remarkable discipline. He told the men not to go to them, and neither does he.

"Joab, hold this line until Benaiah gets here. When he arrives, take your company and leave Abishai and the rest of the men to guard the women. He won't like it, but make sure he does it."

"What about the Philistine captives?"

"Guard them too. Everyone returns with us."

David turned and disappeared into the night before Joab could speak again. He wiped a finger over his eye; sweat and grime were seeping in and burning.

Who was that warrior from before?
Not now. The line.
He looked in the direction of Benaiah's attack.

Shammah checked his arrows once more. The arrowheads were solid iron. They would penetrate light armor with great effectiveness. The first of the Amalekites, seeing that their command tent had fallen and deciding to make a hasty departure, were now approaching the Three, and Shammah's bow was poised and ready. The sheep's-gut cord was rough on his calloused fingertips as he touched it, notched the first arrow, and waited for a target to materialize out of the black expanse of the field.

Only what is necessary and nothing more. Yahweh, God of my fathers, only what is necessary and nothing more. "Pray day and night to your God," his father had told him. *Offer praise to our God and arrows to our enemies.*

Josheb and Eleazar both jumped as a man appeared next to them—a fleeing Amalekite, drunk and terrified. In one practiced motion, Shammah acquired his target, drew the bowstring, and released. The arrow buried itself in the man's chest. He fell to his side, confused, knowing that something had struck him but unsure what or how. Josheb vaulted over the boulders and finished him off before he could react further.

The three of them leaped to their feet and began to charge forward through the darkness. Black figures of fleeing men were highlighted now against the fiery glow of the encampment, so Shammah, on the run, fired his next arrow at the closest one. As soon as it left, he jerked another out of his quiver and heard the twang as it snapped free.

Another arrow, another target, then another. Josheb and Eleazar kept pace with him, waiting to get closer to the enemy before using their weapons. Shammah loosed arrow after arrow until the quiver was empty. He was the only man in David's army who could shoot accurately while running.

"Close up!" Josheb shouted. The three had fought together so many times that they operated by instinct. Hundreds of enemy soldiers were moving toward them now, probably thinking that they could salvage something from the defeat by killing these isolated warriors.

Shammah let Josheb slip in front and to the left of him while Eleazar covered their left flank—a perfect wedge, with Shammah taking the right flank. They would burst through the line of charging soldiers and separate, with each drawing enemies toward himself. For the crash through the line, they would need heavier weapons, like—

"Weapon change! Pikes!" Josheb shouted.

Shammah tossed aside his bow and pulled the pike shafts from the leather quiver on his back. The Three did not use armor bearers because none could keep up with them. Shammah was the biggest of them, and his style of the *abir* was built on strength, so he carried the extra weapons for the group.

Shammah tossed a pike across to Eleazar and handed one to Josheb. Then he held the tip of his own out as he ran through the night, approaching the fleeing soldiers bearing down on them, and he thought of his father's words. *Strength, courage, honor; love those things, my son. Walk humbly.*

The wood was cold in his grip. The enemy was close.

Only what is necessary and nothing more.

The thunderous sound of two hundred more angry warriors racing across the camp split the night air. Benaiah's men smashed into the remnants of the Amalekite perimeter like a herd of hungry predators, desperate for vengeance, cutting down soldier after terrified soldier like so many stalks of wheat.

For a moment, the foreign army looked as though it might make a stand. The Amalekite soldiers to Benaiah's right had not been drinking, and most seemed able to find their arms. But their resistance didn't last long—under the murderous hate of David's army, every Amalekite abandoned his position and fled.

The enemies stumbled and blundered over cookware and packs. Livestock bleated. A few men lashed out at their attackers in their blind fear and killed each other instead. Those too drunk to understand what was happening swung their swords at any shape. Smoke was so thick that many Amalekites thought they were fighting shadowy phantoms from the netherworld. The war cries of the attackers were in coordinated and perfect unison, as David had trained them, giving the impression of a vast force of many thousands of possessed souls.

Benaiah's men surged forward until they came to the collapsed war tent Joab's men had surrounded. David's army was now concentrated in the middle of the camp. The captains met in the center, next to the elated families. To the amazement of them all, not a man had been lost yet.

Benaiah and Joab, panting, bloody, knelt next to a dying fire and began to reform the attack. Benaiah had not expected such resounding success. Even so, the fragments of the shattered Amalekite force had been pushed and channeled into the canyon where the Three held position. Brushing the ground at his feet clear, he hastily set up several sticks and pebbles, representing the positions of all the forces as well as he could, with Joab's assistance. Joab's replies to Benaiah's questions were terse, and Benaiah sensed that something was wrong. But this was not the time for it. When Joab answered too vaguely on the number of men attached to the north flank, Benaiah yelled at him to focus.

In a sudden rage, Joab punched him in the face.

Stunned, Benaiah could only stare dumbly. Enraged, before he could stop himself, Benaiah kicked Joab's knee with such force that Joab fell.

Benaiah tried to hold himself back, but the kick had felt so good he wanted to kick Joab again, to bury his foot into Joab's throat. He wanted blood—wanted it so badly that he didn't care about the shrieking women and children watching them fight. He only wanted to pummel this arrogant man until his face poured blood.

The two of them scuffled like rabid dogs, without strategy or effectiveness, fueled only by hatred for the other. After several violent seconds, a powerful arm grabbed Benaiah's tunic and jerked him away from Joab.

Joab, embarrassed for the second time that night, glared at Benaiah with such loathing that Benaiah almost shook off the hand restraining him and attacked again.

"Stop this now! Control yourselves! You're behaving like children!" It was David's voice, and David's hand that held him, no doubt concerned that Benaiah might kill his nephew. "Son of Jehoiada, I order you to control yourself!"

Benaiah felt his control returning. Battle lust made a man do foolish things, made him kill and rape without knowing what he was doing. But Benaiah had been trained to resist it, and now he had failed to do so. He thought of Sherizah and how close she must have been. Had she seen the fight? He wanted to see her so desperately that he cursed discipline and order.

David, still holding tightly to Benaiah's waist, spoke urgently into his ear: "Benaiah, come with me."

Benaiah let David lead him a short distance away, near a pile of enemy dead to which the men were dragging corpses.

"Your wife is not among the captives. Abigail said she and two others, Deborah and Rizpah, were taken."

Benaiah blinked. Sherizah gone. Yahweh had taken her from him once more.

"We need to press the attack here through the night, but you may take Eleazar and Josheb and find the women," David said.

"What about your bodyguard?"

"Yahweh protects me this night."

Benaiah wanted to add something about Yahweh and his protection but resisted the urge. "Did the women see who took them?"

"A large man. Said he had light skin and looked like an Egyptian. Said he was a cubit taller than any of us and carried a spear larger than a weaver's beam."

Benaiah held his breath. A large man. An Egyptian. He saw hot sand and the sea, dark visions of a massive warrior, the pharaoh's cold stare, maidservants mocking him. It could not be the same man. "Women exaggerate."

"It was Abigail. I believe her."

He held up his war club, covered in the blackened blood of the first assault. David eyed it a moment. "Remember the covering," David said.

"Yahweh has left me! I don't want him or his covering! What god allows a man's family to suffer and his children to die?" The words had poured out of him, and Benaiah was surprised at the depth of anguish in his voice. The group near them had gone quiet. A piece of burning wood nearby snapped, sending a shower of sparks up.

Benaiah regretted his words immediately. This was not the time to shout and moan like a woman, not when a battle was raging and his wife needed to be rescued. *Hurry up, you fool! They are getting away! Why aren't you moving?* He ordered himself to move, but his legs felt like bronze weights. He stared at the ground.

David was still beside him. "I did not know of your suffering, my friend, but I know that Yahweh is for you and not against you," he said.

"You are very sure of that? Even after everything?"

"Even after everything."

Benaiah took several slow breaths. "I fear that Yahweh will never come to me again for what I have done. I did not—"

"I know, brother. I have not always walked with Yahweh either. I have left his council for my own paths and live with that every day. I want to blame myself for all of this," he gestured toward the captives, "but I know that is not what he wants. He only wants me to return to him. Stay focused, Benaiah. You will get her back. Yahweh has promised it, but you need to hurry. Men who waste time lose everything dear to them."

Benaiah started to speak, but his voice caught and refused to leave his throat. Both men stared at the rocks at their feet, listening to the sounds of the battle around them, knowing they needed to keep moving but taking this moment.

David raised his hand and put his palm gently on Benaiah's forehead. In a soft voice, he prayed for Benaiah to accomplish his mission. He prayed for covering in the day of war.

When he was done, they embraced. David stood with him patiently. Benaiah's muscles pulsed now with raw energy. He took a long breath, tasted the smoke on his tongue, washed it with water from the pouch—and then ran. He took great strides past the freed captives, the mercenaries, the celebrating families. The other men were allowed a moment to find their loved ones in the group. Tears, laughter, screams of joy and delight, fathers tackling children, hardened warriors unashamed of their relief and their tears. He looked at the children, laughing and jumping, and imagined seeing his daughters among them as he ran past. *Not there, Benaiah. Neither is Sherizah. Even if I get her back, she will never come to me again.*

One of the men had swept a little girl into the air and kissed her face, causing the girl to shy away from the fearsome and bloody warrior she did not recognize as her own father. The man kept kissing her and clutching her hair and the little girl shrieked in fear, but the man did not care. He kissed her through his blood-soaked beard and held her with powerful arms. A woman stood next to him clutching his waist, as if she wanted him to do the same with her.

They were behaving like fools, and it was the most beautiful thing Benaiah had ever seen. He turned and raced toward the gaping canyon rising in the night ahead of him, thinking of his wife's beautiful dark hair.

The battle had slowed because the Amalekites were in full flight. David and his men would pursue the Amalekites throughout the night, and most of the men, no longer needed in the fight, were now preparing. Provisions were passed out and water bags were filled. Benaiah passed a soldier, nearly hidden in the dense smoke, shouting orders in a foreign tongue and carrying an armload of weapons. It was Keth, performing the task that would receive no glory but was indispensable.

Remember the covering.

The black war club glinted in his hands.

Karak eased himself slightly over the top of the pile of bodies still warm from life and now lying in a heap. All of his men were dead or dying, or soon would be. All of them. An entire army gone because of his foolishness.

The wine still made his mind murky, but the cold air helped him regain his alertness. He would never be able to return to his own lands. He would be the brunt of laughter, called a woman, and forced to haul water from the village well. *That would never happen.* Whatever honor he had left, he needed to preserve for the next life.

Karak had watched the battle from under the pile for an hour. He'd seen the Hebrew general forming a perimeter of men around the ruins of Karak's command tent, moving in perfect discipline and easily slaying Amalek's drunken warriors. He watched as his women captives were lost, along with all of his war prizes and wine—so hard-won but gone forever now. Karak had no men to take them back with.

Lying hidden in the pile of bodies, Karak had caressed the hilt of his dagger, feeling its gentle weight, and felt a hot desire to bury it in the neck of the Hebrew war chief. He waited while the pile of bodies grew around him—all of them his men, men he had failed just as they had failed him. He saw two of the Hebrew commanders fight one another, only to be separated by their leader. It was unlike men of such discipline to do that.

He kept his face low and still as the two generals stood next to him and discussed the escape of the Egyptian. Karak's anger rose as he listened.

The two men stopped talking. One of them walked away. The other stood silently for a moment. Karak could hear his breathing and was able to watch from the edge of his vision as the tall warrior waited in the smoke and gloom. Then he heard him bound away in a steady stride. Karak was alone again.

He raised his head slightly until he could see the huddle of women and children, some of them still frightened and weeping, others greeting their men with joy. Behind him, other Hebrew warriors were holding their positions in the perimeter to keep security, showing remarkable discipline for not charging into the group of captives. He thought again that they were hard men, good fighters, a worthy enemy to lose to. He should have been prepared.

And then something odd happened. For the first time, Karak felt unsure of himself. He feared that he would probably die this night.

He shook his head violently, blamed the wine for these mad thoughts. Why should he fear death? His people believed that there was an eternal war. All men went there—or at least all brave men who had captured plunder and killed their enemies. Some would rule with the gods, and war would rule them all. And now he saw how to prepare himself for a place of honor in that eternal war. He would prove he was not inept. He would kill the Egyptian and the Hebrew commander.

Karak saw the Hebrew commanders kneeling and talking.

One of the men ran off, leaving the other alone, who then rose up and turned in his direction, the sword on his back highlighted against the flames. It was far too large a weapon for a man that size to carry. The Egyptian might have wielded it, but not a man of normal size like this Hebrew.

This was the Hebrew commander. Karak could sense it as one could sense all men of authority when they came near.

The Hebrew general studied the darkness. Karak waited. The man eventually turned his back to Karak, watching a company of his men resuming the pursuit of the remnants of Karak's army. It was now or not at all.

Karak prayed to his gods, begging them for entrance into the eternal war if he killed the Hebrew, hoping it would be enough, in their judgment. If he could just make the eternal war, he would prove himself. If he could just make the eternal war ...

He sprang to his feet, shoving off the bodies that had covered him, and stumbled down the pile toward the Hebrew. Karak funneled his anger into speed, driving his sloppy legs as hard as he could and forcing blood into his veins. The Hebrew would hear him at any moment. He needed to close the distance quickly.

Karak pulled the war axe from his back and held his dagger low in his other hand. A few more paces. He raised the axe and swung, but as he did he grunted. The Hebrew must have heard him, for he collapsed out of the way as the blade sliced across the air next to his head.

Karak could not slow his momentum. His hands vibrated as the axe struck not the Hebrew warlord's head but rocky ground. He thudded against a surprised woman who had been sitting next to the Hebrew, and they crashed to the earth together. He felt her body take the force of his impact hard.

Soft flesh pressed against him as they rolled together. But the Hebrew warlord would be regaining his balance and drawing the enormous blade from his back. Karak pushed the screaming woman away and rolled.

To the left!

The Hebrew's sword nicked his thigh. He snatched a handful of burning embers from the nearby fire and threw them, feeling the sizzle of charring flesh in his palm. It worked: the Hebrew had to raise his arm in defense, and Karak lashed out with his axe in a low swipe. It caught the leather straps of the man's sandals but did not hit flesh.

But the Hebrew was fast! Before Karak could regain balance to swing again, the man darted to his left and brought the sword down hard onto Karak's shoulder. Karak lurched. Blood splattered his face. The cut was deep, nearly severing his left arm, and now it hung useless.

Karak shouted curses, calling on his gods through the pain, his eyes suddenly stung by thick smoke, and he had to move again quickly because the man was charging too fast. He brought the axe up with his good arm and blocked the next blow. But he could not stop the next and felt hot iron slide into his belly under his raised war axe.

He looked down at the sword in his gut. It was a remarkable blade, a huge weapon. No man should have been able to wield it with such speed; it was simply too large. Karak was angry. He could feel blood burbling into his throat and his ears ringing. He gagged, spat it out, watched it drip down the sword. The Hebrew general was looking into his eyes.

Karak smiled at him. He was grateful for that. They would be fighting in the afterlife in the eternal war. There would be no end of their battle, and Karak would be waiting for him. The man who'd killed him had auburn hair. His features were harsh and rugged, his beard cut short, and he had the amber-colored eyes of a lion. There was no mercy in them.

Karak gurgled again, the ringing growing louder, his head beginning to swim. He felt the cold of death begin to take over. The war would be good on the other side. *The war is there, and I will wait for him*, he thought. Pain ebbed, but then as his vision slipped away into blackness, the eyes of a lion bore into him.

He gasped again, terrified.

David watched the tattooed warrior drift away. When he was dead, David pulled the blade out and knelt on one knee, suddenly overcome with weariness. It would pass. It always passed.

It was late. More time had passed since the initial attack than he'd realized. Dogs were coming out of nowhere to ravage corpses. He said something aloud. An order. But what? What had he just said? He shook his head.

Goliath's blade was warm.

Still so much smoke. The wives are safe now. Finish it and we'll all go home.

He wiped his brow with his dirty, matted tunic.

Find the men.

David stood back up. The weariness was gone now, and he gave thanks aloud. "Thank you, Yahweh. You train my arms for war. Forgive the sins of my men and give them power where they fight, this moment, this hour. Do not forget us, do not forget your promise."

He needed to find his men. He blinked and focused. Joab was rushing his troops forward to cover the flank of the Amalekites' retreat to make sure no man escaped. It awoke him from dreaming. Energy surged back into him. He gave thanks again. The day was not over yet. Benaiah would be near the Three now.

Yahweh, cover them.

An arrow swished past Josheb's head just as he tripped the next soldier coming at him. He had settled into a rhythm of lunging forward, and if the enemy was off balance he would press it — if not, he would retreat three steps in order to draw the enemy soldier in. In the darkness, he could barely make out Eleazar and Shammah doing the same.

They kept together without fail. The tide of Amalekites pushed them back through sheer numbers, but the Three were able to hold them. Cowards kept to the edges of the canyon, trying to run past them, but others hungry for glory in the afterlife attacked them in desperation.

Eleazar shouted something over the clashing, but Josheb missed it. He waited for Shammah to repeat it but heard nothing else.

Three Amalekites appeared out of the night in front of him. He caught the first strike, a spear, and tore it out of the soldier's hand. As the man fell forward Josheb leaped onto his back, swung the stolen spear, and crushed the neck of the next man. The falling soldier whose back he rode landed and skidded on the gravel. Josheb stomped his head with his foot.

One more coming, others behind him.

Josheb threw the spear into the man and let him fall against him, using his body as a shield against the arrow that flew out of the darkness from an unseen archer and thudded into the soldier's back. He shouted, threw the man down, and swung the pike in his left hand until it connected with another soldier.

He did not know how many he had killed, but the Amalekites were still coming, and somehow he had strength to keep his blades moving. The ground was slick with the bowels of dead men, and he slipped in the grime. A soldier was screaming in agony on the ground nearby, a wide gash in his belly. Josheb stabbed him in the neck—a mercy.

He shook his head to clear the sweat and to focus, and another group of three emerged. Where was Eleazar? There, with two men on either side of him.

Shammah was there too; he caught the strike of one of them and clubbed him with an axe. An axe? Where did he get the axe? He must have taken it from an Amalekite.

Josheb ducked another attack just in time and thrust his elbow into the soldier's torso, but he was wearing armor, and Josheb's arm burst with pain. His fingers twitched; he felt as if he had just shattered his entire arm, but there was no time to examine it; he had to dodge another blow. A fast jab with the pike into the man's mouth broke his jaw, then Josheb impaled him in the torso to finish it.

Shammah was their rear guard in larger battles, when swarms of men surrounded them and the other two were piercing the ranks, unable to see behind themselves. He proved himself once more, striking down a soldier Josheb hadn't seen until it would have been too late. Josheb was grateful. Then he heard the warrior actually singing, impossibly calm in the midst of the battle, singing as he struck down enemies and protected his brothers.

Each man fought within the carefully chosen movements of the *abir*, controlling his efforts precisely, feeling Yahweh's voice in the chaos, following his lead, feeling the power of the covering.

Some soldiers streamed past them in panic-stricken flight; they could not reach them all—the canyon was a bit too wide for that.

The rest of David's army would hunt them down once the families were safe.

Josheb kept spinning and waiting for another charge, his arm still throbbing from striking the dead soldier's armor. But for the moment, he was alone, and Shammah and Eleazar were finishing off their opponents.

Josheb felt a muscle twitch in his leg. He seized the moment to grope for his small water pouch and drink. The black night was suddenly cold. Or had it been cold, and his nerves and the battle prevented him from realizing it?

His tunic, slick with sweat, stuck to his back, slapping him with a freezing wet feeling each time he moved. The other two came to stand near him momentarily, eyeing the night around them while sipping quickly from their pouches, then retying the top and dropping them back beside their waists.

"How many more of them can there be?" Eleazar panted.

"Can't be more than a few hundred," replied Josheb.

"They're here again," said Shammah, nodding toward the camp. More backlit figures ran toward them.

Josheb saw the form of a man larger than the rest running near the rear of their ranks, and the three of them watched in surprise as he began to drop fleeing soldiers from behind. His weapon rose and fell, smashing against the heads and backs of the Amalekites. They only ran harder, frightened, almost corralling like sheep toward where the Three were waiting for them.

Josheb darted back to the front of the group and raised his pike. The first man he let go past for Eleazar, the next went to Shammah, then he stuck out his leg and tripped the third. The man didn't even resist when Josheb plunged the tip of the weapon into his back. He pulled it free and struck the next one quickly. The three of them drew tightly together now and fought only forward, since they were now unable to swing and spin without hitting each other.

The large figure who had been killing Amalekites from behind reached them, clubbed a soldier to the ground, and Josheb recognized Benaiah, his face twisted in fury.

"Josheb, Eleazar, they have our women."

Eleazar looked as stricken as though an enemy blade had slid past his guard and buried itself in his neck. Josheb's own throat went dry. "Where?"

"I don't know. Could they have come this way?"

Josheb felt sick, remembering. "I saw a small group go into a side canyon, early in the fight." He gestured toward the gap in the distance. "It may have been them. I will go with you. Shammah, stay here and hold them. Can you do it alone?"

"I will not be alone," he said, smiling. "Go get them."

"How many of our men are down, Benaiah?"

"None that I know of. Neither Joab nor Abishai have lost anyone. And you three are here."

"Praise to our God and arrows to our enemies, brothers," said Shammah solemnly. They nodded, and everyone but Benaiah repeated it. Josheb could not help but smile. Shammah always reminded them of their priorities.

Another wave of enemy troops was coming. Shammah would need a moment to prepare, so they hugged each other, unashamed, bid him farewell, and the three of them ran toward the dark canyon.

TWENTY-EIGHT

The fighting raged through the night. The Hebrews combed the remnants of the encampment for any surviving Amalekites and struck them down when they found them. The men with families to rescue battled ferociously, moved with perfect precision, and showed their enemy no mercy. Many Amalekites attempted to surrender but were cleaved apart with iron axes. Smells of blood and smoke followed the battle as it pressed through the woods.

Joab's task was to clear out the open fields at the edge of the forest to make sure the Amalekite camp was secure. It was an arduous and time-consuming process. Joab was splashing his face from a water skin when Abishai appeared out of the smoke.

"Total success. I have not lost a man yet."

"Don't stop," Joab said irritably. "They are not all dead. Keep your company moving forward." He motioned for his brother to follow. "And keep your eyes open for Asahel."

Joab had not seen his other brother all night but knew he would have been told if anything had happened to him. Joab and his troops continued their sweep of the boundaries of the Amalekite camp. They had skirmished all that night with various pockets of resistance, some of them putting up strong fights, but as Abishai had said, David's army had not lost a man. Joab knew that was remarkable, but he was too tired and angry to care. He wanted only to finish this and be done with it.

He tried to focus on ordering his troops but could not forget what had happened with Benaiah the night before. Benaiah would need to go. He had thought so for some time, but their fight during the night had been the final affront. Once this was over, he would tell David. If David did not let Joab do something about it, then he would simply kill Benaiah during their next battle.

Teams were dispatched into the forest to press the search for any who'd thus far survived. Word reached him that a group of several hundred servants had escaped on camels, leaving in the direction of the Negev. Apart from that, most of those who'd tried to escape had headed for the canyon where the Three were waiting for them.

David loves his Three, Joab thought as he watched his troops poking among the undergrowth. As long as they stayed away from the management of the army, they would be useful. But he hated Benaiah bitterly. The fact that he could not explain why he hated the man made him even more furious.

When he was satisfied that the camp and the forest immediately around it was empty of men, he urged his men on toward the canyon gap where the Three had been positioned, clearly visible in the distance now even through the smoke.

From the top of a small rise, Joab could see the area where the Three were to have been fighting. He nodded when he saw the field scattered with bodies and a man still fighting the enemy alone among them.

But there was only one? He couldn't tell who it was from that distance, but he knew that he only saw one man. Had the other two fallen? And where was Benaiah? David had taken command of Benaiah's men and now the warrior was missing.

Jealous, afraid that the others were involved in something he was missing out on, he shouted a change of orders and rushed with his men toward the canyon entrance.

The Hittites had kept up with the surge all night, lugging weapons back and forth across the field. Keth had never seen such a strategy. In most armies, men carried what they wanted to use and would not see an armorer until after the battle. If a weapon broke, a warrior would snatch one from the death grip of a fallen enemy.

Not every man with a weapon needed a replacement, so the armorers had also carried water. That was never the most glorious position on the field. Songs of war would never be written about those who carried water. But without them, there would be no victory. It was a job given to those who did not seek glory, but only wanted to serve. He wished he were able to gain David's favor with a daring assault, instead, or a magnificent stand in the face of many enemies, but he gritted his teeth and told himself to let go of it and trust that David saw his contribution. He believed David to be a good general, and a good general recognized what the quieter elements did.

The first assault needed to be light, so Keth and his men had waited in the forest until ordered to start the resupply. Now that it had been such a total success, the army was simply cleaning up the remaining holdouts, as they had throughout the night. The Amalekite force had been enormous, much larger than they'd thought, but to Keth's amazement, as well as everyone else's, there had been no reports of a single loss in David's army.

He shook his head. It was not for him to understand. He had never worked in such precise units before. These men were experts at what they did, so he would do his job, ensuring that they got what they needed: ten men taking equipment to Abishai, ten to Joab, ten to Asahel, and the rest in reserve.

From his spot on a small mound of rocks overlooking the mouth of the canyon, he could see the entire scene. This was so much different than fighting in the ranks, where there was nothing but confusion and disorder, where you couldn't hear orders even when they were screamed over the din of battle. In the ranks, there was blood spraying at all times as limbs were severed, and a man would be so exhausted and frightened that he could do nothing except plunge his blade forward and hope that the enemy did not do the same.

And the stench. Men's bowels were emptied. The spilling of blood mixed with body fluids was the worst of all stenches. He shuddered.

Here, away from it all, he felt detached, as though he were a god watching the play toys of a child. It made perfect sense from where he was: the lines of Abishai and Joab sweeping the far side of the field, the company led by David moving along the other side, slowly pressing toward the canyon gap in a pincer movement that would concentrate the fleeing Amalekites toward where the three warriors had been placed as a block.

Keth did not know if any man *wanted* to be in the ranks. There was glory, yes, but after a while a man begins to forget about glory and simply wants to live, plant his crops, and make love to his woman.

Too much thinking. He shook his head and focused on directing weapon supply.

Shammah sang only in his heart now, too tired to sing aloud, for every breath was needed to keep his arms moving. The ranks of Amalekites never seemed to end. He fought, dove, slashed, retreated, counterattacked. He had fought them all night, and now dawn had broken. Earlier, he had noticed a herd of camels with riders going past, but since he was busy fighting foot soldiers, he had let them pass. They carried no weapons and looked like servants anyway.

Shammah dropped the last soldier in a group and fell to the ground in exhaustion, groping the earth beneath him, praying and singing. I need it now, I can do it no more, he thought. Find me worthy of the fire.

And yet again, Shammah felt the surge of warmth and heat course through his muscles, as if a spirit had entered and possessed him. He shouted aloud in gratitude. David said the covering came when a man humbled himself and asked for it. It came now, and Shammah praised the one who had sent it. It always left after a time, but it was here now again, sent because Shammah asked for it, as he asked continuously day and night. When no one else obeyed the Law or heard the stories, Shammah was faithful. He knew the covering well.

His palms were raw with blisters, but it did not matter. Under the covering, he felt no pain. The coming of morning light illuminated the vastness of the encampment. Thousands of enemy troops had been there. There was no way to know how many he had fought, and he was not done yet. Hold a little longer, and they will be here, he thought frantically.

Shammah had no idea how many hours had passed, only that the fire had returned as it always did, and he jumped up and charged forward into the gray dawn, striking men until his weapon snapped. He reached around for a sword and, finding none, attacked the next man with his hands.

Shammah punched him in the face as hard as he could, and did the same to his partner. Both soldiers tumbled backward from the blow. Shammah stepped on them, then put his sandal against the chest of the next man and kicked him to the side. The next two he killed quickly, breaking their necks.

Two spears flew through the air toward his chest. He leaped backward, flipped himself upside down, and avoided them. Another spear arced past him, but this time he caught it. The fire was consuming him again, moving his arms and legs with perfect precision. He flung the spear back toward the man who'd thrown it. The iron head struck him, thick armor and all, with such impact that the Amalekite behind him slouched too, impaled on the same spear. Both went down.

The next attack came from the side. Shammah kneed the man in the groin, then drove his fist forward into the man's neck, crushing his throat. The soldier went to his knees gagging, unable to breathe. Shammah spotted a broken shield nearby, its edge jagged and sharp along the break line, and with one swift, hard swing cut the man's head off to end his agony.

He looked up to prepare for the next soldier—and saw no one except the first ranks of David's army.

"Thank you," he said, intending it as a prayer. He searched the ground around him for any kind of weapon. His pike had long since broken and so had his sword. He picked up the blade of a dead Amalekite and waited for the first troops of David's army to reach him.

Joab, out of breath, appeared in front, and Shammah quietly prayed that he would find the strength to be patient with him. "Where are the others?" the younger man said, skidding to a halt.

"Good to see that you're okay, Joab. Lost any men?"

"No. Where are the others?"

"They went after their women. I remained," Shammah said.

"Alone?"

"Not alone."

Joab had stopped listening. He shouted for the other men to stay in their formation. They were covered with dirt and blood, Shammah noticed, but each of them wore a triumphant expression. It had been a total victory. They still had not lost a man.

"David wants you back with the captives while we round up the last of them," Joab told Shammah.

"You'll be chasing them all night," Shammah said. "Many fled to the canyon and we killed them, but the ones who scattered into the forest will take time to find."

Without another word, Joab walked back to the section leaders to give them the update. Not a man lost, Shammah thought. Remarkable. This had never happened before. Someone always fell. But tonight, apart from flesh wounds, there would be no grief. The devastation of their discovery at Ziklag was past. Yahweh had kept his promise.

Shammah was aware that the men were watching him. Word would be spread about the Three and their stand at the canyon. Their legend would grow, and he knew that they would face the sin of pride.

Eyes closed, he opened his mouth to breathe the frigid air and cleanse his lungs of the battle. He prayed for his brothers, prayed for these men watching him now, in awe of his exploits, that they would remember where the victory had come from. And he prayed for the others, on their way now to find their loved ones.

Benaiah.

His eyes snapped open.

Covering for Benaiah in the day of war.

The words etched themselves into his mind so clearly that he knew it was immediately necessary to do it. The man from Kabzeel needed covering.

Physical harm? No.

Something else.

TWENTY-NINE

The Egyptian knew that the group would not last.

All night they pushed through the Judean forests and canyons, heading southwest as much as possible. The Egyptian had led them in and out of narrow canyons and wadis to throw off anyone following. The trade routes were to the southwest, and he would need to reach them to have any hope of escape. Morning had come and etched the sky above them with gray streaks among the stars before revealing enough light to see the canyon path.

By dawn, they had reached the end of the canyon lands and were able to see the deserts of the south, which they would need to cross before he would feel safe and free. He hurried them along.

Now that the sun was out, he knew that the farther they pressed into the desert, fatigued to the point of hallucination, the less likely he would be able to maintain discipline. He threatened death to the captured women if they resisted, then ordered the group to stop for a water break, since there were still many hours to go until the next settlement of Amalekites. But now he faced a dilemma. He did not want to take refuge in an Amalekite village; the people might start asking questions. But if he did not, then all of them would die in the Negev, either by the hand of that Hebrew warlord or from lack of water.

Their escape had been inglorious; the gods had cruelly spared them the fate of death by combat and driven them out into the wilderness with only a couple of whores and no dignity. He was no longer a well-paid mercenary spy in Amalek, but he had many options. He could earn as much if he went to Moab or even back to Philistia before making his first report to Pharaoh.

The woman he had taken earlier was watching him. He spoke to her in her tongue. "Your men are mighty fighters, I will give them that."

She lowered her eyes and waited for the skin of water to come to her. He was not a man who raped; he considered it barbaric. But he was a man like any other. He desired her. She had been compliant in everything until then. Perhaps she would be compliant further.

Sherizah examined her bloody feet and then drank deeply of the water skin when Deborah passed it to her. Sand and grit burned in her throat, and it hurt when the hot water washed over it. The frightening warrior was watching her again. His looks had been growing hungrier, and her silent prayers increased whenever he was near.

One of the ten soldiers began to argue with his companion. Sherizah did not understand their language but knew it had to do with water, since the man was waving his gut skin around and pointing at the offending soldier. The Egyptian ordered them to be silent, but they ignored him and continued arguing until one of them punched the other in the neck.

The struck man fell but pulled out a dagger and lunged for the kill. The others ran to break up the fight, but someone threw a blow that hit the wrong man, and it quickly escalated into a battle of every man against the other. They fought like a herd of wild animals, clawing and biting, savage and undisciplined.

One soldier stayed out of the scuffle. Sherizah watched him slowly move to where the bag of captured gold was lying near a rock, exposed and unguarded. The Egyptian was now in the middle of the fight, trying to break it up, his massive arms knocking men left and right.

The soldier sprang forward, grabbed the bag, and rushed toward the canyons in the distance. But it was heavy, and he was forced to drop his weapons to carry it. If he could get enough of a head start on the group, Sherizah realized, he could disappear into the maze of hollowed gullies and ridges before they caught him. She looked back at the fighting men, still lunging at each other despite the massive Egyptian's efforts. She leaned closer to Deborah and said, "If they run after the man and leave us, we need to escape."

"What if they leave a guard?" Deborah replied.

"We will run as soon as they notice him missing. That will force them to choose which to pursue," Sherizah said. She looked over at Rizpah, who nodded. Deborah seemed uncertain but nodded her head also. They waited.

The first man to notice the missing soldier was the Egyptian. He looked up from the fight and saw the figure racing across the desert with the bag over his shoulders.

The Egyptian bellowed as loud as he could. "He has your war prize!"

The men stopped fighting at the mention of the gold and began to claw at each other to regain their footing. The Egyptian ran to where he had laid his weapons and realized suddenly that the women too were gone. He shouted again at his men, who looked back toward him, saw his pointing arm—and then the fleeing Hebrew women.

The Egyptian had to make a decision: chase the thief first or capture the women. He had no intention of letting either get away. The man would be slow with his bundle and could be caught later, but the women, if they escaped, might give away their location to David's men.

And he wanted that Hebrew woman with the dark eyes.

"Up the hill after them, now!"

The men hesitated.

The Egyptian shouted again. "If you go after the women, you can have them immediately, but hold the one with her hair tied up for me. Just be quick about it. I will get the gold back."

Their faces lit up. Some of them had not had a woman in many months, and these were the chief's women, choice among the captives. They turned and ran up the sandy slope. The Egyptian, carrying only his spear, ran after the fleeing robber, his great strides flying.

He saw the thief in the distance look over his shoulder and panic. The fleeing soldier snagged his foot in a patch of brush and shouted as he hit the ground. The gold pieces crashed across the desert around him. The Egyptian did not slacken his pace. He closed on the hapless soldier struggling to free his leg.

The man shouted for mercy, but the Egyptian buried his spear in the thief's chest, withdrew it, and circled past the man's quivering body without breaking stride. He left the gold where it was, to be picked up after the women were caught.

He ran steadily in the direction of the women's escape. He could see them now; they had already reached the cleft in the rock at the source of the canyon. One of the soldiers had caught hold of the slower Hebrew woman and was tearing at her garments. It was not the woman the Egyptian desired. The woman he wanted was almost to the cliff. She would be his, and he would not share her.

As the man who had reached the first one clawed at her body, the Egyptian saw something fly through the air and strike the soldier. The man jerked backward, and the woman, struggling to gather her clothing, screamed and resumed running up the hillside toward the gap.

The Egyptian looked up. Three Hebrew warriors were charging over the ridge.

THIRTY

Benaiah's sandals pounded the dirt, rocks forcing him to stumble and leap, willing himself to keep running faster. He was bone weary from the continuous fighting, and he knew that Josheb and Eleazar were too. Still, they had to hurry. The leather straps holding his water skin were digging into his shoulders, but he did not care.

They were running along a narrow canyon formed by flooding during spring rains, so it was now dry enough to follow the riverbed and the tracks of their quarry. His breath was labored, and he drew strength from his comrades on either side. They gave him hope that their women would be safe in their arms before long. He could almost see her hair, almost taste her skin, and his blood churned with anger for the man who would dare touch her—and for the sorrow Benaiah himself had been to her.

The canyon narrowed and disappeared as they ran, leading to another series of boulders over which they had to climb. It was frustrating terrain. The Amalekites might be waiting to ambush them around any corner.

They had no idea how many Amalekites there were. This was a strategic nightmare, but there was no choice. Ahead were cliffs, craggy openings, hidden canyons—any number of places for fleeing soldiers to escape.

Josheb, in the lead, threw his arm up, and they skidded to a halt, pitching forward onto their hands and knees behind cover. Despite their heavy breathing, they strained to listen.

A slight breeze kicked up sand around them, but there was no other sound. No shouts, no screams. Josheb leaped back up to his feet and resumed running, Eleazar and Benaiah falling into step behind him. Their eyes searched the ground for any clue about the Amalekites.

At the end of the boulder field, pinched by the cliffs of the box canyon they were in, was the opening to the plains in the distance. Beyond that, Benaiah knew, was a broad slope of sand. That would be the Amalekites' best escape route, if their goal was to scatter across the open plains. The three men looked at each other quickly to confirm and then ran faster, their sandals kicking up dust and pebbles.

The gap approached. Eleazar ran out in front of them, and as Benaiah watched, he suddenly jerked his spear up over his head, gaze fixed on something he could see through the gap in the cliffs. Benaiah and Josheb called to him, but he did not respond.

Eleazar charged forward through the gap, faster than Benaiah or Josheb could run. As Benaiah emerged from the gap himself and could see down the slope, Eleazar was ramming the spear into the chest of an Amalekite who had been standing over a huddled figure.

Next to them, Benaiah recognized Sherizah and Deborah running up the steep slope toward them and away from a group of Amalekites, who were quickly gaining ground on the women.

Benaiah and Josheb never broke stride, racing down the sandy slope in tight formation to their wives. But as he ran, Benaiah caught a glimpse of the giant man at the base of the slope. So it was him, just as he'd feared. The pharaoh's warrior.

The women screamed for help. Josheb and Benaiah sped forward. Benaiah finally reached the slender figure running toward him. He caught her, clutched his wife in his arms. He felt a burning in his eyes, but fought it. There was still a battle ahead. "Are you harmed? Tell me quickly!"

"No, I am unharmed."

She pressed her hands on his face and wept. As Benaiah held her, he looked up to see Josheb checking his own wife, fighting tears but failing.

There was no more time. The Amalekites were closing.

Josheb shouted, "Run back into the canyon behind us! Eleazar, stay with them, Benaiah and I will hold them in the gap — it's too narrow for all three of us. If we fall, you have to get them back. Gain as much distance as you can right now."

"You send me back with the women during a battle?" Eleazar said. But he turned and obeyed, leading Rizpah and Deborah in a sprint through the gap in the cliffs in the direction they had come. Benaiah touched Sherizah's face, kissed her one more time, and whispered to her. She nodded her head and turned away, her eyes red and swollen.

No time. Never enough time.

Sherizah joined the others and rushed back up the slope toward the safety of the canyon. Benaiah and Josheb took their positions in the narrow gap where they could best defend themselves and crouched, weapons ready.

The Amalekites had reached the body of their fallen comrade, and Benaiah could see their faces twisted with hate. Even though they had turned and run like cowards the night before, now they were insane with lust and vengeance.

Josheb held his sword up to his face and closed his eyes. "Praise to our God."

"Arrows to our enemies," Benaiah replied. He glanced quickly behind them. Eleazar was leading the women through the boulders. This would be harder than last night, when they were fighting drunken, disorganized rabble.

The Amalekites rushed the gap. Josheb parried the first spear thrust and shoved his blade between the shoulders of the first man, then twisted and struck the second man's head with his shield. Benaiah sidestepped the charge of the third man, turned, and thrust his spear into the man's lower back. All three Amalekites yelled, vainly groping at the weapons that had killed them. Benaiah tried to jerk his spear free, but to his horror the shaft snapped, leaving the head buried in the dying man. Josheb had leapt back to his position.

Benaiah tossed aside the broken spear. The Amalekite soldiers kept coming. In the distance, the Egyptian stood back, watching the fight, twice as large as either Josheb or Benaiah, much larger even than Shammah, his arms as thick as Cyprus trees.

Images of the time he had fought this man next to the sea came to his mind. Benaiah had been driven back under the merciless onslaught, driven back further, not strong enough to withstand ...

A rush of blood lust, wave after wave, washed over Benaiah until he could hardly see through the red. He shouted hoarsely and ran toward the Amalekites, fresh fire in his body.

"Benaiah! Stay in the gap! It's better to defend!" Josheb shouted, But Benaiah ignored him. David's orders had been for total destruction. He would happily give them that.

Benaiah swung his fist into the face of the next man, cracking the bones. As the man fell, Benaiah yanked the war club from a strap across his back. He had been waiting to use it, and panting, he killed the next man with it. The club dented the stolen Philistine armor the soldier was wearing and crushed his rib cage. The soldier cried out, tears springing to his eyes, but Benaiah drove the club into his throat to quiet him.

Two more approached, trying to come at him simultaneously from two sides, but the club lashed out once more, breaking both Amalekite swords with the same blow. Aghast at their shattered swords, they turned to run, but lunging after them, Benaiah hit both in their lower backs, breaking their spines.

He let the lust for vengeance overtake him. He saw his daughters, the blood on the floor, the face of his wife as she wept and told him what happened years ago.

Josheb broke to the side, drawing away half of the remaining Amalekites. Two carried spears and three swords, but Josheb struck down four of the men almost instantly. The last man lunged at him, and he easily parried the sword thrust with his shield, causing the soldier to thrust high. Josheb slipped his spear low and thrust it into the man's leg. He fell to his knees. Josheb buried his sword to the hilt in the Amalekite's chest and held it there a moment, looking into the dying man's face as he gasped for breath.

The light quickly faded from the man's eyes, and Josheb withdrew the blade and knelt to catch his breath and control the pain. Sand clogged his eyes and sweat drenched the leather armor on his torso. His muscles shook from weariness.

Only one Amalekite remained, and the giant. The final soldier broke into a run. Benaiah chased him, shouting his war cry, and clouted him across the neck, snapping it. The man's cries were muffled in the sand.

Josheb tried to steady his breathing. Only three men remained upright—Josheb, Benaiah, and the giant, who had stood calmly watching the struggle. Saving his energy, Josheb thought. He knew we would be exhausted after battling the foot soldiers.

Benaiah staggered back to where Josheb sat resting in the sunlit sand. The fire that had raged in him had cooled. He was suddenly so tired that he'd almost fainted after the last soldier fell. Not all the men they had defeated were dead; the unearthly screaming of dying men echoed against the canyon walls, calling out for a mercy killing. The Egyptian simply watched them, no expression on his face. Benaiah and Josheb leaned against each other.

"He . . . never joined them," Benaiah sputtered between breaths.

Josheb shook his head. "Saving himself, waiting for us to wear out."

The Egyptian had been leaning on the shaft of his spear, which was decorated with paintings. Benaiah recognized the glyphs that Egyptians used in their artwork, as elegantly refined as the rest of their society. He knew they often decorated their weapons with representations of the spirits of men they had slain in battle. The Egyptian's spear held so many there was barely room for more.

The mercenary looked at them from thirty paces away, arms crossed, holding the spear against his chest. "We have fought before, Hebrew," the Egyptian said in their language.

Benaiah nodded, ignoring Josheb's stunned expression. "It will end differently this time."

"Did you learn more weapons? You would need to."

"How did you learn our language?" asked Josheb.

"He was once a slave in our lands when he was young," Benaiah answered. "He escaped and has hated us ever since. I battled him in front of Pharaoh several years ago for sport."

"Who won?"

Benaiah shook his head. Josheb rolled his eyes.

The Egyptian said, "How did you learn multiple weapons? You had only the sword before."

"From my brothers who have trained me. You battle a different Hebrew than you did before."

The Egyptian looked at Benaiah a moment, then back to Josheb. "You serve the man David, is this not so?"

"Yes."

"Does he pay well?"

"Enough."

Their enemy raised his face to the sun and wiped his brow. "Mercenaries are highly paid in Moab. They raid the highway where the eastern caravans travel. We would do well there. Their kings are desperate to gain a foothold in this country."

"You think that after stealing our women and burning our homes, you can talk us into joining you?" Benaiah scoffed.

The Egyptian shrugged. "It is war. You do the same."

"No, barbarian, we do not," Josheb said. His voice sounded weaker to Benaiah.

"I know what your men do to Amalekite villages. You are no different than they are. Besides," he tilted his head slightly toward Benaiah, "you don't seem the peaceful type."

Benaiah had heard enough. He rocked to his knees and stood, then reached out his hand to help his partner up. "I will take point. Cover my left flank. We can get him in a rush."

Benaiah studied the giant, planning his attack. He did not notice for a moment or two that Josheb had neither replied nor taken his hand. After a silent moment, Benaiah looked down. Josheb was lying still, eyes half open. Benaiah knelt and slapped him across the face. "Jokes come later. I need your help now."

No response.

Benaiah slapped him again; this time Josheb's eyes fluttered and focused on him.

It was then that Benaiah noticed the dark pool under Josheb's back. The sand had absorbed most of it. He rolled his friend over and saw the hilt of a buried dagger. He felt the shock of it, hard. When had this happened? How?

As if answering, Josheb said, "One of the others threw it. I was too slow. I have enough for this last battle. Just help me up."

Josheb's voice was soft, but Benaiah felt in his grip a reserve of strength. He did not even consider forcing him to stay down; Josheb would have crawled to the fight. Benaiah pulled his friend up to a standing position. He tottered for a moment, seemed to find balance with the shaft of his spear, and waited.

The Egyptian warrior regarded them awhile longer. Then he held up his spear. Benaiah remembered that spear well. The head was iron and must have weighed hundreds of shekels.

The wind from the distant sea picked up slightly, tumbling over the foothills and stirring up the dust around them. Benaiah closed his eyes briefly to wait it out, then opened them to find the enormous man bearing down on them. He was so close, had moved so quickly, that Benaiah could only leap to the side. Josheb threw up his shield to absorb the first blow. The Egyptian's spear was flying, first at Josheb, then smashing against Benaiah's chest too quickly to be avoided.

Josheb had rolled away with renewed vigor, then leaped into the air and slashed across the Egyptian's back. It struck a leather strap instead of flesh but was enough to slow the assault.

Benaiah's eyes wouldn't work—the Egyptian had thrown sand into them. He tried to shake off his surprise at how fast the giant moved, knew he should have remembered from before. Benaiah ran from the battle, hating himself for it but desperate to clear his eyes. He stumbled, heard the sounds of weapon on shield as Josheb fought the mercenary, tried to find the water skin lying on the ground. There were cries and grunts behind him, but he could not see. He groped maddeningly for the water pouch.

There!

He fumbled with the skin, found the opening, then poured the water across his eyes. The burn made him cry out, but after the second time enough dust had washed out for him to see.

Josheb, running in a circle, was trying to strike at the man's legs, but the long night of fighting and the dagger wound had slowed him. Benaiah staggered back toward the fight—and watched in terror as Josheb's spear was too slow in a thrust. The mercenary caught it with his shield and wrenched it away. Josheb tried to leap backward, but the Egyptian raised his spear high to deliver a killing blow; there was no way for Josheb, weakened and slow, to avoid it.

Benaiah threw his club. It flew low and hit the giant's waist, an ineffective blow but enough to force the man's spear to veer to the right, missing Josheb's neck but landing on his outstretched leg.

Benaiah threw himself toward his friend, tackling him out of the way of another strike just in time. When they stopped their tumble, Benaiah sprang up, but the Egyptian was bearing down on them again with incredible speed, spear raised. Without his club, Benaiah groped around for anything, found a rock the size of a melon, and hurled it with all his strength.

The stone thudded against the Egyptian's face. He staggered to the side, dropping the spear. He coughed and gagged, sounding like a burbling river. He knelt, clutching his neck.

Benaiah too knelt for a moment and focused on his breathing, his vision swimming. *Stay down, pagan. I need a moment.*

Lying in the sand several steps away was the great spear. Benaiah's club was next to it.

Josheb was not moving.

Benaiah pulled his friend's face close. He was still breathing—he must have passed out from loss of blood. He looked quickly at the Egyptian, still coughing up blood, his head hanging. Then he looked up at Benaiah across the sand, smirking through the blood on his bronze face. Benaiah rolled to his feet. He would end this now.

The Egyptian pushed himself up and stood. The spear was back in his hand—when had he reacquired it? Benaiah could not help but marvel at the spear. The giants of Gath also used them, but they were slow. This man was fast.

Benaiah pointed to the war club lying on the ground near him. "This is from my tribe, Egyptian. I have killed many with it. Including many of your own countrymen. Your civil problems are even worse than ours."

The mercenary's dark eyes flickered toward the club. Then he wiped perspiration and blood from his face and smiled a misshapen smile. Enormous muscles twitched beneath his skin. He made no reply. The sun pounded the sand around them. The fading screams of dying men echoed against the cliffs.

Then the Egyptian rushed, faster than before. But this time, when he kicked the sand to distract him again, Benaiah was ready for it. He rolled to his side and snatched the war club in a single motion. The spiked hardwood tip of the club swung low and caught the Egyptian as he passed. The huge man yelped and buried the head of his spear in the sand to stop his momentum. Benaiah reached back with the club and swung it again, missing this time but forcing the Egyptian to pivot off balance to avoid the strike.

More sand in his eyes; he blinked it out. *Watch the weight shift, the spear is so large he will need to—down now!*

The spearhead whistled next to Benaiah's ear, slicing deeply into his scalp in the same spot as the lion had wounded him. Not serious, he judged quickly, though he felt blood pour from the wound. Keep moving!

They broke apart to reset their attacks and circled. Benaiah was running now, running in a circle, finding strength from somewhere, rotating the war club in his hand. He should have wrapped the grip tighter—sweat was making his hand slip.

The Egyptian, losing patience, lunged with the spear, terribly fast, forcing Benaiah to leap back. But when he did, he finally saw his opening.

As the shaft of the spear reached its full length, instead of using the pause to dart away, as he normally would have, Benaiah jumped forward and, before the Egyptian could recover the enormous shaft, Benaiah had pushed it to the ground with the bottom of his foot. In the same instant, he yelled and smashed the war club with all his strength across the Egyptian's face.

The Egyptian thrashed and released his grip on the spear shaft. It had been a solid blow. The man's face was crushed. He would die from the strike.

Benaiah reached down and grasped the fallen spear.

He would help the man along.

As the Egyptian thrust his hands away from his face to see his attacker, Benaiah drove the spearhead deep into the man's chest. The huge man lurched, toppled, and crashed to the sand.

Benaiah, his vision red with his own blood, shouted and pushed the spearhead further. The man pounded at the shaft and struggled against it, but Benaiah held strong. The Egyptian gasped and sputtered curses. He wrenched against the wound—then, seeing it was futile, he lay still. He glared up at Benaiah and tried to speak, but there was too much blood in his throat.

Benaiah twisted the spear and plunged it again. And again. An Amalekite sword was nearby, so he gripped its blood-splattered hilt and swung it down on the Egyptian's neck, severing his head.

Benaiah strode up the slope with the head, stamping through the sand to the nearest fallen Amalekite soldier—still alive, struggling for his own breath. Benaiah saw the faces of his children through the darkness and blood.

He thrust the head into the wounded man's face. "I have beheaded your Egyptian champion, and now I will cut off your head as well! You will fight no battles in the afterlife!" he shouted, then impaled him with the sword, cursing into his ears as the dying man struggled.

When the Amalekite lay still, Benaiah ran to the next one, working his way up the slope, finding some dead but others alive. Each time, he screamed and spat curses into their ears, then finished them. He would kill every one of them.

He felt a hand on his shoulder and whirled, ready for battle.

It was Eleazar. Behind him were the three wives. Rizpah was next to Eleazar, but Deborah was kneeling next to Josheb, trying to fix his wound. Sherizah was staring in horror at her husband.

Until now, she had never looked at him with fear.

He glared at her, still filled with rage—but not rage at her. Women should not see this. He wanted to strike Eleazar in the face with his club for bringing the women back.

Eleazar held both of his shoulders. "Benaiah! It is over! Let them be!"

His blood was pounding. Sweat poured; his breath was heated and savage. He felt rage, so much rage. He wanted to kill them all. Kill them and kill them and kill them.

"Stop it! Listen to my voice! Stop! They are all dead!" Eleazar had a strong grip. He was not letting go. The power in his friend's grip was enough to force Benaiah to stop. Slowly, he began to fight the vengeance and rage in his heart.

He tried to breathe normally, but his arm was still shaking—so hard that he dropped the club. He looked at Sherizah again, her face awash with fear, and he gripped his elbow with the other hand, desperately trying to stop the shaking. *Cover me in the day of war, Yahweh, cover me in the day of war, cover me in the day* ...

He pinched his eyes shut and fell to his knees, letting the head of the Egyptian mercenary drop next to his sword. He rolled onto his side, panting, eyes closed. The sand stirred and swarmed against him; his hands still trembled with hate. He turned onto his belly and crawled, tasting the sand in despair, then brought his knees up to his chest.

Benaiah opened his eyes and squinted across the blood-soaked sand.

There were children running toward him.

They were screaming, laughing as if they knew he was about to chase them. His beautiful daughters, giggling with delight as they climbed the sandy slope to him.

He sat up and cried out to them. Reached for them. But now they were gone.

Benaiah lowered his head, his eyes closed.

Eleazar sat next to him and put his arm around his neck. The two of them remained still for a while, staring at the horizon. Deborah and Rizpah were working on Josheb's wound. Benaiah could feel Sherizah standing nearby, then felt it as she walked away.

Slowly at first, Benaiah began to weep. He felt it growing within him, moving inexorably to the surface, and he didn't have the strength of will to stop it. Soon great heaving sobs were bursting from his chest. For his daughters. For his failures. For all the things he wanted to say to Sherizah but never had.

Eleazar said nothing. Benaiah felt his arm around him, squeezing tight. Willing comfort to his friend.

Evening came. Wind blew the sand in swirls across the battlefield, stinging the faces of the living, gathering on the silent forms of the dead.

THIRTY-ONE

Keth stepped among bedrolls in the growing dark of the forest. Camp had been made alongside the road under the protective canopy of trees. The Hebrews had found a stash of stolen Philistine campaign tents among the recaptured loot and were pitching them all throughout the forest.

A red sun had risen that morning, meaning storms were on the way tonight. He had even spotted a flare of lightning in the distance toward the Great Sea as he walked the perimeter. David had ordered everyone to rest for the night under shelter, since the Sabbath was the next day—even though many of the foreigners did not observe the Sabbath. Ziklag was, anyway, too far a march for people so exhausted. No one seemed to mind, since nothing awaited them there but silence and ash.

Some men, too tired even to eat their evening meal, had fallen asleep where they sat. Wives and children reclined with them, families sleeping together in oddly huddled masses, and Keth considered the happy confusion a sign of hope and renewal.

Not all slept. Some fathers were extolling their exploits to their children, becoming the hero all over again. It had been a stunning victory. Not a man lost or even seriously wounded—except, of course, Josheb.

And he was expected to recover from his wound.

When Benaiah, Eleazar, Josheb, and the wives had arrived back in camp after a long day's march, Keth had reveled in the pure joy of reunion. There had been cheers all across the camp. Even now, strolling through the camp, Keth heard the legend beginning to grow about the exploits of the Three and the mighty Benaiah. He shook his head and smiled.

The men on the perimeter were alert and ready. They were the men who had stayed at the Besor brook—now rested, fresh, and eager to prove their manhood to their fellow troops.

Picking a route through the people, Keth spotted the campfire he was looking for. He would make another round on watch this night, but first, a fire. A warm fire that would feel so wonderful he would be afraid of sitting in front of it because he might never get up again. The night would be cold, and he had no woman; the fire would be his companion.

Benaiah looked up from the fallen log as Keth sat down. Next to him were Josheb, Shammah, and Eleazar. All of them wore their exhaustion on their faces. David himself would no doubt have enjoyed sharing the company of these men this evening, but Keth had seen him walking toward the perimeter. No war leader he had ever known checked the perimeter watchmen as much as David did.

"Thought you would be asleep by now," Benaiah said to Keth, who reached over and tore off a chunk of meat from the edge of the fire. The smell of herbs and spices watered his mouth heavily.

Keth settled onto a rock, grateful to discover that it had been warmed by the flames. Evening had softened and darkened the trees above them. Warmth was finally coming, and would bring the storms Keth had seen gathering in the distance. "The men who stayed at the brook yesterday are on the perimeter," he said. "I needed to check on them. David goes out there now."

"Good. They will need checking," said Josheb.

Keth let the warm flames lull him. He felt at home among these four. They shared something. He was not sure what. "How are you, Josheb?" he asked.

"He lost blood, but he will make it. Passed out like a woman. I plan on never letting him hear the end of it," said Eleazar.

"A dagger. I have defeated twenty men at once, and a dagger takes me out of the fight. I almost couldn't save Benaiah in time," Josheb said.

"Good fight today," said Eleazar. "Good work on that Egyptian, Benaiah. Largest man I have ever seen. Bet it felt good to finally get him."

"Not nearly as impressive as what I heard about Shammah," replied Benaiah from across the fire.

"Yahweh was with me, but there will be more of them. Word will spread that Philistia is going to war against Israel. They will be like vultures," Shammah said.

Josheb nodded. "Amalek will try again. They won't be content just to lose an entire army to phantoms. If Amalek moves, so will Ammon. Then Moab. All of them will have their eyes on the trade routes to the north and south. If that Egyptian was spying for the king of Egypt, then the Nile kingdom might be coming at us as well. We'll need more than three companies of thieves to stop them."

"Will he be their vassal? David? If Saul is defeated, will he be the Philistine vassal in Israel?" asked Keth.

"He might." Josheb paused, poked at a wound on his wrist. "But if we can forge iron weapons, he will not be their vassal for long."

"The time of battle has passed, for now. It is no longer unclean to lie with a woman. Why are you all still here? Growing fond of me?" Shammah said.

"I should ask the same of you. No warm flesh among the captives?" Josheb answered.

"Even if he knew how to be with a woman, Shammah would probably fall asleep before he got going," said Eleazar. They chuckled. Shammah scowled.

Across the camp, there was occasional laughter. Many were asleep by then, but there was always another campfire going. They would go as late into the night as men wanted to avoid their dreams.

Lightning flashed again, far away. Soon Josheb and Eleazar were sound asleep, leaning against one another. Shammah hunched forward, head hanging. Keth smiled at them. Benaiah, though, was still awake, staring into the flames. His face was unreadable.

A round of laughter from a fire nearby startled Josheb awake. He thumped Eleazar on the head, and the man sleepily stared at him, uncomprehending. "A sight we are," said Josheb.

Shammah had awoken as well but was pretending he had not been sleeping. He rubbed his eyes to look more alert. The group of them sat together, enjoying each other's company. Keth felt privileged that they allowed him to sit among them. Brothers closer than kin — the hardest circle to penetrate.

"For the life of me, I cannot understand why you all are still sitting here. Your women are nearby," Shammah said.

"Good point. Eleazar is beautiful, but ultimately unfulfilling. In the morning, brothers." Josheb rose and left.

"I'm too tired to sleep. I will go stand watch on the perimeter." Shammah stood and walked away, his gentle stride disappearing into the woods.

Eleazar rose to do the same, but before he did, he said to Keth, "Excellent work today, Hittite. Selfless, brave, all of it. We are glad to have you. I overheard David speaking about you this evening.

Wants to give you another name while you live among us. It is a custom of our tribes."

"What name?"

"Uriah. It means 'Flame of Yahweh.' A good, fierce name. Uriah the Hittite."

Keth nodded. "Uriah. I like it. I suppose I will have to learn more about Yahweh if I am to be named for him."

Eleazar walked into the night after the others.

Keth looked again at Benaiah across the fire. It was just the two of them now. Benaiah's countenance had been impossible to read since they arrived back in camp that evening. Keth let the quiet darkness around them settle a bit longer before he spoke up again. "If Israel's army is defeated by Philistia, the entire northern portion of the kingdom will be cut off. What do you think David will do?"

Benaiah shifted his position, probably trying to rouse himself. "I've stopped trying to guess. He is a strange man. Probably write a song about it, then attack Gaza by himself," Benaiah said.

"Perhaps he will move to take the throne. If he was anointed for it, maybe now is the time. Your god Yahweh might be clearing a path for us."

"Our time among the Philistines will be finished soon. That is certain. My guess is that we will go to Judah and establish a city there. We will need a base to operate from in our own lands and among our own people, and David is popular in Judah. Then, if David truly wants to unite the kingdom, once Saul dies he will need to remove any surviving heirs. David will resist that—he is close to Saul's son Jonathan, but he knows it has to be done. Then there is Ammon, and Moab, and now Amalek. They have their eyes on the trading routes, as Josheb said. Many days of battle lie ahead of us."

Keth nodded. This was good. It was why he had come here, why he was here now. He was a man of war, like these men. They wanted peace desperately and resisted it hopelessly. There was nothing left for him in the north. He thought about his own clan for a moment, then pushed it away. He had a new name, now, given to him by his new brothers. Uriah of the Hittites.

"You should go to her, brother. The sun has set."

Benaiah said nothing for a moment. His face was covered in a shadow. "I mistreated her before we parted the last time," he said. "And she saw the battle today. No woman should see her man do such things."

Keth shook his head. What Benaiah said was true: No woman should see that. "Is she still angry with you for mistreating her?"

"I have not asked."

"Why not?" Keth asked.

"I told her I wanted another wife, before I left. To give me sons. We only had daughters."

Keth shrugged. "That is not so bad. You should be able to make peace with her. You will have more chances for sons now."

Benaiah paused long before he continued. "Two years ago, just before I came to David, I was in Egypt, a mercenary for the pharaoh. While I was gone, my daughters were slaughtered and my wife was raped by Amalekites."

Keth closed his eyes, then opened them slowly. The lightning emerged as a white flash through the orange glow of the campfire against the trees. He waited.

"The soldiers forced themselves onto my daughters and then cut their necks, right in front of my wife. They spared her life so that she would suffer by reliving the images of her children being dishonored and slain, but they took turns with her as well," Benaiah said softly.

"Does anyone else know?"

Benaiah shook his head. "No one but Sherizah and I. We came here to escape it. David knew something had happened, but he did not know what until last night."

Keth had seen the altercation between Joab and Benaiah the night before. He had also seen David pull Benaiah aside during the pause in fighting.

Benaiah continued: "I tell you this because ... I feel like I am supposed to."

"I am honored."

Keth watched the trees above, wishing he could somehow comfort his new friend. Only a father, he supposed, would understand that type of grief. He had no family of his own. Keth had seen Benaiah's wife enter a tent before sunset. A happy family reunited, he had thought at the time.

Benaiah said, "After it happened, I heard about David and his army. We came to David, but all I wanted was vengeance. I had neglected my family, sought my own glory, and now I am suffering for it, as they did. Sherizah is lost to me. I never was a good father. Now Yahweh is against me."

"I am sorry, brother." Keth knew it was a senseless comment that did no one any good, but he hoped that Benaiah heard his heart behind it.

Benaiah nodded. "I never told you what my own name meant."

"I asked Josheb. It means 'Yahweh has built.'"

Benaiah closed his eyes. "I don't know what he has built. I only know what has been destroyed."

Keth glanced away from him, up into the night. He decided there was nothing more to say and waited. He watched out of the corner of his eye as Benaiah looked up from the fire and turned toward the west. Lightning flashed again and again.

They listened to the slowly dying noises across the camp: the crackling of logs, the whisper of warm air rolling in from the distant mountains to collide with the storms over the Great Sea, bringing rain and life to the earth around them. Benaiah studied it. Keth watched him and imagined that he was looking past the forest, past the lowland hills and pasture lands, past the deserts of sand to the Great Sea, seeking to swim across it, away from the violence and bloodshed of battle, away from predators who stole in the darkness. He wondered what this god Yahweh was building in Benaiah. Keth's own gods had abandoned him long ago.

He let it go. There would be time to grieve tomorrow. *Too tired now.* He felt at home here, as he had never felt at home in any other place. He closed his eyes and let his dreams come: mountains of the north, a beautiful woman among the captives, the scarlet and purple house where he had uttered the strange prayer that had stopped him from entering.

Need to speak with David soon, he thought. Need to find out what the covering is ...

My hammer strikes the final nail. Cheering, my brothers clap me on the back. There are shouts through the streets. The house is complete at last. My labors have borne fruit. A new home worthy of my new bride, Sherizah. Must go to her now. Light the torch, walk down the dark street to my beloved. The time has come. Our wedding ceremony, finally. She smiles at me, so very shy, so very nervous, always so quiet. The shawl is across her shoulders. I take it, drape it over my own shoulder, assuming the mantle. She is mine now. Mine to protect, mine to cherish. To hold in the sunlight and to hold in the dark nights when the stars are gone and the land is cold ...

It is a spring day soon after, and she is laughing. She sounds like a bird when she laughs. Good day today. Finally alone. Beautiful valley, trees, the river. Her skin is close to my chest. She will have good sons. Does it matter? Not really. Sherizah. Lovely one. How do others take more than one? I do not want this day to end. Our last day together for a long time. There is much to do, much to enjoy, much to savor. I love her. She comes closer to me, and her smooth skin is warm.

"Will you send me a message from Egypt?" she asks.

"You cannot read anyway."

"I want to see your handwriting."

"Then yes, I can send you a message. On a papyrus scroll as a special treat."

"You do not need to go. There is other work. Other men have trades and work their land and have their wives."

She is right. But I must go. I must test myself away from my father's house, must prove myself apart from him and his laws and Yahweh. I love her dearly, but I must go.

She sighs. "Just through winter? And then you will come back?"

"And then I will come back."

"I think you will. You will want this again."

"Confident, are you?"

Her skin is so soft. We lie together under the shade of a terebinth. We delight in each other ...

I return, but leave again. There are many opportunities, many dreams to chase to build myself in the world. We have two children, daughters. Beautiful, but I would rather have sons. She keeps my home, runs my affairs, and I must continue to go away. Back to Egypt.

Years pass. I stay gone, desperate to prove myself, but for what purpose? The Egyptian defeats me in battle; I lose my way, wandering the deserts to find wells I do not own, wandering without my home, my beloved. Her memory starts to fade. I must return ...

Benaiah stayed up late by the fire. He drifted in and out of sleep. But as the night wore on, he could avoid it no longer.

He slipped under the flap of his tent just as the rains finally arrived that night. They were strong, good, springtime rains, not the smattering of snowy moisture that did little to bring the crops out of the earth and remove the winter's grip. The storm was fierce and unknowable and would purge Yahweh's promised land all through the night.

He was careful not to disturb her as she slept. He listened to her breathing a moment, then crawled under the blankets, his body wracked with aches and exhaustion, grateful for the warmth radiating from her. Her breathing was steady and slow. He searched for words but found none. He wanted her to hear words that came from his heart, but he did not wish to wake her.

"Forgive me," he whispered.

Her breath went on as steadily as before. Benaiah moved a hand through the blankets and touched her neck. She did not respond.

Benaiah turned over onto his back. The quiet darkness of the tent comforted him. He closed his eyes and enjoyed the sound of her breathing, wondering if she would awaken during the coming storm.

If she did, he would be there.

He listened to the rain. The wind began to pick up, bringing warm air to clear away the cold so unusual for that time of year.

The Sabbath, day of rest, was tomorrow.

EPILOGUE

The people of David reached Ziklag the next day, but the joy of being reunited was diminished by the reminder of what had happened to their homes—and their lives. David held a council that night, and it was decided that they would move elsewhere. David decided to wait until they had received word of the Philistine attack against Saul before plotting their course.

The defeat of the Amalekites had retrieved a tremendous amount of plunder, and David directed that some of it be sent to the elders of towns in Judah as tribute, since many were still convinced he meant them harm. Benaiah chose men out of the bodyguard to deliver the precious spices and metals.

Two days later, a messenger arrived with news of the defeat of Israel's army, and the worst news of all—that Saul and Jonathan were dead. In his rage, David ordered Joab to kill the messenger. His grief was so great that David withdrew and composed a song, and then sang it long into the night, his men listening and mourning with him.

Many had lost brothers and tribesmen. Now that the kingdom was almost destroyed, they were unsure where to go or what to expect. Israel no longer had a king. David was the natural choice, but Philistia now ruled their lands with an iron grasp.

The following morning, two men arrived in town. One was powerfully built and carried himself sternly; the other was a youth who walked with a limp because of an arrow that had been lodged in his foot. No one knew who they were. Nor did anyone particularly care. They were veterans of the battle and blended in easily with the other refugees streaming in from the north, where the Philistines were capturing villages and overrunning the former kingdom.

Rumors flew that Saul's general Abner was rallying support, but no one could confirm them.

David gave the orders to prepare for another campaign. Many assumed that they would be securing the borderlands from the coming invasions. Those close to the inner circle of the warlord knew otherwise—his objective was the throne of Judah.

Several days after the arrival of news about Saul, the voice still echoed against walls and houses and through the dusty corridors of the ruined city, as it had each night since then.

When it reached the place where men were forging new iron blades, Keth looked up from supervising the work of the Hittites. He paused awhile to listen as the voice mingled with the nightly creaking of the locusts. A man coughed, and his comrades glanced scornfully at him, irritated that he would disrupt the beauty of the music.

It was a lyre, strummed by hands moving so skillfully that at first some of the foreigners believed a captured goddess of the Sea People was in their midst, but those who knew what it was just nodded and closed their eyes.

Keth wondered where Benaiah was. Hopefully with his wife. Everyone had been busy trying to rebuild what they could of the city; interactions among the men had been limited while they pounded nails all day. The work had given them all many blisters, and there would be many more, but for now, everyone was content to listen.

David was playing it again, a song he was calling "The Lament of the Bow."

The voice moaned in melodies too mournful to be understood. Everyone had been forced to learn the song out of respect for the dead, but few truly grasped the words. It did not matter. It was a song of war and loss, of friendships and grief, and of other things men know of but refuse to dwell upon.

NOTE ON HISTORICAL RESEARCH

Anyone interested in further research regarding the places and events in the Lion of War series ought to consider the following materials, which I consulted extensively during the preparation of the novels.

Many of the specific details on movement and weaponry are my own invention, serving the necessities of storytelling and the supernatural elements that can't necessarily be determined by research. Many of the larger battle descriptions, however, are largely faithful to scholarly research. For battlefield tactics, strategies, weaponry, and chronology, the primary source was *Battles of the Bible* by Chaim Herzog and Mordechai Gichon. *The Military History of Ancient Israel* by Richard A. Gabriel provided insight into military tactics as well. For archaeological and anthropological research, I relied primarily upon the classical volumes *A History of Israel* by John Bright and *Bible History: Old Testament* by Alfred Edersheim. Modern sources consulted include *New Illustrated Bible Manners and Customs* by Howard F. Vos and *The New Manners and Customs of Bible Times* by Ralph Gower. For those looking for a well-researched, biblically faithful account of the whole of David's life, I recommend Eleanor Gustafson's *The Stones*.

Other sources consulted that I encourage readers to examine are *David: A Man of Passion and Destiny* by Charles R. Swindoll, *David: Shepherd, Psalmist, King* by F. B. Meyer, *The Life of David* by Arthur W. Pink, and *The Expositor's Bible Commentary*, Frank E. Gæbelein, General Editor.

Many of these books come from a Christian perspective, since I am a Christian. However, I did spend considerable time consulting Jewish sources both ancient (Josephus, *Antiquities*) and modern (materials provided by the Jewish History Resource Center of the Hebrew University of Jerusalem).

The best research, however, is found on site in Israel. I've had a wonderful time getting to know experts on the land, reading books by scholars of all the Abrahamic faiths, and sorting through many known facts on David's life, but none of it fully came alive to me as a storyteller until I spent time in the land itself. Sites that a curious reader must make it a point to visit are Ein Gedi, the Valley of Elah, Tel Gath, the Gilboa highlands, the Negev region, Masada (a possible location for one of David's strongholds), and, of course, the City of David.

ABOUT THE AUTHOR

Cliff Graham lives in the mountains of Utah with his wife and children. He is a military veteran and currently serves in the Army National Guard Chaplain Corps. He travels around the country, speaking and writing about David and his Mighty Men.

You can follow him on Twitter @cliffgraham or on Facebook.

For the author's blog, updates about the Lion of War books and upcoming movie series, author speaking requests, and other general information, please visit http://www.lionofwar.com.

Share Your Thoughts

With the Author: Your comments will be forwarded to the author when you send them to *zauthor@zondervan.com*.

With Zondervan: Submit your review of this book by writing to *zreview@zondervan.com*.

Free Online Resources at
www.zondervan.com

Zondervan AuthorTracker: Be notified whenever your favorite authors publish new books, go on tour, or post an update about what's happening in their lives at www.zondervan.com/authortracker.

Daily Bible Verses and Devotions: Enrich your life with daily Bible verses or devotions that help you start every morning focused on God. Visit www.zondervan.com/newsletters.

Free Email Publications: Sign up for newsletters on Christian living, academic resources, church ministry, fiction, children's resources, and more. Visit www.zondervan.com/newsletters.

Zondervan Bible Search: Find and compare Bible passages in a variety of translations at www.zondervanbiblesearch.com.

Other Benefits: Register to receive online benefits like coupons and special offers, or to participate in research.

ZONDERVAN®

ZONDERVAN.com/
AUTHORTRACKER
follow your favorite authors